A press of canvas carries us out,

half gale from astern.

We're out to teach the British, boys,

a lesson they must learn.

1812 forebitter chanty
anonymous

A PRESS OF CANVAS

a novel by

W. H. White

Volume One in the
War of 1812 Trilogy

PUBLISHING
St. Michaels, MD

Cover art: "Pursuit"© 2000 Paul Garnett
Illustrations © 2000 Paul Garnett

Graphic design and production by:
Words & Pictures, Inc., 27 South River Road South, Edgewater, Maryland 21037.

Printed in the USA by:
Victor Graphics, 1211 Bernard Drive, Baltimore, MD 21223 USA

Questions regarding the content of this book should be addressed to:

TILLER Publishing

P.O. Box 447
St. Michaels, Maryland 21663
410-745-3750 • Fax: 410-745-9743
www.tillerbooks.com

DEDICATION

This effort is dedicated to my three sons to whom I taught, and from whom, in turn, I learned, the art of seafaring. They are my most ardent supporters and critics; and to Ann, my mate on the life voyage we chose together — my source of support, consolation, and the occasional course correction, each as needed. Thank you each and every one for your love and patience with me.

ACKNOWLEDGMENTS

Without the help of a number of special people, this work would not have been possible; I am indeed indebted to the good folks at the USS Constitution Museum in Boston, especially Margherita Desy and Marianne Galvin, for their help in using the resources of that great institution. Also, the librarians at Peabody Essex Museum in Salem Massachusetts. Bill Fowler, author and historian, provided wisdom and insight, as well as some most useful technical information.

Justine Ahlstrom of the National Maritime Historical Society in Peekskill, New York, and editor in chief of the Society's magazine Sea History, was unstinting with her guidance and help in that institution's library, and Peter Stanford, President of NMHS, for not only his incredible knowledge, but also his friendship and inspiration.

Carol Klein, noted biographer and teacher, provided some course corrections early on, and encouragement that the project was indeed viable.

My sister, Linda Wiseman, a scholar specializing in the field of historical interior design and architecture, helped with some invaluable research, adding to the accuracy of the novel, and my three sons lent their names and a few of their character traits to my efforts.

Donald Petrie, most likely the single most knowledgeable American in the field of nineteenth-century prize law, was always available for questions and provided wisdom to me and accuracy to the actions of the American privateers operating in the Caribbean.

John Hattendorf, scholar, historian, and sailor, provided a read and some worthwhile suggestions for improving the historical accuracy of the manuscript, not to mention his graciousness in providing a Foreword for the book.

Any errors that might exist in the yarn you are about to read are mine alone, and can not in any way be attributed to these most helpful experts.

Jerri Anne Hopkins, my editor at Tiller, has been enormously helpful in suggesting improvements in the flow of the story and making the every-necessary corrections that arise from my ability to fool the spell-checker in my computer

Last, but in no way least, my friend, sailing buddy, and co-conspirator, Joseph Burns, lent me not only his name and personality for the character of similar name, but also his encouragement as the work progressed.

If I have succeeded in making this story interesting, exciting, or historically accurate, it is in no small measure because these good folks were unstinting in their willingness to help. Thank you all for making me look good.

William H. White
June, 1999

FOREWORD

W. H. White's evocative sea tale, *A Press of Canvas*, introduces a new character in American sea fiction: Isaac Biggs of Marblehead, Massachusetts. Sailing from Boston as captain of the foretop in the Bark *Anne*, his ship was outward bound with a cargo for the Swedish colony of St. Barts in the West Indies in the autumn of 1810, a difficult and complex moment in American history.

Ships on the sea lanes of the North Atlantic world had been sailing under the nearly constant threat of war for seventeen years during the series of conflicts that had convulsed Europe since 1793. The young American republic, in its attempt to avoid "foreign entanglements," had tried to stand clear of the huge political issues raised, first by the French Revolution and, then, by Napoleon's bid for hegemony in Europe. In the process, Yankee ship-owners discovered that there were great profits for neutrals to make in carrying goods to the warring countries, but it soon became clear that, in such a world, commerce — neutral or not — was part of war. It had been the cargoes of American flour that led to the first great naval battle between the French and British war fleets at The Glorious First of June in 1794. At the same time, both French and British privateers preyed on American commerce as it served each other's enemies. Such attacks finally forced the young republic to establish its own navy and to fight its first battles in the Quasi War with France.

In these same years, the British faced an ever increasing demand for seamen to man warships in their own struggle for survival against France. As many English seamen deserted their own service for the higher pay and better conditions in the growing number of American ships, the British government increasingly stopped American ships and impressed British-born seamen from them. In response, the American government issued certificates of citizenship to protect its citizens, but the British officials found that they were too often forged or too easily negotiated to be believed and the practice continued to the increasing anger of Americans. Despite these continuing irritations, American maritime commerce boomed through the war years up to 1806.

Increasingly irritated by British impressment of American seamen, Congress passed the Nonimportation Act in April 1806. With this Act, Congress was attempting to force the British to stop injuring American merchant activities by announcing America's intention to ban imports of key British goods into the United States. Before U.S. diplomats could use this Act to exert much effect, the conflict with Europe overshadowed the American issues. First, Britain attempted to impose a blockade on French ports. Then Napoleon responded with his Berlin Decree, establishing full-scale economic war against Britain and blockading all trade to and from Britain with the "Continental System." The British continued to impress American seamen, even in American waters. The most dramatic incident occurred in the summer of 1807, when HMS *Leopard* stopped the USS *Chesapeake* to search for British deserters just off the entrance to Chesapeake Bay, opening fire on her, killing the commanding officer, and seizing four crew members, only one of whom was, in fact, a deserter. In protest, President Jefferson ordered all visiting British naval vessels to leave American ports.

Meanwhile, American maritime commerce flourished as it had never done. In 1807, combined imports and exports reached a record value of $246 million, a figure it would not reach again for nearly thirty years in 1835. By November of 1807, Britain had begun to feel the pinch of Napoleon's economic blockade and retaliated with the Orders in Council, requiring neutral ships trading in Europe to obtain a license in a British port. Those without a license, the British government declared, were liable to capture. A month later, Napoleon responded with his Milan Decree, declaring that any neutrals that complied with the British orders were enemy vessels. America's flourishing merchant trade, the largest among neutrals, was clearly caught in the struggle between two world powers.

From this point in 1807, the situation worsened. Hoping to use the tool of economic coercion as a means of forcing the belligerents to recognize the mutual benefits brought by neutral trade, President Thomas Jefferson sponsored passage of the Embargo Act in Congress, prohibiting American ships from trading with any foreign country. Legally, virtually all American overseas trade stopped, but naturally enough, enterprising Yankees found loopholes or merely defied the law in order to continue their profitable trade. While the embargo had relatively little effect on the belligerents, it quickly proved devastating to the American economy. Napoleon also used it to his advantage, claiming in his April 1808 Bayonne Decree that any American vessel that appeared in a French port must have fraudulent papers and was, therefore, subject to French seizure. The embargo remained in effect until nearly the end of Jefferson's term in March 1809. Just three days before he left the office of President to James Madison, the Jefferson administration persuaded Congress to repeal the Embargo and replace it with the Non-Intercourse Act, opening American commerce to all nations, but retaining the prohibition on trade with France and England until one or the other (or both) abandoned policies that damaged American shipping.

A year later, in May 1810, the American economy was suffering even more from the effects of America's own policies than were either France or Britain. When the Non-Intercourse Act expired in the spring of 1810, Congress enacted in its place North Carolina Congressman Nathan Macon's Bill Number 2, authorizing American ships to resume trading with both Britain and France. However, if one side would revoke its policies damaging American trade, Congress declared that it would then prohibit trade with the other, hoping to obtain some concessions for continuing American neutrality. Learning of the passage of Macon's bill, Napoleon responded with a ruse, instructing his foreign minister to tell the United States' envoy that the Berlin and Milan Decrees would be withdrawn after November 1, 1810, on the condition that the American government halted trade with Britain unless the British government withdrew its Orders in Council. In reporting Napoleon's order to the American representative in France, the French foreign minister exaggerated by clearly suggesting that Napoleon had already withdrawn the Berlin and Milan Decrees. Unsuspecting, President Madison accepted the French statement at face value and immediately issued a proclamation reopening trade with France and declaring that trade with Britain would end in February 1811.

Caught in the war between the two largest maritime empires, American trade remained under direct attack from the French, while the British continued to impress seamen from American vessels. The United States had fallen for Napoleon's ruse and was on the verge of both cutting off trade with Britain and adding to the forces that were fighting Britain. This was clearly a French-manipulated threat that used the United States in Napoleon's war against Britain, but it was also a dangerous and very difficult moment for America's merchant ships and seamen.

It is at this moment that Isaac Biggs left Boston in *A Press of Canvas*, and provides, through the art of historical fiction, a seaman's viewpoint on the months that led up to the American declaration of war against Britain in June 1812.

John B. Hattendorf
Ernest J. King Professor of Maritime History
U.S. Naval War College
November 1998
Newport, Rhode Island

Sail Plan of a Square-Rigged Ship

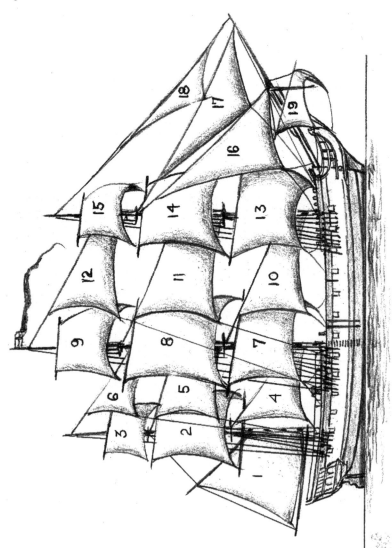

1. Spanker
2. Mizzen Topsail
3. Mizzen Topgallant Sail
4. Mizzen Staysail
5. Mizzen Topmast Staysail
6. Mizzen Topgallant Staysail
7. Mail Course Sail
8. Main Topsail
9. Main Topgallant Sail
10. Main Staysail
11. Main Topmast Staysail
12. Main Topgallant Staysail
13. Fore Course Sail
14. Fore Topsail
15. Fore Topgallant Sail
16. Fore Topmast Staysail
17. Fore Topmast Outer Staysail
18. Jib
19. Spritsail

PART ONE

On Board
ANNE
1810

CHAPTER ONE

A Storm Is Brewing

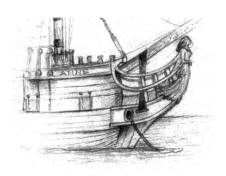

"Biggs, find Mr. Clark, if you please, and ask him to step aft." Captain Jed Smalley continued his pacing of the quarterdeck of the bark *Anne*, casting an occasional glance at the sails hanging limply aloft, reflected almost perfectly with the image of the ship in the brilliant, but dead calm sea. Isaac Biggs, Captain of the Foretop, had been taking his ease with some of his fellow topmen in the scant shade offered by the vessel's deck house when Smalley sent him to find the first mate.

"Aye, sir." He said aloud, and to himself, *Something must be gonna happen. Maybe the Cap'n figgers we gonna get a breeze o' wind. 'Bout time, I'd reckon.* He stood and walked forward, squinting as he left the shade, and the full force of the Caribbean sun, low in the sky and bouncing off the quiet sea, hit his eyes. He noticed with pleasure, and some relief, that the deck no longer burned his bare feet as he made his way forward, and the tar caulking the seams no longer oozed from between the long leaf pine boards.

As he gained the fo'c'sle, he could smell that Cook was getting close to having the evening meal prepared. Isaac could only imagine how hot the galley must be, and the air around the Charlie Noble stack shimmered as the cooking heat rose from it. First Mate Sam Clark was sitting with some of the foredeck hands on the butt of the bowsprit, and Biggs watched for a moment as the jib boom on its outboard end described lazy circles in the air from the gentle rolling of the ship.

"Mr. Clark, Cap'n wants you on the quarterdeck, if you please. Sent me to get you." The mate looked up at the young topman. He stared for a moment at the curly dark hair, the earnest penetrating eyes, and the easy smile that always seemed ready to expand into a full grin. The mate smiled in spite of himself and stood.

"He say what he wanted?" There hadn't been anything requiring the mate's attention for the two days they had been becalmed, and even though he knew it would be unlikely for Captain Smalley to have shared his thoughts with a foremast hand, his curiosity got the better of him. He could see the tall, whip-thin form of the captain some 130 feet away, still pacing his domain, and he wondered how he stood the black frock coat he habitually wore at sea, regardless of the weather.

"Not to me, sir. But then I guess he figgered it wasn't none o' my business. He ain't been off'n the quarterdeck since the breeze quit, though, 'at I've noticed. Probably concerned 'bout gettin' into St. Bart's afore someone else gets our cargo for the return." Isaac watched the sails overhead as he spoke; they still showed no signs of life, not even the t'gallants some 140 feet above the deck. Not a breath of air was stirring.

The two stopped as they passed two of the bark's longboats, lashed down tightly, and covered with taut canvas, bleached white by the tropical sun. Isaac, seeing his friends still taking their ease, rejoined them in the shade as Sam Clark continued to the quarterdeck.

"Think we're gonna get us some breeze, Cap'n? The men been scratching the backstays and whistling until they's lips hurt. You'd think we'd have more wind 'en we could handle from all o' that. I cain't recall them nor'east trades droppin' fer this long down here. Might be gonna change. Mebbe get some weather."

Smalley had stopped his pacing, and stood at the larboard rail staring at the horizon to the east. He continued watching the horizon, while his first mate stood patiently behind him, waiting. Clark could see the sweat running down the captain's neck and the queue in which he habitually wore his gray hair was damp from it, the black ribbon drooping. Hatless, the tall, almost gaunt skipper suddenly turned, squinting at his mate with deep-set pale eyes that most took as blue, but were in fact gray, in a weathered face that had seen the sea in all her moods over the nearly forty years he had been at sea. His jaw line showed a stubble of white bristles — not from slovenly habits, but from an inability to see close at hand without his spectacles. And he did not feel that wearing spectacles while he shaved was appropriate. He had been captaining vessels for 25 of his 48 years — everything from small coastal vessels to a few brigs, schooners, and this bark, *Anne*, his favorite, and also the largest.

"Yes, Mr. Clark, I think we might get a breeze this night. And from the look o' them clouds startin' on the eastern horizon, mebbe even some rain inta the bargain. You can let the men enjoy a song after supper if they's a mind, as I figger we'll be workin' with no time for gaiety and cavortin' soon enough." Smalley's baritone voice was quiet, as always.

Underscoring his words in an ironical counterpoint, the silence of the day was broken only by the slatting of sails and the slap of unstrained sheets and halyards as *Anne* rolled in the gentle swells. Sam Clark knew better than to doubt this man's sea-sense; he had sailed with him for five years now and had yet to see him err when it came to anticipating the weather.

"Aye, sir. I'll give the second the word; it'll most likely be his watch that's shortenin' sail later."

Clark left the quarterdeck and the captain continued pacing, glancing from time to time at the eastern sky. Absently, Smalley watched Clark's compact form head forward, not thinking about anything in particular, but aware of everything going on aboard his ship. One part of his brain again gave thanks that he had this strong leader and excellent seaman as his second in command. He noticed, without thought, that Clark stopped and spoke with a few sailors, his powerful arms gesturing aloft, and, as he turned his face eastward over the larboard side, his light-colored beard glowed as the lowering sun shone through it. The captain expected that the wind would come in more from the east than the north, and said to himself, *Be nice if'n we might could get them steady half gales back we been enjoyin' since Boston. This don't look like it to me, though. Reckon they might just be some weather over yonder. Be takin' in a passel o' this canvas before long, I'd warrant.*

The *Anne* had all her canvas set — courses, tops'ls, t'gallants, and the spanker on the mizzen; all hung as slack as wash on a Vineyard clothesline. The stays'ls and jibs forward and the sprits'l under the rakish bowsprit were motionless and it might seem to the casual observer, and certainly to some of the landsmen aboard, that thinking about shortening sail was, at this point, a waste of effort — indeed, even foolish.

The rattle of the pumps brought his mind back to the immediate present, and he looked up the deck where he could see, just abaft the capstan, two men working the handles for the pumps, manned for about an hour during each watch to keep the holds and bilge as dry as possible. He noticed that Clark was now deep in conversation with Second Mate Joe O'Malley and Third Mate Ben Jakes, both good sailors, but only the second was the kind of leader Smalley wanted in his ship. Jakes was a smarmy little man with a scraggly beard and a mean cast to his eyes. Even in the heat of the day, his tarpaulin hat was pulled low on his narrow brow, hiding his eyes as they darted everywhere but at the person with whom he spoke. He did not inspire trust from anyone, least of all the captain. Snippets of conversation drifted aft.

". . . Aye, if Cap'n Smalley's lookin' . . . breeze, I'd bet on it. Seen . . . before . . ."

"Thinks . . . men need sompin' to do . . . shorten down? My maintopmen surely don't need no practice . . . tell Biggs . . . his crew aloft . . . ain't no wind yesterday, ain't none today and ain't none tomorrow, neither. Man's gotten . . . sun, you ask me."

"I'll let you know when . . . later . . . supper . . . jest lettin' ya know . . . get yer boys together."

Biggs stood up and stepped over to where the mates were talking. After waiting for a break in the conversation, he looked at Clark. "Did I hear something 'bout shortenin' down later?" At a nod from Clark, he continued "I'd best get my boys fed if . . ."

Clark cut him off. "Ain't no rush, Isaac. Cap'n said be after supper and mebbe a song. No need to rush none."

Smalley smiled to himself; that young foretopman was always ready to work, and eager to advance himself. *Reckon he'll make a fine mate — mebbe even a master — someday. Good man, that. I could use a dozen like him.*

He watched as Biggs, dismissed by the first mate, joined one of his foretopmen and moved over to sit on one of the 24-pounder carronades, straddling the short barrel. Biggs rested his large, scarred hands on the bulwark in front of him, unconsciously flexing the muscles in his forearms as he stared out to sea, watching the horizon. So intent was his gaze that the fellow with him remarked.

"Isaac, what's that you're lookin' at so hard? Ain't nothin' out there 'ceptin' flat calm water."

"Cap'n thinks we gonna pick up a breeze o' wind here soon enough, and I'm tryin' to see what it is he sees makes him think that. Stuff I need to learn my own self, if I'm gonna ever sail as mate. Must be them low clouds over yonder. Looks like it could rain, you ask me." He leaned over the rail, looking at the water and the black sides of the ship with the white painted gunports.

The ship had been painted before leaving Boston for this run to St. Bartholomew and he knew she still looked Bristol. The gunports, mostly there to deceive, did include four that opened to reveal the 24-pounder carronades, short barreled and with a range of scarcely more than a pistol shot. They were lethally effective when properly served and loaded with bits of iron, nails and chain; unfortunately, there were few aboard save Mr. O'Malley who knew how to handle them, and the owners, New Englanders all and parsimonious to a fault, felt there were far better ways to spend money than on powder and shot for practice. Let the Navy handle that. Besides, if a French privateer or British man-of-war really wanted to cause trouble, those four carronades would not slow them down much.

There seemed to be little defense against the British "right of search" boarding parties which could strip a ship of vital crew members in a trice. The British had been busy with the French for the past several years, but instead of that ongoing war distracting the English Navy from American ships, it focused the attention of any short-handed Royal Navy vessel squarely on American merchant vessels. The conflict required a constant supply of seamen to sail the king's ships. And in the eyes of the British, a supply of skilled sailors existed for their pleasure on American ships like *Anne*. A cry from the masthead of "Sail ho!" could mean an opportunity to speak a homeward bound American, or the potential for the British to board them on the premise of looking for British subjects avoiding service in His Majesty's Navy. This had become an increasingly frequent occurrence in the past several years, and a problem that many ship owners and captains felt should be handled by the American Navy. If it led to war, so be it.

Smalley, while not having experienced the British "right of search" first hand, agreed with his fellows that something must be done, and soon. Already ships that had been regulars on the Indies run were heading off to Europe or Russia where there was less likelihood of problems with the Royal Navy. Smalley had captained a score of successful trips to the Indies for his owners, but still felt the uncertainty that always showed up about two or three days before the anticipated landfall. That landfall this time would be St.

Maarten, just to the northwest of his destination and occupied by both the Dutch and the French. The likelihood of crossing tacks with a French privateer leaving or returning to port was a consideration, but he was more concerned about a British ship, and this was, in part at least, why he had been on the quarterdeck for most of the past two days.

Designed to carry cargo in many forms, *Anne's* deck areas and holds were packed with a variety of barrels, casks, crates, and puncheons filled with goods for the market in St. Bartholomew, a Swedish colony and free port. Some contained fish, beef, and butter; others were in fact empty — the clean barrels were themselves the trade goods. From time to time, the cargo included boots, shoes, and hats. The return trip would find the holds filled with barrels of molasses for the thriving rum distilleries in New England, and brown sugar for both American consumption and re-shipment to Europe.

"Dingding, ding." The ship's bell called the captain back from his reverie, and he watched his men appear on deck for supper and their evening ration of rum. The heat was beginning to tell — or maybe it was the boredom from being becalmed — but small fights and arguments were breaking out; it was only a matter of time before one or another of the men brought forth a knife. The men of the larboard watch were eating so they could relieve their mates in the starboard section at 6:00. Smalley looked at the eastern sky for the hundredth time in the past two hours and saw his suspicions were about to be confirmed.

"Mr. Clark," he called to the mate. "We'll hand the t'gallants now, if you please. And trim for an easterly."

The mate glanced at the horizon, and saw that once again Smalley had anticipated the weather accurately. "Aye, sir. And don't look to me like they'll be any singin' this night, 'ceptin' mebbe the wind." His brow furrowed in concern.

Indeed, even as the captain spoke, the water had begun to stir; little ripples and ruffles disturbing the reflected image of the ship which appeared in the molten glass of the still sea. The temperature reacted to the cooling easterly breeze as it started to fill in, and the men on deck moved as one to the weather rail, to feel the relief on their sweat stained faces and arms. Hats off, and the sweat drying on their faces, they stood with their shirts pulled open, feeling the cooling gentle breeze on their skin; a few laughed, while others just enjoyed the sensation quietly. Captain Smalley had a reputation for being conservative, and the preliminary shortening sail prior to a blow instead of during it was one of the manifestations of his conservatism, and one appreciated by his sailors.

"Mr. O'Malley," hollered the mate as he started forward, "Let's get all hands on deck, if you please. We'll be shortening sail directly." Seeing Third Mate Ben Jakes, who had neither opened his shirt nor doffed his hat, loitering near the 'midships capstan, he nodded and spoke.

"Mr. Jakes, have your topmen stand by to go aloft — and see if per chance you might be able to keep up with the foremast hands. The only topmen slower than your crew are the bunch on the mizzen, and Jackson's landsmen are afraid to let go of the jackstay and beckets."

Jakes bridled at the remark, but said nothing save "Aye," tugged his hat brim further down, and went to ensure that his men were ready at the weather shrouds when the word to shorten was passed. The traditional rivalry between the hands working aloft on the three masts had transcended normal competition, resulting in several fist fights and more than a few incidents involving the ever-present seaman's knives which, fortunately, resulted in only minor wounds. The other mates, of course, were well aware of this contest of the seamen's skills, and used it constantly to their advantage; a certain benefit to the ship was that sails were usually smartly handed, furled, and set.

The hands had begun to break off from their pause at the rail and take their positions when the order to shorten sail went out. The waisters gathered amidships to handle halyards, sheets, and braces, pulling the big square sails around either to fill them, or spill the wind from them so the men aloft could furl them. As O'Malley and Clark saw that the "heavers" were in position at the foremast, he signaled Biggs and his men aloft. The t'gallants, being the highest sails on *Anne*, were usually first to come in when the weather started — not only did the yards have to be lowered and the sails furled to the yards, but the masts had to be either housed or struck down into the lower rigging. This was frequently difficult and dangerous. When non-emergency shortening was being accomplished, it was often done from the foremast to the mizzen, one mast at a time. This generally was quicker as enough men were available as 'heavers' at each mast when done individually, as opposed to breaking up crews for halyards, sheets, clew tackles, and braces at each mast.

Biggs' men were at the topmast cap and on the rope ladder leading to it from the top of the lower mast. Seeing this, Clark blew his whistle and shouted for clew lines to be hauled up and halyards to be let go. As the yard moved down the t'gallantmast, the sail drooped from its clewlines. Immediately the yard came to rest on the top mast cap, the men jumped onto it to haul up great handfuls of sail, securing it along the spar. As soon as the sail was securely furled, the order came to "ease jumper stays, standby to house the t'gallant mast." Biggs' men watched below to ensure the necessary lines were in hand, then, on order from Biggs, pulled the dog from the topmast cap and the t'gallant mast slid down the lubber hole in the topmast, coming to rest against a stop so that only a few feet of it showed above the topmast. There it was made fast securely.

The foremast jacks were then released by Biggs to go below, and most slid down the backstays to the deck. Even before they reached the deck, the maintopmen had started to perform the same tasks on the main t'gallant mast. Biggs watched for a few minutes as Jakes continually harangued his men, more often distracting them than inspiring them to greater speed. As the clewlines for the main t'gallant were hauled up, the sail's middle moved up toward the yard producing a "draped" effect which made it easier for the men on the yardarm to haul up the canvas and secure it. It seemed as though the job was going smoothly, in spite of the third's "encouragement." Biggs knew that Jakes had a great deal more deep water time than he, but he also knew that most on board thought Biggs was a better sailor.

As he made his way forward with his mates for supper, Isaac Biggs recalled the men who had taught him to hand, reef and steer. Of course, his father, a Banks fisherman who had taken young Isaac to sea at the tender age of eight, had been the major influence. Isaac remembered the skipper of that schooner, Mr. Rowe; a real sailorman he was who had sailed the deeps, and had only taken up fishing later in life. He had found in the lad a willingness to learn and an enthusiastic pupil who eagerly absorbed all that he saw and heard. It was he who had arranged for the boy to secure a berth as ordinary seaman on a brig out of Salem bound on the coastal route south. A bully mate had convinced Isaac that mind-ing his business and staying out of reach was the way to not only stay alive but also to advance, and within a short while, Biggs had been made an able seaman.

Still youthful and unwelcome ashore with the older men, Isaac, while becoming a most competent sailor, was sadly lacking in worldliness. His Methodist upbringing had taught him taverns were no place for a young Marblehead sailor, and aside from the half rations of grog provided him due to his youth, he had yet to taste the sweet potions of the ale houses. A succession of coastal ships added to his education, and ultimately to his current berth as captain of the foretop here on *Anne*. Watching others over the years, men he respected, had taught him that it was easier to lead men from in front, than by pushing from behind with a starter and shouts. The men liked his easy-going style and instinctive leadership and bent to their tasks with a will.

Captain Smalley, with whom Biggs had sailed for almost two years, had noticed his development and natural ability aloft as well as with his men, and was waiting for the opportunity to find him a berth as a third on a sloop or brig. To that end, Smalley had encouraged Sam Clark to instruct the topman in the art and science of navigation, and the reports he received from the mate confirmed his hopes for the lad's potential.

The third on *Anne*, Ben Jakes, was a poor leader of men and weak of character. Any man who felt regular use of a starter necessary would not, in Smalley's opinion, ever rise to command. Smalley also suspected that Jakes was involved in some underhanded dealings aboard, and did not trust him. Jakes was, however, an excellent seaman, and for that, the captain found him useful.

The wind was rising steadily now, and it was obvious to even the landsmen aboard that some dirty weather was indeed afoot. The t'gallants were in their gaskets and their masts struck down. The ship was responding to the trimming of sheets and hauling on the braces; she moved quickly now through the still calm sea as gradually, the wind's song in the rigging rose from a whispered caress to an insistent whine. The sky became darker — an ominous darkness which was beyond the growing dusk. Heavy clouds were beginning to move rapidly across the sky, increasing the gloom of twilight. The main topmen were back on deck, and were headed for the galley and their evening meal, debating the relative rapidity of handing their respective sails. In all likelihood, they'd be back soon — either to relieve the starboard watch or to reef tops'ls and courses if the wind continued to build. *Anne* began to heel to the wind, and the occasional burst of spray from the now building seas wet the decks.

Second Mate Joe O'Malley made his way aft toward the quarterdeck, moving his lanky form down the now canted deck in a rhythm dictated by the seas as they attacked the windward bow of *Anne* and rolled down the side of the ship. He noted the men working under the direction of First Mate Clark securing the carronades against the bulwarks. This action would be justified by the deteriorating conditions; a loose gun could wreak havoc on a tossing deck. The men had shortened the gun tackles and the barrels were slanted up against the bulwark and tied in place with heavy hemp line. Once secured in this manner, it would take more severe weather than they expected to move them.

O'Malley stepped onto the quarterdeck and headed for the wheel, where the helmsmen's stance and concentration provided a marked contrast to their inactivity earlier that day. O'Malley considered adding another pair of seamen to the wheel, then decided it could wait awhile. As the leader of the starbowlines, he was responsible for ensuring that the ship was properly manned while his watch was on deck. He checked the slate on which were recorded the regular casting of the ships log; after a string of "0"s and "1"s, it was good to see an "8" written on the slate just a few minutes previously. He estimated the wind at about thirty knots already, and knew that if it continued to increase, sails would again have to be shortened.

Spray was now blowing across the quarterdeck, making the watch turn their faces away from time to time when a heavier gust carried the spume over the deckhouse. It would surely get worse before it eased any. He watched the ship's boy turn the glass and move forward to the bell; five strokes could be heard before the wind carried the sound to leeward and away. The larboard watch was on deck and taking their positions at lookout, and at the sheets and braces, ready for the inevitable commands necessitated by the rising storm. O'Malley saw Ben Jakes, late yet again, heading for the quarterdeck to take over the watch until eight bells, when O'Malley would return to manage the ship until midnight. Jakes relieved his superior with few words exchanged in the face of a rising wind and their mutual antipathy.

Having assumed the watch, Ben felt the ship shiver slightly as a larger wave shocked the windward bow, and a burst of green water flew down the deck. The door to the deckhouse closed as O'Malley disappeared inside, narrowly avoiding a surge of water down the companionway. *What a night this is going to be*, thought Jakes, buttoning the top button on his oiled canvas jacket, and jamming his hat even further down on his head. *This is only going to get worse.*

He was right; the storm continued to deepen as he alternately stood by the helmsmen and paced up and down the quarterdeck. The captain had apparently decided to hold the sails currently deployed, at least for the time being, trying to make up some of the time lost in the calm; his orders to the watch were quite explicit and woe to the mate that countermanded them without damn good reason! Shortly before he was scheduled for relief, Jakes saw two of his maintopmen appear by the covered area abaft the deckhouse where the waisters and idlers were allowed to shelter in bad weather. Watching them for a minute or two, he realized they were arguing about something; hearing what was out of the question. Then he saw one of the men turn toward him and shout something; the wind carried the words away as soon as they were out of his mouth, but their implication was clear.

Ben Jakes had some unsavory characters in his watch and had found them useful in carrying out some of his less-than-honest chores. Those same men also found that Jakes could be helpful to them on occasion as well, and the resulting symbiotic relationship was usually at cross purposes with the goals of the captain and the owners. On a ship the size of *Anne*, many of these "deals" and goings-on were known throughout the fo'c'sle and mates' mess, but it was often better to ignore things that didn't affect you if you wanted to avoid an "accident." The captain and first mate suspected that Jakes was behind some of the problems they had experienced in the six months since he joined the ship, but none were as yet serious enough to override the fact that he was a very good seaman, and could be counted on to act properly when the situation required it. So far, his primary "business" appeared to be selling ships' stores and extra equipment ashore and, while it certainly was not desirable, it was common enough practice in both the merchant fleet and the Navy that it could be overlooked for now. If it developed into a greater problem, he could be paid off and put ashore.

Raising his voice over the increasing whine of the wind as he moved toward the two, Jakes shouted, "What are you two lubbers doin' hangin' about back here? You're s'posed to be for'ard."

One of the men, an older topman with a natural sneer to his face shouted back, " We can get there quick as ever you please should we be needed there, but we wanted to have a word with you."

They stepped into the deckhouse to continue the conversation at a more moderate tone. "Well, here I am. Have yer word."

"Biggs is gettin' to be more of a problem than ever. He was mentioning again to the first this afternoon that a lot of his spare line and blocks was gone missin' and that idler, Billy, 'at works as the captain's steward was standin' right there with his ears flappin' like wings. We wouldn't want our "business" to get snuffed by a nosy mate. If Billy happens to mention it in front of Cap'n Smalley, Clark mightn't have a choice but to close us down and God knows what else. What do ya think?"

"I think Biggs might have an accident aloft. There's some dirty weather makin' up tonight and my guess is the tops'ls and courses will have to be reefed during the evening watch. I'll . . . " Before he could finish the thought, Joe O'Malley appeared on the ladder, heading for the quarterdeck where he expected to find Jakes awaiting relief from his watch. A look passed between Jakes and his men that said, "He heard it all — now what?"

O'Malley instead spoke up and said, "I figgered you'd be aft, Ben. What are you doin' in here? A little weather botherin' you?"

"Just chasin' these two back up for'ard, Joe. And you needn't worry 'bout me and weather; I seen more than most. You here to take the watch now?" The menace in the third's growl was clear.

Ignoring the tone, O'Malley moved on, speaking over his shoulder to Jakes. "Aye. Let's get on with it before it gets any worse out there. I wouldn't want you to have to stay out in this any longer than necessary." They stepped outside, Jakes ignoring the jibe, accompanied by the two topmen who, with a look at Jakes, disappeared forward. O'Malley led the way to the quarterdeck, and turned when he got to the binnacle. "What was that all about?" he said. "You doin' 'business' at sea now? I thought you only traded in port. I would mind me ways at sea; there's no place to lay up if it gets stormy, if you get my drift."

"I would keep me nose in me own damn business, were I you, Joe O'Malley" snarled Jakes. "You gonna relieve me or stand there spoutin'?"

"You're relieved. But I'll warrant I see you again before the middle watch. We'll be shortenin' down, way this wind's risin', is my guess."

Jakes turned and moved forward, going around the deckhouse to the pin rail at the foot of the mainmast where his two sailors waited. "Well?" asked the older of the two, who had assumed the role of spokesman for these two miscreants.

Jakes studied his crony for a moment before responding. "He's thinking he knows more 'n he does. Don't worry about him. I think that foretopman, Biggs, is going to have to be taken care of though. Maybe I should have a word with one of his men later. If this weather holds, it's just possible that Biggs might have an accident while he's out on the foretops'l yard. That'll ease his sheets and at the same time cut us some slack with Clark. O' course, we'll be ashore in a couple of days, and sometimes men have trouble when they're drinkin' and carousin'; anything might happen."

CHAPTER TWO

Preparation for Trouble

Having resolved the matter in his own mind, Jakes moved forward and, ducking the occasional green water and now almost constant spray flying down the main deck, headed for the fo'c'sle hatch and a sailor on whom he thought he might depend for help in Biggs' crew of foretopmen.

Entering the crew's berthing area just forward of the galley, Jakes looked around, trying to pierce the gloom and smokiness. The contrast of the atmosphere in the fo'c'sle with what he had just left on the main deck was dramatic. The air here was close and fetid, filled with smells of food recently consumed, burned whale oil from the lamps, unwashed, sweaty bodies, and smoke from the cheap tobacco most seamen used. The creaking and groaning of the ship could be heard more clearly down here, without the screaming of the wind. In less boisterous weather, the water rushing past the bows made a comforting, restful noise which a landsman might favorably compare with a mountain stream. The noise heard now from the water meeting the bow was anything but comforting, and would be, to a landsman, positively distressing!

Jakes checked the few hammocks swinging with the roll of the ship without success. His man was not here; Biggs, however, was. He and Jakes saw each other through the fog of the cramped space. There were no words spoken; it wasn't necessary. Biggs, though able to get along with just about anyone, could barely tolerate Jakes, whose dirty dealings and underhandedness had no place aboard a ship, and were certainly not what Biggs would seek in an officer were he in a position to choose — which of course he was not. Jakes, jealous of Biggs' favor with the other mates, and more particularly the captain, had a burning desire to be rid of him, or make him look incompetent in any way he could. He didn't like being compared to an able bodied seaman and coming up short in the comparison. With a snort of disgust at not finding his man — or at finding Biggs — Jakes turned and left the forward living compartment. He stopped in the galley to scrounge some leftovers from the pensioner serving as cook on this voyage, and found Billy, the ship's boy, helping him clean up.

"Billy," he said. "Run up on deck quick as ever you can and see if you can find Reese for me. Tell him to meet me at the foot of the foremast. And step lively!"

The boy ran out, heading for the ladder and leaving Cook to finish the clean up. Needless to say, Cook was not pleased at having his helper taken from him. Being old, and a veteran of numerous passages including six 'round the Horn, Cook had seen mates like Jakes time and again; they never came to any good, and usually had to "lead" their men from behind with a starter or rope's end. If Jakes was looking for Reese, Cook thought to himself, there was something in the wind that wouldn't do anyone but Jakes any good. Not wanting to get on the bad side of the short tempered third mate, Cook said nothing, but thought he might mention his premonition to Mr. O'Malley or Mr. Clark when next he saw one or the other.

Third Mate Ben Jakes left the galley gnawing absently on a piece of hardtack; he did not see the look Cook threw in his wake, and had he, probably would not have cared a whit. He seemed impervious to the hate and discontent he routinely aroused in both the foredeck sailors and his fellow ship's officers. Stepping out on deck again, he realized that, even in his short absence, the weather had deteriorated; green water was rolling down the deck with more frequency and violence. The wind had increased noticeably, and the lee bulwark was just inches from being continually awash. Glancing aloft as he worked his way aft to meet Reese, he saw the courses and tops'ls straining at their buntlines and sheets. The braces on the yards were stiff as iron bars and the mainyard had the beginnings of a bow in each end. Shortening down was going to come quicker that he had guessed. *Good thing the carronades already been secured,* he thought. *I better tell Cook to get some weather cloth around the livestock. Deck's gonna be under water, these waves keep buildin'.* He wrinkled his nose as he passed to leeward of the pen holding some chickens, a couple of pigs, and several lambs. Even with the breeze up, the odor emanating from the "floating barnyard" was strong. The animals stirred nervously, huddling together as the lambs bleated soulfully, sensing as they did the approaching weather.

It was full dark now, and the low flying clouds obscured any light that might have come from the heavens. Rain was beginning to fall, blowing horizontally in the howling gale and mixing with the salt spume in the air; it was getting on towards being a really dirty night! He saw Reese standing just aft of the foremast, his canvas jacket buttoned to his chin, and a raggedy tarpaulin cap pulled down low over his face. His bare feet seemed rooted to the deck, and his natural seaman's ability to adapt to the motion of the ship allowed him to stand in the scant shelter offered by the foremast without so much as resting a hand on the pin rail next to his hip. Indeed, his wiry form seemed adequately protected by the girth of the mast, though his tarred braid stood off to leeward as the occasional gust of wind caught it. Reese wiped a small, almost delicate hand across his face, momentarily ridding his stubbled cheeks and close-set eyes of the mixture of rain and spray.

"You wanted to see me, Mr. Jakes?" Reese's unnaturally high pitched voice seemed to carry clearly in spite of the noises surrounding them. "I was just thinkin' we're gonna be shortenin' down right quick now. I was hanging here on deck 'cuz Biggs likes us to be first aloft when a sail change is called. I noticed the Captain aft talkin' to Mr. O'Malley just now; hadda be 'bout reefin' tops'ls and courses. If this keeps gettin' worse we're . . ."

The last thing Jakes wanted to hear was that O'Malley and the captain were deep in conversation; had O'Malley mentioned what he had overheard from Jakes and his two sailors?

"Shut up, Reese, and listen to me." Jakes' growl provided a strange counterpoint to the nasal whine from Reese, and he raised his voice even though he was practically touching the foremast jack. "You can even an old score tonight if you're up to it. You might even get to be captain of the foretop — you will if I have anything to say about it."

"Biggs is captain o' the foretop, Mr. Jakes. You know that. I shoulda been. I got more time aloft than he's got at sea, but the first picked him when the Swede paid off in Boston."

"That's just the old score I was thinkin' of, Reese. If something were to happen to Biggs when we're reefing tops'ls later on, like a weakened becket up there, he might just go overboard. I'd see to it

that you were named to replace him. It would be a big help to me."
His conspiratorial smile, and a wink from under the brim of his hat
put one in mind of a shark about to enjoy a tasty meal. "There's
always room for one more hand in some of my business dealings
ashore, but I need someone I can trust and count on to help me
when I ask. Think you might be . . ."

His words were cut off by a particularly violent gust of wind-
driven rain and spume, followed by the ship lurching so hard that
both men grabbed for the pin rail to steady themselves.

"I sure would like to be captain of the foretop, like I deserve, Mr.
Jakes, but if you're askin' me to pitch Biggs overboard, I don't
think I kin do that. He ain't a bad sort, and he is a pretty fair
hand."

"You wouldn't be pitching him overboard, you muddle-headed
lubber!" Jakes started backwatering, realizing he might have
picked the wrong man to enlist in his plot. He had to convince this
man to become a confederate now that he had tipped his hand.
Accomplishing his objective without Reese would not be impossible, but it wouldn't do to have Reese talking to his shipmates about
the third's murderous intentions. Having gone this far, Jakes had
to either enlist his assistance or ensure that Reese did not share
his new insight to the third mate's mindset with any of his shipmates.

"Listen, Reese, all you have to do is cut one of the beckets up
on the foretops'l yard — not all the way through — just enough so
it won't hold him when he puts his arm through it. The weather'll
take care of the rest, and since you'll be at the other end of the
yard, you'll be clear of it, if someone asks. He might not even use
a becket, if he holds the jackstay. You know that men fall from
yards in bad weather from time to time. Hell, I'd bet you even saw
it more 'n' once."

A cloud passed over Reese's face as the memory of just such an
incident came to his mind. Jakes watched him carefully and realized he could lose his complicity if he allowed his conscience to
bubble up anymore. Reese spoke again, before the third could seize
the initiative.

"Mr. Jakes, I can't do what you want. You're right. I've seen
men fall from the yards. One fell who was right next to me on the
main tops'l yard on the old *Pride* out of New York, back in the year
four, I think it was. I watched him grab for the mainyard footrope

as he fell and missed. He landed on the pinrail and I still 'member the sound when he hit; the Cap'n said he broke his back. No sir, I wouldn't want to see that again. You better find yourself another foremast jack to cut that becket."

Jakes realized Reese was about to turn and end the discussion. He had to do something to get his help, or climb up to the tops'l yard himself and cut a becket. He could handle that easily, and, he realized, should have done so from the outset. Now he had to do it himself, and on top of it, he had a sailor who knew of his intention to cause Biggs to have an accident. "Reese! Just keep in mind you could have something go wrong up there too. . . 'specially if someone hears about our words here."

Reese staggered away toward the forward hatch, timing his movements to match those of the ship as she labored through the now heavy seas. The third mate watched him disappear in the rain and spray, then moving carefully over to the windward shrouds, swung up onto the ratlines, heading for the foreyard and a becket that needed to be dealt with.

CHAPTER THREE

Tragedy Strikes

"All hands on deck!" The first mate and Second Mate O'Malley were hollering down the hatches, rousing the men to heave out and get topside. Since the watch was about ready to change, it being nearly midnight, the men were quicker on deck than might have been expected. However, they were still rubbing the sleep from their eyes and hitching up their trousers. Shoes were not an issue; most were barefoot and had the splayed, callused feet to show for long periods of shoeless sea time. Shoes and boots were for going ashore, and for use at sea only in the colder parts of the globe.

The captain's appearance on the quarterdeck shortly before had precipitated the call. As was his habit, he spent most of the dark hours when the weather was making up or already bad on the quarterdeck. He trusted the seamanship of his mates, but it was his ship and his responsibility. He was known to have taken a turn at the wheel from time to time just to "see how she felt," particularly after a sail change. Like most men of his experience, he truly believed that a properly trimmed and managed ship would "talk" to a knowledgeable seaman through her wheel, and like many captains, he had favorites among the seamen qualified to steer. In touchy situations he would tell the mate which he wanted; this night might yet become one of those situations, but for the moment, any four men qualified to handle the big wheel would suffice. The wind and resulting seas had picked up to the point where two were required on each side of the big helm just to keep *Anne* on course without shivering the sails, or worse, backing one or more, as the wind fluked around a couple of points either side of east.

Dirty ain't in it, he thought as the leeward rail scooped up another wave and rolled it down the lee side of the deck nearly waist-deep. The wind had increased its wail to a constant scream now, and the low racing clouds totally obliterated any possible light from stars or moon. The spray whipping down the deck had some sting to it and maintaining footing was getting to be more and more difficult, even to the experienced hands in *Anne*. The new men, mostly landsmen who had given up farming or store keeping to go to sea, found it impossible to move down the deck without holding on to the safety lines Clark had had rigged earlier in O'Malley's watch. Additionally, since this was the first really bad weather to hit them since they left Boston, many were feeling its effects. Captain Smalley had seen several earlier in the watch chasing a yard of puke to the rail. *This night'll give 'em their sea legs, or they'll never get 'em,* he thought. Fortunately, most of the men who would be working aloft were all good hands and he had confidence in their ability to do their jobs while maintaining one hand for themselves and one for the ship.

In response to the orders Smalley had issued moments before to Sam Clark, the mates were sending men to their positions for shortening sail — again. He would see how his ship rode under the shortened sail before he would significantly alter course to scud before the storm, or heave to. They were still more or less making their heading, and if he could safely continue, they would make St. Bartholomew in good time, in spite of the two days lost to the calms. He would shorten more than was necessary, leaving a stays'l up for'ard as an acknowledgment of the essentially beam winds. He heard Clark's whistle as the men assembled at their assigned positions.

This time, he thought, it would not be a simple chore, as it was when they furled the t'gallants some six hours before. Now the wind was up, the sails straining in their buntlines and the braces and bowlines taut as ever they might be. The waisters had to brace the yards around to spill the wind from the sails so the topmen could reef or furl as necessary. Timing for the evolution was critical, and a false move aloft or the early release of a halyard or sheet on deck could result in loss of life. The first sail to be dealt with would be the mains'l, or as most called it, the course. The yard was hauled around to spill the wind, and the sheet was eased. The men aloft, under Ben Jakes, moved out on either side of the yard, both hands on the jackstay, and feet shuffling crablike on the footropes. When they reached their assigned positions on the yard, Jakes bawled out the order to furl. Leaning over the yard, now with an arm through a convenient becket, the men grabbed the wildly flapping canvas and hauled it up over the yard, tucking it between their bodies and the yardarm. Once it was up, brails and gaskets were passed and the sail was secure. On order from below, the topmen moved up to the topmast and the main tops'l yard which the waisters were already beginning to ease down. When it was lowered sufficiently to tie in a reef, the men went out on the yard and repeated the ballet they had performed on the main yard, effectively reducing the sail area.

As the job finished, the maintopmen came down off the mast, some by "riding the backstays," others more conservatively down the shrouds and their ratlines. The foremast hands started aloft while the waisters and heavers moved forward on the gyrating deck, trying to maintain their footing, sometimes knee-deep in the water rushing down the length of the ship, and find a secure hold on their assigned halyard, brace, or sheet. The foretops'l and course would be furled, leaving only a forestays'l up to give the ship some weatherly ability. To say the work was dangerous was understatement at its finest; the thrashing canvas could knock an unprepared man off the yard in a trice. From there, the next stop was the deck or the sea. In either case tonight, a fall was a death sentence; there was no way a man in the water could be found even if a boat could be put over the side without foundering in the heavy seas.

Working beside his men on the foreyard, Isaac Biggs kept one arm through a becket, his splayed bare feet seeming to grip the footrope. As the forecourse was hauled up by the men below, he and his other foretopmen took handfuls of the stiff canvas sail and tucked it between the spar and their bodies, much the same as the men on the mainmast had done. When they had all of the sail thus hauled up — not an easy task by any means — they would pass the gaskets and secure it to the yard. As the sail area was reduced, the ship seemed to stand a little straighter and labor less, but the frenzy of the elements was not diminished a whit; in fact, up on the foreyard, the storm seemed more ferocious than below. The roar of the wind made it almost impossible to hear a shouted word unless it was from the man next to you. The rain, driving horizontally, made everything slick, and the footropes under the yard were swaying crazily with the motion of the ship, amplified ten-fold at the main or foretop.

The fores'l was almost furled now, and after taking the final few tucks, the topmen would pass the gaskets around the spar and sail. After that, they would move up to the tops'l yard and furl that sail. The men worked at their task without thought of the peril of their jobs — it was instinctive to keep an arm through a becket, or hang on to the jackstay while engaged in this dangerous enterprise. Biggs felt a hand grabbing at his soaked nankeen shirt and the footrope jerked under his feet. He turned to look at the man next to him, Reese, thinking he was trying to get his attention by pulling at his shirt, and to his surprise, saw no one next to him on the yard. Reese wasn't there! There were only five men on this side of the yard. The footrope was swaying crazily and he heard a faint shout over the scream of the wind. Biggs realized the screaming he was hearing wasn't just the wind and, following with his eyes the additional sound to its source, saw Reese, wide-eyed in fear, hanging onto the footrope, suspended over the deck with nothing but wind and rain between him and perdition. Reese looked up at Biggs imploringly. Isaac could see his shipmate's mouth forming words, and only by listening carefully could he make out, "Help me, Biggs!" Reese was screaming it, but the wind snatched the words away before anyone could hear them. Biggs loosened his hold on the becket and eased himself down to where he was almost sitting on the footrope.

Grabbing a handful of Reese's shirt, he shouted at him, "Take hold o' my hand, Reese! You got to let go of the footrope; I won't drop you." Reese, clearly terrified, had a death grip on the footrope. There was not a chance in Hell he would let go of the only thing between him and the deck!

Suddenly, Biggs saw another of his foretopmen beside him on the footrope reaching for Reese's arm. With a secure grip on it, he pulled up and Reese, realizing he would not now fall, let go of his hold, making it possible for the two men to pull him to a sitting position on the footrope.

When they were standing up and holding on to the jackstay, Biggs shouted at Reese, "What happened, Reese? Did you slip?" For answer, Reese moved down the yard a few feet and picked up the becket he was using while furling the foresail; it was in two pieces, and even in the driving rain and pitch darkness, Biggs could see it had been cut so that only one strand of the three normally there would take the load imposed on it. Naturally, as soon as Reese had leaned into it, it parted and, losing his balance in the violent motion of the mast and pummeled by the shivering sail, he fell. It was only through his experience and quick reaction that he was able to grab the footrope, and save himself from a certain death. The words Reese shouted were indistinguishable, but the look on his face, white with the realization of his close call, was not. Biggs motioned to him to go down to the deck and he and the remaining foretopmen finished furling the sail quickly. After moving further aloft, to the tops'l yard, with his men to perform the same task there, he made a final check to ensure everything was secure and as was his habit in weather good or bad, Biggs took the fast way down, sliding down the tops'l downhaul to the deck. He was followed by two of his men, the others preferring the windward ratlines as safer in bad weather.

Biggs and his men found Reese heading aft on the heaving deck, oblivious to the seas sweeping it, and the wind driven rain and spray making the atmosphere palpable. They caught up to him as he grabbed onto the pin rail at the foot on the mainmast, more to keep from washing down the deck than for balance. Seeing the look on his face, Biggs and one of the men who accompanied him took his arms and steered him to the after end of the deckhouse, more or less out of the wind and water. In the darkness and frightful weather, neither the waisters handling sheets and braces for the men furling the mizzen tops'l and reefing the spanker, nor O'Malley who was supervising the task, were aware of anything save the chore at hand.

"What the Sam Hill are you doing?" shouted Biggs as they ducked into shelter. He wiped his dripping face, pushing back his sodden curls, as he peered deep into his fellow topman's eyes.

"I know how that becket came to be cut like that, Biggs. It was Jakes done it. I know. He wanted me to cut it so you would fall. I didn't play his game and he must'a' found someone else, or done it hisself." The older man's eyes again grew wide, this time in anger.

"That's serious business, Reese. If it ain't true, Jakes'll rightly have your ass." One of his mates from the foremast looked hard at him and then at Biggs, to whom they all looked for leadership. "Why do you think Jakes done it, and not someone else?"

"Jakes told me afore the watch changed that if I helped him, he'd make me captain of the foretop. Said Biggs would fall and that no one would be the wiser, long as I kept my mouth shut." Reese forced his words out through clenched teeth. "I told him I wouldn't be part of killing someone, least of all Biggs. Then he said I better watch my own self, or I'd have an accident. I'm gonna gut that whoreson."

Isaac's brow furrowed as he considered the problem. "Hold on now, Reese. Let's see what Mr. Clark thinks about this. We'll get to him as soon as Jackson's men finish on the mizzen. He'll know what to do. For now, we got to go on watch."

The final part of shortening sail was coming along nicely, and the ship was starting to once again behave like the lady she was, handling the sea with dignity and grace. While still the occasional wave did thunder down the deck, making use of the safety lines imperative, walking and working on deck again became possible. All that remained was to tie in a reef on the spanker, the big fore and aft sail rigged to the mizzenmast. O'Malley stood on the after end of the quarterdeck, next to the sheet for the big mizzen boom, waiting for the men on the peak and throat halyards to take their positions for easing same. He would signal the helmsmen to bring her up a trifle so that the mizzen would shiver some and allow the sail to come down enough to tie in a reef.

Seeing that all was ready, he blew his whistle and waved his arm; the men on the wheel brought the ship's bow closer to the wind. If they brought her up too high, they ran the risk of backing the reefed main tops'l and stopping the forward motion of the ship; if they didn't get the bow up enough, the men tying in the reef on the mizzen would have to deal with a sail that might as well have been carved from wood as made from flexible canvas. O'Malley watched the helmsmen and the main tops'l; he saw the tops'l begin to shiver, and shouted to the men at the wheel.

"Hold her there . . . meet her!" His words were barely audible over the sounds of the storm, but the men hanging onto the ship's wheel heard and obeyed. Unfortunately, at that moment, the wind decided not to cooperate and shifted a point to the south. This caused the tops'l to back, briefly, but more importantly, the shift caused the mizzen to shiver violently. O'Malley, seeing that the tops'l was backed and that the ship was in danger shouted to "Pay off!" and "Let her head come down!" Captain Smalley had also seen the situation developing and had stepped to the wheel to add his weight to the effort of the four men trying to correct the problem before *Anne* had lost headway, or worse, begun to make sternway, a condition which could tear off the rudder. O'Malley, seeing there was nothing he could do in that direction, looked at the mizzen boom and saw one of his men hanging on to the sheet tackle, trying apparently to tame the wildly thrashing sail. Shouting "Hang on!" he stepped aft without a second thought to grab the hapless seaman before the boom shook him into the sea. He had managed to get a hand on the sailor's trousers to guide him to the deck when, with a stunning crash, the sail filled. With the sheet tackle loose, there was nothing to stop the sail as it filled, and the heavy block slammed into the second mate. Backwards over the taffrail he fell, his head pretty well stove in. For the hands under the mizzen boom, time stopped as they watched O'Malley tumble into the churning froth of *Anne*'s wake. Instantly, he was gone.

The cry "Man overboard!" sprang from half a dozen mouths simultaneously. The words were unnecessary. Both the captain and Mr. Clark had seen the accident, but their instinctive reaction to heave to and get a boat in the water had to be overcome tonight; no small boat would make ten feet before foundering. The captain shouted above the storm at his mate, "I don't think there's anything we can do for him. I can't risk a boat and crew in this sea, and bringing *Anne* to would do no good without we put the cutter over."

"Looked to me like his head got stove in by the boom, Cap'n. My guess is that he was dead when he cleared the rail," the mate said, trying to ease his and Captain Smalley's frustration and guilt over being unable to rescue their shipmate.

Clark moved aft and took charge of the stunned, now leaderless men. His calm and commanding presence brought them back to their unfinished task, and they moved to carry out his orders.

"Ease the halyards now. Lively there. Reefers, get your reefs tied in smartly now." And finally, "Take up the slack in the halyards. Belay and secure."

CHAPTER FOUR

Burial at Sea

"Mr. Clark, pass the word for the crew to assemble in the waist for the memorial service, if you please. I am going to my cabin. Please join me for a word or two, and when the hands are mustered, have Mr. Jakes send Billy for us and we'll lay Mr. O'Malley's spirit to rest."

"Aye aye, Cap'n." Clark turned to Ben Jakes who was enjoying the warm and pleasant weather at the rail near the quarterdeck. He had a self-satisfied smirk on his face, and seemed to be thinking that things were going quite well for Mr. Benjamin Jakes, Third Mate, and soon, he thought, to be named second mate. "Jakes, since you seem to have taken on as acting second, call the hands to attend the service for O'Malley. When we get done with it, I'll want to have a word with you in private."

As Jakes started to move off to muster the crew, Clark turned and disappeared into the deckhouse, heading for the captain's cabin as he had been ordered to do. He went down the ladder to the berthing deck and headed aft through the mates' dining compartment. The captain's door was closed, and Clark knocked once on it, getting a response almost immediately. He walked into the cabin, and stood with his hat in his hands waiting for the captain to look up from the chart he was studying at his writing table.

"Sit down Mr. Clark. I was checking our position and figuring when we might expect to pick up St. Maarten. Near as I can see, we didn't lose too much to the storm, and with this nor'easterly holding steady, we should see the mountains during the morning watch — probably at first light — tomorrow. Means we'll be in St. Bartholomew by supper time, assuming we don't run afoul of any privateers and have to run for it."

"Aye, sir. I understand from the carpenter that the hold is

drying out. Says the water we shipped during the storm never damaged the cargo since we got on the pumps right quick and kept the level down. Without we unload the holds, I can't check the hull for damage, but I'm thinkin' there won't be much when we do. Maybe a little caulkin' be necessary, but we'd still be shippin' water if there was more 'n that. The usual hour a watch on the pumps has kept her pretty dry. Aloft, as you know, we made out pretty good; only problem was the maintops'l yard splittin' and Jakes's men replaced that yesterday, right after the storm blew itself out. No, I think old *Anne's* in pretty fair shape."

"That she is, Mr. Clark. That she is. I'm more concerned about the men than the ship right now, though. With O'Malley gone, we need to have a new second, and I'm not real easy with putting Jakes into the job. I don't trust him, and although he's a fine seaman, the second's job is more than seamanship, as you know. I'm thinkin' that maybe we won't name anyone to the position until after we get to St. Bartholomew. We might find us a better man there, and we shouldn't have no trouble making the island without a second. You and Jakes'll just have to take up the slack."

"That'll be no problem for me, Cap'n. I'll take O'Malley's watch with the starbowlines. Jakes'll have to pull a little extra weight too, but I'll take him out of the maintop to free him up some. I don't know who we'll put on as captain of the maintop, but I guess Jakes can make that selection. I want to leave Jackson on the mizzen — he's got him a bunch o' landsmen with him, and they need to be watched pretty close so's no one gets hurt. What are you gonna do if you don't get a new second in St. Barts? I don't think we wanta sail home without a qualified second mate. Also, O'Malley was pretty good with the carronades, and Jakes don't know the gun tackle from the touch hole on 'em. We need someone what knows guns as well."

"Aye, that we do. I'm sure we'll find some men in St. Bartholomew who'll ship as gunners. The second concerns me more, but there's nothing I can do about it at sea. I guess we'll have to see which way the wind is blowin' when we get there. Let Mr. Jakes know he's not going to be named second mate. I don't 'spect he'll be real pleased. He's been kinda puffin' some since the weather cleared. Guess he thought he'd slip right into it. I wish I trusted the man, but you know as well as me he's selling ship's stores ashore. I'd like to catch him up in it and have done with this whole mess once and for all. I can't put him ashore on suspicion, so until we catch him, I think we'll let him stew for a while; maybe he'll slip up."

"Yessir," nodded Clark. "Biggs, the Captain of the Foretop, was tellin' me just the other day 'at he was missin' some blocks and spare line he kept for emergencies on the foremast. Said none o' his men moved 'em. One of the maintopmen musta said something, 'cuz Biggs seemed to think Jakes had something to do with the stuff goin' missin'. I also heard some scuttlebutt that Jakes was involved with a foretopman fallin' durin' the recent weather. Nobody's hurt or missin' so's it couldn'a been much, and Biggs ain't said a word to me 'bout any of his men fallin'. I think we'd best keep a weather eye on Mr. Jakes for the next few days."

On deck, the men were assembling from throughout the ship. Since it was late in the morning watch with fine weather and moderate seas, there was only routine maintenance being performed, and the men not on watch were sewing clothes, dozing, and taking their ease forward. They stood in a loose formation, more in groups based on jobs, as was their habit when mustered, in the waist of the ship, forward of the quarterdeck to await the appearance of their captain and the start of the memorial to their late second mate. While only a few men had actually seen the accident, all had heard, and were genuinely sorry to have lost O'Malley, for two reasons: O'Malley was well liked throughout the ship by almost everyone. He was known as a friend, and could be counted on to lend a hand when needed, even though a ship's officer. They also grieved because, in all likelihood, Ben Jakes would be named second in the natural progression of things; if not permanently, at least until the ship returned to Boston or received word from their owner's agent confirming or denying the advance. Of course, only a small few of the men knew that there was a reason why Jakes should not have the promotion.

With the death of O'Malley, Reese's problem seemed to pale, and neither he nor Biggs had yet talked to the first mate about their suspicions that Jakes had tried to murder a foretopman. In fact, with the passage of a few days, the incident had not seemed quite as pressing as it had when Reese came off the foreyard with the intent to "gut that whoreson." Maybe the becket had not been cut, maybe it was frayed and worn, and the strain put on it by the topman in the storm had sufficiently weakened it so that it parted

. . . or maybe not.

Regardless of the problems of the past, the men were indeed glad that a burial service was to be held for Mr. O'Malley; a sailor left "unburied," or without a memorial, was understood to return to the ship, haunting and bedeviling the crew. No proper captain would forget such a duty, and the men knew that Captain Smalley took such responsibilities seriously.

Jakes, seeing that most of the crew were now here and waiting, called to Billy with an attitude that befitted his assumed role of second mate, "Run down to the Cabin quick as ever you can and tell the captain and Mr. Clark the men are mustered." His eyes darted around the ship, taking in the assembled crew and lightly brushing over the youthful messenger as if he were unworthy of the mate's attention.

Billy turned and dashed into the deckhouse and clattered down the ladder. He almost stumbled in his zeal to do Jakes' bidding, and instead of knocking on the captain's door, more or less fell against it with an embarrassing thud. Mr. Clark opened it, and realizing what had happened, smiled.

"A simple knock will do in the future, Billy."

The color rose in the boy's neck and face. He stammered out the message from the deck, and turned to go, lest he embarrass himself further.

The captain, carrying his well-worn, dog-eared prayer book and followed by the mate, headed topside to begin the burial at sea, but without a body to bury. Smalley wanted to get this behind them all as quickly as possible, and while he had handled this same chore many times before in the twenty-five years he had been a captain, he always dreaded it. While he was privately a religious man, and read his Bible faithfully, he wasn't a parson and was uncomfortable reading scripture aloud and pontificating on things spiritual.

He was probably made most uncomfortable by the memory of having to say the words over the body of his captain that awful day in 1782 when he woke up in the cockpit of a navy brig with the surgeon's mate leaning over him. The memory rushed back as he climbed the ladder to the deck. He recalled that the body next to him was what remained of his captain, recognizable only by the tatters of the jacket on his torso. His head was gone, and much of his upper body burned. Smalley could not help but bring to mind the final moments of the exchange of broadsides with a British man o' war, and the sight of the captain as his upper body took the full impact of a white hot "hot shot," decapitating him in a fountain of blood and turning his shoulders into a torch that burned brightly but mercifully briefly. That was the day his hair had started going gray. He shook his head, and stepped out into the sunlight.

At the edge of the quarterdeck, he took a minute to look at the faces of his men. He had been through some pretty nasty weather, and even an encounter or two with privateers with some of them, but he had never had to lay to rest one of their shipmates. Their faces returned his stare expectantly, and he heard the first behind him cough discreetly and clear his throat.

Better get on with it, he thought, and began thumbing through his prayer book for the appropriate passages. When he found them, he marked them with his index finger, holding the book in two hands, and looked back at the men for whom he was captain, mother, father, judge, and occasionally parson. His normally gaunt face seemed even more drawn, his eyes deeper in their sockets.

"Men, before we get started with the service for Mr. O'Malley, I want to tell you what a fine job you all did in the unpleasant weather we experienced the other night. Without your quick response to the mates and your skills, so recently learned by some of you, we would not have fared as well as we did. Together, we kept *Anne* sailing safely, and while not always toward St. Bartholomew, we didn't lose a lot of time over what we lost to the calms some days ago. I have heard that a foretopman almost fell during reefing that night, but since apparently no one was hurt, and as no one has come to Mr. Clark, I guess all's well."

Out of the corner of his eye, he caught the glance Ben Jakes directed at Biggs, who was standing with his foretopmen on the windward side; the color had briefly drained from Jakes' face. He recovered his composure as quickly as he lost it, but the scowl that appeared on Reese's face did not go away. The topman shifted, as though to take a step. The captain noticed Biggs put his hand on Reese's arm, and then the moment passed; there was probably no one else on the ship, including Sam Clark, who noticed the exchange.

"As you all know, we are here now to give Mr. O'Malley a proper burial. You are all aware that he was killed and knocked overboard while reefing the spanker the other night. There was nothing that anyone could have done to prevent it, or save him. Mr. Clark and I both believe that he was dead before he hit the water, and heaving to would have been for naught. Let us now bow our heads and put his spirit at peace.

"God is our hope and our strength, a very present help in trouble. Therefore we will not fear, though the earth be moved, and though the hill be carried into the midst of the sea; though the waters rage and swell and though the mountains shake at the tempest of the same.

"There is a river, the streams whereof make glad the city of God; the holy place of the tabernacle of the Most Highest. God is in the midst of her, therefore shall she not be removed; God shall help her and that right early.

" Be still then, and know that I am God: I will be exalted among the nations, and I will be exalted in the earth.

" The Lord of hosts is with us; the God of Jacob is our refuge.

" Out of the deep I have called unto thee, O Lord; Lord hear my voice.

"O let thine ears consider well the voice of my complaint.

"My soul fleeth unto to the Lord before the morning watch; I say before the morning watch.

"O Israel, trust in the Lord, for with the Lord there is mercy, and with him is plenteous redemption.

"And he shall redeem Israel from all his sins."

The captain paused for a moment from his reading. He removed his spectacles, saw that he still had the attention of the men, and moved to the leeward rail of the quarterdeck. Facing the sea, he returned the spectacles to his face, checked the page in his prayer book, and raised his voice to its quarterdeck command level.

"Remember thy servant, Joseph O'Malley, O Lord, according to the favor which thou bearest unto thy people, and grant that, increasing in knowledge and love of thee, he may go from strength to strength, in the life of perfect service, in thy heavenly kingdom . . ."

"Sail ho! Fine on the windward bow." The disembodied voice of the lookout standing in the foremast crosstrees effectively ended the service; for two or three heartbeats, even the breathing of the ship's company stopped; the easy motion of the ship on her southerly course belied the urgency of the lookout's words. He called out again.

"Deck there. Sails on the wind'ard bow. Showin' topmasts fore 'n' aft."

PART TWO

HMS ORPHEUS
1810 - 1812

CHAPTER FIVE

A Meeting at Sea

"She's to leeward, sir, about four leagues. Showin' t'gallants and tops'ls," the lookout shouted down in response to the question from Lieutenant Oliver Fitzgerald of His Majesty's Navy. Lieutenant Fitzgerald had the morning watch on the Fifth Rate HMS *Orpheus* sailing the Leeward Island station.

So far this cruise had been quite unremarkable, and he hoped that perhaps this ship, seen only minutes ago from the crosstrees of the foremast, would provide some diversion, and maybe even a French prize. As the officer in charge of the forward six guns, three on the larboard side, and three on the starboard side on the weather deck, he hoped for some action. His crews needed some practice, and Captain Harry Winston, of rather parsimonious leanings, was firmly convinced that shooting at contrived targets was a waste of time and effort, not to mention shot and powder. His opinion was that crews learned fastest when someone was shooting back at them, and so spent little time in actual shooting. He did, however, have lengthy dull drills of "dumb show" wherein the great guns were run in and out to simulate firing. The crews, as well as his officers, did not feel this provided much benefit beyond learning the motions involved; some of the new men had never heard the crashing roar of one of the frigate's 26 eighteen-pounders, not to mention the thunder of a 32-pounder carronade, of which she had eight.

"Mr. Blake, step up to the main tops'l yard, if you please, and tell me what you see." Lieutenant Fitzgerald did not particularly care for the midshipman assigned to his watch. Blake was a good looking young man of seventeen years, well muscled and tall for his age, and quite bright. He had been at sea now for five years, first as a boy, then with an appointment to midshipman from a captain who had taken a liking to him. He most likely would pass for lieutenant in two years when the Board would hear his oral examination, and it bothered Fitzgerald that he had done well without the political connections so common in the Royal Navy. While he was loath to admit it, Lieutenant Fitzgerald would have struggled to attain masters mate without some heavy shore-side pushing by an uncle, well connected in Whitehall. He rarely missed an opportunity to send the lad aloft — usually higher than necessary — or on a fools errand.

"She's still hull-down, sir, but I can see courses fore and aft. Four leagues, I make it, and closing. It appears she's born off some, and if we do so as well, we'll close even faster." Midshipman Blake further annoyed his lieutenant with the speed at which he attained his lofty perch and the completeness of his report, giving Fitzgerald little room for criticism or complaint.

He managed, however. "When I need the instruction of a midshipman as to how to close a strange vessel, I will let you know. Until then, Mr. Blake, restrict your answers to what you were asked!"

He added, for good measure, "Her flag, man. What flag does she show?"

The response was immediate. "None, sir. No colors. Not even a house flag."

Captain Winston, a seasoned commander who had made an excellent record for both himself and HMS *Orpheus*, chose that moment to appear on the quarterdeck. His presence was immediately felt by all on the quarterdeck. Without looking at him, the watch knew with certainty that their diminutive captain would be in full uniform, clean-shaven save for his mutton chop whiskers, and capable of instantly assessing the situation. That he was a harsh man who firmly believed in the power of the cat was offset by his superb record of taking prizes, and his well respected ability as a seaman.

"What do we have, Mr. Fitzgerald. I assume you had already sent your midshipman to find me?" Winston raised one bushy eyebrow at the portly young lieutenant, a gesture that spoke volumes to any unlucky recipient.

As the color rose in his face, Fitzgerald noticed beyond the captain that Midshipman Blake was about to step onto the bulwark from the main shrouds. Turning slightly, the lieutenant of the watch raised his voice and put as much authority as he could muster into it.

"Mr. Blake, you needn't go find the captain, as I had instructed you. He is here. Instead, find the gunner, and have him step aft, if you please."

Recognizing that his lieutenant was barely competent, and that the young mid had just been aloft, Captain Winston turned to face Blake.

"Mr. Blake, what is your opinion of that sail? What would you do to close with her?"

"Sir," Blake began to stammer. An eyebrow began to rise. Responding to the officer of the watch was one thing; responding to the captain was another one entirely, especially Captain Winston. It was unusual to have this captain address a midshipman directly, especially in front of the watch lieutenant, and it slightly unnerved him. "I would ease sheets enough to bear off some. That would close her faster, but maintain the weather gauge in the event she was not friendly." He saw the eyebrow return to its place, and a smile begin to play at the corners of the captain's mouth. He gained some confidence. He went on, his words accelerating enthusiastically. "She could be an American merchant going to one of the neutrals down here."

"Very well, Mr. Blake. It appears that you have been learning your lessons well. Now go and fetch the gunner, as Lieutenant Fitzgerald asked. Quickly, if you please.

"Mr. Fitzgerald, if you agree with your midshipman, you might give the order to ease sheets, and bear off a trifle. When we're closer but still ahead of him, we will tack the ship and maintain a position from which we can cross his bow if it proves necessary. In the meantime, let us see what we have found here. Opportunity awaits us, perhaps."

The sails were now plainly visible from deck, and although the ship itself was still below the visual horizon, from the maintop she would show her hull. Fitzgerald looked at the captain, picked up his long glass, and said "With your permission, sir, I will have a look myself from the maintop." He did not wait for an answer, but moved smartly forward to the weather shrouds at the break of the quarterdeck.

The captain watched his junior lieutenant struggle up the shrouds, noting the strain on his none-too-clean britches as he climbed slowly to the top. His strength had not kept up with his girth, and as a result, the effort expended climbing to the fighting top of the mainmast caused him to lean on the rail up there and pant for breath for a full minute before he ever put the glass to his eye. He remained on the top for longer than was probably necessary, and when his breathing returned to normal, he headed back down to the spardeck, then aft to the quarterdeck.

The gunner had already appeared, and was waiting patiently for Mr. Fitzgerald. The word had traveled throughout the ship very quickly, and the men were eagerly awaiting the determination that this was a potential prize. They were gathering near their battle stations, in obvious anticipation. The gunner had his own ideas of what it was, and was ready for orders which would confirm his thoughts.

"She appears to be a merchantman, sir. No colors, but I would guess American from the way she crowds on sail. Bark rigged. She shows gunports, but I would guess that from the stowage of the cargo on deck, that if there are any guns aboard, there is no room to work them." Fitzgerald wiped his sweating, red face with a dirty handkerchief, feeling he had covered the subject, and waited for an acknowledgment of that opinion from his captain.

Winston barely looked up; the eyebrow shot to the limit of its range. Almost as if to himself he spoke so quietly, his words were for the lieutenant alone. "Mr. Fitzgerald, assuming she doesn't have, or can not serve her guns is perilous at best, and suicidal at worst. Let us assume she is heavily armed until we know otherwise."

Once again, the red in Lieutenant Fitzgerald's face deepened, and to mask his discomfort, he turned and walked to where the gunner was waiting; he instructed him unnecessarily, "Gunner, have shot and powder brought on deck, and let the carpenter and bosun know that we will be tacking and then clearing for action, if you please."

Orpheus was now bearing down rapidly on the ship under her lee bow. The vessel was clearly visible from deck and had herself borne off to improve her speed. While fast, she proved an unequal match for *Orpheus* and in time, the two ships were almost within the range of an eighteen pounder. Watching the relative position of the two ships, the captain waited until he felt the time was right and spoke quietly to the officer of the watch.

"Mr. Fitzgerald, we will tack the ship, if you please. And do it smartly as we must hold our position on her windward bow after we have reversed course."

Fitzgerald barked to the bosun, who having heard the captain's words had already started forward. "Bosun, stations for stays, if you please. Clew up the main course, and smartly now."

Bosun Tice had, in fact, begun sending men aloft and was chasing others to their sail handling positions on deck. Seeing the main and foretopmen on their respective yards, he bawled, "Course clewlines, 'eave together now. Braces 'aul."

The ship slowed perceptibly and began to head up toward the wind as the helmsman responded to orders from Lieutenant Fitzgerald. "Keep her full for stays. . . careful, man. Don't bring her to 'igh." He nodded at his transplanted Russian sailing master, a warrant named Ivan Smosky, indicating all was ready and to bring her about.

With the courses clewed up, and the ship close hauled, Smosky bellowed for all to hear, "Ready about . . .lee the helm . . . ease your jib sheets . . . cross trim the spanker. . ."

As the ship headed up and into the wind, he again yelled "Mains'l haul!" and to the helmsman, more quietly, "Keep her up, lad. Let her come around easy now."

Orpheus passed through stays smoothly; had she not, more than one would have felt the cat. The courses were let down, and braces hauled to fill them on the new tack. Tops'ls filled, and as the jibs and stays'ls backed, they were sheeted home on the new tack. The frenzy of activity slowed at the same rate that the ship accelerated, and soon the bosun reported to Smosky, "all lines coiled down and ready to run."

Captain Winston saw that his ship was almost exactly where he wanted her, to windward and slightly ahead of the stranger. He was positioned to fire a broadside if necessary, or bear off ahead and deliver a raking fire.

"We'll beat to quarters, now, Mr. Fitzgerald, if you please."

The sound of the fife and Marine drum playing "Heart of Oak" filled the air, punctuated by running men eager to have some action, and anticipating the possibility of a prize. Captain Winston watched as the ship was cleared for action. The spar deck guns that he could see, including six nine-pounders aft and a brace of ugly short-barreled thirty-two-pounder carronades were run out, loaded, and had slow matches burning in the tubs next to each, a backup for the sometimes temperamental flintlocks. Royal Marines were in the tops with muskets, and the doctor and his assistant were set up in the relative safety of the midshipman's berth, aft and well below the fighting decks. The crew had taken to referring to the area as the "cockpit," recognizing the similarity to the blood soaked arena of like name. The medical team would later move forward on the orlop deck where the ship's hospital could be set up when necessary. While he couldn't see from the quarterdeck, he knew that bulkheads would be coming down on the gun deck to clear the way for movement, increase the light and to provide less material for the always possible and often lethal splinters that could fly in the event his ship took a hit during an exchange with an enemy. Reports were coming to the quarterdeck regarding the preparedness of various parts of his ship, and the captain was satisfied that they could fight, and, he hoped, fight well, should it be necessary.

The first lieutenant came to the quarterdeck after checking the ship, and reported that all was ready.

"Very well, Mr. Burns, you may bear off a trifle to take us to within musket range, if you please. I shall return directly."

With that, the captain strode off the quarterdeck, and headed below to put on his number two uniform. Not as fine as the number one which was reserved for obligatory shore visits to dignitaries and visits aboard from his Admiral, Sir Francis Lafory, his fighting uniform was more than impressive to most. He knew his steward and personal servant, Paisley Cochrane, would have the clothes laid out on his bed, properly brushed and already rigged with epaulettes.

He entered his cabin, noting the interior bulkheads had already been removed and most likely carefully stowed with most of his furniture. The two eighteen-pounders with which he shared his cabin were manned, their slow matches lit. His uniform was in fact laid out, and Cochrane was fussing with the cockade in Captain Winston's hat, squinting through close-set eyes in his ferret-like face, and muttering under his breath that his efforts were rarely, if ever, appreciated, and why did he spend his life in a constant struggle to make an ungrateful captain look as proper as the Royal Navy required. Winston, of course, was completely used to Cochrane's comments, muttered or otherwise, and ignored them, saying only, "We should be finished with this action in a matter of hours, Cochrane, so dinner will not be delayed too long. I am sure you can manage to keep it hot. Remember also, if you please, that First Lieutenant Burns and two of the midshipmen will be joining me for the meal." This last was purely for Winston's perverse amusement, as the surly steward was nothing if not painfully punctual. Twenty-five years as ship's boy and steward, almost ten of them to Harry Winston, had developed in him an ability to anticipate and a concern for his master found only in a superior man servant and occasionally in a wife.

Cochrane replied that he would have "No problem with managing, sir," and left the captain to change, muttering as he disappeared into the gloom of the gun deck.

Winston saw immediately upon his return to the quarterdeck that *Orpheus* was now less than a cable's length from the object of his attention. The two ships were sailing more or less side by side, with the stranger to leeward. Captain Winston studied her for a few minutes. Because of the angle, he could not make out the name or her hail port; he could see, however, that her deck did indeed have significant amounts of cargo stowed about it. He also saw that most of the ship's company was on deck or aloft, trying to squeeze as much speed as they could muster from the breeze. The captain of the ship was watching him carefully, occasionally using his long glass for a closer inspection.

"Mr. Burns, you may hoist our colors, if you please. Let us see what response that might have."

As the British Naval Ensign fluttered to the peak of the mizzen, Captain Winston stepped onto the bulwark at the mizzen shrouds, and holding his speaking trumpet to his mouth, shouted across the water, "This is His Britannic Majesty's frigate *Orpheus*. What ship are you and where are you bound?"

The answer came back in a New England twang, "We are an American ship out of Boston, the *Anne*, with cargo for St. Bartholomew. Jedediah Smalley commanding. You are crowding us, and causing us to alter our course. Stand clear."

The American flag sprung into the wind from the spanker gaff.

"Heave to at once, captain, and prepare to receive a boarding party." Captain Winston then turned to his first lieutenant. "Lower the cutter. Take Mr. Blake and three well-armed Marines as well as the boat crew and go over there. I am sure there must be some British subjects aboard. We could use a few experienced hands."

Raising his voice, he continued, "Gunner, fire a gun to windward, if you please. Let them know we're serious."

Practically before he had finished saying the words, the air was filled with the crash of an eighteen-pounder long gun firing to windward. Smoke blew back across the deck, momentarily obscuring the forward part of the fo'c'sle. The captain watched the *Anne*. Nothing seemed to be happening. No one was headed aloft to back the main tops'l or course, and the ship maintained its speed, in fact, bearing off slightly to try to gain more speed. The eyebrow twitched, and began a slow ascent. Again, he stepped onto the bulwark.

"Sir. I order you to heave to in the name of the Royal Navy. I am sending a boat across to you."

For a response, *Anne* swung open her two starboard side gunports showing the snouts of two ugly twenty-four-pounder carronades.

"Mr. Burns, have Mr. Fitzgerald fire a gun across her bow, and run out the larboard battery, quick as ever you please. The man must think he can bluff me with those carronades. Perhaps he will rethink his strategy with a ball across his bow, and a look at the open end of a dozen and more eighteen-pounders."

As if to punctuate his remark, the number two gun fired, and he watched as its eighteen-pound ball splashed up a small geyser in the water a scant fifty feet in front of the *Anne's* stem. Almost simultaneously, the clatter of the port side gunports opening could be heard, followed by the rumble of twelve heavy gun carriages moving to their firing positions. Without looking, Winston knew the tompions were out, and the open muzzles staring across at the other ship at virtually point-blank range had to be a daunting sight. Apparently, it was. Men were going aloft on *Anne's* mainmast and he saw that the ship was easing up to bring the wind forward of the beam so she could be hove to. Sails were shivered, and *Anne* gradually slowed and then more or less stopped, rolling slightly in the now crossing seas. Harry Winston smiled wolfishly, and turned back to his quarterdeck.

"Mr. Smosky, we'll heave to now if you please. Mr. Burns, you may lower the cutter as soon as we have stopped." As the two moved to obey, he turned and strode to the leeward side of the quarterdeck, where he watched the other ship carefully to be sure there would be no surprises. Behind him, he could hear the commands and sensed the actions being taken to bring his ship to a stop.

"Main and tops'l braces haul. Trim sheets. Trim jibs and spanker. Up helm. . . meet her. . . steady there. Belay all."

The clatter and shaking of sails slatting and lines running through blocks combined with the shouting of the men handling the sails ended abruptly, leaving a quiet punctuated only by the gentle sound of the waves slapping on the side of the rapidly slowing ship.

Orpheus now lay dead in the water less than a cable length from *Anne*. Both ships' companies watched as the cutter swung out from its chocks and was lowered efficiently into the water on the leeward side. The crew clambered down the side of *Orpheus* and sat at their oar positions, while Mr. Burns took his position with Midshipman Everett Blake in the stern sheets.

CHAPTER SIX

Impressment

"Give way together now, lads," Lieutenant Burns spoke quietly to his crew. He was naturally soft spoken and felt that yelling, or even speaking loudly unnecessarily, was contributory to confusion and thence to error. He had been a lieutenant for almost ten years and had taught himself the discipline early on after a long three years with a screamer as first lieutenant. His commanding presence and quiet manner inspired confidence, but not camaraderie. And it could be menacing as well. The crew of the cutter dipped their oars into the sea and the small boat headed smartly across the two hundred yards or so of open ocean toward the waiting *Anne.* The gentle rolling motion of the sea rocked the cutter as it moved perpendicular to the waves, and the distance closed quickly.

With oars tossed smartly, they bumped against the tall side of the American ship. There was no sign of the manropes which normally would be thrown over the side to assist anyone clambering up the boarding battens fastened to the outside of the vessel.

This is not going to be easy, thought Blake as Lieutenant Burns, looking up to the men lining the bulwark, ordered them to drop down the manropes. There was a pause, a few men disappeared briefly, and in absolute silence, the requested ropes dropped over the rail. Burns grabbed both at head height and stepped agilely onto the bottom batten. He moved quickly up the ship's side and Blake watched as the men parted to let him step from the bulwark onto the main deck of *Anne.* Blake and the three Marines followed in rapid succession, leaving the boat crew in the cutter now tied alongside.

Lieutenant Burns led the party aft to the quarterdeck, assuming correctly that the tall man, elderly with mostly gray hair and a black frock coat, standing there was the captain. He had to pass through a gauntlet of men to get there, and noted that their expressions were consistent; rage mixed with uncertainty with a touch of fear thrown in. The Royal Navy lieutenant held himself erect, trying to appear tall and imposing though he was only of moderate height with a noticeable paunch that preceded him. His hand rested easily on the hilt of his sword. He stepped onto the quarterdeck, and introduced himself, realizing as he spoke that the man was not nearly so old as he had originally thought; the gray hair was deceiving.

"Good morning, Captain. I am Lieutenant Joseph Burns, First Lieutenant of His Majesty's Ship *Orpheus*. This is Mr. Blake, our senior Midshipman. We are responsible for determining whether you have any British deserters aboard, and for returning them to service in His Majesty's Navy. Muster your crew amidships, if you please."

"I am Captain Jedediah Smalley. I do not welcome your visit, and protest most vigorously your thinly veiled attempt at piracy. My crew are Americans, born and bred, and I doubt you will find any legitimate candidates for impressment among them. However, in the interest of getting you off my ship as quickly as possible, I shall assemble the crew as you ask. Mr. Jakes, my third mate, will escort you.

"Mr. Clark, Mr. Jakes, assemble the crew in the waist, if you please." Smalley's lips formed a thin line across his drawn face, and the blue-gray eyes blazed out from their sockets like sapphires hit by the sun.

The two Englishmen watched silently as the men of *Anne* gathered in ragged rows around the mainmast. The snippets of conversation carried aft by the wind indicated that the crew shared their captain's feelings about the boarding and search; the men knew that any one of them, for a trumped up reason, could be carried back to the British man of war to serve an unspecified term of enlistment. The men's glances darted between their mate and the British officer, and while their words were angry and brave, their eyes betrayed their true feelings. The Royal Marines, resplendent in their red jackets and "clayed" white pants, accented with glistening black boots and cartridge boxes, stood by at the break of the poop, ready to quell any potential disturbance at the earliest indication. Their muskets, with gleaming bayonets reflecting the sun's rays in blinding brilliance, provided a mute reminder that resistance or other trouble could end in bloodshed. A nod from Mr. Clark indicated to the captain that all the men except the helmsman were assembled.

"Mr. Burns, the men are assembled. You will make your inspection as quick as ever you please, thank you, and be gone. Mr. Jakes, take His Majesty's Lieutenant to the men, if you please."

The sarcasm was not lost on Burns, but he chose to ignore it, and merely nodded at the midshipman to step forward with Jakes, their appointed escort.

"If any of you men are British subjects, step forward now, and save us the bother of finding you. Because find you we will. With your cooperation, both you and we will be able to proceed apace." Burns' normally quiet voice was raised enough to be heard by all, but still quiet enough to carry a noticeable degree of menace. His demeanor indicated he was serious and would brook no nonsense. He stood rigidly in front of the sailors, peering intently at them through close-set eyes, his stare unwavering, and to some, unnerving.

Of course, none of the men moved. Lieutenant Burns approached the first man in the line in front of him. "What's your name, sailor?"

"Able-seaman Gerald Reese. I was born in Boston, Massachusetts, July 23rd, 1781."

"Boston was still under British rule in 1781, Reese. That would make you a British subject. Once an Englishman, always an Englishman." Burns was quick witted, and could turn a subject to his advantage easily. "Step over there, if you please." He pointed to the bulwark where the British press gang had received their hostile welcome.

With a startled and fearful cast in his eyes, Reese glanced at Jakes, then set his full attention on his first mate, Mr. Clark. He was obviously unsure of what to do, and at first, remained rooted to the deck. His entire body began to tremble, and a trickle of sweat made a track down his weathered face.

Could this be happening to me? I ain't British. . . What am I going to do? This long-nosed dandy and his Marines could take me and any of 'em should they want to. Reese's thoughts rushed through his confused mind. Ingrained through years at sea of doing what he was told, acceptance and obedience of an order took over; his feet moved without a conscious thought and he started to take a step in the direction the officer had indicated.

"Reese, stand fast." Clark roared out the order to his sailor, who once again became rooted to the deck, a look of utter confusion masking the spark of joy at his potential salvation. In a quieter voice, the first mate, who had joined in the little procession at the rear, spoke to Lieutenant Burns.

"You may recall, sir, that America declared her independence from England back in 1776, and at that moment any British subjects living in America either the took the opportunity to run away to Canada, or become Americans. Probably wasn't no Britishers living there much past then, and I'd reckon precious few visiting, save for the lobsterbacks." This last comment included a glance at the three standing rigidly by the mainmast.

He went on, "Under your idea, there would be no Americans over the age of twenty-eight. An idea what is clearly preposterous. This man is no more a British subject than you are an American, perish the thought."

Burns had rarely been "one-upped" by a colonist, but he gave in this time. He checked half a dozen other men, finding all American born and bred. Turning to move into the next rank, he heard a whisper in his ear.

"This next one's a Britisher, sir. Came from Wales, I'm thinkin'. Not a bad topman, either, but a bit of a trouble-maker. Maybe some of that Royal Navy discipline would help straighten him out."

Burns turned back, seeking the source of this new information. He nearly stepped on the man assigned to escort him; a furtive glance shot out at him from beneath a tarpaulin hat, and shifted immediately to the row of men, then back to Burns and finally retreated to study the deck at his feet. He recalled the man's name was Jakes. Looking back at the men, Burns was now face to face with a short, sunburned man of about twenty years, good looking, and apparently strong. Curly dark hair, dark eyes, and a slight smile gave him the appearance of innocence and a relaxed demeanor spoke wordlessly of his confidence.

"Where are you from, lad?" Burns lowered his voice to a friendly, almost conspiratorial level.

"Marblehead, Massachusetts, sir. Born January 12th, 1790. I am American."

"Your accent sounds a bit Welsh to me, sailor. Sure you're not from Wales?"

"Aye, I'm sure. They could be a little accent from my parents. They left Wales for America in 1787, and I was born in Marblehead where they settled. Other than sailing, I have never left New England; I ain't even been east of the Bermudas."

Burns' stare went right through the young sailor. After a moment of silence, he spoke.

"I don't believe you. Consider yourself a British seaman, now assigned to HMS *Orpheus*, from this point on." He motioned to one of the Royal Marines standing by the mainmast, who immediately stepped out smartly and escorted the new British seaman to the bulwark.

"Hold on there, Marine." Burns turned to the departing men. "You, the Welshman, what's your name?"

The American sailor turned around and just stared, wide-eyed in fear, at the officer for a moment. It was apparent that the enormity of the event had just hit him, and he was stunned. His confidence had abandoned him. With a visible effort, he gathered himself, collected his wits, and spoke clearly, "Isaac Biggs . . . and I'm American, not Welsh." His curly hair was plastered to his narrow forehead with a sudden outpouring of sweat born of an abject fear. While his words were calm, his voice had a tremor, further testimony to his terror of what lay ahead.

"Biggs, you're a British sailor now, so we don't much care where you're from or not from. And when you address an officer of His Majesty's Navy, you use 'sir'. Am I clear?" Midshipman Blake was exercising his own authority; it couldn't hurt to make his position and responsibility clear to this new man. He might turn up working for him, and this would give him a jump on establishing his authority.

Any color left under the tan on young Isaac Biggs' face faded completely; the sweat ran unchecked down his cheeks and neck. His head was spinning with the enormity of this horrific turn of events. *I don't belong on that ship . . . mebbe I shoulda got one o' them citizenship certificates they was sellin' in Boston after all. Heard they wasn't worth the paper they was printed on though . . . what can I do? How'm I gonna get back to Marblehead . . . see my folks . . . what's gonna happen to me? I'm cap'n o' the foretop on* Anne, *not some Royal Navy tar gettin' the lash . . . God help me.*

Frustrated by his inability to affect his future, Isaac glanced over the bulwark, contemplating his chances overboard; he decided against it. He shifted his gaze to the frigate, rocking gently, her guns still aimed in deadly silence right at *Anne*.

They're pointin' right at me, he thought ruefully and decided to do what he had been told — at least for now, and only to stay alive — maybe there'd be an opportunity later to regain his life. He rested a hand on the bulwark, steadying it and trying to regain his composure. And waited.

Burns and Blake, followed by Jakes, continued down the line of men, asking each questions designed have each man talk. Burns watched their eyes; sometimes he could tell more from a man's eye contact with him than ever he could from their words. He found two more men; a waister claiming home was Baltimore, and a mizzen topman, a landsman, who probably was from England, but claimed New York as his home. Tyler, the waister, was barely old enough to shave, and burst into tears when escorted to the bulwark by the Royal Marine, who finished the short trip by dragging the shaking, sobbing boy. Nobody on *Anne* really knew the topman, named Pope, as he was both new on board, and had kept to himself for most of the voyage. Each of the pressed seamen was sent under escort to collect their scant seabags and returned to the main deck quickly.

Completing their tour, Lieutenant Burns and Midshipman Blake turned aft to the quarterdeck. As they stepped up the short ladder, Captain Smalley moved to the top of it, effectively blocking their further progress. Burns stopped, a step from the top, while the young midshipman peered around the back of his superior, trying to fathom why he had stopped. The captain's voice solved the mystery for him.

"Unless you plan on searching my vessel looking for more of my sailors on which to visit your miseries, you have no further business here, sir, so I'll thank you to stay off of my quarterdeck. You may leave my ship if you are finished with your evilness. I suspect there will come a day of reckoning for you imperious scoundrels, and I truly hope it will be soon, and that I am there to see it. Good day to you."

"Thank you for your cooperation, Captain, I shall note it in our log. You Americans are going to learn that without England you have nothing; you should be grateful to us. Arrogance rings hollow, without the hope of supporting it. You will learn your place, however — soon, I think — and my hope is that *Orpheus* will be involved in teaching you. A good day to you, as well, sir."

Burns, equally angry at this upstart American, turned so suddenly to return to the bulwark and his cutter that he knocked into his midshipman. The young man was embarrassed, but Burns, in his anger, barely noticed. He wanted no further incident; it was not to be, however.

As he clambered onto the high bulwark, a belaying pin from the mainmast pin rail was thrown with some expertise, and landed with a hollow thud in the middle of Burns' back. It might have been aimed for his head, and had he not stepped onto the rail at that precise moment, the outcome would most likely have been different. As it was, the blow sent him sprawling to the deck. The three Royal Marines brought as one their muskets to full cock, and swung them around, looking for a target. One felt he had found the perpetrator and fired. The shot rang out, quelling the short-lived cheers and catcalls from the still assembled crew. The silence was sudden and complete, then broken by the thump of a body hitting the deck, and the ensuing scramble of the men, some taking cover from further shooting, and some rushing to the aid of their fallen shipmate.

Lieutenant Burns, having regained his feet, put his hand out, crying "Hold! Cease your firing!" and stopped the other two marines from creating more chaos. He watched as the American seamen lifted their mate and carried him below.

"Have you not caused enough trouble already, Lieutenant? I told you to get you and your men off my ship. Should you not leave now, I will not be responsible for the actions of my crew. And yes, I realize that should there be more trouble, we risk a broadside from your ship. That would not help you, however. Therefore, I suggest you get down the side now and away from my ship!" Captain Smalley was under control, but barely, and his shaking voice and obvious effort to maintain his composure gave credence to his words. He turned away, giving orders, as he did so, to get *Anne* underway. The niceties of waiting for the cutter to load and leave his side forgotten in his rage.

The British boarding party climbed over the bulwark and down the narrow steps to the waiting boat. The three new man o' warsmen, realizing that they had absolutely no choice, and nowhere to run, also climbed down into the boat and took seats between the oarsmen under the watchful eyes of the Royal Marines, who had already proved they would shoot to kill. The crew pushed off, and as they did, the crew of the *Anne* not engaged in making sail once again lined the rail, hurling epithets and jeers at the Britishers, and encouragement to their stunned former shipmates, now pulling away. The boat crew and the passengers were silent, each keeping his thoughts to himself. Burns saw the three American faces going through the mental torment that so many others before them had suffered; fear of the unknown, fear of the reputed discipline and related floggings common in the British Navy, and sorrow at leaving their shipmates in *Anne*. He knew that each also wondered whether they would ever see their families and homes again. The young one, Tyler, he recalled, was completely terror stricken; the boy's eyes darted everywhere like a trapped animal, seeking a friendly face, or perhaps a way out. The tears he had shed earlier had left salty tracks down his smooth cheeks. An occasional sob escaped his lips; his hand brushed across his eyes frequently, wiping away the fresh tears that, unbidden, continually appeared.

Midshipman Blake broke the silence as the cutter neared the frigate. "You three men will be assigned to different messes and watches so you will adapt to the Navy way faster. Our sailors will teach you, and hopefully you will learn quickly. Captain Winston does not suffer fools gladly, and will brook no nonsense. A word to the wise should suffice."

All three men just looked blankly at him. The impact of his words did not register, and he softened his voice a little when he said, "Are you men attending to what I said? It is possible that learning quickly will save the skin on your backs."

They nodded dumbly, their eyes uncomprehending, their expressions unchanged.

The cutter was now alongside the frigate, and the manropes were down and waiting for them, unlike at the side of the American. Lieutenant Burns was first up the side, followed by Midshipman Blake, the three former American merchant seamen, now about to become full-fledged Royal Navy sailors, and the Royal Marines. The boat crew made fast the bow and stern to tackles lowered to them for the purpose, and then climbed out themselves. By the time the first lieutenant had reported to the quarterdeck, the boat was out of the water and headed inboard to its chocks on the spardeck.

"We found three men, sir." He answered the questioning look from his captain. "A Welshman, and two Englishmen. I'm told the Welshman is a fair hand, a topman in fact, and quite able. The other two will most likely need training. I believe I will put the topman in the starboard watch with Mr. Blake, and the other two in the larboard watch with Midshipman Davis. They will also need to be assigned to gun crews."

"Very well, Mr. Burns. Let us get the ship underway as quick as ever you please. Have the surgeon look them over from stem to stern to ensure they are fit, and have them make their mark in the ship's articles. Then strip off those American clothes, hose 'em down, and have Mr. Beckwirth issue them slops, mess gear and a hammock. You may have the bosun see to their assignments on the Watch, Quarters, and Station Bills. You might have someone show them below, as they will be of no use to us when they get lost aboard. I shall be below. You may have the crew stand down from Quarters."

The orders were being given almost before Captain Winston had left the quarterdeck. As he descended the ladder and headed aft to his cabin, he felt the ship bear off. He could hear the *whoomp* of the canvas as sails filled, combined with the running footsteps and shouted commands of the men making sail. He felt the ship begin to move through the water, and gradually gather speed.

Cochrane, his whip-thin form standing sneering imperiously in the doorway, was waiting for the captain when he walked into his cabin. He had naturally been berating the carpenter's men who had the bulkheads almost completely restored, and Captain Winston barely acknowledged their presence, save to glare at them impatiently while they finished their tasks.

The men put the last peg in the bulkhead, and headed forward, to a final high pitched sally from Cochrane who had noticed the captain's look. "Next time I'll expect this job done by the time the captain comes below, you layabouts." The steward, while trying to sound threatening, actually was whining. The carpenter's men, like most of the crew, ignored the captain's steward, thinking of him as a little more than a pest, but when there was some inside scuttlebutt to be gleaned from befriending the man, they accepted his abuse and surliness. It was a matter of pride to Cochrane that he generally knew, but only occasionally told, what he heard at the meals he served in the captain's cabin. He suddenly realized that the captain was speaking to him, and turned to see his commanding officer standing in the middle of his sleeping cabin in his small clothes.

"Where is my at sea uniform, Cochrane? I can't go on deck in my small clothes. Are you ready for my dinner guests?"

"I have your uniform right here, sir. I was just brushing it for you. It wouldn't do to have the captain looking shabby. As to dinner, it can be ready as quick as ever you please. I have yet to hear the crew called to dinner, though and I didn't expect you'd want to start quite so early." He looked at his captain, a hand on his hip, and scowled, but he didn't quite come off as he had intended.

Almost as he spoke, the ship's bell rang, and with the ship settled down full and by on her course to her assigned sector, the men finished restoring the vessel to her peaceable appearance and changed the watch. Running feet overhead and muffled curses from the petty officers added some emphasis to the event.

"You may tell Mister Burns and Midshipmen Blake and Murphy that I will expect them at two bells. I will wear my sea-uniform for dinner, so you may brush and stow my number two again, if you please. Now go and see to dinner." Winston, as always, dismissed his steward's occasional tantrums as the price one must pay for a superior servant.

Cochrane made his standard exit, muttering about ingrates under his breath, and wondering half aloud why it always fell to him to bear the brunt of their lack of Christian charity. Captain Winston had turned and, as was his practice, ignored his steward.

CHAPTER SEVEN

Assignments

Biggs stood with his fellow Annes on the larboard gangway of His Majesty's frigate *Orpheus*. He looked first aloft, seeking to orient himself with a familiar sight. He was most familiar with the maze of spars, ropes, and sails, and felt that if he could correlate what he saw on the frigate to what he knew from *Anne* and other ships, he would be able to acclimate faster. He took in the lofty spars, noting that the rigging from one ship to another is generally the same; only minor differences exist which oft-times reflect the wishes and experience of her captain. Biggs satisfied himself quickly that he would have little trouble aloft should he be assigned there; in fact he hoped he would. He did not want to be on one of the ship's big guns. He knew nothing about them, but had heard that in battle, the other ship frequently aims at the guns of the enemy to put them out of action. That seemed an inherently dangerous place to be.

Moving his eyes back to the more immediate environs, he saw *Anne* sailing off to the south.

Wonder if I'll ever get back aboard her, he thought, noticing that still his hands were shaking. His thought was echoed aloud by Pope, and young Tyler began again to whimper. The enormity and finality of their situation had hit them, and Pope's words made them all realize that in all likelihood, there was probably little chance that any of them would ever get back aboard *Anne,* or even see her and their mates again. Except for the occasional choked-off sob from Tyler, they watched in silence as *Anne* gradually disappeared over the southern horizon.

"You ever seen so many men on a ship, Biggs?" Pope observed. They all looked fearfully around the deck after tearing their eyes away from the quickly departing bark. It looked as though there were sailors and marines everywhere, aloft and on deck. What they could see of the weatherdeck between the gangways over the waist seemed also to be literally alive with men. Both men, seeing the yards manned as they were, mistakenly assumed that such was always the case, and that men were stationed aloft in the Royal Navy even when not actively working the sails. Other men, on the spardeck, stood in groups near their assigned positions, ready to haul a halyard, brace or sheet as needed. It occurred to all three of them that finding room to swing hammocks for this many men must be indeed a challenging proposition.

In fact there were two hundred and four men not counting the forty Royal Marines, six officers and warrants and seven Midshipmen all assigned to HMS *Orpheus*. Still her captain felt he was short-handed, and when the opportunity presented itself, would seek additional sailors from other ships, in the grog shops, or in the brothels ashore. It was always good to have men over and above the minimum required to sail and fight the ship; extras provided replacements for battle casualties and could man a prize crew. It was usually desirable to sail a prize into a friendly port rather than tow it in so the ship did not have to leave her station. And then there were the desertions ashore, a common problem throughout the fleet, and perhaps a trifle more frequent on Captain Winston's ships due to his forthright and, at times, brutal ways.

"I'm Philip Tice, Bosun. Pick up your dunnage and come with me." The three American sailors were jerked from their reveries by a very large man in his mid-thirties wearing a blue short-waisted jacket with brass buttons which had not visited their corresponding button holes in some time, and dirty — they might have once been white — nankeen trousers. Hard eyes over a bulbous red nose fixed each of the new Royal Navy recruits in a shriveling stare. He was shod in leather shoes, something the men weren't used to seeing in American merchantmen. Muscular hairy forearms stuck out from the ill-fitting jacket, and one over-large hand — almost a paw — held a short length of twisted rope, stiffened and bound with twine. Biggs had seen a starter before; he recalled Ben Jakes had frequently used one. Somehow, seeing one on a British man of war surprised him. There were to be more surprises for all of them. Tice turned and started forward, continuing to talk to the three over his shoulder.

"You'll be assigned to watches, messes, and quarters stations. Learn them, and when you 'ear the drum beat to quarters get to where you're s'posed to be as fast as ever you can. You'll get one time to get lost aboard; after that you'll find the cat licking your back. Right now, you lot get down to the surgeon so's 'e can check you out — make sure you ain't diseased or nothin' and fit for duty on a King's ship."

They followed the bosun forward, along the gangway where, by looking down, they could see some of the starboard eighteen pounders on the weatherdeck below them; he took them down a ladder onto that deck with all its cannon. The first thing any of them noticed was the gloom; amidships, under the gangways it was sunny, but here, under the fo'c'sle, it was dark and it took a while for their eyes to adapt. What little there was filtered in from the open area under the gangways on the spar deck. Long guns lined both sides of the deck, and most of the eighteen-pound iron balls and each gun's supply of powder bags had yet to be re-stowed. They lay in neat arrangements by several of the guns, and it occurred to the Americans with a sudden and shocking clarity that Captain Winston had been prepared to fire the guns at *Anne* had there been sufficient provocation. Biggs remembered how the muzzles had looked from *Anne* when the guns were run out; they looked just as deadly from this end. He had not realized how big they actually were, and how much damage one of those huge iron balls could do to the hull and rigging of a ship, especially if fired from the almost point-blank range at which *Orpheus* had lain from *Anne*.

The group continued forward; Biggs stopped and looked back when he heard a solid sounding *thump*, followed by a grunt. Tyler, busy gaping at the guns, had walked squarely into the foremast where it passed through the deck. Embarrassed and bruised, he looked around to see if anyone had noticed his blunder. The remaining gun crews and a few powder monkeys had certainly seen, and were enjoying a laugh at his expense. As he ran a hand cautiously over his face and through his shaggy non-descript hair, he silently thanked the heavens that it was dark enough that they could not see his red face! At least his quick exploratory probing had discovered no obvious damage!

Down the next ladder they went, and Bosun Tice waited at the bottom for them.

"This is the gundeck, and you'll sling yer hammocks with yer messmates."

The bosun caught the look that passed between the three Americans; if this was the gundeck, why were the guns on the deck above? Biggs shook his head, confused, and nudged Pope.

"Gundeck, aye. Guns were topside — you see any down here, Pope?"

"Too dark to see much of anything, but I guess this'd be what we'd call the berthin' deck. Mind yer head there."

The bosun ignored his charges and kept moving; he continued his instructions.

"Leave yer dunnage 'ere, and I'll take you down to the orlop where the medico oughta be about now. Come on, step along now and follow me."

Another deck lower they went, further into the bowels of the frigate. The gloom turned to dark, and the occasional purser's glim became the only light. Pulling aside a curtain, Tice motioned the men inside what appeared to be a small room. There was a table, several cupboards mounted on the bulkhead, and three men who were apparently asleep in hammocks slung to one side of the room. The light was better here, bright by comparison to the orlop deck, even though there was only a single oil lantern giving off a smoky yellow light and a few small candles mounted in tin holders, called purser's glims. A short stocky man, patently unkempt, in what must have once been a white shirt but was now stained with brownish blotches across the front, stepped out of the shadows when the three men entered. He saw the bosun just outside his curtain.

"Come in Mr. Tice. There's nothing here to hurt you. This is a place of healing." The sarcasm was heavy in the surgeon's voice.

"Aye, sir. I've heard that from others — most of which got pitched over the standing part of the forecourse sheet with a good Christian burial read over 'em. It'll be a cold day in Hell when you get your hands on me — that or when they ain't no choice," he added lugubriously. Tice looked around the curtain, maintaining a safe distance, and noting with a smile the rising alarm in the faces of the three seamen standing by the table.

"These three come off'n that American merchant we stopped back a bit. They's British what was shirking their duties in the Royal Navy 'idin' out on foreign vessels. Mr. Burns found 'em an' brought 'em over. Cap'n wants 'em checked out just like always — make sure they ain't carryin' no disease and they got all they's parts in the right places."

As he finished speaking, he let the curtain fall back into place and over his retreating footsteps, the men heard, "You men get yourselves back up to the weatherdeck quick as ever you can, once the medico's done lookin' you over, and find me. Doc, don't be takin' too long with these coves; they's work to be done."

"Stick out your tongue, lad." Tyler started so suddenly his feet nearly left the deck, as the doctor selected him for "lookin' over" first. "Ain't no reason to be jumpy, son. I most likely won't hurt you."

Tyler did as he was told, wide-eyed in fear and jumping at every touch of the surgeon. The other two took their turn, and after a cursory examination, the doctor pronounced them fit and sent them on their way to find the Bosun.

As he had promised, Tice was on the weatherdeck berating a couple of men; he stopped when he saw the three Americans and called them to him.

"You lads get over 'ere quick as you can; we got to have you sign the ship's articles — you can write yer names, I collect." This last was not a question, and the bosun did not expect an answer, but of course, Tyler missed that and responded to Tice's retreating form, "Of course, sir, we've had schoolin'."

The bosun merely threw a withering glance over his shoulder and continued to lead the men aft and back down below to the pursers' office.

"This 'ere's Mr. Beckwirth, purser. He's in charge of your pay, and without you don't sign the Ship's Articles makin' you a member of the ship's company, you ain't gonna get no pay." He pointed a stubby finger at the large book which Beckwirth had opened on the table.

"Make your mark right here, lads, and I'll fill in your names for you, if you ain't able." Beckwirth smiled at the men as he showed them where to sign with the quill he handed to Biggs.

Each having written their names in a reasonable hand, turned to the bosun expectantly.

"Let's get you down to . . ." He was interrupted by the sound of the ship's bell and the fife playing the *Nancy Dawson*. "That'd be the call to dinner and grog. You can go get yer dinner and yer ration. Galley's forward on this deck. Grog's in the waist on the weatherdeck."

When the three new hands reached the open area of the weatherdeck again, they were blinking like nocturnal animals suddenly caught by the sun. Their eyes quickly adapted to the brightness of the day. They saw a line of sailors by the foot of the mainmast and joined it. As the line moved forward, they met some of their new shipmates. They were handed cups of grog mixed to the Royal Navy's standard of one third water to two thirds rum. The men moved back below to get their meal, one man from each mess going to the galley to bring the food back to his mates. Since Biggs, Tyler and Pope were not yet assigned to a mess, they had to more or less fend for themselves and Biggs sent Tyler off to find the galley and get some food for the three of them.

When Tyler returned, he found the Americans on the berthing deck sitting with a few British sailors, and joined them.

"Yer the lad what came face to face with the foremast a bit ago, what?" One of the men had apparently been finishing up his chores on a gun earlier, and had witnessed Tyler's mishap. His accent was difficult for Tyler to understand at first, and he didn't immediately respond. When he finally figured out what the man had said, he again colored, and unbidden, his hand touched the newly risen lump on his forehead. A round of laughter, acknowledging his admission, added to his discomfort, but he joined in, hoping that it was the right thing to do. It was the first time he had laughed since being pressed, and it sounded slightly hysterical. The conversation moved on to other subjects, including pressing sailors.

"Aye, I was pressed by a shore gang in Portsmouth, in Mother Carey's place it was . . . bastards didn't even wait for me to finish me business; just barged in an snatched me right out o' the snatch, they did. Har har." Wallace paused in his tale of impressment to laugh at his own mental image of being pressed. He continued, still smiling. "Must be well past two years ago now. You'll find the Navy ain't such a bad place; I don't recommend trying to jump ship. 'Course if you try and they catch you, you'll be on the gratin' afore noon with the cat scratching yer back. You do what yer told, smartly, and don't get in Fitzgerald's way, you'll be righty-oh. That man don't know his arse from a tops'l sheet, and takes it out on any Jack tar what crosses his path. So mind yer helm when he's about."

Biggs thought their new friend, Wallace, might be giving them some good advice, and attended closely his words. It developed that

Wallace, who seemed sincerely good-natured, was a topman on the mainmast, and had been to sea all his life. He had sailed Indiamen and coast-wise traders since a boy and had rounded Cape Horn three times. Middle-aged and sea-wise, he was about to sign on to an English whaler headed for the Pacific when the Royal Navy interrupted his rendezvous at Mother Carey's.

He continued to describe the daily routine and hazards of life on a man of war, interspersed with personal observations, philosophy, and homespun wisdom. He admitted two concessions to the Royal Navy which included wearing what passed, barely, for a uniform, and shaving most Sundays for the inspection before church services. Of course the subject of press gangs and sailors serving in the navy against their wills weighed heavily on the Americans' minds, and Tyler kept pushing the good humored British sailor to talk more about the pressed men on *Orpheus*.

"How many of these men are here against their will, Wallace?" Tyler in his youthful innocence didn't quite realize just what he was asking.

"You want me to count the officers, too, or just the jacks? Tyler, right? Lookee 'ere, Tyler, ain't one among us wouldn't rather we was 'ome with our families or lady friends than bein' 'ere on a ship with a flogger fer a cap'n, and a bunch of officers what'll likely get more 'an a few of us kilt sooner than later. We lose men ever' time we go into port, what with desertions an' all. And the Yellow Jack. The ship sends out a gang or two to find the ones what left — or any others what'll fill their berths. Ain't particular 'bout whether the ones they grab know a tops'l from a spanker; they can learn, and learn they do with the cat o' nine tails 'angin' over they's heads. The lucky ones, they get the Jack and wind up in a shroud. No, boy, I don't 'magine you'll find much what'll put you in mind of that American merchant you come off'n."

"What of the mates, Wallace? You ain't said nothin' 'bout the mates." Pope spoke up for the first time. It seemed as though his accent had become a little more pronounced, and Biggs thought to himself that perhaps he was more recently from England than he admitted.

"No mates in the Royal Navy, sailor. We got lieutenants and midshipmen. You already seen the first lieutenant and Mr. Blake — he's a midshipman, and not a bad sort. Lieutenant Burns, the first, 'e's one you want to watch out fer. You never know with 'im wot's gonna happen. 'E can change 'is course as easy as kiss my hand. As long as 'e's back aft you ain't got to worry. It' s when 'e comes for'ard that you want to look to yer duties. An' when 'e talks quiet, there'll likely be trouble fer someone. Tol' you afore about Mr. Fitzgerald, an' the other lieutenant, Mr. 'ardy, — well, you'll see 'im soon enough; 'e's not a bad cove. Captain's a flogger — a bad sort. Ain't always fair-minded, either. 'E does make damn sure the purser don't short our prize shares, though. Which you lads'll be needin to pay off yer debt."

The mention of 'prize shares' caught their attention. So did the mention of 'debt'.

"Debt? What debt. We ain't been here long enough to get into debt." Pope looked at Biggs, who was equally as mystified as his shipmate. "How could we be into debt already?"

Biggs shook his head. "He didn't mean now, Pope. We ain't in debt. How could we be?" Obviously, this British sailor must be wrong.

"Oh, you lads're in debt all right. You got slop chest clothes, didn't you? You got a 'ammock, didn't you? You got a cup and dish, right? You didn't think they was given ya out o' the kindness o' 'is Majesty's 'eart, now did ya? Har har. No, you lads already owe Beckwirth more'n a month's wage. An' knowin' 'im, the King'll never see a farthing o' what you gonna pay for them slops. 'At's that way it works, though; don't matter what ship you're on." Wallace and his mates laughed at these Americans; how could anyone be that naive!

"That don't seem right, Wallace; we didn't want to be here, and they wasn't nothin' wrong with our own clothes. We're learnin' more an' more now. But you mentioned 'prize shares'. You mean we get prize money?"

Biggs, having never been in a hostile situation at sea except on the wrong end, and then only once — recently — had no idea the crew shared in the spoils of war.

"A good cruise with Captain Winston'll get you £50 or £60. He looks for Frenchies with cargoes 'eaded for 'ome. Sometimes we find a Spaniard too. If we can take 'em without what we got to burn 'em, the prize crew'll sail 'em into Jamaica or Antigua, or some-times Nassau. I guess they sell the cargo." He paused, then con-tinued with a smile, "That barky you was on woulda' made a nice prize. The pickins' been a little scant this trip. We'll find us a fat

Frenchman yet. Scuttlebutt is we're headin' over toward Hispanola. Likely to be a prize or two there."

Dinner was finished, and the men sent their dishes and cups back to the galley. Wallace rose from the chest he sat on and headed up through the weather deck to the brilliance and fresh air of the spardeck, and the fo'c'sle. For lack of something better to do, Biggs, Pope and Tyler followed along. As they reached the slightly raised fo'c'sle, Bosun Tice appeared.

"Biggs." Biggs turned, suppressing a response.

"You're assigned to the Starbowlines — on watch now. Report to Jack Toppan at the waist. 'E's the Petty Officer in charge of the watch. You been assigned to the maintop. You 'ave some time aloft, I collect?" This last was rhetorical as the assignment had been made and it would not do to question the wisdom of a warrant officer in His Majesty's Navy. "Take Tyler with you. Pope, you'll be in the larboard watch. Yer messmates'll show you the ropes." Without further word, Tice moved off, heading aft to ensure work necessary to the maintenance of the frigate in Bristol fashion was being carried out. Biggs and Tyler followed, heeding the instructions they had been given.

They found petty officer Toppan standing with a group of sailors at the foot of the mainmast. Actually, they heard him before they saw him; he was in the process of questioning, at the top of his lungs, the ancestry of one of his sailors who had unfortunately blundered where the watch captain could see him. Jack Toppan was a stocky man short of stature but long on wind; it was said he could shout orders to windward in the height of a gale, and make no mistake, the orders would be heard. He sported a droopy mustache and the long sideburns that seemed to be so popular with the ladies of the time. While not spotless, his uniform was in better shape than any of the men they had seen so far and it lent a certain amount of authority to his words and actions. A scar of indeterminate age ran from his ear, the lower part of which was missing, and down his neck, disappearing into the top of his jersey. Tyler stared at it, transfixed.

"Mr. Toppan, sir, I am Isaac Biggs and this here's Michael Tyler. We're off'n the *Anne*. Bosun Tice told us to report to you for watch." Biggs had waited until the diatribe seemed to die off before speaking. In fact, Toppan had merely paused for breath and was about to launch another tirade when he was interrupted. He turned to see the source of the voice.

"First off, don't call me 'sir'. I ain't no officer; I work for me pay. If you got to, you call me Toppan or Jack. Better you don't call me anything — just do what I tell you, smart-like and right the first time. I ain't got no time for slackers or landsmen. Either of you got any time aloft?"

"Yessir . . . I mean . . . I do. I was captain of the foretop on *Anne*. Tyler was a waister, but I know my way around aloft." Biggs was thinking about the men he and the other Americans had seen in the rigging, even though no sails were being handed or set. He decided that staying out of harm's way was probably the best way to avoid trouble.

"Then get up to the main yard. You too, Tyler. No time like the present to learn you a useful trade. Captain of the top is Coleman on this watch, and 'e could use a couple of hands. Lost one overboard in some nasty weather a few days back. Got another in 'ospital below. Been runnin' short since. And when the watch changes, go find the purser — 'at's Mr. Beckwirth — and sign the Articles, if'n you ain't yet. 'E'll be most likely in the gunroom or lookin' for one of the ship's boys. Har har har." Toppan leered and the men around him laughed on cue at the comment.

Tyler blinked, and his eyes met those of the petty officer. "We already done that. Wrote our names proper, and without no help, we did." The youngster was still proud of that fact, but Toppan and his men missed the retort, laughing.

Biggs did not laugh; Biggs was already on the bulwark heading for the ratlines, but Tyler was rooted to the deck. The comment Toppan had casually thrown out about a topman falling overboard struck him like a hammer blow. The longer he thought about it, the wider his eyes became and the more convinced he became that there was no way he could force himself to climb the ratlines and work like a monkey in the rigging; he knew he would fall, it was only a matter of time. He looked aloft, and began to shake. He stared at the petty officer.

"Uh . . . sir . . . uh, I mean Mr. Toppan . . . uh, I mean . . . I can't work aloft. I don't know how. Bein' up high scares me. I was once on a cliff at home and I looked down at the water and nearly fell over. I can't . . ."

Toppan listened to the rush of words for a few seconds then cut him off with a look. The voice, when it came, inspired young

Tyler to even greater levels of fear, and caused the tears to well up in his eyes.

"Lad, you weren't attending what I said. I just told you to get up to the main top with yer mate there. 'At's where I need another 'and and 'at's where you'll be workin' on this watch. Let me give you a 'and up."

The petty officer roughly grabbed Tyler, who made no effort now to hide his tears, and manhandled him to the bulwark and threw him at the shrouds. Had Tyler not grabbed the ratlines he most surely would have been overboard. After clinging for dear life to the thick tar-coated shrouds for some time — to him it seemed like forever, but not nearly long enough — he glanced at Jack Toppan. Then he began to slowly climb up; his fear of being aloft had suddenly been overcome by his fear of what would happen if he didn't obey. It took a concentrated effort for him to release his grip on the shrouds as he climbed, ever so slowly, up the rigging, each step taking him further from the relative safety of the deck.

After what seemed an eternity to him, Tyler felt hands reaching down through the lubber's hole at the main top. Biggs got a firm grip on the lad's shirt and literally pulled him up through the hole in the platform which the more seasoned topmen called the lubber's hole. Men accustomed to working aloft went up the futtock shrouds to the top, shunning the safer, but slower lubber's hole as unseamanlike. Tyler was shaking so badly that he could neither speak nor stand up; he sat on the floor of the fighting top, hugging his knees. He kept his eyes tightly closed, but the tears continued to course down his cheeks unabated. Biggs took the boy gently by the arms and stood him up.

"Open your eyes, Tyler. Don't look down yet, just look around. Look there. You can still see the top hamper of *Anne* from up here. See? Over the larboard side."

The boy unscrewed his eyes to look. He wiped them dry and, while he did hang on to the rail of the fighting top for dear life, he looked at Biggs, then at the other topmen who had watched his display, and finally at the horizon and the disappearing ship which had been his most recent home.

"Biggs, what are we gonna do? We don't belong on no British Navy ship. What's gonna happen to us?" The lad was barely in control, and he stared wide-eyed at his friend — his only friend in the world. His voice shook with fear.

Biggs had had similar thoughts; now was not the time to share them with Tyler, and he figured he better do what he was told and try to stay out of trouble. He passed this wisdom along to Tyler in a low voice.

"Keep your eyes on your work, Tyler. One hand for yourself and one for the ship. Make sure you have a good step afore you take it, or it'll likely be your last. Do what you're told and don't talk back to no one. One ship's much the same as another — just flyin' a different flag. At least bein' up here'll keep you from havin' to work on the guns. Now that looks dangerous. You'll get to like it up here."

Tyler hadn't completely bought into the concept yet, and he was skeptical, but figured Biggs had worked aloft for many years and must know. He tentatively tried a look down at the deck. Reeling, he quickly decided that was not a smart thing to do, and resolved not to do it again.

Coleman had moved in to the top from the furled sail on which he had been resting.

"I'm Coleman. Toppan send you up 'ere?"

"Aye." Biggs turned to face his new boss. Coleman was young, Biggs thought he was about the same age as he, and pleasant. His light colored hair was tied in a braid down his back, and a gold ring hung from his ear. He was missing several teeth, the result of either a fight, scurvy, or a navy surgeon. He was quick to smile, and his blue eyes danced and his ruddy cheeks puffed in genuine mirth. Biggs decided he could like this apparently easy-going young man. "Tyler here ain't never been aloft afore, and he's a little scared. My name is Isaac Biggs. . . from Marblehead. That's in Massachusetts."

"You can keep Tyler with you. Teach 'im what 'e needs to know. Just don't let 'im fall; 'e'd be the second in just over a week. I can't lose no more men; It's a bloody 'andful brailing up the mains'l even with a full crew. Those lubbers on deck don't 'ave an idea about 'auling the clewlines when I tell 'em. Toppan thinks. . . well, you'll see soon enough. Keep an eye on the boy, an' keep 'im next to you on the yards."

The watch eventually ended. Tyler was becoming used to being aloft now, and had even ventured out on the mainyard followed closely by Biggs. He maintained a death grip on the jackstay and beckets, and moved ever so slowly, but he had done it, and was proud of his new accomplishment. His tears and trembling had stopped. Then he had to go back down the shrouds to the deck below; that necessitated looking down. He slid his feet down through the lubber's hole and found the ratlines. Very slowly he started down the windward shrouds; the fact that a dozen and more sailors were watching him and laughing was of less importance to him than finding the next rung of the rope ladder which, with the shrouds, made up the ratlines. By the time he hit the deck, the group had increased in size; those who had missed his performance were filled in by the others with colorful embellishments and all laughed heartily as he jumped off the bulwark. Tyler, realizing he had little option, and thrilled to have made the trip without incident, joined in.

CHAPTER EIGHT

A Letter to Marblehead

Dear Mother and Father:

I hope this letter finds you both well and getting along. I wish I could say that all is well with me and that we're soon to be on our way home from St. Bart's. It was my bad luck, along with two other sailors from *Anne* that the bark was stopped two days out of our destination by a British warship, and three of us were pressed into the Royal Navy. Your son is now a topman on an English frigate engaged in a war with the French.

You can only imagine — or maybe you can not — the terror we all felt when that warship ordered us to heave to and did the same her self, about a cable's length away with all those cannon poking out of the side right at us. And there was a lot of them — huge gaping muzzles what could of tore the poor *Anne* to matchwood. Looking at them was terrifying, I can tell you. Made some of the men start shaking just out of fright. Captain Smalley was some mad, fit to be tied in fact. He wanted no part of heaving to or letting them Brits come aboard, but he didn't have no choice in it. Reckon he was some scared on top of it. I can tell you I surely was.

As you know, the British are famous for stopping almost any ship and plucking seamen from her ranks to fill out a crew. This time it was our very bad luck to be selected. When the officer, a Lieutenant Burns, came aboard with armed Royal Marines and ordered Captain Smalley to muster the hands, most of us figgered we would not be taken on account of which we are American. To Lieutenant Burns, that don't signify, and he pulled me and a cove named Pope and a young boy named Michael Tyler out of the crew and drug us off to the frigate. The Marines even shot one of the Annes afore we was in the frigate's boat. I didn't see who the poor cove was, and I can tell you I was terrible frightened — though not as bad as young Tyler was. That poor boy was crying and carrying on something awful. The Marines had to drag him physical right off'n the ship. And then, he was told he would work aloft with me, and he got even worse. I was some frightened my own self, but not about being aloft. And then we both got put on one of the long guns for when we go into a fight — quarters they call it — and I ain't happy about that at all. Seems like it might be right dangerous being there. I surely don't want to upset you, but you ought to know what is what.

This ship is big — they's about two hundred fifty men aboard, and sleeping room is something nobody's got. Seems like everything is done in a rush and with a whole lot of men. They beat a drum to tell the hands what to do for everything, eating, going to our fighting stations, muster and all. To me, the tunes, if you could call them that, all sound the same, and it's some hard to figger out what I'm supposed to be doing without I ask someone. We're still finding our way around, and figgering out who's who, and who we got to look out for. Over the month and more we been here, we ain't had a run in with any of the officers yet, but they's a few others what ain't too friendly nor helpful. Tyler's still real fearful of everything, and while he's getting better at going aloft, it takes him a awful long time, and even longer to get out on a yard. I try to help him, and been telling him how to do it, but he's just too scared.

And afore we was even aboard an hour, we was told we were in debt, on account of having to buy our plates, cups, hammocks, and clothes. Course not one of us had even a coin, so the cove that's in charge of those things, the purser, give them to us, but never said nothing about we got to pay for it out of what they pay us. We found that out later from some sailors. Somehow don't seem fair, you ask me. But that's what I reckon everyone what comes aboard got to do.

Some of the men we met so far ain't too bad. Fact is, some are real nice and kind to us. One cove, Robert Coleman, is captain of the top — like I was on *Anne* — and he and one of the others aloft — a fellow named Wallace — been real nice. Turns out, Wallace was pressed same as us, and he's a Brit! I'd reckon about half the foremast jacks aboard are pressed, or on what they call 'tops'l bail'. That's when a magistrate tells someone he's going to sea or jail. Most of them pick going to sea over jail, though I can't imagine the conditions here are much better than in a jail somewhere. Coleman seems like a easy going cove, about my age, and seems always to got a smile on his face. Wears his hair in a braid like a lot of them aboard here. Coleman is who I work for, and it ain't real bad. Seems to like me, and I guess he knows by now that I know my own way around aloft. Wallace, he's one what was pressed — I can't tell you where, but ashore — he's been to sea most of his life mostly on whalers and merchants. Don't take real well to the Navy life, but seems to be getting by all right. Don't seem to take a lot of they's rules real serious, and it's got him whipped more than once.

The officers what I had truck with don't seem too bad, though a couple of them don't know a sheet block from a boomkin. Take out they's stupidity on the foremast jacks, which makes for hard duty. The first lieutenant, a cove named Burns — he's the one what pressed us off the *Anne* — he seems like he knows what he's about, and most of the time he seems fair. Some of my friends tell me to wait, on account of he ain't when it comes down to it, but I ain't had no problems with him. Some of the boys, midshipmen they are — like officers, but they ain't — seem so stupid it's a wonder they can find the bow without being took there. Captain Winston is a bad sort, though most of the men think he's a fair hand in a fight, and while I ain't seen it, they say he's a right fine seaman as well. I ain't had the occasion to meet him, but I remember seeing him when first we come aboard from the *Anne*. Standing there on the quarterdeck, he was. A little cove with a noticeable nose, and his hair worn in a longer queue than even Captain Smalley. He sure stood up straight, probably trying to make himself look bigger than he is, and dressed in a fine uniform with gold braid and shiny buttons. And gold hanging off his shoulders. He was pacing up and down, but when we got on deck, he stopped and stared right at us. Looked like he was about to lay into some unlucky cove. Most of the lads we've met say he's real lucky and that he's done just fine in taking enemy ships in a fight. I mentioned he was a bad sort, other than in a fight, and he is just that. He calls the men together more'n once a week to witness punishment — flogging — and seems like it's getting to be more often. I sure hope I can miss that. I've watched quite a few in the short time I been aboard, and it is sickening to behold.

Every time he has someone flogged, all hands got to be there to watch, and I truly hate it. I found it makes me sick to see a man whipped like you wouldn't even whip a mule, but most of the hands seem not to mind. Guess they are used to it. Don't think that's something I can ever get used to. So far, ain't none of the Annes gotten the lash. One thing, I noticed that Lieutenant Burns seems to flinch every time a stroke is laid on. I don't think he takes to it much as Captain Winston does. Course, neither one of them have to listen at night to the ones what got whipped. It's truly awful to hear the groaning and crying out that they do both in they's sleep and when they's awake. Must hurt something powerful having your back flayed open, sometimes right down so as you can see the bone. And they ain't nothing anyone of us can do about it. Those what got flogged just got to get through it on account of they's back to work the next watch. Unless the surgeon says they's too bad cut to work, but that don't happen too often. I hear the captain don't take real kindly to him pulling men what been flogged from the duty.

I hope you won't think ill of me, but as awful as the flogging is, and as sick as it makes me to watch, it seems like I can't draw my eyes away when it's going on. And that makes me even sicker to my stomach. I can't understand it, and it causes me no end of worry. I hope I ain't becoming like the Brits, but I don't reckon I can ever get used to it like they seem to be.

I don't have any idea of how I can post this, or even when. Fact is, I don't have much of an idea of what lays ahead. Seems like a long time ago I was captain of the foretop on *Anne* and learning navigation from Mr. Clark so I could maybe get a third's berth one day and maybe after that keep moving up. That's what Captain Smalley said I might do. All that's gone now, and I got no idea what is gonna happen next. Ain't no mates in the Royal Navy, and they ain't gonna let a foremast jack learn navigation. I been praying like we used to at home, and I got hopes that something will come of it, but I hope it don't take too long. Sooner or later the *Orpheus*, that's the name of this frigate I'm on, is gonna run into a Frenchman and we're gonna have to fight. I ain't looking forward to that one bit. I got to stop this and take the watch now. I'll try and figger a way to get this posted somewhere.

Don't you worry none about me on account of I'll be all right. A prayer for me might help some, though. You take care.

Your loving son,
Isaac Biggs
November 21, 1810

CHAPTER NINE

Punishment

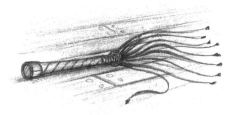

Several months passed. The Americans were absorbed into the crew of *Orpheus*, and had, superficially at least, become British sailors. Even Tyler seemed less afraid and had made a few friends among the British man o' warsmen. *Orpheus* sailed her assigned sector in solitary splendor, catching neither Frenchman nor Spaniard, and only once seeing what was assumed to be a French merchant briefly from the masthead.

Daily, during the afternoon watch, the ship beat to quarters and the crew exercised the great guns in dumb show. Captain Winston's policy of not wasting ammunition in effect in the early part of the commission was now eased since they had had no actions in which to use the shot and powder aboard, and he allowed the guns to be fired at floating targets on a weekly basis. The crew came to look forward to these real firing exercises, even though each crew had only three rounds to use at each practice due to the shortage of good, corned black powder in the Indies. The gun crews, as well as the officers and midshipmen, vied with one another for accuracy and speed of fire. Since the targets, composed of barrels and scraps of wood nailed together in a free form sort of mass, floated by at whatever rate of speed the ship was sailing, crews had varying lengths of time during which their individual guns would bear.

At first, as might be expected, the rate of fire and the accuracy was abysmal; accidents occurred at every gun almost every time the ship fired. Mishaps, ranging from burns to broken bones to a crushed foot, kept the surgeon and his mates busy. Captain Winston was fatalistic about them.

"As long as we're running the drills," he said to Lieutenant Burns, "we might as well give everybody some practice. The sail handlers and officers are learning to move faster and work the ship to better advantage, the gunners are gaining some skill and accuracy, so too should the surgeon and his mates be provided an opportunity to practice their trade."

Gradually, the rate of fire improved along with the accuracy, and often by the time the target was in a position where the after guns would bear, there was little left for them to train their pieces on. As the skill of the men went up, the number of accidents, as well as the severity of them, went down. After a few months of practice, the surgeon was heard to complain that his men had little do in the dark and confining cockpit where they were required to set up a make-shift hospital each time the ship beat to quarters.

The entire crew became acclimated to the crashing roar of the great guns and the organized bedlam involved in firing them. Even Lieutenant Fitzgerald's crews, on the forward six pieces, began to develop some respect for their officer, and those guns, each manned with ten seamen and a gun captain, became the bench mark that the other crews strove to beat. Of course, Lieutenant Fitzgerald took as much of the credit as he could for the success and strutted about the ship like an overstuffed popinjay. On the positive side, however, he was less of a bully to the midshipmen with whom he came in contact. Rarely did he abuse them when they came to the quarterdeck to shoot the noon position, and while he knew little more than they about the art and science of navigation, he tried to be of modest help to them when they had questions. The other officers took the positive change in their brother with a smile, and most felt that there would be no long lasting improvement. As Lieutenant Burns was heard to observe one day at dinner in the gunroom, "A leopard will not change his spots."

Except for the men in his own gun crews, the ship's company felt little of the benefit of Mr. Fitzgerald's success. He continued to be as unpleasant and unknowing as ever, and the petty officers and warrants had constantly to swallow reactions to his usurping their authority in routine events.

Biggs, who had been assigned to a gun crew in addition to the main top as his quarters station, was sent aloft along with Coleman, Wallace, and eleven other men to reset the reefed main top-s'l. He returned to the deck as quarters was piped down one day, and watched from the gangway as Tyler got into an argument with another seaman, one who happened to be on gun two. Tyler had been put in a gun crew and in spite of practice, the men could not seem to combine accuracy with an acceptable rate of fire. No one would later recall what the disagreement was about, but most did agree that one of Fitzgerald's men fired the first verbal sally. As the disagreement reached full cry, the man from gun two pulled his knife and started for the gun captain on Tyler's gun, a man named Ezra Spicer. Tyler had been in the van of the argument until the knife came out; at that point, he moved away, and the knife-wielder started for the other man, not caring who he cut. Tyler chose his moment, then from behind, whacked the man with a rammer from one of the nearby guns. It was only a heartbeat later that Lieutenants Fitzgerald and Burns appeared on the scene. When Tyler's rammer struck the sailor, the knife dropped from his hand and was immediately picked up by his intended victim, so that what they saw was not an accurate representation of the circumstances; Spicer was holding the knife, and Tyler, still holding the rammer, had obviously just hit his shipmate in the head. Tyler and Spicer were ordered below in irons; the victim, since he had not been observed in the commission of a crime was sent back to his duties by way of the surgeon, and the crowd, wanting not to be the focus of either Fitzgerald's or Burns' attention, melted away rather than correct the misapprehensions of either lieutenant.

The pressed sailors from *Anne* were soon to personally experience the major difference between the American merchant fleet and the Royal Navy. While most American sailors had heard the tales of swift justice and floggings, none of the men late of *Anne* had witnessed such punishment before coming aboard the British frigate. They had seen floggings many times over the months they had been aboard *Orpheus* and each had been sickened by it; it seemed arbitrary and unfair to them. The warnings they had been given at the start were right; Captain Winston used flogging as the answer to any discipline problem.

Now the Americans were about to witness the ritual again, only this time, one of their own would play an active role. The day after the incident at Tyler's gun, the men were called to muster in the waist. This had become an all too frequent occurrence under Captain Winston. The Marines were also assembled, and fully decked out in their red coats and white pants. Bayonets gleamed on their muskets and the line they formed was razor straight.

The petty officers lined up their men in ragged rows; midshipmen and the ship's officers formed neat ranks on the forward section of the quarterdeck, immediately aft of the mainmast. Captain Winston stepped forward and stood with his officers at the rail facing the crew and spoke the now familiar words again.

"This muster is to witness a captain's hearing and subsequent punishment if so ordered. You will remain silent and in ranks." He raised his voice slightly and continued, "Master at Arms, bring forth the prisoners."

None were surprised to see five men, including Tyler and Spicer, the gun captain, half dragged and half marched to the front of the crew. Beside Spicer, the American sailors knew one of the others, but two were complete strangers to them. Tyler, of course, was well known not only to the Americans, but to many of the British sailors as well. Most who knew him thought him a friendly youngster who made them laugh, caused no trouble and did his job; he would probably make a fine sailor-man one day.

He stood there, beside Spicer, with the other prisoners, his hands in irons, head down and totally beaten. He trembled visibly and a constant flow of tears streaked his grimy cheeks. His protestations of wrongful accusation had fallen on deaf ears; after all, two King's officers had "witnessed" his action with the rammer. Captain Winston looked at the group for a long minute and then spoke to the master at arms.

"Read your charges, Master at Arms. Let's get on with it."

There were two cases of drunkenness, one insubordination to an officer, and the two gunners. The master at arms, having read the first three charges came to Spicer. He prodded him forward as the charges against him were read.

"This man, Captain, is accused of threatening a shipmate with a knife, and it was only a matter of timing that he didn't follow through with the threat. Lieutenant Burns and Mister Fitzgerald witnessed and thwarted the attack in the nick of time."

The captain looked at Lieutenant Burns and said, "What about this, Mr. Burns. Did this man attack his shipmate with a knife?"

"No sir. He was only holding the knife when we arrived on the scene. In fact he didn't appear all that threatening to me. More like he was just holding it."

"I would have to agree, sir. The man made no move to stick his shipmate." Unnecessarily, Lieutenant Fitzgerald corroborated the story.

"Spicer. What do you have to say about all this, hmmm?" The captain didn't seem all that eager to seize the man up.

"It's like the lieutenants said, sir. I had just picked it up where

Tompkins dropped it, sir. Wasn't gonna stick him. Wasn't necessary since Tyler had just whacked 'im with the rammer."

The eyebrow shot up, stayed aloft for a heartbeat, then returned.

"Very well. Since it appears you were not about to cut your shipmate, I am suspending your grog ration for two weeks for arguing. You're dismissed, Spicer." The captain seemed willing to listen, and Tyler, who was next, looked up at him, and smiled nervously, wide-eyed and hopeful he would listen to him as well. Winston turned to the master at arms.

"This, then, must be Tyler."

The warrant again stepped forward and spoke.

"Aye, sir. He is charged with violation of Article 32 of the Articles of War, in that he beat another, his shipmate, with a rammer, sir. He also is charged with fighting and disorderly conduct. I believe Mister Fitzgerald and Lieutenant Burns saw the blow, and there is no question about what happened."

"What is your job on *Orpheus*, Tyler?"

"I'm a main topman on the starboard watch, sir."

"Bosun Tice."

"Sir."

"Who is the watch petty officer and captain of the main top on the starboard watch?" The captain was looking for someone to speak up for the boy.

"Toppan, sir. And Coleman is the captain of the maintop."

"Do either of you have anything to say for Tyler . . . in his defense? Did either of you see the incident the Master at Arms described?"

Toppan spoke up. There was no question he would be heard; he fairly bellowed his response.

"The boy is one of mine, sir. 'E come aboard from that American merchant a 'alf a year back. Scared to death 'e was sir, when I sent 'im up to the maintop. Seems to be used to it now though, and 'e's not a bad 'and. I saw the end of the fight, sir, and seemed to me 'at Tompkins 'ad a knife. Tyler didn't start nothin'. I doubt 'e could. Sir."

"Thank you Toppan. Lieutenant Fitzgerald, is Tompkins up and about?" Receiving a nod in affirmation, he continued. "Have him come forward, if you please."

The man shuffled forward from the assembled crew; there was

no mistaking him. He still had a slightly glazed over look in his eyes and a bandage wrapped 'round his head. He stopped well away from the captain and Lieutenant Fitzgerald. He wore purser's slops that fitted his large frame poorly and kept his eyes averted, furtively shifting between the deck and the horizon.

"What can you tell me about this, Tompkins? How did it come to pass that you got knocked on the head?"

"Aye yer worship. Me an' Spicer, off'n gun five, was havin' a little disagreement over something. Tyler was standin' there, and then 'e left, I thought. Next thing I know, sometin' cracks me skull. Knocked me cold, it did. Shouldn't 'it a man from behind." A little exaggeration couldn't hurt his case.

"Does anyone else have anything to add to this story?" The captain paused. The ship remained silent save for the creak of the rigging and the gentle rushing sound of the water as it slid by the hull. "In that case . . ."

"Sir. I saw the whole incident from the gangway, sir, and nobody's told it right."

The eyebrow shot up, and remained.

"What have we here, Lieutenant Burns? A sea lawyer, perhaps?" The captain left no doubt that he had already made up his mind and did not appreciate the interruption. The first lieutenant stepped to the quarterdeck rail so as to more clearly see who had had the audacity to speak up so plainly.

"Who said that? Come forward and speak up." Burns spoke in his usual quiet voice, but every man jack on the spardeck heard him, and heard the menace and challenge that the words carried. There was a pause. Then the same voice spoke again.

"Me, sir. Biggs. Able seaman, maintopman starboard watch."

"Weren't you one of the men from that American we stopped a few months ago?" Seeing Biggs nod and about to speak, Burns went on.

"That would make you a former shipmate of the accused. Is that why you're speaking up, or do you have something to add?"

Winston's eyebrow returned to its resting place, and a smile, ever so slight, began to play at the corners of his mouth.

"No sir . . . I mean, aye sir . . . I do have something to add. I saw the whole thing from the gangway. We had just secured from firing the great guns, and I seen Tompkins start an argument with some of the men off'n gun five. When he pulled a knife on one of them — Spicer, I reckon it were — Tyler hit him a stroke with a rammer. Tyler likely saved Spicer from bein' stuck by Tompkins — mayhaps even killed. Why, Spicer didn't even have his knife in hand. Couldn't have fought back at all. I know Tyler, sir. He wouldn't start anything."

"Captain, that's not how Mr. Fitzgerald and I saw it. We were, in fact, right on the weatherdeck, not up on the spardeck looking through the gangways into the darkness. It was apparent that Tyler, here, had indeed hit Tompkins over the head with the rammer smooth as kiss my hand. And when I looked at Spicer, I saw the knife in his hand, not Tompkins'."

The captain had heard enough, the start of his smile vanished as quickly as it had appeared. He looked down at Tyler.

"I will not tolerate fighting of any kind on my ship. Save your fight for the Frenchmen when we find 'em. Tyler, you're relatively new aboard so I am going to do you a favor. I am going to teach you about discipline in the Royal Navy so as you won't soon forget it." He turned to the bosun.

"Three dozen, Bosun."

There was no reaction from the crew; they had heard the same punishment ordered countless times. Tyler, however many times he had heard it ordered, had never before heard it associated with his name, and audibly gasped. Then he sobbed. His head was bowed, and his small frame, wracked with sobs, seemed to shrink even smaller.

With the punishment meted out to the other three men, Captain Winston had ordered a total of over sixty lashes with the cat o' nine tails to be swung by one of the bosun's mates. The main hatch grating was rigged to the gangway with its lower part secured on the weatherdeck. Stout line was brought out and the first of the prisoners, a man named Crelock, was stripped of his shirt and had his hands tied to the top of the grate. Bosun Tice brought out the red baize bag and stood to one side, waiting with the bosun's mate who would deliver the punishment.

Captain Winston removed his hat, as did the officers and midshipmen. He then read in a strong voice completely devoid of emotion, the Articles of War appropriate to the offense, in this case, drunkenness, and finished by saying to the Bosun, "One dozen, Mr. Tice. Do your duty."

Tice nodded at his mate, and the bosun's mate took the cat out of the proffered red bag and stepped forward, checking to be sure he had ample room to swing the lash. He raised his arm and smoothly brought it down. The nine strands of the cat whistled as they flew toward the unlucky sailor's back. When they landed, it was with a sharp crack punctuated by a sudden intake of breath.

While all of the men aboard had witnessed punishment with the cat, none could help but put themselves in the place of the sailor seized up to the grating. No one made a sound; the silence was broken only by the slap of the knotted leather strands of the cat across the now bleeding flesh. The sailor, Crelock, groaned involuntarily as the lash fell, his back now a mess of pulped skin with bone showing, but not once did he cry out.

At the completion of the twelve strokes ordered by the captain, Crelock was cut down and taken forward by his mates to treat his raw back. The next miscreant was brought forward and after being ordered to strip, was seized up to the grate. The captain again doffed his hat, read the appropriate Article of War, and ordered the bosun to "Do your duty." A different bosun's mate stepped forward to take the whip. Winston wanted fresh arms wielding the lash so as to maintain the quality of the punishment.

The scene was repeated yet again before it was Tyler's turn to be tied to the grate. None had been awarded as many strokes as had Tyler, and most of the crew knew he could not endure more than twelve or fifteen without losing consciousness.

Tyler, in fact, had nearly passed out just watching the other men receive their punishments; he had no delusions about his own ability to withstand the whipping. The pain he would experience was compounded in his mind by his innocence, and knowing that he was to receive almost twice as many strokes as the preceding three men, it became an unendurable turn of events. His eyes took on a wild look, glancing around the ship, and into the faces of his mates as if looking for an advocate who, at the last moment, might indeed save him from his horrific ordeal. No one moved, or met his eyes. His sobbing had stopped, and his tears were replaced with steady streams of sweat running from his hairline down his face and neck, disappearing into his shirt, already dark and stained. His trembling renewed with increased vigor, uncontrolled and violent.

The master at arms had removed Tyler's irons and dragged him forward to stand in front of the grate. The boy remained motionless, save his uncontrollable trembling, and his eyes, red and swollen, darted wildly about the scene, never settling long on anything or anyone.

"Strip." The word seemed to galvanize Tyler into action, and before the bosun's mate could grab hold of him to tear the shirt off him, Tyler screamed, "Nooooooooooooooo. . ." Turning, he leapt for the bulwark, and in a flash, he was over the side and falling head first toward the blue Caribbean Sea.

Nobody moved a muscle, so stunned was every man aboard. Neither the master at arms, nor the bosun's mate with the cat, nor the captain had ever experienced anything akin to this action. They were momentarily speechless. No one had ever jumped overboard before in the face of a flogging.

Suddenly everyone began talking at once. All the men who could get there, ran to the rail to see if they could see him. In the confusion, two voices rose above the general din.

"He can't swim! Throw him a line!" This was his old shipmate, Isaac Biggs, looking frantically for a loose coil of rope to throw to his friend, now floundering around in the wake of HMS *Orpheus*. The other voice was louder and more authoritative.

"Heave to the ship. Swing out the cutter." The captain's words were barely out of his mouth when the sailing master, Smosky, issued the orders which would bring the ship to a stop so that a boat could be lowered. Men moved quickly to their sail handling positions, and from the maintop, Biggs, alternately watching his young friend in the water and the job at hand, could see his friend floundering in the water astern of the frigate. Before the ship was stopped, however, he lost sight of him and feared the worst. He could hear Captain Winston ranting on the quarterdeck.

"Get that man back aboard! No one beats a punishment on my ship. I'll have him flogged around the fleet for desertion. If he doesn't drown, he'll wish he had when I get through with him. I'll personally flog the skin off his back. GET THAT BOAT OVER, NOW!"

HMS *Orpheus* had stopped; the cutter was in the water with a crew and Midshipman Blake sitting in the sternsheets. They pushed away from the ship and began rowing back along the wake, trying to hear cries from Tyler or directions from the ship. Unfortunately, no one on the ship could see Tyler any longer, and the crew was again silent. The boy had disappeared.

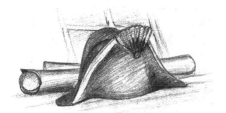

CHAPTER TEN

English Harbour, Antigua

The island of Antigua broke the horizon and was duly recognized by the lookout in the foretop, acknowledged by the officer on the quarterdeck, and caused all hands currently on deck to leap into the rigging for a glimpse. The bosun and carpenter quickly restored order and returned the men to their pre-dawn duties, which included washing, holystoning, and then flogging dry the deck. As the sun broke out of the calm turquoise sea, the deck was nearly dry and lines were being recoiled. The men were beginning to think about queuing up for breakfast which would be piped in another hour. The sighting of their destination and the knowledge that it was only a matter of hours away brought a new air of vigor to them, and a level of excitement not yet experienced on this so-far quite ordinary cruise. There had been no prizes or battles; the last close contact had been with the American *Anne* well past six months back. There had been some sightings thought to be French, but they were so far hull down that *Orpheus* had been unable to close them. The crew's frustration and resulting testiness had been echoed by the officers, and *Orpheus* was not a happy ship.

"Mr. 'ardy's compliments, sir, and we have in sight Antigua off the larboard bow, five leagues distant and not yet visible from deck." The midshipman sent to inform Captain Winston of their landfall made it through his report without stammering, a fact of which he was suitably proud.

Fourteen years old and in his second year as a midshipman, Mr. Charles Duncan had been sent to sea by a father with a minor position in the district government and thus enough influence to secure his son a midshipman's appointment. There was little hope in the Duncan family that young Charles would make a success of his budding career, but at least his being at sea reduced the number of mouths to feed and bodies to clothe. Charles' stammer came from a combination of factors, not the least of which was an appalling lack of confidence which his time in the sea service had finally begun to abate. His small stature and pock-marked face frequently made him the butt of jokes and recipient of unsavory jobs, but, as he kept telling himself, taking abuse in stride built character.

"Very well, Mr. Duncan. When I have finished my breakfast, I shall be on deck. Unless there is a reason I should come now?" The captain never made it easy for the midshipmen, or anyone else for that matter.

"Uh . . . yessir . . . I m-m-mean, no sir. There is n-n-nothing else, sir. Lieutenant Hardy d-d-didn't say nothing . . . I m-m-mean anything about c-c-coming now. Sir." Young Duncan's discomfort fed on itself and with his face turning crimson, he turned on his heel and walked squarely into the door which he had only moments before most carefully closed.

"Excuse me, p-p-please," he said, either to the door or the captain. Captain Winston uncharacteristically laughed out loud at the boy's clumsiness, and sent him back to the quarterdeck without further comment.

As the midshipman returned to the deck, he heard seven bells struck. He knew he'd be relieved soon and would then be able to return to the mid's berth — and his breakfast. He looked forward to getting away from the constant scrutiny of the quarterdeck, and the resulting criticism. Glancing up the deck, he saw the men from the larboard watch rolling their hammocks tightly and stowing them in the netting provided for the purpose along the bulwark. The practice afforded some protection from a musket ball, and cleared out the lower deck for cleaning. He briefly thought the sailor's lot might be an improvement, but quickly disabused himself of such ideas.

After a meal of ship's biscuit, burgoo, and today, cocoa, the starbowlines, including main topman Biggs, were turned out to clean the berthing and gun decks. Since the sea was calm, and the weather bright, the gunports were raised, pumps rigged and the decks washed down. They would be holystoned and ultimately flogged dry with swabs, as had been the spardeck a few hours before. Working a holystone across the deck was a hands and knees job, and the men talked and joked about their officers and midshipmen, a popular pastime when none was within earshot.

The Navy had changed with the ever-growing need for sailors and the direct manifestation of this was a marked reduction in the loyalty and regard of the officers for their men. While many of the Tars were fiercely loyal to their ships and captains, there were also many who were anything but, and it was these who would have been hard pressed to understand the kind of loyalty and respect that Admiral Nelson had commanded, and the willingness of his sailors and officers to sail into the face of danger with nary a thought of personal safety.

Of course, many of Biggs's shipmates were pressed, but most had adapted to the Navy and felt that aside from the ever-present danger, it was as good a way as any to make a living. For several, duty in the Royal Navy came in a different form; their service began as "tops'l bail," and like the men gathered by press gangs, they had little choice in service but were equally "Royal Navy." They were indistinguishable from any other tar. They all knew that if things got too bad, desertion was an option, and many took that road, but frequently wound up caught, tried, flogged, and back at sea. The punishment did not seem to be a deterrent, and whenever there was a chance of getting some liberty, even for a few days, the subject came up.

Biggs did not join the conversation and foolery brought about by the landfall. He was thinking about his friend Tyler, and that frightful day some months past. He recalled the shock that went through the entire crew when Tyler had jumped, rather than face the cat. Flogging was a way of life in the British Navy and most sailors took the punishment as ordinary routine fare. It was most irregular to have a sailor question the practice, and unheard of for a sailor to jump to a certain death when sentenced to a flogging. The American sailors did not feel the same way; flogging was less frequent in their Navy, and rare indeed on most merchant vessels. The crews of both were volunteers, not conscripts, and there were other ways of punishing a man when out of line.

The ship had lain hove to for nearly two hours. Captain Winston eventually had calmed down, and called for the cutter to return. Since they hadn't found Tyler, or any trace of him, it was safe to assume he had in fact drowned or been consumed by one of the large sharks which frequently appeared in the vessel's wake. The boat was hoisted back aboard and the ship again made sail.

Biggs, in the off-watch section, came down from the maintop

and, with the master at arms, made his way forward to the berthing area where he and Tyler had swung their hammocks for the past four months. Picking up Tyler's scant belongings and his seabag, the master at arms had offered them to Biggs.

"You want any of this stuff? You were his mate and it's only right you should get first pick."

"Not on your life. He had nothing I need. Give it back to the purser for the slop chest. He can charge it against the pay of the next soul what gets pressed . . ." Isaac's voice was hard; his eyes, fixed on the master at arms, flashed like flint in a firing pan. He balled his fists and began to form more words filled with the vitriol that had suddenly bubbled up.

A look from the master at arms had silenced his youthful and angry tirade. Isaac's features relaxed quickly as he realized how close he had come to being seized up to the grating and given a taste of the cat for his outburst. He would miss Tyler; he knew that their being pressed had caused his death just as surely as though he had been shot on *Anne* by one of the Royal Marines. His resentment mounted, and he still had difficulty containing it. Before he got himself even closer to a flogging, Isaac walked away without a word, but he silently promised himself that somehow, some way . . .

Scrubbing his holystone harder with each stroke, he focused now on Lieutenants Burns and Fitzgerald. He owed it to his dead shipmate to even the score, and, while he had no idea how an ordinary seaman could, he figured that an opportunity might present itself He wondered what he would do. He saw the futility of trying to settle things with either Burns or Fitzgerald, but they were the problem, and he would wait for an opportunity. He forced his mind back to the present, and the darkness from his face.

"You think we'll get ashore, Wallace?" Biggs' mate on the main-top had become a good friend and advisor, frequently keeping Biggs from crossing a line which would have earned him more than a few stripes across his bare back.

"Maybe, and I surely am hopin' so. We got us a chance, any-way, bein's 'ow this 'ere island's so full of Royal Navy as to be Portsmouth with palm trees. Not much chance of a cove runnin' 'ere — 'ceptin' into the arms of one o' the local lovelies. Antigua's a right lively spot and the natives 'ave always been friendly. No need for a place like Mother Carey's, though they're there. 'Patience and 'olly's' is a fine place to lay up out o' the weather. One o' the quartermasters what's friendly with Cook told me we'll be takin' on water and stores, so it's likely 'at some of the men'll be gettin' ashore, if only to jackass casks and barrels to the boats. Mebbe Cap'n Winston might put the ship 'out of discipline' if they ain't gonna be no one gettin' ashore." Wallace stopped when he saw the blank look on Isaac's face.

"What's that you said 'bout discipline, Wallace? Ain't we got enough o' that what with the regular floggin' and cut grog rations an' all?"

Wallace laughed. "Not like that 't'all, Biggs. 'Out of discipline' means at the ship is open to visitors from ashore. Cap'n's done it afore 'ere. We can get the ladies to come to us, 'stead o' the other way 'round. Things can git *a bit rowdy aboard*, 'corrdin' to some o' the officers." This last he said in a fair imitation of an aristocratic English accent. The others laughed, recalling some of the occasions of which Wallace spoke.

Wallace had stopped his holystoning to contemplate on and then answer Biggs' question; he received a stroke with the bosun's starter across his stern-end as a none to gentle reminder to "get on with it."

"How 'bout it, Bosun Tice. We gonna get ashore here?" Biggs did not make the mistake of stopping his work, and didn't look up.

"I know what yer thinkin', Biggs. Lemme tell you; Antigua's not a real good place to run off. It's the homeport of the fleet in the Leewards, and there's more Marines here than ever you seen. Why they'd grab you up quick as kiss my hand, and Admiral LaFory ain't got a sense of humor 'bout sailors what desert. I've heard of deserters bein' flogged 'round the fleet. Been involved in one of them my own self. Damnedest thing too; man was dead when they brought him aboard. He'd already been given nigh onto a hundred strokes on four ships, but the sentence called for him to get a dozen an' more of the bosun's finest on each an' every ship in the harbor. We was in Plymouth at the time and there was prob'ly 'half a dozen fifth and sixth rates and three seventy-fours in. We strung 'im up to the grate and I give him a dozen me own self. I was a bosun's mate then, back in the year four it was. When we cut 'im down, they put 'im back in the boat an' strung 'im up on *Alert*. Did it right 'round the fleet, they did. No, this ain't the place to think about jumpin', Biggs. You neither, Wallace."

The story had mesmerized the men, and the work had pretty well stopped. Tice started a few and growled at a few others and the scrape of the holystones was heard again. The men had already been told that the great guns would not be exercised today while they were sailing into Antigua; this meant that when the decks were finished, they might rest until the watch changed at midday. For some, this meant sleeping or just sitting around on the weather deck or gundeck telling stories; for others, it meant an opportunity to mend clothes or make a new shirt from material tucked away waiting for the right moment.

As *Orpheus* closed on the island, in addition to land and green vegetation being visible from deck, the masts of a host of ships came into view. Captain Winston was on the quarterdeck, in his number two uniform as was his custom when entering port. He fully expected to be called to the flag ship, but even if he was not summarily summoned, he was obligated to pay a courtesy visit on Admiral Lafory and he planned to change prior to embarking on that mission.

The quarterdeck had become a hive of activity; there were no less than three midshipmen, Sailing Master Smosky, First Lieutenant Burns, and Lieutenant Hardy who still had the watch. Of course, as was the norm, two quartermaster's mates were at the ships huge wheel taking direction from Mr. Smosky, and the bosun hovered nearby.

"Mr. Tice, a leadsman in the chains, if you please." The captain, who had arrived on the quarterdeck moments before, turned to the watch officer and added, under his breath, "Or were you planning to divine the depth, Mr. Hardy?"

Captain Winston always used a leadsman when coming onto a harbor, even one marked with buoys as the cut into English Harbour had been for quite a few years now.

The calls of the leadsman were relayed back to the quarterdeck as the ship moved closer to the harbor. Adjustments were made in the course to remain in the unmarked outer channel based on the depth reported, and *Orpheus* moved at a stately pace past the headland and into the twisting, but given the prevailing winds, easily followed entrance to the main harbor.

"You may hand the courses, now, if you please, Mr. Smosky. Leave tops'ls, jibs, and stays'ls flying. Mr. Tice, you may prepare the best bower." The captain's orders created a flurry of activity;

men were sent aloft to brail up the big courses while others hauled on braces and clewlines to assist the topmen with the heavy sails. T'gallants had been furled the previous night in keeping with Captain Winston's usual habit and, since they would be entering harbor this morning, had not been reset at dawn. As the courses were clewed up, the frigate slowed perceptibly as she moved forward under just her stays'ls and tops'ls. The chant from the forechains continued showing the ship with plenty of water under her keel. Other men removed the lashings from the big bower anchor catted to the starboard bulwark, and would stand by awaiting the order to let it hang free, and ultimately, to let go.

A ship entering a port where the fleet is at anchor is always under the closest scrutiny; seamanship, smartness, and a smooth working crew make for an impressive entrance. The lack of any one of them will tell, and not only the captain, but any member of the ship's company would be subject to comments and ridicule from everyone from the Admiral to pub keeps. Needless to say, Captain Winston was acutely aware as he brought *Orpheus* around the headland that every eye was on them, and even if Admiral Lafory was not personally on deck, someone from his staff was and would report in detail to him.

"Mr. Hardy, make our numbers now, if you please. And our colors." For once, Hardy was ahead of the captain, and the quartermaster had the flags already on a halyard ready to fly. Almost before the captain finished speaking, the flags were snapping in the warm breeze. He looked for and found with his glass the flag ship. She had responded to his numbers and was flying the signal "Captain repair on board" with *Orpheus'* numbers from her mizzen crossjack yard.

Wonder what that's all about. Winston allowed only a part of his mind to ponder the summons from his boss. The rest he kept squarely on the matter at hand. *Orpheus* was moving through the anchorage now; the men aloft standing taut and ready for the commands that would bring the ship more or less close-hauled and then safely to anchor. The sailing master and bosun were close at hand, waiting for the orders from him, and anticipating the timing by watching the progress the ship made through the anchored ships.

"Bring up her two points. Mr. Smosky, haul your braces and bowlines." Winston had picked his spot to anchor and was heading toward it. The chant from the leadsman in the chains continued, showing ample water.

"Back the fore tops'l, Mr. Smosky, if you please." The order was relayed forward and Winston could see the yard coming around as the waisters hauled the braces. Suddenly the tops'l shivered and then, with a crack, filled backwards. It blossomed out around the topmast and again the ship slowed.

"Gunner, a salute to the flag as we pass, on my command." This was not only appropriate, it was essential. Deference to the senior officer with all the trappings of Naval etiquette required six guns in salute. Generally, the flagship answered the salute with her own guns, and Winston could see men standing by her larboard guns in readiness.

"Stand by . . . fire." The starboard forward-most gun erupted in flame and smoke, roaring out the appropriate salute. It was followed immediately by the next gun in line, then the next, and so on until six powder-only loads had been expended. The salute was answered as expected with four crashing booms from the flagship's thirty-two pounders.

"Take in the stays'ls, Mr. Smosky. Quick as ever you please. Mr. Tice, stand by for'ard. Quartermaster, bring her up a point, if you please." The ship responded to the course change and the further reduction of sail by heading closer to the wind and slowing even more. Now headway was almost nil, the fore tops'l backed and the main tops'l and spanker barely drawing.

"Hand the main tops'l, smartly now." Smosky was attending and had the order relayed to the men in the waist and on the maintop as the captain said the words. The backed fore tops'l had been braced around to maintain its braking effect as the ship approached the spot where they would anchor. The men forward were standing by stops on the now hanging anchor with an ax awaiting the order to let go.

Captain Winston was watching the water from the leeward side of the quarterdeck. It was barely moving past the ship's side. Satisfied with their speed, he glanced around the ship, ensuring he was in fact where he wanted to be. He called to the bosun.

"You may let go the bower, now, Mr. Tice." The bosun raised his arm and waved. Forward, the ax swung, the preventer holding the anchor was cut, and with a mighty splash, *Orpheus'* best bower sped to the sandy bottom of English Harbour, Antigua. The frigate stopped her forward movement and swung around as the anchor took a strain, bringing her bow into the wind.

"Carry on, Mr. Hardy. Mr. Burns, I'll see you in my cabin, if you please."

The captain strode off the quarterdeck and through the hatch to the gundeck and his cabin. Behind him, the cutter and long-boat were being readied for the water; the spanker and tops'ls were disappearing as the topmen and waisters furled them, and men not involved in those activities were gazing about the harbor, looking for old shipmates on the nearby vessels, and hoping they would get the opportunity to get ashore. Biggs, still at the main-top, had never been in Antigua and was astounded at the bustle and ebullient atmosphere of the place. He had also never seen so many British men o' war in one place before, and the two line of battle ships, both old seventy-fours, but none-the-less impressive. He had never seen so large a ship, and here were two, HMS *Worcester* and HMS *Gloucester.* The latter carried the blue ensign and command flag of Admiral Sir Francis Lafory, commander of the Leeward Island Station.

His work furling sails and putting harbor gaskets on the t'gallants, tops'ls, and courses was done, but Biggs stayed aloft to enjoy the view and observe the activity both on *Orpheus* and the other ships nearby. He saw the cutter swung out from its chocks amidships and lowered to the water on the starboard side. The crew clambered down the side of the ship and he noticed they were in matching jackets and hats. Their pigtails were neatly plaited and tarred. They made a Bristol appearance. The longboat likewise was lifted and swung out. That boat was secured to a warp and boom off the larboard side, but was not manned. He wondered about that.

Shortly, the captain appeared on deck; he was resplendent in his uniform; the epaulettes on his shoulders signifying his rank as Post Captain with over three years seniority, fairly glowed in the brilliance of the morning. His blue jacket with the gold braid was spotless, and showed well the effort Cochrane had expended in brushing it. His white breeches and ceremonial sword reflected the sun light and dazzled the eyes. He was followed by Mr. Burns, Biggs observed, who was still was in his sea-going rig. Paisley Cochrane brought up the rear of the small entourage carrying the captain's dress hat. He fussed with the cockade, uttering unintelligible sounds as he did, gave the hat a final, and totally unnecessary brushing, and placed it firmly on Captain Winston's head, fore and aft, as was becoming increasingly popular, rather than the old fashioned 'athwartships' style used by Admiral Lord Nelson. The captain adjusted the hat, spoke a few words to Cochrane, who stalked away with a glare at his master. Biggs could see the man's lips move, but from the maintop, was unable to hear the words. He was sure, though, that they weren't "By yer leave, sir."

The topman watched as Burns escorted his captain to the rail on the starboard side. A brief exchange followed, and Winston fairly leapt onto the rail and dropped down to the channel for the main shrouds and thence into the waiting cutter. No sooner was he settled in the stern sheets than the boat pushed off and the coxswain called the oarsmen to their duty. The boat, Biggs thought to himself, made an impressive sight as it stroked across the water towards *HMS Gloucester* and the waiting admiral.

CHAPTER ELEVEN

A Change of Plans

Shortly after six bells of the afternoon watch, the harbor lookout spotted the cutter returning to *Orpheus* with the captain in the stern sheets. The lookout hailed the quarterdeck, giving the midshipman stationed there sufficient warning to prepare the necessary reception for Winston's return, thus avoiding a potentially painful breach of naval etiquette.

Hearing the bustle and preparations for their captain, Biggs and Wallace left the group on the fo'c'sle with whom they had been discussing the pleasures of shore leave in Antigua, not to put too fine a point on it, and headed up to the maintop where they would be able to see and hear most of what transpired. The primary question in their minds was getting ashore, followed closely in priority by the issue of fresh provisions. They assumed that Captain Winston would tell at least Lieutenant Burns what he had learned on the flagship, and having overheard the conversation, Biggs and Wallace would be in a position to break the good news to their mates.

The quarterdeck hailed the small boat as it drew closer, and received the response "*Orpheus*" from the coxswain, indicating that indeed the captain of that ship was on board and intending to come alongside. Sideboys, a Marine drummer, bosun mates with pipes, and the first lieutenant would be required, and the midshipman sent one of the ship's boys to find Lieutenant Burns, passing the word for sideboys and the bosun mates himself.

The cutter drew alongside the frigate, the crew tossed their oars, and with pipes trilling, the drum rolling, and the sideboys at rigid attention, the captain appeared over the rail. Burns met and welcomed his captain rather excessively, the men in the maintop thought. They watched as Winston stopped and said to Burns in a voice that carried easily to the top, "Have the officers assemble in my cabin as quick as ever you can, if you please."

"Somethin's goin' on, Biggs, and I'm not sure it's goin' to be for the better. Either Winston got 'is bloody arse chewed out by the admiral, or 'e's gone and gotten new orders for us. In either case, I'm bettin' we'll not see the inside of a pub here." Wallace had experience and spoke with conviction. Biggs believed him. The men slid down the backstay to the spardeck, and rejoined their mates on the fo'c'sle to see what would develop. The ship seemed unusually quiet, and it was almost a relief when eight bells rang out and the crew was piped to supper.

It was during the second dog watch when Cochrane appeared on the weatherdeck, headed below to a storeroom. Wallace, Biggs, and several other men were lounging on one of the long guns telling stories and smoking when they saw him and called him over.

"What's going on in the Cabin, Cochrane?" Wallace came right to the point.

"You know I can't tell you that, Wallace. Captain Winston'd 'ave the 'ide flayed off'n me back if 'e thought I'd even whispered what I 'eard. But I will tell you, you men ain't goin' to be goin' ashore this time. We got barges comin' 'longside tonight with provisions an' water so as we can weigh anchor at first light . . . but I . . . you didn't 'ear that from me. I've already told you too much."

"Where're we goin', Cochrane?" This time one of the other men asked what was on all their minds.

"Like I said, I've already told you more'n I shoulda. You men know I don't blab what I 'ear in the captain's cabin — and I can tell you, I 'ear most everything. In fact, sometimes Captain Winston asks me what I think of this or that. 'E didn't have to ask me tonight though. 'E had all the officers in there and fairly kept me 'oppin' bringin' 'em this and that. Coffee, brandy, biscuits, sweets . . . I'm tellin' you, I was in and out of there so much I could barely keep track of the conversation. I reckon the admiral's got us joinin' up with a couple ships — a brig, I'm thinkin' and mebbe a frigate, sixth rate for sure. Goin' to intercept a bunch of Frenchies comin' up from Guadeloupe. Sounds like they . . . no I can't tell you more'n that. You just forget what you 'eard and who you 'eard it from. Which is to say, it weren't me."

"COCHRANE! Where's that coffee?" The captain's voice carried easily to the waist and made Cochrane jump, caught doing what he should not have been, and keeping the officers waiting on top of it. With a quick glance over his shoulder at the cabin, he scurried off to complete his errand as quick as ever he could.

Biggs, Wallace, and their mates looked at each other, and then rose as one, heading for the fo'c'sle. They found Toppan and Coleman with a few other starbowlines staring across the harbor toward the town where faintly could be heard the beginnings of a raucous evening as the sailors from other ships arrived at the docks of English Harbour.

"Don't get yer 'opes up, then, fellows. There's work to do tonight if we're to be under way at first light." Had a spar dropped from the foremast to land at their feet at that very moment, the men could not have been more surprised, nor would they have attended more closely the words Wallace spoke. He told them what they had heard, without revealing the source, and when he finished, they all spoke at once. Naturally, Toppan's voice seemed to float above the others.

"What the bloody 'ell are you blowin' about, Wallace? We ain't gettin out o' 'ere tomorrow. We got stores to get aboard, and leave to enjoy. Why, I meself heard Burns sayin' to Mr. 'ardy just after dinner that 'the men'll be goin ashore tonight and I hope not too many jump ship as we'll be needin' 'em to bring on stores over the next few days'. 'Sides, I 'spect a little dark eyed young lass seen us come in and be waitin' on me ashore. Probably pacin' up an' down the dock wonderin' why I ain't come to git 'er yet."

"Well, Jack, I don't 'spect even the petty officers'll get ashore tonight. Word we heard was takin' stores aboard from barges tonight and sailin' on the tide." Wallace wasn't going to let Toppan enjoy his dream even for a moment.

The group continued to discuss the veracity and reliability of the unknown source Biggs and Wallace had until Tice and his bosun's mates began bawling for the crew to "Muster in the waist, and don't tarry!" Starters and canes encouraged the ones who lagged, and soon the entire crew, including the Marines, were assembled, toeing the same deck seams they had used to form on for witnessing punishment. Hushed voices wondered aloud what was going on and conjecture ran rampant. The officers suddenly appeared at the rail of the poop, and Captain Winston, still resplendent in his finest uniform, stepped forward and spoke.

"Men of *Orpheus*. I know we just came in and are in need of stores, and some time ashore. All of us. But it is not to be. We will be joining with *Amethyst*, thirty-two guns, and *Jolie*, a twelve-gun brig captured only last month from the French to attack and capture a merchant fleet which is reported to be homeward bound with only two thirty-two-gun frigates and a brig as escort. We will load stores tonight, and be under way on the first tide thereafter. Lieutenant Burns will see to the loading."

The absolute silence that greeted this disastrous tiding reflected the stunning effect Winston's words had on the men. Shocked, open-mouthed stares searched the faces of the assembled officers, and were met with looks which did little to cover the disappointment they also suffered.

Lieutenant Burns let them stand and stare for the moment it took for the shock to hit home in each man, then stepped forward to the rail and spoke in a voice that demanded immediate attention; he did not yell, but raised his voice enough to be heard by the men in the furthest ranks and got their attention with his tone.

"Men," he said. "We will be loading stores tonight by watch. The starboard watch is due to take the deck in about half an hour. They will work loading from the barges we expect shortly and at eight bells, the larbowlines will take over, and starboard watch will lay below. This will continue until we have taken on sufficient stores, powder and shot, and water for this commission. It is likely we will see action, and be in a position to take prizes, and every man jack of you has to do his job perfectly. When we come back to English Harbour, there will be sufficient time for shore leave, and spending some of your prize shares." This last was greeted with cheers and stamping of feet.

The lookout in the foremast shrouds hailed the deck. "Deck there! Barges off the larboard bow pulling out from shore. 'Eaded this way, they are too."

Whether he had finished or not, this ended the first lieutenant's speech, and he dismissed the watch below while the starbowlines rigged single and double whips from the main and fore yards to swing the casks and crates aboard. They would be removed to the holds by human chains and stowed under the supervision of Mr. Beckwirth and his purser's mates. Powder and shot would of course be stowed in the magazines under the watchful eye of the gunner and his mates.

It was full dark, about one bell on the evening watch, when the barges were secured alongside at the waist. The two longboats which had towed them out returned to shore at once to pick up another barge or two while the first were being unloaded. The sailors of the starboard watch and all the idlers began the arduous task of swaying up the necessary stores and man-handling them to the lower decks. Midshipmen and officers were stationed at intervals along the way to ensure that all the provisions made it to the purser's storerooms, and that there were no slackers. The job moved smoothly. At midnight when eight bells rang out, the sentries made their reports, and the larboard watch took over from the exhausted men. Those who were relieved found out of the way places to collapse and sleep for four hours until they were rousted out again. From time to time, Captain Winston would silently appear; it might be at the waist where the whips were swaying the barrels aboard, or it might be in the hold, looking over the shoulder of Mr. Beckwirth as he tallied in a precise hand each item stowed. But for the most part, he paced back and forth on the quarterdeck obviously deep in thought. He had changed into his at-sea uniform, giving credence to an imminent and hasty departure.

CHAPTER TWELVE

The Next Morning

The new day broke, not with the bright Caribbean sun dancing across the waters of English Harbour, but with a gradual lightening of the gray sky, heavily overcast, and showing promise of rain before the day was out. Men and stores littered the deck of HMS *Orpheus*, a silent testimony to the night's frantic activity of preparation for a rapid departure. There were still members of the human chain passing barrels and crates below to the hold where an exhausted Warrant Beckwirth still tallied each new arrival with his usual precision and directed its stowage, assisted by the carpenter and his mates. The last barge had been towed away by a longboat only half an hour previously, and men of both watches, not otherwise immediately needed, collapsed where they stood until called again to finish striking the materiel below. Captain Winston and Lieutenant Burns stood on the quarterdeck watching as the deck gradually became cleared of all the goods necessary for sustenance of ship and crew, and once again took on the appearance of a man of war of the Royal Navy.

"As soon as ever possible, pipe the men to breakfast. The tide will begin to ebb soon and I want to take advantage of it. *Amethyst* is to meet with us before noon, and *Jolie* will be weighing anchor directly. Since she's slower, we have some time, but dallying will never do." Winston turned and headed over the to larboard side of the quarterdeck, his sacrosanct dominion, cutting off any thought of discussion or comment from Burns.

"Aye, Captain." Burns spoke to his retreating form, and watched as the captain began pacing forward and aft, deep in thought and apparently planning the day's events and the upcoming fight. He saw Paisley Cochrane waiting patiently at one end of the quarterdeck with a cup of coffee for the captain; when the pacing took him past his steward, Winston took the proffered cup without word or look, and Cochrane returned to his pantry below to prepare breakfast, for once without comment.

The last of the casks swung below, and already Bosun Tice and his mates were stirring the exhausted men of the larboard watch to begin the daily ritual of holystoning and washing the decks. Tice had already had the captain's coxswain sand the larboard side of the quarterdeck so as not to disturb the captain's regular morning walk, but the gangways and weatherdeck had been so littered with stores that the daily cleaning would have been impractical at best, and impossible at worst. Burns called to him now.

"Mr. Tice. You may pipe the hands to breakfast now, if you please. We will be making sail after the change of the watch." Burns watched for a few moments as the bosun started a few of the crew with his cane and then piped the watch below to their breakfast. By the time they finished eating, the larbowlines would be finished with the decks and would be sent to their meal. Tice, ensuring that one of his mates was keeping a watchful eye on the men on deck, went below himself for breakfast.

Biggs and his messmates, topmen all, had retrieved their food and were sitting on chests in the gundeck eating and discussing the pending commission against the French merchants and their escorts. Taking a bite of a ripe melon which had come aboard last night and thus was wonderfully fresh, Biggs asked the more experienced men about what they could expect dealing with three French men-of-war.

"Depends," responded Coleman ambiguously. "They could strike their colors soon as we show up, or they might just decide to take us on and then it would be a sight you won't soon ferget. I remember still my first fight with another ship. On the *Frolic* brig it was, under Cap'n 'arbrace. Not much of a fighter was 'e, goin' mostly after merchants, but that Frenchy give us a tussle, I'll tell you. Brig, she was, like us. Shot away our foremast and knocked out 'alf our larboard guns. We gave 'im a 'ot-shot from a carronade and 'it their magazine. What a bang! Wasn't nothin' but scrap wood and cordage left floating. What crewmen didn't get 'emselves kilt in the action got 'emselves blowed 'igh as our mainyard when that magazine went up. 'arbrace put over the only boat what wasn't broke up to look for survivors, but not a one did we find. Lost a lot o' me mates in 'at one, I did. Won't soon be forgettin' it, neither. No, Biggs, you'll 'member yer first one same as me — same as all of us."

The men nodded and looked seriously at each other as they recalled their own baptisms by fire. Fingers absently fiddled with earrings, pigtails or whatever came to hand; some faces grimaced as, in their minds, they heard again the crashing roar of cannon and the tearing of wood, all punctuated by the screams of their wounded or dying shipmates.

Biggs had stopped chewing, so rapt was his attention to Coleman's story. He sat there, mouth slightly ajar, and a line of drool pooling on the piece of melon he held. Never in life had he imagined such a picture as Coleman's story inspired. He blinked as his thoughts came back to the present and swallowed. Wiping his chin with his sleeve, he wondered aloud how *Orpheus* would make out if the French decided to fight, which was, of course, most likely.

"We'll get 'urt, and no mistake about it. There'll be splinters flyin' and if the Frenchies get in some lucky shots, we might get a long gun or two dismounted or lose some rigging. Them kind o' things add mightily to the butcher's bill, and the surgeon's mates'll be busy in the cockpit with dismounted arms 'n' legs. Har har." Toppan laughed at his own grisly joke. The others merely smiled, having seen first hand the carnage caused by a naval battle. "No matter about that," he continued, "Ain't a Frenchman on the seas we can't take as a prize easy as kiss my 'and. Make no mistake. You don't get shot outta the top or what we lose the mainmast, you'll likely live to tell yer tale to yer kids." His speech lost some of its bravado as he unconsciously ran a finger down the scar on his neck. He caught himself and smiled at Isaac, knowing the young New Englander had seen the gesture, and self-consciously grabbed up a piece of pork and popped it into his mouth.

One of the bosun's mates came through the gundeck encouraging the men to finish their food as "We'll be makin' sail quick as ever, make no mistake." Biggs stood, leaving the remainder of his pork and fruit to his mates. Suddenly his appetite wasn't quite as voracious as it had been, and he felt the need for some fresh air. Wallace went on deck with his fellow topman.

"Don't you worry none, Isaac. Things'll be happening so fast you won't have time to think about anything but sponging out your gun and gettin' aloft when they call us. If we're goin' to board, you'll be aloft anyway to tie up their yards when you can so you won't get killed goin' over on deck." Wallace's words seemed to provide little of the comfort they were intended to, and Biggs, grim-faced, decided that he would do his job and not worry about the future.

Isaac noted that the weather had not improved any; in fact it looked as though the heavens might open at any minute deluging them with rain. The wind had picked up some, and was starting to whine in the rigging; the surface of English Harbour was showing flecks of white as the calm water of last night picked up a short chop. *Orpheus*, like the other smaller ships in the harbor began to work at her anchor rode, impatiently lifting and bowing as though engaged in some elegant minuet, eager to put to sea.

"Hands to stations for making sail and up the anchor." Tice's voice carried forward and was followed by the pipe calling the crew to their positions for getting under way. Men ran to the capstan amidships, putting the twelve bars in the numbered pigeonholes around the top of the big drum and lining up four deep on each bar. The ship's boys ran forward with the messenger and under the supervision of a bosun's mate, secured it to the massive hawser leading to the best bower. At the signal from the quarterdeck, "Heave short the anchor," the capstan turned, the men marching round and round, stepping without thought over the messenger, and the fiddler perched on top played to keep them in step. The continuous loop of the messenger came in, pulling the anchor hawser which disappeared below to the cable tier where the carpenter's mates supervised its stowage. When one end of the messenger was amidships, the boys freed it and ran forward with it again to attach it to the hawser, timing their efforts so the men on the capstan would not break their rhythm. The fiddler's tune was insistent, encouraging the men to "Haul away lively-like," and "Stamp and go."

"Anchor's at short stay, sir." The hail from the bosun's mate on the fo'c'sle was readily audible on the quarterdeck, and the captain stepped forward and looked aloft, reassuring himself that the topmen were in position on all three masts and were ready to let go the sails. A smart departure was even more important than coming in smartly, and Winston was damned if he couldn't take *Orpheus* out with the best the Royal Navy had to offer.

"Mr. Smosky, stand by to make sail, if you please." Winston's quiet tone belied the angst he generally felt getting under weigh under the scrutiny of the admiral. His hands alternately clenched and relaxed at his sides and he seemed unable to stand still. "Mr. Tice, heave around and signal up and down, if you please."

Tice's bellow started the capstan moving again, and from the quarterdeck, Winston could see the hawser begin to take a huge strain, noting as it did, that it gave up what seemed fully half its girth under the tremendous load. Still, the ship didn't move, though the men on the capstan labored mightily. Tice called for more men to assist, and a handful of idlers who had been unemployed up to now jumped in to help on the bars. Still nothing happened.

"Get one more pawl. She'll break out. Put yer backs into it!"

The previously regular clicking of the pawls on the capstan had stopped; only occasionally could be heard the single click as one dropped into place, holding the messenger's bight from slipping out and losing the strain on the hawser. Smosky looked to the captain for instruction. Without orders from captain, he could not drop tops'ls until the bosun called the anchor clear.

"Anchor appears to be fouled, sir." Tice informed the quarterdeck of what was becoming increasingly obvious.

An eyebrow shot up. "Thank you, Mr. Tice. You may 'vast heaving for now, but be ready to take a strain as quick as ever you can when I signal you. For now, however, you may give us a little slack, if you please." Winston knew what he had to do, and while it was a relatively uncommon maneuver, he had successfully done it more than once in his career of command.

The captain's face was composed, confident in what he was about to attempt. "Mr. Smosky, we'll have to sail it out. Haul braces to set the tops'ls on the larboard tack, and let go when you are ready. But we'll be clewing 'em up smartly when she starts to swim."

"Aye, sir." He turned and blew his whistle, following it with a bellowed "Starboard braces, haul!. Tops'ls, lay out and loose. Let fall. Lively now, boys. Tops'l sheets, trim. Bear a hand there!"

Orpheus' head fell off to starboard as the tops'ls caught the wind and she began to ease forward.

"Put your helm down, quartermaster. Mr. Smosky, you may clew up, now, if you please."

The orders were given, and the ship, brought up by her helm and the tension on the anchor cable, jerked the anchor free. "She's aweigh, sir. Fiddler, start yer playin'." Tice wanted to be sure nothing further went awry, and the regular click of the pawls told him that the anchor cable was indeed coming in smoothly. The captain nodded at the sailing master, who again blew his whistle and bellowed.

"Cast loose the tops'l clewlines. Set the spanker and stays'ls. Stand by the courses. Braces haul. Trim your sheets."

Orpheus paid off smartly on the larboard tack. Winston stood by the quartermaster at the helm giving direction.

/ "Ease her off a trifle, son. Let her come around smoothly. Feel the wind." Then louder to Smosky, "Braces haul, Mr. Smosky. Mind your sheets. We'll be comin' right 'round. After we're clear you may let go the courses." He glanced at the flagship where colorful signal flags were whipping from the hoist on the mainyard. "Mr. Blake. What does the flagship have up? Make ready your response."

"Sir, she's showing our number and 'well done', if you please, sir." Blake didn't need his book for that one.

"Very good, Mr. Blake. Kindly acknowledge." Winston allowed himself the luxury of a barely perceptible smile; the admiral had obviously seen what he had done and approved of his seamanship. A good beginning for this commission, to be sure, and perhaps a harbinger of things to come. The captain dwelled on that thought for a moment; the smile broadened. He forced himself back to the matters at hand; the smile disappeared, unnoticed by any. This was not the time to bask in small victories.

The ship was now moving under tops'ls, spanker, jibs and stays'ls toward the harbor entrance. She approached the narrow cut and swung gracefully into it. The cry of the leadsman in the chains floating aft to the quarterdeck showed ample water, and *Orpheus* followed the twisting channel out of English Harbour with the ebb tide and an easterly fresh breeze billowing her sails.

As they cleared the channel, the lookout at the foretop hailed the deck.

"On deck there! Sail ho. Two points off the starboard bow. 'Pears she might be *Jolie*. A brig at any rate."

Burns, who had been standing by while the captain took *Orpheus* to sea, turned to a midshipman who was at the moment unemployed.

"Mr. Murphy. Step to the maintop and confirm that the ship is in fact *Jolie*, if you please."

The young man ran to the main shrouds and fairly leaped into them, scrambling aloft like a monkey, so eager was he to please. When he arrived at the main yard, he realized he had forgotten, in his haste to get aloft, to bring a glass, and while he could see the brig with his naked eye, he had no hope of making out enough detail to determine if she was in fact *Jolie*. He turned to the first man he saw on the yardarm.

"Biggs, quick as ever you can, nip down and get me a long glass. Smartly, now."

Biggs nodded at the boy, and looked at Coleman, who smiled his understanding of the youthful midshipman's plight. Grabbing the main backstay, the topman was quickly on deck and approached Mr. Burns standing on the quarterdeck.

"Mr. Murphy's compliments, sir. Seems as if he ain't brought a glass aloft. Sent me to fetch him one."

Burns' incredulity at his midshipman's stupidity drew only a long look aloft and a slight shake of his head, but he said nothing and handed Biggs a glass with a leather strap attached at either end. Biggs took it with a mumbled "Thank you, sir," and moved quickly to the main shrouds, the glass swung 'round his shoulders.

Murphy quickly put the glass to his eye and studied the brig. From the maintop, she was hull up and quite obviously French-built. Her sweet lines told of a fast ship, able to adequately cope with the mounting seas. He noted she had not shortened down yet and was indeed under a press of canvas. He hailed the deck.

"She appears to be French-built, sir. Most likely is *Jolie*. Showing tops'ls and on the larboard tack."

Burns waved his acknowledgment and stepped to where the captain was standing by the wheel. Winston nodded his confirmation of the report from the maintop without comment. He stepped forward and spoke to the Sailing Master.

"We'll have the courses now, Mr. Smosky, if you please." He looked aloft and thought for a moment, then added, "And t'gallants as well." To himself he decided, *We could surely give her t'gallants and still eat her up in an hour, two at most, but young Jason Smithfield over there needs to be taught some respect. Youngest lieutenant I ever heard to get promoted to commander so quick and master of a fast swimming brig like* Jolie.

"Beg pardon, sir?" Burns appeared beside him with an inquiring look about him. Apparently, the captain was not thinking entirely to himself. He turned to his first lieutenant and smiled thinly.

"Nothing, Joseph. Merely thinking that this would be young

Smithfield's first taste of an action as captain. I know he distinguished himself as first lieutenant on *Amethyst*, and saw some successful actions with Captain McCray, but it surely is different being the master." Winston balled his hands into fists, resting them on the rail. He looked out over the gray expanse of water and his eyes seemed to be focused on something over the horizon.

The captain's expansiveness made Burns open up a little himself, and he shared with Winston something that had been on his mind for some months, now.

"I am hopin' we'll have a large measure of success on this commission, Captain. I need some notable action behind me if ever I'm to see a promotion to my own ship. Young Jason over yonder was in his first midshipman year when I was thinkin' 'bout passing for Master's Mate. Rankles a bit to see him with his own ship, a French built sweet swimmin' one on top of it. I guess havin' an uncle in Whitehall helps a bit, too."

One bushy eyebrow lifted slightly, then returned to its resting place. "I seem to recall hearing somewhere you had a cousin in a position to give you a boost now and again, Joseph. When word reaches London that we have taken a host of French merchants after capturing or burning their escorts, I am certain your cousin will have no trouble in securing a brig or sloop for you to command yourself. You have only to see to your duties and be certain the ship is ready for whatever may come, and I will recommend you personally to Admiral LaFory."

"Thank you, sir. You are most kind. You may count on me." The conversation was hauled short by the quartermaster coming up to Burns and after touching his forelock with a knuckle, requesting permission to throw the log. The moment ended, and formality returned to the quarterdeck, leaving nothing in its wake of the conversation.

"Aye. Throw the log, if you please, quartermaster." Burns watched as the man picked up the reel with the log line wrapped around it. He set the chip askew, made sure the trip line was free, and turned to the boy at the thirty-second glass.

"Are you ready with the glass, boy?" A nod and "Aye" confirmed that the timer was in fact ready. "Stand by to turn."

The quartermaster dropped the chip over the side, clear of the turbulence of the wake. As it hit the water, he cried out, "Turn!" and watched the reel as the line spooled off it smoothly. For thirty seconds there was no sound on the quarterdeck as the ritual ran on. Then the boy on the glass said, "Stand by . . . nip!" and the quartermaster pinched off the line where it left the reel. Looking at the knots tied into the line, he turned to the officers and announced, "Nine knots, two fathoms, sir."

"She's moving smartly, Mr. Burns. Keep this course, if you please. Don't worry about *Jolie*; she'll have to keep up as best as ever she can manage. I am going below. You may set the watch and have me called when *Amethyst* is sighted."

With that, Captain Winston turned and left his quarterdeck to his second in command and the starboard watch.

CHAPTER THIRTEEN

Rendezvous

The three Royal Navy men-of-war sailed in company for two full days and nights, waiting for the wind and seas to moderate enough for the captains to heave to and meet on *Orpheus*. The other frigate, *Amethyst* had met them on the first afternoon, only slightly later than anticipated, and had fallen in with *Jolie* and *Orpheus*, sailing in a ragged line abreast. Winston had determined that a well-thought-out attack on the French fleet would include using *Jolie* as decoy, but had not yet been able to gather Captains McCray of *Amethyst* and Smithfield of *Jolie* aboard his ship to lay out his plan. The frigates had shortened down to tops'ls and reefed courses to allow *Jolie* to keep up with them as they headed to the north-northeast in search of the Frenchmen. Lookouts were posted at the topmast trestle trees in all three vessels, and changed hourly to ensure eyes as sharp as ever possible would see the top hampers of the enemy before being seen and the surprise turned into a stern chase.

Winston had figured they would sight the topmasts of the French fleet on the third day — certainly no later than dawn on the fourth — given the fact that the merchant ships would be unable to maintain the same press of canvas of which a frigate would be capable. Intelligence sent to Antigua on a fast schooner had indicated to the admiral's staff that the ships had sailed from Martinique three days prior to *Orpheus'* departure from Antigua; with the easterly blowing as it had for two days, the French convoy would have likely been heading something south of east before turning north to ensure a clear passage past the British held islands in the Leeward chain. This would give the British ships time to meet their quarry in the deep ocean. It was Winston's intent to cut them off as they worked their way north, and do it well away from any possible assistance from either French or Spanish warships. Hence, he took his ships north, out into the Atlantic.

By dawn on the third morning, it was apparent that the wind was moderating as were the seas. Winston knew this before ever he came topside; lying in his swinging cot he could feel the easier motion of his ship and hear the diminished whine of the wind through the masts, yards and rope aloft. He determined that this would be as good a day as any to get the other captains together, and the sooner the better. He went on deck, instinctively glancing aloft as he stepped up onto the quarterdeck. He spoke to no one and walked to his place on the leeward side. He paced fore and aft for some minutes, deep in thought, and then called to Lieutenant Fitzgerald, who had the watch.

"Mr. Fitzgerald, I shall be in my cabin taking my breakfast. After the crew has been fed, we will signal *Amethyst* and *Jolie* to heave to and call the captains aboard. It is my intention to have you and Mr. Blake handle this maneuver without my or Mr. Burns' comment. Naturally, we both will be close aboard should you have difficulty, but I suspect that you will manage nicely."

Without further comment, and leaving a speechless Fitzgerald gaping after him, Winston again glanced aloft and then around his entire domain, missing nothing, and headed below where he expected Cochrane would have his morning meal of coffee, toast, fruit, and pork laid out on the dining table in his cabin. Fitzgerald shook himself and gathered his wits; his brow furrowed in concentration, he spoke sharply to his midshipman.

"Mr. Blake, kindly check the signals book for the appropriate hoists and have the quartermaster prepare them and hold them at the ready." He paused, thinking of what else must be must be done. "Pass the word for the gunner." This to fire the necessary gun to windward to call attention to the signals.

Shortly, the warrant officer responsible for the guns appeared on the quarterdeck. Midshipman Blake was first to notice him, and started to give him the instructions he felt necessary.

"That will do, Mr. Blake. I believe I can manage to communicate our needs to Gunner Chase without your assistance." A stunned midshipman moved back toward the wheel with a quiet "Aye, sir" and covered his astonishment and his embarrassment for his officer by looking aloft. "Mr. Chase, prepare a wind'ard gun for'ard to be fired on my signal, if you please, after the crew has been fed. We will be heaving to directly thereafter, so kindly use no topmen in the gun's crew." He turned back to the quarterdeck, indicating the conversation was at an end, and, remembering he needed additional help, spoke to no one in particular, "Pass the word for Mr. Smosky and Mr. Tice." The men on watch in the waist could be heard calling forward and below for the two warrant officers without whom Lieutenant Fitzgerald had little hope of successfully completing the maneuver the captain had ordered. At that moment, the hands were piped to breakfast, and Lieutenant Hardy appeared on the quarterdeck to relieve Fitzgerald so he could go to the gunroom for his own meal. The watch was turned over, and Fitzgerald left with the admonition "Just keep her full and by as she goes, Mr. Hardy. The captain wants someone competent on deck to heave to and be on the quarterdeck when the other captains come aboard. Blake and I will return directly." He turned and walked away, full of himself, and did not see the astonishment which turned to a smile on Hardy's face.

The wind had backed to the northeast, and continued to moderate to the point that heaving to became almost redundant, the ships were moving so slowly, but the captain had said "Heave to," and heave to they would. Fitzgerald had returned to the quarterdeck after his breakfast in the gunroom with the other officers. From the expressions on the faces of his fellow diners when they came topside, he had spent a good part of the meal expressing his thoughts on the captain's confidence in him and the obviously greater things that were in store for him as a result. Many of the officers secretly hoped for a disaster that would haul short this troublesome braggart once and for all. He was the kind of man who took all the credit but never the blame, usually finding a scapegoat on whom to lay the credit for his own malfeasance. Fitzgerald turned to Blake, who had also rejoined the watch on the quarterdeck having enjoyed a rather more pleasant breakfast in the midshipmen's berth with the other mids.

"Go and tell the captain that I am ready to heave to and signal the other ships, if you please. Be sure to say 'with Mr. Fitzgerald's compliments'. Before you go, have the quartermaster standing by with the signal."

A quick "Aye, sir" and Blake was gone, first to instruct the quartermaster as directed and then to inform Winston that Fitzgerald was about to heave to the ship. When he returned, he saw the flags flying from the mizzen tops'l yard, and looked forward, expect-

ing to see the gun crew on the forward-most windward gun standing by with the lanyard in hand and the gun run out. They were
not, nor were the sail-handlers at their positions aloft or in the
waist. Nobody had called them yet, and in spite of the advance
notice from the officers, the crew would not be assembled until the
quarterdeck gave the word to the warrants and petty officers. First
Lieutenant Burns was not in evidence either, and of course, Captain Winston had not yet come on deck. It occurred to Blake that
Mr. Fitzgerald might be getting a little ahead of himself, but as he
had been chastised before by his lieutenant for making suggestions, he kept his own counsel and waited to see what might happen; he smiled secretly and the gleam in his eye, which he could
not hide, did not betray him.

"They seem not to see the signal, Blake." Fitzgerald sounded
genuinely perplexed as the other ships continued sailing their
course in apparent oblivion to the signal flapping lazily from
Orpheus.

"Perhaps a gun to wind'ard would draw their attention to it,
sir." Blake tried very hard not to sound as if only an idiot would forget something so basic, and Fitzgerald, in his growing angst, took
the suggestion at its face value.

"My God, Blake. Where in the name of all that's holy is the gunner? He was supposed to be standing by with a ready gun. Pass the
word for the gunner . . . and Mr. Smosky."

It was during this outburst that the captain and first lieutenant
chose to appear on the quarterdeck; they each smiled inwardly,
their faces giving nothing away, and moved to a position where
they could observe. It would be unlikely that they would offer assistance as the three ships were virtually hove to already, so light was
the wind. The sails were drawing, but had not been spread full
since the wind abated, given the plan to stop for the captains' meeting.

Warrant Officer Chase appeared in the waist. Fitzgerald saw
him before he got to the quarterdeck and bellowed loud enough to
be heard clearly all the way to the end of the jib boom, "Mr. Chase,
why hasn't a for'ard gun been fired to wind'ard as I requested?"

The answer came back at similar volume, "You said, sir, on
your signal. You ain't signaled yet."

Fitzgerald turned purple. Blake, the captain, and first lieutenant struggled to suppress grins; the rest of the crew on deck

didn't bother to make the effort. Their response ranged from smiles to outright laughter, which Lieutenant Fitzgerald tried very hard to ignore.

"You may fire to windward now, if you please, Mr. Chase." The report of the gun sounded so quickly it was obvious that Chase had followed his earlier instructions and had the gun ready, only awaiting his signal. Since all on deck had heard the exchange between the deck officer and the gunner, the gun's crew had already moved into position at their gun from the pinrail around the foremast where they had been lounging awaiting the order.

Amethyst and *Jolie* reacted promptly to the gun and each backed their foretops'ls, rounding up a few points as they did so. *Orpheus* sailed on; the order had not been given for the topmen to lay aloft and consequently, sails were not backed. It was only due to the lightness of the breeze that Fitzgerald could correct his error without sailing out of sight before *Orpheus* was hove to. Naturally, this correction included berating both Sailing Master Smosky and the Bosun Tice for being as ill-prepared as was Gunner Chase.

Captain Winston stepped closer to the junior lieutenant and spoke so quietly that none but Fitzgerald might hear.

"You surely won't win any praises from the boat crews bringing their captains across; we could have been several cables closer had you hove to when you signaled them to."

The captain was not one to mince words, nor did he suffer fools gladly. Fitzgerald's performance had been a comedy of errors and Captain Winston became highly exercised when any king's ship, but most particularly his own, did not perform with the highest level of competence and seamanship.

"The warrants let me down, sir. They were not ready as I had instructed them to be, and Tice had no men aloft to back the tops'ls . . ."

The eyebrow shot up, then returned. His eyes glowed in anger, and his expression, when the young lieutenant saw it, stopped his pathetic litany of excuses in mid-sentence. Winston spoke quietly, but there was an ominous undercurrent to his words.

"You mean they didn't pull your chestnuts from the fire, do you not, Mr. Fitzgerald? You were in charge, not them, and your abilities, or rather your lack of them, will likely keep you a lieutenant until the Admiralty sends you ashore once and for all. As for now, kindly turn the watch over to Mr. Hardy and retire to your cabin until I send for you."

"Boat ahoy!" The cry came from the waist of the frigate where Bosun Tice, knowing what was happening had already assembled the appropriate sideboys and bosun mates to properly receive the visiting captains.

"*Amethyst*," came the reply, indicating that the captain of that ship was in fact in the boat, and the rendering of proper honors would be expected. As a Post Captain in the Royal Navy, he was entitled to four sideboys and four bells sounded on the ship's bell as he stepped over the side. All of the pomp was carried out flawlessly, and Captain Winston, now at the waist to greet his guests, escorted Captain McCray aft, admonishing Lieutenant Burns as the two captains stepped away to "Bring young Smithfield aft to the cabin as quick as ever he gets aboard, if you please."

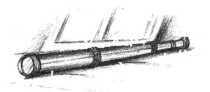

CHAPTER FOURTEEN

First Contact

Isaac Biggs and his fellow topmen lounged on a furled stays'l at the maintop, awaiting orders from the deck to set t'gallants. The men had remained aloft after getting under way from the captains' meeting since they were not on watch and were enjoying the cooling breeze which was considerably less noticeable on deck. Biggs noticed the seeming haste with which the visiting captains departed *Orpheus* and the rapidity with which sail was made on all three ships. Smosky seemed to have a genuine urgency instilled in him and heightened anticipation moved quick as a summer squall through the ship's company. They were actually going to fight the French, and more importantly, much more importantly, there would be prizes in which they would all share.

"When do you think we'll catch up with them, Coleman?" Biggs' level of enthusiasm was no less than the others even though he was not a British sailor, but an American pressed into service. He still would experience the danger, the excitement, and was entitled to a share in the prize money when it was distributed. The men had practiced on the great guns, and several had been close at hand when Gunner Chase had allowed to the first lieutenant that he thought the crews could actually maintain an acceptable rate of fire while at the same time, hit more or less what they were aiming at. There was no one on board *Orpheus* who was not eager to go to battle and take some prizes.

"Maybe tomorrow, Isaac. Believe me, it'll come quicker than ever you would expect." Coleman thought for a minute, absently fingering his gold earring, then added, "Even though you know it's going to happen, and yer even eager for it, it'll seem a surprise when it does. You mark my words." His normally smiling face was flat and expressionless. Isaac pondered his friend's enigmatic words.

The rest of the day passed uneventfully. The wind continued to be light out of the north-northeast and the three ships maintained their line abreast formation as they moved southeasterly in search of the French merchants and their escorts. The logs showed four and five knots at each half hour interval, and the watch on the quarterdeck felt the captain's frustration as he tried in vain to gain an extra knot of speed. The ships had all set most every sail they could; tops'ls and t'gallants, and in the case of *Amethyst*, studdings'ls on the windward ends of her main and fore yards. When the wind did pick up, they would be busy indeed to get some of the sail in before it could do any damage, but that was an acceptable risk to each of the captains, given the limited opportunity to catch up with a sizable French fleet.

As night fell, the wind did indeed pick up some, and the ships were now moving nicely with the log showing over eight knots at each throw. Captain Winston seemed pleased with this, but was careful not to show the crew that his enthusiasm matched theirs. He felt it necessary to maintain an air of aloofness from the men and his officers, not only to maintain his natural separation from the two groups, but also to keep everybody attending the ship carefully. He did call the evening watch together as they assembled to relieve their mates.

"Men, I fully expect to see the French at first light on the morrow. That is not to say we could not see a light from them tonight if they are showing any, and those of you posted to lookout duty must be more than usually vigilant. Should one of you catch a glimmer from anywhere forward of the beam, you must let the officer on the quarterdeck know as quick as ever possible." He paused, looking at the eager faces, each filled with excitement and anticipation. Few showed any concern or fear. He reached into his jacket pocket and held up the golden coin he pulled out. It glinted dully in the moonlight and held every eye. Winston swept their faces again with his gaze and continued to hold the coin aloft as he spoke. "To the lookout that first sees a sail, or a light that turns out to be the enemy, will go this guinea." This last he thought might inspire those at the mast heads to stay awake for the duration of their trick at lookout. There was considerable nudging, smiling, and a few risked murmuring, as each of the men thought of the delights a gold guinea would bring ashore until petty officer Toppan, responsible for the starbowlines, commanded "Silence!" in a voice that left no doubt among the members of his audience that to continue talking and skylarking would result in a meeting with the cat.

The watch was dismissed to carry out their assigned duties, and for once, there was no reluctance to go aloft on lookout duty. The lookouts were still assigned in one hour turns to maintain their sharpness, and even the normally deck-bound waisters and idlers were seeking an opportunity to win the gold guinea. Even though they were not assigned to lookout duty per se, the topmen all headed aloft to their stations, determined that they would see the lights of the fleet first. Biggs and Coleman moved almost to the cap of the topmast, resting on the main tops'l yard while they scanned the horizon across one hundred eighty degrees. The wind continued to build during the watch, and by midnight, when the starboard watch was relieved, the ship was scudding along at ten and more knots, reaching in a now northerly gale, which allowed a more easterly course.

As a concession to the increased wind, the t'gallants had been handed before midnight, their poles struck down, and still the topmasts groaned and whined under the enormous strain placed on them. The shrouds and backstays were taut as iron bars, and Biggs commented to Coleman as they reached the deck that reefing or handing the tops'ls in this wind was best left to the larbowlines as, in his opinion, someone would surely get hurt.

Hardly had the men gotten below and into their hammocks when there was a loud bang followed by a crash. These sounds were followed immediately by Toppan's bellow for "All hands lay up on deck!"

"Have we started the fight?" seemed to be on everyone's lips. They pulled on trousers and climbed the ladder to the deck they had just left to discover that the fore tops'l had blown out and the sail was shredding itself while the topmen struggled to get it contained. Coleman and his maintopmen leaped into the shrouds of the main mast and headed aloft almost before the bosun had finished bellowing orders to get the main tops'l handed before it too blew itself to ribbons. The larbowlines were already aloft which made it rather crowded on the yard, but Biggs, Coleman, and two others climbed quickly on up to the main topmast, ready to assist their shipmates with the sail as the waisters on deck eased the tops'l halyard, lowering the yardarm, while others on deck heaved mightily on the clewlines and buntlines pulling the sail up in the middle like a droopy bag. This bag, however, was full of wind, and gathering it in and securing it to the yardarm was no small task. With the extra hands, however, the job was accomplished, and the ship responded to the reduced sail.

Meanwhile, on the quarterdeck, Captain Winston was discussing with Smosky whether or not *Orpheus* could safely carry reefed tops'ls and full courses as was Winston's preference, or whether they should reef both as advocated by the sailing master. The captain wanted to give nothing away in the way of speed, and he knew if they didn't catch up with the French fleet in the next day, their chances of finding them would diminish greatly. He was prepared to cast aside his usual cautious early reefing to attain this end, and while Smosky was most likely correct in his assessment of the wind and conditions, he bowed to his captain, muttering under his breath in his native Russian as he walked away.

The ship continued to career through the night, and occasionally, the watch on deck would catch glimpses of lights from both *Amethyst* and *Jolie*, the latter struggling to maintain the speed of her sisters, and straining her rigging to its limits. Toward daybreak, Winston came on deck and instructed Lieutenant Burns, who had assumed the watch a few hours before. He assessed the conditions, and made up his mind.

"Signal the others to shorten sail now. Use the lanterns as well as flags, if you please, but no gun to wind'ard. If the French are where I expect them to turn up, a gun would most assuredly give us away. I want to see what the light brings." He turned to Bosun Tice who was on the gangway just forward of the quarterdeck. Having heard Winston's orders to Lieutenant Burns, he stayed close for the next orders which he guessed would be for him. He was right.

"Mr. Tice. We will reef the courses now, if you please. We'll continue under reefed courses until we have sufficient light. Kindly carry this out with a minimum of noise. Until I know where the French are I do not wish to give our own position away with a lot of bellowing and caterwauling."

"Aye, sir." Tice moved forward, speaking to his men and starting a few of the slackers with his cane. They were aloft in a trice on the fore and mainmasts and orders were given on deck to haul clewlines and braces in a normal speaking voice. The wind made it difficult to hear to commands, but the men were well trained and had carried out the maneuver so many times that orders were almost superfluous. Certainly the topmen needed no bellowed orders, as the starbowlines had the watch and were well experienced in their jobs.

The ships in company had likewise reefed and slowed; Captains McCray and Smithfield knew that plunging into the dawn at breakneck speed would be ill-advised and so had been expecting the command to shorten sail.

As the dawn broke, the lookout in the foremast, standing on the tops'l yard hailed the deck.

"Eight. . .no, nine sail!. A point to leeward and hull down. Make that ten sail!" He could not hide the excitement in his voice, anticipating as he was the thought of battle at long last, with its resultant prize shares and the golden guinea which he could now claim.

The words had barely been blown away by the wind when the captain was dashing forward, long glass in hand, headed for the foremast shrouds. As he reached them, he slung the glass over his shoulder and leaped agilely onto the bulwark and stepped into the rigging. He moved aloft with the sureness of foot and grace of a man of fewer years, surprising several sailors who had not before seen him go aloft. When he reached the foretop by way of the lubbers hole instead of the futtock shrouds, a concession to his age, he did not pause, but continued on to the topmast. He stepped onto the tops'l yard and swung his leg around a shroud to steady himself while he brought the long glass to bear on the strange sails.

"My guess is French, sir." The lookout was so excited he could barely contain his exuberance, and spoke his opinion, unasked, to the captain. Continuing, he said, "I seen Frenchies afore, sir. They set stays'ls different than us. Sheet 'em sloppy on top of it."

Winston was pleased to have found his enemy where and when he had expected. He said nothing nor did the young seaman notice the eyebrow as it rose quickly, then disappeared behind the long glass. Lowering the brass and leather instrument, the captain said, "I think you are right, young man. You have keen eyes. I promised you a guinea, and a guinea shall you have." He returned the glass to his eye and studied the fleet for several minutes longer, then without further comment to the astonished lookout, Captain Winston stepped onto the rope ladder to the foretop and arriving there, reached for the lower backstay and came down as smooth as any topman would. He went to the quarterdeck, finding most of his officers already there. Word had spread, and to say they were eager would be gross under-statement.

"Quartermaster, we will have the signal 'Enemy in sight, two points to leeward', if you please. Also show 'Alter course one point to windward', and 'Make all possible sail'. There will be no gun for this signal, Mr. Burns. Bosun, have the men piped to breakfast, if you please. I expect we will be engaged by mid-morning. Mr. Smosky, let us shake out the reef in the courses and set the mizzen and main stays'ls, if you please." Almost as an afterthought, he added, "Uppers as well as the lowers, I think. It'll strain her a mite, but speed now is quite essential."

The captain paused, looking around to see that everything he ordered was in fact being carried out. He turned to Burns and spoke again.

"I shall take my breakfast in the cabin now, Mr. Burns. Bring her up a point and let me know at once if anything changes. Also the moment the French are hull up from aloft."

The first lieutenant responded and turned away to issue the necessary orders to sail handlers and the helmsmen. The crowd of officers on the quarterdeck dispersed heading to the gunroom for their own breakfast. The ship was at a fever pitch and Burns knew that beating to quarters would be a formality as all the men would be at their battle stations with the ship rigged for fighting prior to the first notes of the "Heart of Oak."

He thought to himself that this would be the telling action of his heretofore uninspiring career, and hoped that not only would he conduct himself in the manner expected, but that his actions and conduct would be noticed and forwarded on to the Fleet Admiral for further forwarding, with a seal of approval, to London and the selection board for commands. While Burns had seen some action off the coast of France, and again in the Leeward Islands — this latter under Captain Winston — neither had been sufficiently bold to gain flag notice, he recalled. The first had been when he was still a midshipman and had resulted in the taking of a French brig and her merchant consort. This might have been noteworthy had not the ship he served on been a thirty-eight-gun frigate, easily capable of thrashing a modest brig, which they had indeed done. The second was on *Orpheus*, and was of similar stripe, only without the benefit of a prize as the brig had caught fire and burned to the waterline and the merchantman was so badly damaged that it was incumbent upon Winston to sink her.

Joseph, you're finally going to be tested, he said to himself. *This action we're heading into will be a major undertaking, with the three of us facing at least three and possibly four French fighting ships and potentially armed merchants. There's going to be damage and death aboard* Orpheus *as well as the other two, but I know the confidence is high in both the gunroom and the fo'c'sle; after all,* Orpheus, Amethyst, *and* Jolie *are British ships manned by British crews and as such, are arguably the best in the world since the halcyon days of Drake. We have that strong tradition behind us, and I am confident that the men of* Orpheus *will do nothing to diminish that glory. I surely hope I do not either.* He paced up and down the quarterdeck, watching as sail was crowded on his and the other ships, racing them to a favorable position which would maintain the weather gauge on their enemy. He noticed with some chagrin that he had started to sweat, and a trickle of wet ran uncomfortably down his back.

Burns had sent Midshipman Blake to the foretop to watch the French ships with a long glass, admonishing him to inform the quarterdeck of the slightest change in their position or course. From deck could barely be made out the top hampers of the nearest ships, and Burns felt confident that the distance was great enough that the British ships would not be noticed for a while yet, giving them the opportunity to close the distance and work more to weather before having to chase down their quarry.

Time passed; the three men of war worked further to windward while still closing the French fleet, albeit not quickly. The French were still hull down, and while their t'gallant masts and in a few cases their topmasts were visible from the deck of *Orpheus*, their actions indicated that either they thought they were still alone on the high seas, or the approaching ships would not threaten. As the sun rose higher in the sky, Biggs questioned the delay.

"Why don't we just go right at them and get on with it?" His inexperienced impatience caused Coleman and Toppan, who had just come aloft to see what he could see, to smile.

"It's real important that we 'ave the weather gauge, Isaac. That way, Captain Winston decides when 'e wants to start the action, not them damn Frogs. When the captain decides we're far enough to windward that we can swoop down on 'em, 'e will. And you'll see your action." As an after thought he added, "Probably faster than ever you wanted, once it starts." His voice held a somber note, and he unconsciously touched his scar. Toppan had seen a great deal of action with a variety of captains and knew Winston was one who favored Lord Nelson's strategy of "Go right at 'em and board 'em in the smoke." Before he did that, however, he would be sure he was tacitly in control of the situation. From the main top, where the three men watched, the French masts were plainly visible, and it was surprising that the French lookouts had not yet noticed the British ships.

"Something's going on on *Jolie.*" Coleman had noticed that the little brig had born off and was sailing large, almost fully before the wind, heading for the nearest of the French ships. The men noticed also that *Orpheus* was flying a hoist of flags from her mizzen yard. Toppan had enough time in the Navy to recognize many of the flags and the meanings of various combinations. He spoke to his companions.

"Those flags we're flying . . . you see? *Jolie* is flying like ones. I would imagine Winston's telling the brig to sail down there. Lookee there, would you! She's puttin' up a Frenchy flag . . . and some numbers. Could be that she's going to make them Frenchies think she's one of em. If it works, they'll let 'er right in among 'em."

As *Jolie* gained some distance, about half a league, *Amethyst* and then *Orpheus* bore off and headed downwind also toward the enemy fleet. Suddenly, the fife and drum could be heard, playing the stirring "Heart of Oak," signaling the call to quarters, and the three men went to their battle stations. The ship was cleared for action; bulkheads below were removed to gain greater access to spaces as well as minimize the opportunity for fire and more importantly, splinters which could fly amazing distances, spitting a man like a pig. Sand was spread across the weather and spar decks to allow the men to maintain their traction when the decks were covered in blood; shot and powder cartridges were run up from the magazines by the powder monkeys to be placed by each gun, and the galley fire was extinguished, again a precaution against an enemy shot breaching the galley bulkhead and spreading the fire. The nets were rigged over the decks to protect the gun crews and sail handlers from falling blocks, spars, and other tackle which could be brought down by a well-aimed shot and could crush a man's skull like an egg shell. Gunner Chase was making his rounds to be sure that the guns were all unlimbered and properly prepared to be loaded, which command would come from the quarterdeck at the appropriate time. He sent one of his mates to report to the first lieutenant that all was ready. The bosun's mate had just made a similar report, and the carpenter informed the officer that the bulkheads had been struck below and the pumps were manned; the captain was duly informed that his ship was indeed ready to fight.

"Pass the word for Mr. Chase." The captain wanted the gunner himself. When he appeared on the quarterdeck, the captain spoke quietly to him.

"Mr. Chase, I would like you to have a bow chaser loaded — load a light powder charge, if you please — and place a ball to the wind'ard of *Jolie* and slightly astern of her. Kindly sight the gun yourself. I do not wish to give Captain Smithfield cause for alarm, but I do hope to make the French think we are in pursuit of the brig." He turned to Mr. Smosky.

"Sailing Master, maintain the sails we have set, but leave them a trifle slack. I am not looking to close with *Jolie* just yet, but we must look to the French as though *Orpheus* is a slab-sided Dutch-built lugger that could not catch their fleet-of-foot brig, and we must be convincing in our performance."

It hurt Winston to refer to his fine sailing frigate as he had, but the French captains would find out in due course just how fine a ship his *Orpheus* truly was.

Smosky went off to see to the easing of the sails, just enough so they would not draw well, but from forward would look as if they were indeed full and doing well their jobs. He noticed Bosun Tice gathering some men to carry a spare tops'l yard to the quarterdeck. They balanced it on the taffrail, stout lines were affixed to either end, and then the yard was pushed into the water, the lines paid out, then secured on deck. Smosky smiled in spite of himself; dragging the spar would act like a brake on *Orpheus*, slowing her down substantially and adding to the illusion that she was sailing for all she was worth, but was unable to make up on *Jolie*. *Amethyst* seemed to be employing the same charade to equally good effect and was maintaining her position relative both to *Jolie* and *Orpheus*.

As Smosky watched this action on the quarterdeck, he saw the captain turn to face forward and wave his arm; with a less than deafening roar, the windward bow chaser fired. Smosky looked up in time to see the shot land in a small geyser to weather and astern of *Jolie,* exactly as Winston had requested. *Amethyst* fired an equally well placed shot just to leeward of the apparently fleeing French brig.

"The last ship in line is coming to weather, sir. Appears to be the brig." The lookout's shout had confirmed Winston's unspoken thought that firing at *Jolie* would undoubtedly give substance to their deception. Another shout from the lookout indicated that one of the frigates was also altering course, trimming sails to move more to weather and provide succor to their fleeing countryman.

"They have taken the bait," Winston exclaimed to Lieutenant Burns, as they watched the two ships move further away from their merchant charges, which, judging by the sails visible from deck — they were hull down — seemed to be continuing on their east-northeasterly course with now but one thirty-two-gun frigate to guide and protect them.

"Hold her steady, now, quartermaster, keep her on course. We don't want to catch up too early." There was no chance that the French vessels could gain the weather gauge on the British, but they would have to have time to try, and in the process, separate themselves further from their merchantmen. Winston had to time this maneuver correctly, cutting adrift the towed spar and trimming his sails at precisely the right moment to sweep down on the French with *Orpheus* positioned to present her broadside. He waved his hand forward and was rewarded with another roar from the windward bow chaser, followed by a splash to windward of *Jolie,* closer than last time, but still a safe distance away.

The French ships — the ones coming to the aid of *Jolie* — had now broken out their colors and a hoist which could have meant many things, but probably was telling *Jolie* to sail toward them for protection, which she was doing at a great rate. As the distance closed, the crews on *Orpheus'* weather deck craned their necks to see out their open ports, waiting for the order to run out the guns and fire, and not understanding why their ship was sailing so poorly. The French ships were clearly visible now from deck, and while still just out of the accurate range of any gun on *Orpheus,* were tempting targets for the British gun captains.

Biggs, aloft with the other topmen awaiting the order to shorten to battle sail, watched, fascinated with the dance being performed by these ships. The strategy was discussed as it happened at the maintop, and Winston would have been pleased to know his topmen were enjoying his efforts. They watched as *Jolie* drew closer to the French brig, maintaining her windward position and thus control of the situation. Naturally, the French captain felt no threat from *Jolie*, and so was unconcerned with his leeward position, and the lack of control it carried with it. Suddenly, Coleman elbowed Biggs, and pointed at the brig.

"Lookee there, Isaac. *Jolie*'s taking down the French flag. There she goes. There's the British battle flag. I imagine that Frenchy's about to b'foul 'is britches."

The American topman watched, thrilled, fascinated, and more than a little fearful of what was coming. He remembered his friends' words of yesterday about an action's start coming as a surprise even when a body expected it, and now suddenly, here it was. A wave of nausea swept over him, then passed.

As the Royal Navy ensign whipped to the gaff, *Jolie*'s larboard broadside belched fire, sending grape and chain shot through the smoke, flying like a scythe over the deck of the Frenchman. The battle had begun.

CHAPTER FIFTEEN

"Fire as You Bear"

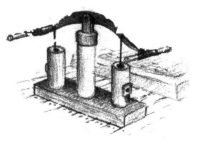

Jolie's broadside had caught the French man-of war completely off guard. While the captain had cleared for action as he altered course to help what he thought was another French brig, the guns had not yet been charged with powder and shot, nor had they been run out, and many of his crew were leaning on the bulwark, laughing and enjoying the spectacle of their countryman outsailing the British frigates. The mixed broadside of grape and chain shot had done its gruesome task well, clearing men and standing rigging from the Frenchman in a shower of splinters and body-parts.

Jolie wore around quickly, presenting her other broadside to the stern quarter of her target. The guns crews ran across the deck, manning the already charged and run-out guns. The deafening roar of six eighteen-pounder carronades, the accompanying smoke, and the knowledge that their guns were playing a vital role in the taking of the French fleet, encouraged the crews to work faster, and indeed, the guns were ready to fire again in just over one minute thirty seconds.

After firing her second broadside, *Jolie,* using her diminutive size and superb maneuverability to good advantage, "spread her wings" and headed back downwind. Now she sailed away from the staggering French brig and the shocked and ill-prepared frigate, and toward the remaining escort which had not had the advantage of witnessing the recently played-out charade, being below the effective horizon. Captain Smithfield hoped this third French vessel would be as unprepared as had been her sisters. *Orpheus* and *Amethyst* would take up the fight now and finish what *Jolie* had started.

Captain Winston bore down on the nearest of the two ships, the damaged brig which had tasted *Jolie's* iron, while Captain McCray in *Amethyst* matched his move, heading for the as yet unscathed frigate, a trifle further away, but to leeward.

"Load and run out your guns, Mr. Chase." The order rang out from the quarterdeck, and was answered by the unmistakable rumble of four-thousand-pound gun carriages, twelve to a side, being man-handled into the stops with their muzzles run out of the gun ports.

"Mr. Smosky, we'll reduce to battle sail, if you please, sir." Winston couldn't sail into a fray with as much canvas as he had aloft, and while it had been necessary to close the enemy quickly, it would now be a disadvantage to maneuvering and maintaining a position for effectively exchanging broadsides with the Frenchman. Courses were furled and the tops'ls set full again; about half the jibs and stays'ls remained in case it became necessary to sail to windward. The topmen on all three masts moved with the speed and sureness that came from practicing this very maneuver, and quickly *Orpheus* was under her fighting canvas. With his speed now diminished, Captain Winston sailed his ship directly for the wounded French brig, presenting a small target for her broadside guns.

With a roar and a belch of flame and smoke, the French guns spoke, poorly laid and raggedly fired. The shot, for the most part, landed wide or short of *Orpheus*, but two balls did come aboard; one buried itself in the foremast, the other flew down the larboard side of the spar deck, wounding several and dismounting a quarterdeck carronade.

Captain Winston barely noticed. Oblivious to the cries of men injured as the carronade overturned, and the splinter from the carriage which flew past his shoulder, his only concern was putting his ship in the most favorable position to inflict the most devastation to his enemy.

"Bear off! Haul your braces, ease sheets, starboard guns, standby . . . fire as you bear!" Winston bellowed his commands, taking no chance that they would not be heard. Looking aloft, he ordered the Marines in the fighting tops to open fire as they came within musket range. He did not have to tell them where to aim; exposed gun crews, and quarterdeck officers were the prime targets. *Orpheus* bore down, away from the wind until she was almost dead before it, and presented her entire starboard broadside to the relatively undefended starboard quarter of the Frenchman. As the forward guns fired, the ship continued to come around, opening up the rest of the battery, and each gun fired in turn. Even with barely a cable's length between them, Winston had time to bring his ship back onto the wind before the Frenchman could counter the move.

The French ship's ability to maneuver was severely reduced. Indeed, as those on *Orpheus* who could watched, the main mast began to lean aft and to leeward. As if in slow motion, it fell, landing on a bias across the quarterdeck with the topmast in the water trailing all manner of lines, spars, and canvas astern. The drag caused the brig to fall off to leeward, helping *Orpheus* gain further advantage to windward. The French sailors sprang into the mess with alacrity, and with axes cut away the remaining shrouds and the tangle of halyards, sheets, braces, clewlines and buntlines in a frenzied effort to loose the mess dragging alongside and effectively killing any chance the ship had to maneuver or even sail effectively. Captain Winston seized upon this opportunity in a trice.

"Braces ease, trim your sheets . . . trim the bowlines!" Again bellowed orders from the quarterdeck. More quietly to the quartermasters at the wheel, "Bring her up two points." *Orpheus* responded as her sails were trimmed. Winston watched as her long jib boom led the bow of the ship back to windward, which, in a few minutes, would unmask her larboard guns for an additional broadside before he would lay alongside and board.

"Larboard guns, fire as you bear!" From the quarterdeck, Winston could see Chase moving along the larboard battery, from gun to gun, checking the elevation of each piece, talking quickly to the gun captains, making sure the slow matches were trimmed and properly burning to ignite the powder in the touch holes of the long barrels in case the sometimes finicky flintlocks malfunctioned. The bow guns spoke, answered in kind by the French guns. Better served this time, but still ragged in their firing sequence — no doubt due to the number of men still involved in cutting away the remains of the main mast — their shots took a toll; the larboard bulwark smashed in two places, splinters flying and finding their marks in human targets. One ball scythed through most of the shrouds on the foremast leaving only a few puny strands holding the lower mast aloft. Still others slammed into the hull with jarring impacts. A long gun was dismounted and overturned, killing several of its crew in the process. Lieutenant Fitzgerald, let out of his cabin for the engagement, but not yet back in the good graces of the captain, stood by his forward guns, encouraging his crews and generally acting the part of a responsible officer. When the eighteen-pounder was hit, pieces of hot iron flew in all directions, and one struck the lieutenant in the shoulder. So intense was his concentration on his tasks, he barely noticed, and was surprised to smell something close at hand burning. Gunner Chase noticed and remarked with no more alarm than had he been discussing the weather, "Sir, your jacket is on fire." One of the many buckets of water placed throughout the deck for such emergencies was hastily thrown in the young lieutenant's direction, extinguishing the smoldering coat, thoroughly soaking the young man, and eliciting a few smiles from the men who saw the officer get wet down. The amusing interlude lasted only a second or two, as now the guns were being fired as fast as ever they could be swabbed, loaded, and run out again.

After the ship had been put under fighting sail, Biggs and the other topmen had assumed their positions as haulers at guns close to the mainmast so they could get back aloft quickly should the need arise. The view out the gun port was not nearly as all encompassing as from the maintop, but anyone who looked could see that Captain Winston was sailing *Orpheus* on a closing course with the French brig, and that if the Frenchman withstood the point blank broadsides, the Marines and sailors of the boarding party would be ordered to stand by with the pikes, cutlasses, pistols, and muskets with bayonets which had been placed at the ready in strategic locations along the main deck when *Orpheus* was cleared for action. Glancing aloft, Biggs saw that the Marines in the fighting top of the mainmast had found the range and were systematically picking off the sailors and officers on the exposed deck of the enemy frigate. Marines on the foremast were following suit. Of course, the French Marines, aloft on the foremast of the brig, were also doing their best to shoot the British officers and sailors who were exposed, and while they weren't having the same degree of success the Royal Marines were enjoying, their fire made moving about the decks somewhat risky.

The noise was continuous now; the two ships were separated by barely one hundred yards, and both had what remained of their full broadsides engaged, firing independently at point-blank range. The roar of the cannons was augmented by the staccato exclamations of the Marine's muskets from both sides, the shouted orders of petty officers and commissioned officers directing their men in barely intelligible commands, and the cries and screams of the wounded and dying on both ships. The entire scene was shrouded in the thick smoke generated by both ships' guns. As Winston moved his ship into position for the grapnels to be thrown which would secure the hulls together, he turned to Midshipman Murphy, the officer in charge of the quarterdeck carronades.

"Belay the ball shot, Mr. Murphy. Now is the time for grape. Concentrate your fire on the Frenchman's quarterdeck, if you please."

He watched as the small canvas bags containing hundreds of bits of iron, musket balls, and other deadly projectiles were rammed home and fired. The effect was startling; men fell on the brig, others ducked behind any convenient cover and while the captain continued to direct the action in the open, he did move into the lee of the helmsmen. The Frenchmen, realizing that boarding was imminent, grabbed up hand weapons and, seeking the protection of what was left of their bulwark, waited for the inevitable.

"Topmen aloft!" The order jolted Biggs, who had been heaving on his part of the gun tackle in a rhythm set by the rest of his crew. He whacked Coleman on the head to get his attention, pointing to the maintop. The two leaped for the ratlines and scrambled to their sail handling station. Six other maintopmen appeared, and when questioned as to the whereabouts of their fellows, only shook their heads mutely.

"Standby to board!" The command could be clearly heard now that some of the firing had died down. The Marines and their muskets at the fighting tops were targets for the French marksmen, and musket balls whizzed by the topmen as they moved to the outer end of the main yard waiting for a yard on the Frenchman to come within reach. Once that occurred, they would secure the two yards together, ensuring that the ships would not drift apart, even if the ropes securing the decks together were cut.

"Boarders away!" Biggs grabbed for the bitter end of the French foretops'l yard as it came within his reach. Coleman handed him a length of line, and the two men quickly tied the spars together. As Biggs finished his task, he glanced forward in time to see one of the British foretopmen catch a musket ball square in the face, and plummet silently to land athwart the two ships' bulwarks, an all too clear reminder of the accuracy of the French marksmen. All of a sudden his own mortality became apparent and Biggs clambered in from the end of his yardarm to the fighting top in an effort to at least put some distance between himself and the French marksmen. Coleman followed close behind.

From his less exposed perch, Biggs watched below as First Lieutenant Burns led the boarding party over the bulwark at the waist, landing on the French deck, sword in hand. From their position aloft, the topmen could see that the French had suffered more severely than the men of *Orpheus*. The decks were red with blood, and a significant number of bodies lay strewn about the deck — most exactly where they fell. He was most surprised by the number of disembodied limbs, clearly visible from the maintop. The boarding party split almost immediately upon gaining the French deck; one group, led by Lieutenant Burns headed aft for the quarterdeck, and the other, led by Lieutenant Hardy dealt with the men in the waist of the ship. Pikes, bayonets, and cutlasses swung, clanging on opposing weapons, and often landing with a soft thud on exposed flesh. The guns were silent now, their crews engaged in hand to hand combat. As he watched, Biggs saw Burns engaged with a French officer at the rise of the quarterdeck. When the Frenchman, backing up, stumbled, Burns took the opportunity to slash him and moving quickly, stepped over him and onto the quarterdeck of the now severely damaged brig.

"Smoke from the Frenchy!" Coleman bellowed to the deck. He wanted to be sure that any officers still aboard *Orpheus* saw the smoke; if it was emanating from anywhere near a magazine and spread, the resulting explosion would not only sink the Frenchman, but would also sink *Orpheus* as surely as would a fire in her own magazines. Lieutenant Fitzgerald heard the warning and saw the smoke, but there was little he could do save to be sure the captain was aware. He started back to the quarterdeck with this in mind. Coleman and Biggs watched from the maintop as the portly, red-faced and powder-grimed lieutenant hurried in his unique lumbering gait down the deck, stepping over fallen men and equipment. He reached the ladder to the spar deck and was half way up when suddenly, he stopped. He looked up, a startled look on his face, and pitched over backwards to the deck below, where he lay unmoving and silent, his blood pooling on the deck under his head and shoulders, victim of a Marine sharpshooter in the French foretop.

Lieutenant Burns, a spent pistol in one hand, his sword in the other, was handling himself with skill on the French quarterdeck; he had dispatched two officers, and was continuing to work his way aft, when a cry went up from half a dozen voices at once.

"She strikes! She's struck!" He looked up at the spar, hastily rigged to the quarterdeck taffrail when the main went by the boards, on which the French had attached their colors, and saw that the French tricolor had indeed been struck, cut down by someone's sword stroke and was hanging over the stern rail. Whether the halyard was cut by a Frenchman or Englishman was neither known nor did anyone care; the fighting ground to a halt, and the captain, knowing that to continue was fruitless, walked to Lieutenant Burns and offered him his sword.

"Sir, I am Captain Jean Faitoute, commander of the brig *Toulon*. My ship can no longer fight. I offer you my surrender with the wish that what remains of my crew will be treated 'onorably and those who need it will be provided with medical attentions."

"I can not accept your sword, sir. I would be honored to accompany you and any of your officers you wish to bring to *Orpheus* and Captain Winston, where arrangements can be made to assist your surgeon should help be needed. I fear we should move as quick as ever you please, though, sir, as I believe your ship is afire." Burns' words caused the French captain to look forward over the length of his ship, and having quickly assessed the situation, he nodded to the Englishman and gave a series of commands to what remained of his crew. Burns' concerned look and tensioning of his sword arm produced a slight smile on the captain's face, and a comment in his heavily accented, but proper English.

"Do not fear, sir. I 'ave not told my crew to take up arms again. Only to extinguish the fires if they can do so. Let us go and see your Captain 'Ween-ston'."

Burns led the way and the French captain, accompanied by his senior lieutenant, slightly wounded, made their way slowly forward. All the while, the two French officers surveyed the damage to their once proud ship, talking quietly to each other as they pointed out particularly devastating carnage. They reached the amidships area and climbed across what was left of the bulwarks to the British ship, where Captain Winston, having seen them coming, greeted them cordially at the waist.

"I welcome you aboard His Britannic Majesty's frigate *Orpheus*, sir. I am Harry Winston, commanding. My surgeon is at your disposal. I would suggest that delay in getting your men aboard my ship would be imprudent as it would appear that your ship is afire, and should it reach the magazine, we all should be in dire straits. I give you my word that your officers and crew will be treated kindly as long as they behave themselves." Winston's face remained unsmiling and impassive, but his eyes darted between Faitoute and the burning brig.

Flames were now visible, and once the remaining sails caught, the conflagration would be unstoppable. Men of both nationalities were moving rapidly to the British ship, and soon the decks were quite crowded. The wounded French were removed to the orlop deck where the hospital was set up, and both captains knew they would be treated not according to their nationality, but to the severity of their wounds.

The lines securing the ships together were cut free, and as the burning brig drifted off, aided by her remaining but untended sails, Captain Winston gave orders to his men to ease *Orpheus* up, sheeting sails as necessary and get some distance between the British frigate and the mortally wounded Frenchman. He called for Gunner Chase.

"Have the larboard guns sink her, Mr. Chase, if you please. A broadside or two at her waterline should answer nicely, I think." During the relative quiet after the battle, Winston had heard the continuous clanking of his own pumps as men labored to keep ahead of the sea entering their hull through what were probably shot holes or, at least, weakened planks. Sending the gunner on his way he called out, "Pass the word for the carpenter."

As the ship's carpenter showed up on the quarterdeck, the larboard guns spoke; the range was not quite point blank, but still close enough at under half a mile so that most of the shots found their mark. Winston quietly watched the burning frigate as the iron hit home, quite oblivious to the warrant awaiting his attention. A second volley was fired, and she began to list to windward, taking on water in her badly damaged hull. To a seaman, watching the death of a fine ship was always cause for sadness, regardless of the vessel's nationality. Suddenly, the captain realized that the carpenter was standing nearby, waiting to be recognized.

"Ahem, ahh, yes . . . how is our own damage Mr. Lacey? What of the water level?" Winston cocked an eyebrow expectantly.

"We are holding our own with the pumps, sir. About two and a half feet in the forward hold, but not rising. Aft there's a trifle more, but the pumps seem to be keeping up with it, sir. If the weather don't make up any, we'll manage, and with luck, get the holes plugged. She's took some hits larboard side low, but I've a crew working on 'em now." The normally taciturn man had spoken more at one time than most had heard him do before, but the captain did not notice, so intently was he watching the French brig in her death throes.

"Very good, Mr. Lacey. Keep at it, and let me know . . ." The explosion cut off his sentence, and for the moment, his thought. The burning brig's magazine had evidently been touched by the flames, and the resulting detonation was terrific. The foremast of the ship went straight up forty or fifty feet before it lazily toppled over and fell with a silent splash into the water. The center of the ship heaved upwards, buckling and releasing sheets of flame which immediately ignited any remaining deck furniture. The fire on deck was short-lived; the main thrust of the explosion had ripped out her bottom, and most every head on *Orpheus*, French and English alike, watched silently as what was left of the frigate rolled over and sank. The only sound was the sizzling as the ocean quenched the fires, and quickly the sea resumed its timeless motion as though there had never been a proud ship disturbing the waves. Bits of wood and rigging floated to the surface, a testimony belying the sea's apparent emptiness. The bosun stepped onto the deck and without waiting for recognition, cleared his throat and spoke.

"Sir. The larboard shrouds on the lower foremast been mostly shot away. I've some men working on 'em, but I do not think she'll stand the strain of a larboard tack until we've rigged new 'uns. The foretops'l is shot full of holes, and we need to bend on a new un. Likewise the foretopmast stays'l and main topmast stays'l." Tice's jacket was torn and spattered with blood. His forearm showed a gash extending beyond the blood-soaked handkerchief tied around it, the result of a splinter which, while obviously painful, Tice ignored.

"Very good, Mr. Tice. See to it, if you please. And you might let the surgeon have a look at that arm when you've a moment. We will hold on this course for now, but I will need to wear soon if ever we're to take those merchants. And heaven only knows what has happened to *Jolie* and *Amethyst*." His words and tone gave credence to the urgency of his need to finish this action. Turning to his second in command, he continued.

"Mr. Burns. Take Captain Faitoute to your cabin. You will move into Mr. Fitzgerald's cabin until we return to Antigua. Make room for his officers as best you can."

Jean Faitoute bowed at the waist to Captain Winston and acknowledged his hospitality.

"Sir. I am most grateful for your 'ospitality, but before I go with Lieutenant Burns, I should like to 'ave a word with my doctor as to the condition of my crew. Would you be kind enough to 'ave 'im sent for?" Winston nodded at Midshipman Blake, who had heard the exchange and immediately went off in search of the French doctor.

Orpheus was now sailing large on a course which would never in life close with the rest of the French squadron, and Winston was concerned. He summoned Smosky and when the Russian sailing master arrived, the captain said, "We must wear ship if ever we are to catch the merchants. Mr. Tice's men will not be done any time soon with the larboard shrouds. Furl all sails for'ard of the mainmast, save the foretopmast stays'l and set main and mizzen t'gallants. As quick as ever possible, if you please. We will wear the very instant the foremast is no longer in danger of falling."

Smosky left, calling out orders as he moved forward. His place on the quarterdeck was taken by two doctors, one British and one French. The latter, his bare arms red with blood, spoke in rapid French to his captain. The other waited as Winston saw his orders to Smosky were being carried out.

"What is the butcher's bill, Doctor? And what of the Frenchmen?"

"We have ten dead as of now, sir. There are a few others what won't make it to dark. The wounded number over thirty, and range from crushed feet and hands to bullets what got to be dug out. As to the French, I can't say. Their own doctor has been taking care of them, and has not yet asked for any help from us."

"Very well. I will be down to the orlop deck straight away. Offer any assistance to the French medico, if you please. Inform the sailmaker we shall need shrouds. I expect there will be more before this day is out."

Another voice caused the captain to turn; he smiled inwardly as he listened to Bosun Tice.

"We've got the foremast secured, sir. All the sail is furled and I 'spect we'll have some shrouds rigged to larboard within an hour or two. Meantime, I had 'em rig some temporary cables; they won't hold no sails yet, no sir, but they'll surely hold that mast up, by my eyes."

"Very good Mr. Tice. Keep the men working." He raised his voice, his eyes searching out the sailing master. "Mr. Smosky, the bosun tells me the foremast is secure. Kindly wear ship."

Following his "Aye, sir," Smosky issued orders which would cause the ship to swing her stern through the wind's eye, maintaining her headway and sailing off in pursuit of the French merchantmen, and *Jolie*. Yards were braced around, the spanker reset, and, after she was full and by on her new heading, studdings'ls were added to the main and maintops'l yards. *Orpheus* fairly flew across the wind, returning to her previous course, but now without her foresails and jibs. With the ship on the larboard tack, the foremast would never stand the strain of sails until strong new shrouds were run from the foretop, through the deadeyes, and secured with lanyards to the channels outside the hull of the ship. Additionally, the twelve-pound ball lodged in the lower part of the foremast required attention, and the carpenter would sister timbers to the mast, strengthening the spar so that it could take the strain of wind and weather. With a new foretops'l bent on to the yard, and human damage notwithstanding, *Orpheus* would be nearly whole before she saw more action.

CHAPTER SIXTEEN

A Blessing in Disguise

"Sail! Sail broad on the larboard bow!" The lookout in the maintop hailed the deck, and was immediately joined by a midshipman sent up from the quarterdeck with a long glass to determine the identity of the newly sighted vessel. *Amethyst* had not as yet joined her sister, and the hope was this would be she.

"Deck there! Hull and rig appears to be French. Under shortened sail . . . rigged with a jury foremast . . . no colors yet." Midshipman Murphy put the long glass up to his eye again, waiting to see if the French ensign would break out from the mizzen. The quarterdeck waited less patiently, and there was a quiet on deck, as the hands wondered if they were about to do battle again. The strange ship was in the wrong place to be the remaining escort for the merchant ships and there were no other sails on the horizon.

"French colors it is they're showing now, sir." Murphy called to the deck. A pause of several moments, then, "Wait . . . they're taking it down." Questioning glances were cast to windward as the sails of the ship became more and more visible from deck. No flag could be made out from the quarterdeck and Murphy's cry had begun a delayed reaction, with the ship again beating to quarters and clearing for action. Barely had the crew repaired the damage from their first engagement, fixing hull and knotting and splicing rigging, and the new foretops'l was still being bent to the yard. The ship could fight, but the lack of the sail would put them at a disadvantage both in maneuvering and speed. The stranger continued to close with *Orpheus*.

"Mr. Burns, we will come up some. While I can't hope to gain the weather gauge on her, we will be in a better position to defend ourselves without exposing our entire larboard side. See if you can encourage the sailmaker and bosun to bear a hand with that foretops'l." Then to the mid standing near at hand, "Pass the word for Mr. Chase, if you please."

The gunner showed up almost at once and Winston instructed

him to have all the guns load chain shot, aim high, and fire at the top of the roll. This was to damage the Frenchman's already damaged rigging, hopefully to take down another mast, completing what *Amethyst* had apparently begun. Chase hurried off to ensure his gunners mates were told and the larboard battery was loaded and run out.

"What ho, masthead?" Winston yelled to the midshipman still perched in the fighting top of the mainmast.

"Something's going on on the quarterdeck, sir. Wait, sir, they're running up another flag . . . it's the British ensign, sir, and the French one's right below it."

"Stand easy, Mr. Chase." The captain's voice and the relief it contained could be heard fore and aft. "Mr. Burns, unless I am greatly and sadly mistaken, that is McCray in the Frenchman; he has taken her as a prize. Mr. Murphy, do you see *Amethyst* anywhere?"

"No, sir. Nothing to wind'ard."

As he spoke, the French ship bore off, and paralleled *Orpheus'* course about half a league off. Flags broke out at the mizzen jackyard, and a gun fired to windward, unnecessarily drawing attention to them. Burns had a glass to his eye and called out the flags. Lieutenant Hardy translated.

" '*Amethyst* burned'," he read, " 'French frigate under my command. McCray'."

This revelation triggered a flurry of commands from Winston, who settled quickly on a plan of action, realizing that the turn of events was indeed a blessing, though a costly one.

"Ease your sheets and braces. Your course is east a half north, Mr. Burns. While it appears that McCray has lost his ship, we can use this French frigate to our advantage in the balance of our commission. Bring us closer yet, if you please. Stand by to lower the blue cutter. I shall go aboard and assess his situation and explain my plan to him. You will continue on this course under tops'ls until I return. Mr. Tice, call my coxswain, if you please, and have the cutter ready at the waist."

A string of orders emanated from the quarterdeck, preparing the cutter for launching and shortening sail. This latter called the topmen from their quarters stations and sent them aloft at the run, to furl the reefed main course, the foretops'l not yet being ready for use, and get the t'gallants handed fore and aft and their poles struck below.

After completing their duties, Biggs and Coleman watched from the maintop as the cutter was put overboard and the captain clambered over the bulwark and down the side of the ship. While much of the conversation on the quarterdeck had escaped them, the two ensigns showing on the Frenchman had not, and Coleman interpreted what they watched for his shipmate.

"*Amethyst* must be lost, Isaac, and they've moved bag and baggage onto the Frenchy. Looks like Cap'n McCray gave 'em what for, though. That topmast spar they've rigged up as a foremast gonna slow 'em down a bit. See that, there's men working rigging a new jib boom too."

"Aye. The hull looks tore up too, Coleman. You can bet they're pumping watch and watch." One of the other topmen joined the conversation, adding, "She looks a trifle down by the stern to me."

The cutter bumped alongside the damaged ship, and from the maintop, the men could see Captain Winston welcomed aboard by Captain McCray. As they watched, the two captains headed forward, pausing at the foremast, before moving aft again and disappearing below when they reached the quarterdeck.

Lieutenant Burns had the men stand down from their quarters stations, and work continued rigging the new foretops'l while *Orpheus* and the formerly French frigate sailed close by one another toward the prize awaiting them to the east. The men at the maintop had been instructed to keep watch on the quarterdeck of the other ship and to inform Burns the moment their captain appeared.

After the turn of two glasses, Coleman hailed the deck.

"Lieutenant Burns, sir. I can see the Cap'n on the Frenchy. 'E's headin' for the waist. Looks like the boat crew's gettin' ready to shove off."

A wave to the masthead acknowledged the observation, and the first lieutenant ordered the man ropes rigged on the lee side, and the sideboys called out to render honors to the captain. As the cutter made its way around the stern of *Orpheus*, Burns could see his captain in the stern sheets wearing a satisfied, if not smug, expression. He hurried to the waist to greet Winston as he climbed quickly up the battens on the ship's side. Doffing his hat in a salute to the sideboys and quarterdeck as the bosun's mate trilled his pipe, Captain Winston took Burns' arm, and immediately headed aft.

From aloft, Biggs and the topmen could hear him instruct Smosky and Tice to "Clap on a press of canvas, as much as she'll carry, if you please," in a tone that was more animated than usual, and out of character for the normally taciturn commander. The orders were bellowed out by the sailing master and bosun, and the topmen had no time for observation; they were busy as you please setting the main course, t'gallants, and finishing the work on the foretops'l so it too could assist in driving the ship to her ultimate goal with all possible speed. A glance at the other frigate showed them following suit, and cracking on as much as her damaged spars could stand.

CHAPTER SEVENTEEN

Rum Capers

The two ships, *Orpheus* and her new sister, *Etoile Noire* — for that turned out to be the name of the frigate McCray took — sailed east a half north in pursuit of the French fleet under a vast spread of sail; the wind had held for them, moving the men-of-war at nearly ten knots, even with their wounded spars and, in the case of *Etoile*, a jury-rigged foremast. A palpable feeling of excitement brought both ships' crews to high spirits and eager anticipation for the prizes and resulting riches that awaited them, hopefully just over the horizon. The overcast had given way to rain, foreshortening visibility and as Coleman put it to Isaac, "Likely 'idin' what we done from them other Frenchies."

With the starbowlines as the watch below, Biggs and his mates lounged under the fo'c'sle deck, sheltering from the weather and comparing the distinctions in their lives before and after the prize shares from the capture of the French fleet would be cashed out. The conversation was one that carried over from their dinner discussion with their mess mates. Biggs had not been as verbose as his companions, choosing rather to listen, and keep some of his thoughts to himself; thoughts indeed of his former life aboard an American merchant ship. His introspective posture and silence continued as the conversation turned to former ships on which they had served, almost as if echoing his own secret thoughts. Wallace noticed his friend's dour look, and asked him point blank, "'Ow'd you happen to be on that merchant barky we stopped all them months ago, Isaac?"

Biggs, remained silent for another moment, and thought about the life he now had, filled with dangers, unthought of before his impressment. He smiled, as he recalled better times. Times on *Anne,* and Captain Smalley and his other shipmates. Even Third Mate Jakes didn't seem so bad now with some of the Royal Navy for comparison.

"Where I grew up," he started, "pretty much everybody was either a fisherman or deep waterman. My Pa fished the Banks with a cap'n called Mr. Rowe, and I useta go out with 'em when I was just a kid from time to time. Cap'n Rowe musta thought he might could turn me into a fisherman, and he saw to it I learned to hand, reef, and steer. When I'd had me some schoolin', he got me a berth on a Salem brig runnin' to New York and back. After I'd made some trips on her and some other coastal vessels — schooners and brigs, mostly — I went out again to the Banks with Pa and Mr. Rowe. I reckon my Mother got him to take me on, since she wasn't none too happy 'bout me bein' away so much on the deep water. Fishin' was fine fer some, but it didn't hold no attraction fer me. I wanted to sail the deep. I 'member comin' in after Pa and me talked on that and Mr. Rowe, he said if'n I needed any help gettin' a berth, he knew some men still sailin' from his days in the deep water that might help me out. It was four years an' more past now, that I found the *Anne* sittin' out in President's Roads — that's in Boston, you know. A fine vessel she was, outa Marblehead, just like me; she cut a fine picture settin' out there. I got myself a ride out in a wherry carryin' out some last minute stores. Bein's how she was fixin' to get under way quick as ever she finished takin' on a crew, the mate was happy to sign me aboard. Started out an able seaman. I was cap'n o' the foretop when Lieutentant Burns pressed me. Mr. Clark, the mate, he was teachin' me 'bout navigatin' so's I could move into a third's berth when one come open." He paused, thinking how drastic was the change in his life. Coleman, always a willing listener, wanted more. Perhaps something about the ale houses and taverns of Boston.

"Some change fer a lad used to schooners, brigs, an' fishin' smacks, you ask me. I reckon Boston gave you some 'igh times afore you sailed though, eh?"

"Never once even went into a coffee house or tavern. Didn't need to. I went out to *Anne* soon's I got there, and signed on. Didn't need to go to a rendezvous to find a berth, an' most of 'em are held in taverns and the like. Cap'n Smalley — he didn't need to get crew that way most o' the time; 'bout everyone on the waterfront knew a berth on his vessel would be a good one. A fine seaman, he is, and I ain't never heard of him floggin' a man. Fact is, he jest runs a good barky. Ain't a bit like Cap'n Winston."

"Aye, as it may be, but 'e gets us the prizes. You'll see soon enough." Coleman's praise of his captain had a most sincere ring to it. Wallace nodded in agreement.

"What you gonna do with yer share of the prize money, Isaac? Might amount to a lot. I'll tell you, I aim to live the good life ashore, long's it holds out." He nudged Coleman and winked. This had obviously been discussed before. "You got a plan?"

Biggs thought for a moment before replying.

"I don't know what I aim to do, yet. Don't figger to stay here, if I can help it. Don't know how I can get myself off, and I ain't yet spent a lot of time thinkin' on it so I haven't a thought about how to go about it, but I'm thinkin' surely the money'll help. But more immediate, how do you think we're goin' to get into the fleet to take the prizes? I'm bettin' most of those merchants is armed — at least old *Anne* was, to be sure. We couldn't practice with the guns much; scuttlebutt was that the owners wouldn't pay for shot and powder for practicin', but we had 'em, and most knew how to run 'em in and out, load and prime, and the mates could sight 'em. We'd never try to stand up to a frigate, to be sure, but that's on account of we usually sailed alone, and Captain Smalley knew we were outgunned most of the time. But a fleet is a different tale again; we can't be takin' on all of them at once, even with *Etoile* helpin', can we?"

"Isaac, ain't you learned nothing in the past year and more you been aboard this ship, lad?" Toppan had joined the group and was amused at Biggs's continued naiveté. "Why would you ever think that Captain Winston don't 'ave a plan to catch those Frenchies by surprise and take the whole lot of 'em without firin' a shot? With a mite of luck, the brig *Jolie* 'as run off the last man-o'-war, and those merchants'll be just sittin' there like chickens to a fox, an' us an' *Etoile*'ll just sail up, show our colors, and those Frog masters'll strike their colors quick as you please, they'll be in such a rush to save their own 'ides."

"Jack, how'd you expect *Jolie* could run off that frigate? She'd be outgunned two or three to one and not stand a chance. One broadside from the Frenchy and she'd be headin' for some French port as a prize — what was left of her. I've learnt that much aboard here. I know Captain Winston wouldn't take on a seventy-four by hisself either." Biggs' eyes got hard and the color rose in his face; he bristled at still being thought of as something other than a man-of-warsman; while he didn't like being a pressed seaman in a

British ship, he still thought of himself as a sailor-man, and a good one at that, and capable of performing all the chores set out for him on this British frigate, and well.

"She ain't goin' to take on a frigate, you pea-brain. All she has to do is show the flag and the frigate'll chase her; *Jolie* can outsail damn near anything that swims, she can, and Captain Smithfield likely will lead 'em on a merry chase, while we come up and take our prizes. By the time that French frigate skipper realizes he ain't gonna catch the brig, we'll be sailin' 'em into Jamaica or back to Antigua to collect our shares. Mark my words, Isaac, it'll be sweet as kiss my hand."

"I can't believe the Frenchies'll let two British men-o'-war just sail into the middle of their fleet, Jack. How're we gonna do that?"

"You can bet your arse that Captain Winston's got a plan for that. He ain't shared it with me or asked for my advice yet, but I'll warrant he ain't gonna just sail in there, tip 'is 'at and say 'howdy do'. 'E don't 'ave the luck 'e's 'ad taking prizes without 'e always seems to 'ave a good plan." After thinking for a second or two, he added, "I'd bet a fair piece that the Frenchy Captain McCray took gonna figger into it some way or other."

Indeed, Jack Toppan's experience with Captain Winston stood him in good stead and had he wagered, he would have done quite well, as that was exactly what Captain Winston and Captain McCray had planned. The only fly in the ointment was the whereabouts of the other French frigate and *Jolie*; had the formerly French brig been successful in luring the frigate away from her charges? Had they heard the sounds of the recent action, and smoked the ruse? Time would tell. For the immediate present, however, a whole host of plans of varying degrees of complexity, reality, and absolute silliness pervaded the foredeck conversation on *Orpheus* and even the normally dour Winston would have laughed aloud had he heard most any of them. His plan was simple, obvious — at least to him — and eminently workable, even if *Jolie* had been unsuccessful in her efforts.

The routine of the ship, always an underlying theme in a British man-of-war continued apace; the men went about their duties with no more conscious thought than they might give to the sound of the wind in the rigging. Cleaning, maintenance, knotting and splicing the rigging and their own clothes carried on. Dinner was piped, grog issued, the watch changed and throughout it all, the lookouts kept eager weather eyes glued to the gray slash of the horizon for the flash of white that would be the top hampers of the French fleet. The intermittent rain and overcast did not make their task easier, but no one had to remind the men that fortunes stood in the offing for most of them, and had a lookout missed a sighting so that the fleet was seen first from the deck, you may be sure that his mates would make his life miserable for all eternity, not to mention the flogging that would be imposed.

Four bells in the afternoon watch had just sounded; the watch below had long finished their dinner, but the officers were still at table in the gunroom and, save those on watch, the mids were dining and cavorting in their mess when the lookout's cry galvanized the quarterdeck into action. The knock came on the captain's door within a minute or two of the sighting being confirmed by the midshipman who was sent aloft for that purpose.

"Mr. Hardy's c-c-compliments, sir, and we have sighted the Fr-Fr-French sails, sir. H-h-hull down and t-t-two points to leeward." Midshipman Duncan's stammer was not improved by his excitement over the prospect of prize shares and the still-present flush of victory from the recent action. He stood ramrod straight just inside the door — he left it open, remembering his blunder the last time he was in the Cabin as a messenger from the quarterdeck — and awaited the captain's pleasure.

"Very good, Mr. Duncan. Tell Mr. Hardy I shall be up directly, and show a proper signal to *Etoile Noire* if you please. Firing a gun to windward will not be necessary." He could not resist adding, "Mind the door." A twinkle in his eye was proof positive that Duncan's previous visit, though a week and more distant, was still in mind, in spite of the other more weighty matters he had been dealing with.

On the quarterdeck, and indeed, throughout the ship, there was a great bustle of activity, though most of it non-productive. Duncan conveyed the captain's message, and was instructed to have the quartermaster rig the flags for "Enemy in sight, two points to leeward." No gun accompanied the signal, but *Etoile* acknowledged it immediately; obviously their lookouts were as alert as the ones on *Orpheus*. Hardy sent Midshipman Duncan back to the foretop with a glass to keep an eye on the Frenchmen and report any changes promptly to the deck.

He moved quickly to his position, used as he was in being

"mastheaded" for various minor infractions which called for spending the balance of his watch, not at the main or fore top where he was now sitting, but at the highest yard rigged, frequently the main t'gallant yard. He had gotten to actually enjoy the view and motion there, and did not mind being sent up. Indeed, the solitude and relief from the almost constant harassment had made the tops a refuge for the young mid. On more than one occasion, the upper yards had been fairly alive with midshipmen mastheaded for various minor missteps, but since their nemesis, Lieutenant Oliver Fitzgerald, rest his soul, was no longer in a position to award punishments, Charlie Duncan figured that might ease in the immediate future.

Winston appeared on the quarterdeck, suddenly at Lieutenant Hardy's elbow, and his words startled the young officer.

"Pass the word for Mr. Burns, if you please, and the bosun." He turned the two men on the wheel. "Bring her down a point, make your course east. Quartermaster, make the signal 'Execute plan on my order'." To Hardy he added, "We'll ease sheets and braces, now, Mr. Hardy if you please. Maintaining our speed will be important for the next hour or so." He still had not divulged his plan to any but his first lieutenant, but Hardy thought nothing strange in the order. When Burns and Bosun Tice arrived on the quarterdeck, he moved to the leeward side, away from the others and spoke to the bosun.

"Mr. Tice," he said, "In a short time you will make the ship look like she was badly beaten, but sailable. We'll have the yards all ahoo and sheets slack. No stays'ls or jibs, I think." His eye twinkled uncharacteristically when he added, "Wouldn't do to strain the weakened shrouds and stays. Gunports both open and closed will add to the illusion, but do not run out the guns. Use as few men aloft as possible, and do not allow the others to stand about visibly on deck. We must look as though we are short-handed — the way a prize might be."

Tice caught on immediately and smiled. "Aye, sir. I think we'll make a good show of it. Let me round up my petty officers and we'll be ready when you give the word." He turned forward after putting a knuckle to his forehead, and with the rolling gait of a man who has spent his life at sea, moved up the deck to begin readying the ship for her part in the charade which would put the frigates in the middle of the French fleet. Winston noted that the gash on Tice's arm had been cleaned and the handkerchief replaced by a proper bandage, indications that the surgeon or more likely, given Tice's well-known aversion to the man of medicine, one of his mates had finally caught up with him.

"Send for Captain Faitoute, if you please, Mr. Hardy." The captain wanted to be sure that there would be no complications from his prisoners when they closed with the French, and with Lieutenant Burns, he awaited the French captain's arrival on the quarterdeck, while the ship was prepared to capture Faitoute's countrymen, their ships, and their goods.

When the French captain appeared on the quarterdeck, Winston smiled at him, a trifle patronizingly it appeared to some, and asked how he did.

"And how are your wounded, Captain? Are the medicos patching them up? I apologize for not dining with you, but I have been rather occupied of late, and a formal dinner was not a luxury to be enjoyed today."

"Thank you for your kind words, sir. My men are being adequately taken care of — those 'at are still alive. We 'ave lost several more from their wounds, and I fear more will follow. Do not concern yourself with the meal, sir. I assure you, I was fed satisfactorily with my officers in the gun room. May I inquire as to why you sent for me?"

"I am about to go into action again with your countrymen, sir. I would like your assurance that neither you nor any of your men will interfere with the running of *Orpheus* or I will be forced to lock you below on the orlop deck. It is quite safe there, and out of the way of harm."

"I will not interfere, Captain. As to my officers or men — those that are able at least — I can not answer for them. If you are concerned, perhaps you should do whatever you think best. I . . ."

The conversation was interrupted by the arrival of the bosun, who waited patiently, but in the line of sight of his captain, knowing he would get the captain's ear as soon as he was seen.

"Yes, Mr. Tice. Are you quite prepared, as we discussed?"

"Aye, sir. The men are ready for some play-acting as soon as you give the word."

Winston turned to Captain Faitoute. "Sir, I would ask that you go below and see to your own safety. It would not do to have you injured, or, heaven forbid, worse, while you are under my protection." Turning to Hardy, he continued "Mr. Hardy. Find the Captain of the Marines, if you please, and inform him I would like the French sailors and officers — the healthy ones at any rate — escorted to the orlop deck where they shall be guarded until the imminent action has been decided."

The French fleet was clearly visible now from deck, and the captain issued more orders. "Quartermaster, signal *Etoile Noire* to execute the plan. Mr. Tice, let us begin. Get your men started."

As he watched, *Orpheus* was transformed into a wounded prize; the sails were eased by their sheets and braces, buntines and clewlines slackened, yards were cocked and skewed in a manner no seaman would find acceptable, and sailors began to disappear from view on deck, heading to the main deck where they would be out of sight behind the bulwarks until the proper moment. As a final touch, Winston ordered the French flag shown at the spanker gaff with the British ensign below it, clearly denoting that *Orpheus* was the prize of the damaged, but proud frigate flying the Tricolor at her gaff. He maintained his position to leeward of *Etoile*, further enhancing the appearance of captor and prize. Hopefully, the probably skittish French merchant masters would happily accept the illusion Harry Winston had so carefully crafted.

"Masthead there — any sign of *Jolie* or the second frigate?" The cry came from Lieutenant Burns, hoping that a brief respite in the rain might have given a sharp-eyed lookout a glimpse of the two ships.

After a lengthy silence — it seemed as though the entire ship's company was awaiting the answer with the quarterdeck — the lookout at the fore t'gallant yard yelled down.

"I thought I saw a top hamper to wind'ard. Sir. 'Pears ten miles an' more distant. Might could be a frigate, but I cain't make it out good. It looks like it's rainin' pretty 'ard where they's at. Cain't see 'em at all now."

"Well, Captain, if it is the Frenchman, he's likely not to cause us concern for a while, I'd warrant." Burns wasn't going to let a single French frigate spoil his day. "Looks like the rain's going to begin here momentarily again as well. Should hide us from him as well."

A few men standing nearby caught the optimism in Burns' tone, and it quickly spread forward, with a ripple of chatter.

"Silence fore and aft. Mr. Tice, take note of any who feel moved to noise. We'll deal with them later. Gunner, load your pieces. Captain of Marines, have your men stand by to go aloft. Clear for action quietly, if you please." This last order was mostly out of habit; the men had been at their quarters stations almost since the fleet had come into sight and were as ready as could be. The decks had again been sanded, but the nets had not been rigged to catch falling debris from aloft as their presence would enable the French — assuming they were alert — to smoke their caper and, while it was unlikely that any of the ships could outsail either *Orpheus* or *Etoile*, Winston did not want a stern chase.

The hours passed and the two ships bore down on the French merchants as fast as the "wounded prize" could sail; they passed the afterguard and as McCray's frigate, under French colors, went by, a cheer, muffled in the now torrential rain, went up from the quarterdeck of the merchant and was joined enthusiastically by the hands forward. McCray and his officers waved their hats in acknowledgment of the welcome as did Winston from his own quarterdeck. Since the merchantmen were under shortened sail — apparently an order from their escorts given before they left to deal with the intruders — sailing through the now disorganized fleet was readily accomplished, and soon the two frigates were in the van.

On signal, they separated, *Orpheus* bearing down a point and *Etoile Noire* heading up similarly. The topmen were called to their stations and without so much as a shout, yards were squared, sheets, braces, and bowlines tensioned and sails were handed and reefed to a battle configuration; two men-of-war, serious and threatening, appeared where there had been a wounded and sloppy French frigate with her damaged prize. The frigates matched the pace of the merchants.

"We'll have our proper colors now, Mr. Burns, if you please." He raised his voice. "Mr. Chase, you may open all the gunports and run out your battery. Load the windward bowchaser with a powder charge only and stand-by for my order."

Winston watched as *Etoile* followed suit, and the Royal Navy ensign snapped to the mizzen peak of both ships in the fresh breeze.

Biggs and his fellow topmen were fascinated as the scene around them unfolded. Here they were, just as Coleman and Toppan had predicted, in the middle of the French fleet without a shot fired. Coleman nudged Biggs with his elbow and pointed at the nearest merchant ship.

"I'd give 'alf me prize share to see the look on their faces now; what do you think, Isaac. They gonna fight or strike?"

"I surely don't have an idea, but I most earnestly hope they'll not decide to put up a fight." Biggs had learned in his relatively short military career that a ship in a fight is a most dangerous place to be, and now that he was headed fair towards a sound financial footing, he did not want to be taking any risks which might interfere with his getting off this man of war and back into a nice quiet merchant ship.

Interrupting his thoughts came the voice of the lookout in the crosstrees of the foremast, "Deck there! Sail bearing down from wind'ard. Hard to tell through the rain, but it 'pears to be a frigate. Cain't make a flag, but looks like she's a'comin' on hard."

Before either of the topmen could comment on this new turn of events, a windward gun on *Orpheus* spoke, emitting a roar and a great cloud of acrid smoke. The topmen jumped at the sudden noise, even though they had expected the gun to fire.

"Now we'll find out." Toppan nodded knowingly at Coleman, smiling at the perplexed look on Isaac Biggs' face. "That gun was to suggest to the merchant skippers that we intend to fight, unless they strike. If they throw in now, the nearest will fire a leeward gun, and lower their colors. If they're gonna fight, they'll still fire a gun, but at us. You watch now, if they take too long, Captain Winston'll put one across the nearest ship's bow, seein' if he can encourage them to make up their minds. If that frigate comin' down on us is that other Frenchy, them merchants might think they gonna be saved and not strike; fancy them thinkin' one frigate gonna be able to protect 'em from the likes o' us!"

A few quiet minutes passed while all hands waited for a reaction from the merchant captains. Then a gun, neither on *Orpheus*, nor on a merchant fired. In fact, until it fired again, nobody was sure from which ship it came — only that it came from the windward side. Then it spoke again, and this time, there could be no mistake. The roar was followed by a splash close astern of *Etoile Noire* and the source was readily identifiable; the second French frigate had closed the range, and seemed determined to do what they might about saving their charges. Her bow chasers fired again, and a hole appeared in *Etoile's* foretops'l. The French frigate was clearly acting out of desperation, her captain seeing his entire career bursting into flames before his very eyes. Firing a bowchaser at the broadside of a man-of-war is the act of either a very desperate man or a very stupid one. McCray waited, as the French came on, then *Etoile* responded with a well aimed broadside, a mix of ball and chain shot. When the smoke blew away from the two ships, the result was immediately visible; the Frenchman had lost his foremast and his main topmast. The wreckage of the topmast and yard was fouled in the mizzen rigging, and the foremast was dragging over the starboard side, causing, as they watched, the ship to bear off drastically, rolling her rail down to the water. One more shot came from the now badly wounded Frenchman. *Etoile*'s wheel disappeared in a cloud of splinters; the two quartermasters' mates just disappeared — completely. While McCray was attempting to get men below to steer by hauling on falls attached to the rudder head, the sailing master was directing men to heave on the sheets and braces in an effort to keep the vessel from rounding up, head to wind. Come up she did, however, and without a means of quickly steering his ship, McCray was helpless to stop her. *Etoile* reached stays and stopped, her reefed tops'ls and courses instantly backing and as they filled began to move the ship backwards through the water.

Orders rang through the ship, clearly heard on *Orpheus*. The crew watched in helpless horror as the ship was caught all aback. McCray was a splendid seaman, and his crew had the tackles rigged to the rudder post as quickly as humanly possible. Sheets were slacked, braces hauled, and stays'ls backed to get the ship out of stays, and stop her backward motion. Gradually, *Etoile* eased off the wind, but, as the report McCray received on the quarterdeck confirmed, too late; with the sudden sternway, the rudder had sheared off. His ship was out of control. For the moment, she was headed downwind, and would remain that way for as long as his crew could manage the braces and sheets. He needed time to rig a jury rudder; a sweep made from an extra tops'l yard and some lumber would answer; rigging it would take time.

The French frigate was forgotten; her crew had their hands full and would not be a problem for a while. On *Orpheus*, orders rang out from the quarterdeck in a steady stream. Biggs and Coleman, along with the foretopmen, were ordered to clew up courses and stand by. They watched as the men on deck made ready lines and grapnels.

"They look like they're gettin' ready to board the Frenchman, Bob. Why don't he just sink her, and be done with it?" Biggs said what was on all their minds, and Coleman didn't have an answer. Jack Toppan was below, bellowing at the waisters and idlers to "Bear a hand there, you lay-about farmers!" and so was unable to share the wisdom gained over many years as a man-of-warsman. The topmen watched and suddenly it dawned on Coleman.

"Boarding that Frenchy don't answer, mates. Were goin' to board *Etoile!*" Already, *Orpheus* was easing up, and was less than a cable's length from her rudderless sister and closing as they watched. Matching speed was important, and Winston's voice carried very clearly to the maintop.

"Ease the sheets on the foretops'l; mind your braces there. Brace those headyards square! Let go the bowlines!" The scene on deck was that of a carefully choreographed ballet — men moving quickly to obey the orders issuing in a steady stream, lines being hauled and sails responding and alternately billowing and shivering as their yards were braced around to control the ship's speed. Gradually, *Orpheus* closed to within a pistol shot of *Etoile Noire*, then closer still; grapnels and heaving lines were thrown and the two ships were joined, side by side.

Winston yelled to his junior captain, "Get your sweep rigged. We'll keep you out of trouble. Leave your tops'ls set in a single reef and furl everything else. You might keep some of your starboard battery manned, and I shall man a few of my larboard guns."

A wave, a deep bow, and a smile came from the *Etoile*'s captain. Words were unnecessary, and would be saved for later when the action was replayed over cheese and port in Winston's great cabin on *Orpheus*. Biggs watched the maneuver open-mouthed. Never had he seen anything like it. Not only was this an extraordinary display of seamanship, it demonstrated lightning-quick thinking on the part of Captain Winston, putting the young topman in mind of his former captain, Jed Smalley, probably the only other man he knew, in his limited experience, who might be capable of such a maneuver. He looked around; the French frigate was still struggling with her spars, and the merchants sailed on, for the moment reprieved from their ultimate and ignominious fate and, most likely, equally fascinated by the display of British seamanship they had just witnessed.

CHAPTER EIGHTEEN

The Bull and Feather Tavern

"You don't say! I never heard anything so remarkable in all my days. This Captain Winston must be a splendid sailor. But how did you manage to get all eight vessels into a safe harbor?" The gentleman — at least he was dressed like a gentleman in a forest green jacket and vest with fawn colored trousers — was enthralled with the tale told by these men, sailors from the British frigate *Orpheus*. He had heard their detailed and thrilling account of the capture of the French fleet without a single interruption, save the refilling of tankards as required to keep the story rolling along like a ship under full sail in a t'gallant breeze. His brow occasionally furrowed over deep set eyes and he tugged at his mutton-chop whiskers as he listened intently, pondering how he might use his newly acquired knowledge.

The man made a habit of frequenting Nassau's taverns, especially the ones visited by sailors. The sailors' visits were generally in pursuit of liquid and physical refreshment; his were in pursuit of information. His sources always seemed to know which waterfront taverns were currently popular with the sailors, and which with the officers. He also knew from experience when the visiting seamen had something to share with him. To the sailors just in from the sea, a willing ear and open purse were guarantees of stories and information. As long as the tankards were kept filled, and he occasionally interjected comments or opened wide his eyes to indicate his continuing interest, he was assured of talkative sailors long at sea and eager for a new audience to impress with their derring-do. The story he was hearing now was certainly as impressive as anything he had heard in the recent past, and demonstrated clearly that this Winston chap was a captain of some substance, a man whose actions would bear further investigation.

"We put an officer, masters mate, or midshipman on each one with a few prime 'ands, and of course a 'andful of marines." Toppan was explaining. "The French crewmen who didn't want to 'elp us sail the ship were put in the 'old under guard and kept there. A few usually volunteered to 'elp after some days with the rats and wet of the 'old. As long as we 'ad no weather or Frenchies come callin', sailin' the prizes in was as easy as kiss my 'and, and 'o course, *Orpheus* and *Etoile Noire* was right there for most of the time. Since we was nigh on to due east of New Providence, it was an easy run in, and *Etoile,* bein' a prize 'er own self, took a few of the prizes down to Antigua, to get refit right along side o' her. Too bad, I'd say, cause they missed out on comin' inta New Providence. I mean to tell you, we got some attention sailing into Nassau with four French ships as prizes. The doxies lined the quaywall, they did. Ain't seen nothing to equal it in three years on the Leeward Island Station. Why, when we come ashore, we 'ad to push through 'em just to get to the taverns. Course not all the 'ands pushed *through*; some picked 'em a pretty one and did they's pushin' later. Hor hor." Toppan laughed at his own crude humor, and was joined by the other men at the table, save the gentleman, who smiled indulgently; his eyes, though, showed no mirth.

"I am not quite clear on why the French merchantmen struck without a fight. You say they never so much as fired a shot?" The gentleman's incredulity showed in his voice as he looked with hooded eyes down his hawkish nose, but the implication was lost on the sailors who by now were feeling the effects of several tankards of the coarse local rum, and were only too happy to tell again of the capture of so many prizes at one time.

Coleman took the stage. "After Captain Winston laid *Orpheus* right alongside *Etoile,* we kept an eye on those French bastards, we did. Not just the frigate, mind you (though she was fallin' astern pretty quick and was soon out of range), but the merchants also. We knew at least some of 'em had cannon, and with us lashed tight to a ship what couldn't steer, we was in no position to fight." Coleman paused to take a drink, and Biggs chimed right in.

"Or even steer much. Cap'n Winston had brung us up some so we was goin' more or less the same way as the Frenchies was, so we just all sailed along together. Strange, it was, I'm telling you." The gentleman nodded encouragingly. Biggs continued.

"I don't know why they never tried to sail away from us. We couldn't have done much about it, save leave *Etoile* to fend for herself and go after 'em. The only one of 'em showed any fight came down on us from weather and fired off a few guns — they sounded like nine-pounders — but the range was too long. *Etoile* let off a few eighteenpounders and took a chunk off'n they's jib boom and splintered some o' they's bulwark. I think the Frenchy lost interest after that, cause they bore up and kept their distance."

"What happened to the frigate. Did you ever see it again? You haven't mentioned her since you told me about *Etoile* losing her steering. Surely your captain didn't just leave her adrift and go on his merry way?" Their friendly benefactor was paying attention to the details, making sure he missed nothing of substance. His eyes shifted from one sailor to another as he waited. Coleman picked up the story.

"Most of the time we was 'elping *Etoile*, we didn't see 'ide nor 'air of her. She'd drifted astern, what with 'er foremast and 'alf her main down, and 'er mizzen riggin' all ahoo. Good thing, I'd say, seein' as 'ow we couldn't a done much about her right then. No, Cap'n McCray got *Etoile* rigged with a jury rudder — wasn't 'alf bad, neither, I don't mind sayin' — and we cast 'er off. We sailed down a trifle then, and turned the leeward ships around, makin' 'em 'eave to so's the cutter or longboat could put a prize master and crew aboard. Then they 'ead 'ere for New Providence. We knew that's where we was 'eaded from Cochrane — he's the Cap'n's steward and tells us what's what, ya know." Coleman smiled at his own interruption, and the recollection of a most extraordinary event. When he continued, his serious demeanor had returned.

"A shot across they's bows usually convinced 'em we was serious, and colors came down quick as ever you like. *Etoile* was doin' the same thing with the three vessels to wind'ard. I heard 'em fire only a handful of times, so I don't 'magine they 'ad anymore difficulty than we did. Once we 'ad em all 'eadin' in the right direction, with British skippers and topmen aboard, and the marines keepin' the Frogs quiet in the 'old, it was easy as ever you please."

Jack Toppan continued the story. "Me an' Isaac, 'ere, was sittin' on the main tops'l yard. I don't know who seen 'er first, but there she was plain as day, jury-rigged masts and all. She was carryin' a press of sail, considering her make-shift masts an' all, and headin' up high enough to close with us. I couldn't believe she was actually sailin' what with 'er foremast and 'er main topmast shot away. They got spars rigged quick as ever they could, you ask me. I even said so to Isaac, 'ere. I said, 'Lookee there, Isaac, that's bound to be that Frog frigate. I'll warrant 'e's lookin' to even the score.' Course, we told 'em down on the Quarterdeck quick as you please, soon as we seen 'em. The Cap'n — 'e's 'ad men flogged for missin' seein' a ship like that. Lookouts wasn't lookin' out, I'd warrant, but Biggs an' me, we saved 'em from a whippin', we did. Anyway, he's comin' right along. Course, the deck 'ad been told already. Captain Winston bore off a mite and 'eaded right down on that vessel, 'e did, and before you could say 'ease yer sheets', 'e 'ad Mr. Chase fire off the bow chasers at 'er. We was still long on the range, and the shot fell short. Still the Frenchy came at us; we was about bow to bow. Isaac 'ere, 'e saw a puff o' smoke from her and we saw the shot land well to leeward of us. Mr. Chase kept firing the bow guns, gettin' closer and closer to the vessel. Then Mr. Smosky, 'e's the master, brought *Orpheus* up a couple o' points. We was some kind o' busy then, what with reefing the tops'ls and clewin' up the courses, so we couldn't watch what was goin' on down on deck, but I knew we was gettin' ready to give 'em a raking broadside, soon as the range was good.

"When the starboard guns fired, I was watchin' that Frenchy, and I saw what was left of 'er rig come crashin' down. Cap'n sails us 'longside smooth as kiss my 'and. Then 'e boards 'er and quick as you please, they struck. Reckon they'd 'ad enough fightin' for a while. We put a few men under Mr. Duncan — 'e's a midshipman — aboard and take that French frigate in tow. Now we got us a frigate — or what's left o' one — as a prize inta the bargain. After about a day or so, someone see's smoke comin' out o' the deck on the Frenchie. They's crew what was 'elpin' our men clean up the deck got below and put the torch to 'er. Not much we could do, and poor Mr. Duncan, 'e went an' got 'isself kilt by 'em. We got most o' the men off'n 'er with the boats, and then cut 'er adrift to burn. They'da been some prize money 'ad we brung 'er in, but I 'eard Mr. Burns tellin' one o' the other officers we likely would get 'ead 'n' gun money, since they was able to get the muster books and 'e knew what guns she was carryin'. I guess that's somethin'." Toppan paused, taking a long draught from his tankard. The gentleman waited patiently and then voiced a final thought.

"So you saw no other ships on your way in, I collect?"

"Well, we did see a couple of schooner-rigged vessels a ways off, pretty near hull down, they was, but they either didn't see us — I don't know 'ow they could have missed us, bein' five ships pretty much together the way we was — or they weren't interested. Coulda' been some coastal traders, though they looked faster than that, you ask me." Coleman thought again about the two ships they had seen, and added, "No, thinkin' about it now, they coulda' been privateers. French most likely, I collect."

"You lads might not have heard the news just yet, as you've been at sea, but they could have been American, just as easily. England is at war with the Americans. Just last month those scoundrels from the colonies declared war against us — ungrateful wretches, it would appear. Something about seaman's rights or some rubbish. I have it on quite good authority that there are a number of private warships here in the Caribbean from a place called Baltimore. They have been raising 'Old Harry' with some of the merchant vessels flying the British flag."

The color drained from Isaac's face; he was thunderstruck. America was at war with England and here he was on a British frigate, and looking at the possibility that he would be called upon to fight his own countrymen! His jaw went slack and his eyes grew wide as the gentleman told them the news. Now he absolutely had to get off *Orpheus*. He ran a hand through his curly hair, then over his face as if trying to wipe away a cobweb and, with it, this shocking news. He barely heard the rest of the conversation. He noticed the other men were looking at him, expectantly.

"Isaac, you're an American. What do you think about all this?" Coleman was first to realize their friend was in an awkward position. "What are you gonna do now that. . ."

He stopped mid-sentence as a pair of youngish women approached the table. One, the men saw was fairly attractive, the other less so.

"You boys are surely serious, 'ere." The less pretty one spoke in a hard street accent, and the other smiled at Biggs, an invitation implicit in her expression. "Why not buy a couple of ladies a drink, and we'll 'elp you celebrate your good fortune."

Jack Toppan looked up, at first startled as he had not seen the women approach, then pleased at the prospect of furthering the evening's entertainment. The gentleman stood up, obviously less than pleased with the interruption of his conversation with these most talkative sailors.

"I must be on my way," he said, not unpleasantly. He adjusted his jacket and hitched up his trousers. "I certainly enjoyed visiting with you men. I do hope I haven't upset you with my news of the difficulties with the Americans. Perhaps we'll meet again, if your ship is to be in Nassau for a while . . ." He let the unasked question hang, waiting for a final piece of information which would further his knowledge. He didn't have to wait for more than a heartbeat or two. Coleman fairly jumped at the opening.

"I 'eard the cap'n tellin' Lieutenant Burns that we'd be 'ere for a fortnight and then back out. Course that mighta changed now when they 'ear 'bout the war. I collect things mighta got knocked into a cocked 'at with that. Probably won't be getting our shares anytime soon I'd reckon. I 'ope Mr. Beckwirth is plannin' to give us advances; I surely won't last a fortnight without I get some money." A chorus of agreement from the other sailors indicated a similar potential shortage of funds.

Their friend nodded sympathetically, smiled, and turned to leave. He stopped after but two steps and called one of the girls to him. A whispered conversation ensued, followed by what appeared to be his offering her a small bag, which she readily took and dropped down her bodice, returning to the table smiling broadly.

"Your gentleman friend must like you boys. 'E wants that you 'ave good time, so drink up." She motioned to the pub keeper who delivered two brimming tankards and a small cask of rum to the table. He set the tankards down in front of the two women, and the rum he placed in the middle of the table. Coleman and Toppan wasted no time in filling their own tankards, casting appreciative glances at the two women. Biggs remained almost motionless, still in a state of shock over the sudden change in his circumstances; a slight tremor had taken hold of his hands and the glass spilled as he lifted it.

"Either of you got a friend?" Toppan knew he didn't want to be left out when the pairing off began, and as the senior member of the group, assumed the role of leader naturally. It would be much easier now to even up the party than later when they would all be three sheets to the wind.

"What do you think, darlin'? 'Becca here surely ain't going to take on two of you, and neither am I. Why it would wear us out, sure it would. You just stay put right 'ere, and I'll be back before you can miss me." She winked at 'Becca and rose, moving quickly to the rear of the tavern.

Coleman watched her go, enjoying her stern view and elbowed

Biggs who, though still in a fog, was beginning to notice that the lady sitting next to him had her hand on his leg. He barely acknowledged his friend, and in spite of his efforts to control it, his shaking hands gave away his feelings. He had been caught quite aback by all of the events of the past several minutes and more, and it was taking some time to sort through it all and make sense of it. First a war, then this young woman sitting next to him and *touching* him. It was beyond his experience. 'Becca recognized his confusion, not knowing that she was only part of the reason for it, and, rightly assuming him out of his depth, thought to herself that she would enjoying 'showin' 'im the ropes' a little later.

When the other girl returned, she had with her a most ordinary looking woman, older than she and showing it, but with a quite extraordinary tophamper. Stringy brown hair framed a narrow face with wide spaced eyes and a flat nose. Her lips were unnaturally red, and her cheeks showed pink blotches, the result of hastily applied paint. Other make-up was caked on her chin and throat. Their earlier companion made the introductions.

"This 'ere's me friend Abby, an' me own name's Sara. Abby's not busy at the moment and would be most obliging if you invite her to join the party."

Abby smiled, showing a paucity of teeth, but the wide spaced eyes crinkled at the corners with her smile. She sat down next to Jack Toppan, moving close to him on the bench, and giving him the opportunity to appreciate her ample bosom as she reached for a tankard of ale.

"O' course she can join us." Jack was never one to be bashful where the ladies were concerned; his eyes never left her more obvious but most endearing qualities. Coleman made room for Sara, and the men, save Isaac, chattered excitedly as they drank, and thought of the pleasures that lay in the offing. Biggs' reticence went unnoticed until, after several more rounds, each of which raised the level of boisterousness, the group broke up, moving off in pairs as they headed for the rooms the girls called home. 'Becca took Isaac, now out of one fog and into another, by the hand, leading him to the stairs as his eyes once again grew wider.

Coleman, staggering a little himself, noticed his friend's expression. "It's righty-oh, Isaac. You'll see . . . gonna be sweet as a t'gallant breeze on a smooth sea."

Biggs nodded, and allowed the girl to lead him up the stairs.

Toppan showed no ill-effects from the vast quantities of rum he had consumed and, being experienced in the way of things ashore, moved eagerly ahead of his comrades. The other two men made their way haltingly up the narrow stairs, and stopped when they reached the landing at the top.

'Becca guided Isaac into the first room in the dark hallway. He glanced back at his comrades, his eyes darting quickly around the hall, as if looking for an escape. A tug on his sleeve moved him and he followed the girl inside, still looking after his shipmates. The two other men were going into separate rooms further down the hall. 'Becca closed the door, ending his view of his mates, and he turned to face her, his eyes adapting to the darkness of the room, illuminated only by the light of a few candles burning, one on a chest of drawers, and two on a window seat next to the bed. The bed and the chest shared the limited floorspace with an unstable looking chair which heeled on a pair of poorly repaired broken legs like a ship rail-down in a blow.

"Now what, 'Becca?" Isaac seemed to regain some level of sobriety as his immediate future — or at least what he was beginning to realize would be his immediate future — began to solidify. He looked questioningly at the girl, his head reeling.

During his several runs to the Caribbean on *Anne* with his American shipmates and Captain Smalley, Isaac had never been in this situation before, though he had certainly heard a host of tales and sea stories about what he surmised he was getting into. None, however, had prepared him for actually dealing with himself as the main player in this story. His strict Methodist New England upbringing had all but precluded the possibility even entering his mind, and now here it was quite literally staring him in the face. He could, and had many times, handled gales, with their screaming winds and enormous seas, calms, and disasters at sea; he functioned through his fear, showing a steady and reliable pattern of actions that gave his shipmates confidence in him. Now he was alone in a room with a young woman with but one purpose in mind and he was virtually paralyzed with fear; all thoughts of the recently declared war, and his own predicament forgotten.

The woman's quiet words soon calmed the young man, and before the dawn showed red in the eastern sky, he had joined the ranks of other sailors who had visited this room before him.

CHAPTER NINETEEN

Letters Home

M y dearest wife:

It has been some months since I've written, and God alone knows when this letter will find its way to you. I pray that when it does, it finds you in good health, and spirits, secure in the knowledge that I will be home within the year instant, and with some considerable wealth. We have enjoyed extraordinary good luck and have only recently captured an entire French squadron of merchantmen sailing fully laden for home. We had to fight their escorting frigates — there were but two, and a brig — and we had help from Captain Edwin McCray in *Amethyst*, and Jason Smithfield with a recently captured brig, *Jolie*. Unfortunately, in the fighting, there were a number of lives lost, and *Amethyst* herself was lost with a large number of hands. Captain McCray was able to board and capture the French frigate, *Etoile Noire*, before *Amethyst* was lost, so the Frenchman sailed with us under British colors. Captain Winston hatched a brilliant plan which the enemy did not smoke until it was much too late, and right into the middle of the French merchants we sailed. I tell you, Samantha, it was glorious. These poor blighters never knew what happened. To be sure, a few tried to get off a shot or two at us, but to no avail, and we rounded them up, heaved them to and put our prize crews aboard. Being well to the north as a result of our chase, we sailed four of them straight west into New Providence while McCray took *Etoile* and his three ships south to Antigua. They were all rich prizes, and should provide a plentiful purse for all hands, including yrs. truly.

Unfortunately, we shall receive no reward for destroying the French brig which was burned and sunk; however, the frigate *Etoile Noire* was a prize herself, and the other frigate, while lost, will provide Head and Gun money since we were able to save the muster books and knew her armament as well. Captain Winston allowed to me that I had acquitted myself quite well in the action and would be passing on favorable comments to Adm. LaFoury.

The fleet remained in New Providence for nigh onto three weeks, with the hands getting some much needed leave. *Orpheus* was put right as rain from the wounds she suffered at the hands of the French, and the cargoes, after cataloguing and bonding by the British Magistrate here were, for the most part stripped off the merchants. The French crews were given their parole, promising not to take up arms against British forces, and will remain for the time being on New Providence. We have not seen Smithfield's little brig, *Jolie*, since she sailed off to provide a diversion so we could catch the French merchants un-escorted, as it were, and Captain Winston and I fear she has been lost with all hands.

Do you recall young Oliver Fitzgerald? I'm sure you must; an unfortunate looking, rather portly, young chap, and our junior lieutenant. I know I've written you of some of his misfortunate escapades. Well, he will be suffering the wrath of Captain Winston and the taunts of the gun room no more. He was shot dead in the recent action against the French. A most disagreeable event as it left us even more short-handed than already we were. Even with his frequent missteps, he had brought his battery of six guns to an excellent state of accuracy and speed, and though he would most likely never have made commander and certainly not post, he filled an important role among the lieutenants here. Captain Winston had the good grace to bury him separately from the crew after the action — gave him a little status, you know, and while he never had it in life, he finally was elevated in death.

The action was a great relief for all of us, especially the men, as it had been too long since the ship had fought, and discipline was being maintained only through virtually constant floggings. You know that Winston firmly believes in the use of the lash, contrary to my tradition, but it seemed as if even for him, this was too much. You recall I wrote you about that young sailor we pressed a year and more ago from the American vessel, and who leaped overboard to his death when confronted with the lash? (I can only hope that the missive found its way to you intact.) Surely we've had no more incidents like that, so inured to floggings are the British sailors — they have come to expect it as a routine part of life at sea. I don't think it needs to be that way. There must be a better way to maintain order without resorting to whipping a man as if he were an animal. I have participated in entirely in too many of these inhuman punishments. I will depress you no more with such unpleasantries. On to other items of recent import.

We were informed while in Nassau that England is now at war with America. I don't imagine it will signify here in the Caribbean, except as to provide us with more opportunity for prizes. Can you imagine that upstart country declaring war against His Majesty? I have it on good authority they have barely a dozen men of war, and few of those are crew'd and fit for sea. We heard in New Providence of some small private vessels which are reported to be at large, but they should be of little bother. I should imagine the Americans will be suing for peace quick as ever they can, once they taste a few broadsides from some of the King's ships. I should not be at all surprised were it to be over by the time you receive this letter. A bit of good news to cheer you, my dear.

You will be most proud of your husband, I am sure. You know how I have pined for promotion to Commander and my own ship. Well, I have been given a command! To be sure, it is of a temporary nature, and I am surely not yet Commander, but I collect from Captain Winston it will lead to a permanent assignment if all goes well. Let me tell you the whole of it.

Some days after we arrived safely in Nassau, Captain Winston received word from a fast schooner sent from Antigua that we were to bring two of the French prizes to Adm. Lafory there. Apparently, McCray had got in and told him of the French fleet's makeup and he's taken it into his head to add to the ships under his direct control there. So Winston tells me to pick a few men from *Orpheus* and fill in with French prisoners who will sail with us and bring the larger of the merchants to Antigua, after a suitable length of time to repair damage to both the ship and the men. Well, my dear, I can tell you my joy knew no bounds. Even when I was informed that never would we have enough crew to sail the ship in any but the mildest weather nor to defend ourselves if attacked, I simply smiled and directed my midshipman, that fool Murphy, to employ an impress gang from the garrison here and pick us some prime hands to fill in. I should add that *Orpheus* was well depleted of crew, between the casualties of battle and the desertions which occurred soon after landing in New Providence, so there were several impress gangs working already to supplement her own dwindling ranks. Midshipman Blake was assigned the other ship, and I am officer in charge of the fleet, even if it is only two ships. We are two days at sea now with extremely moderate weather, though the northeast breeze seems to be holding for now allowing us to run our southing now and thence east to Antigua. I can be thankful that the wind and seas are moderate, as we have the most ungodly collection of hands aboard. I doubt there's time to make a crew of them. Except for those from *Orpheus*, the ones who know ships don't speak English, and the ones who speak what might pass for English don't know a sheet from a gun tackle. I may have given young Biggs, a hand from *Orpheus*, more than he can manage with a quite inept crew at the maintop. They are extraordinarily slow in doing anything aloft and poor Biggs appears quite frustrated. The hands on deck are barely better, but there at least, a fall or mis-step is not a deadly event. We shall sail on and pray for continued easy weather, and a shift in the wind more to the north, with no contact with any privateers, or, perish the thought, a French, or one of the few American, men of war. Hopefully, young Blake will be able to manage his ship, stay with me, and will arrive in due course at Antigua, still in company and still relatively intact.

I will try to write more as time permits during this passage so this brief chronology will find a ship leaving for home upon our arrival in Antigua. I may have neglected to mention the ship's name — the one I am captain of, that is. *Fleur* it is, and it means flower in French. I suspect it will not be changed, particularly if Adm. Lafory is going to put her directly into service.

For now, my love, I will end as I feel I should be on deck. I am now and will always remain

> yrs. faithfully,
> Jos. Burns
> July 30, 1812
> on board *Fleur*, at sea

* * * * * *

D ear Mother and Father:

I hope that you have not been too worried about my fate since last you heard of my whereabouts. I can only hope my letter explaining how I came to be on a British frigate arrived and caused you little concern. I have found that one ship is more or less like another, save the people aboard, and of course the floggings. The Royal Navy seems to spend a great deal of time whipping its sailors. So far, I still have escaped the lash, but I am sure I mentioned when last I wrote that one of the other men, a boy actually, who was pressed with me, actually jumped overboard rather than suffer a whipping. I can tell you, I do pine for the days in *Anne* with Captain Smalley. Even that Mr. Jakes, the third, wasn't so bad, now I think about him. I imagine he would fit right in here in the Navy though. I am hopeful that I will be able to leave this ship soon — at the first opportunity, I'm thinking — as now I have or will have quickly I hope, some money, though I know not how much. My messmates tell me it will be a great deal. Men have left the ship with much less; in fact I hear that a dozen and more jumped while *Orpheus* was in New Providence, and the marines could only find about half to bring back. I am certain they do not wish to be aboard that ship now. Quite a few others came down with a fever they call the Yellow Jack and expired in what seemed like no time at all.

How is the fishing, Father? Are you managing to avoid the British ships on the Banks? I do hope so. They seem to be quite uncaring about who they steal to sail their ships. I hope that all is well at home in spite of the war which I am told has begun against the British. I recall when I left on *Anne* so long ago (it seems) that many were saying a war would be the only solution to the problem. I remember Captain Smalley talking to our first mate, Mr. Clark, about it too. He said there were some what didn't want to fight because it would cost them money, what with their trade with England and all. Seems to me they're putting the cart before the horse. I collect none thought the war would be begin quite so soon, and surely it puts me in a fix, as I am on a British vessel. Hopefully I won't be called upon to fight against my own. I have lain awake for many nights pondering what I shall do, and have so far come up with naught. I can only hope it don't come to me having to fight Americans. Let's hope it don't come to that.

I should tell you that we have just come from capturing a French fleet — prizes they call them. When they're sold, the crew shares in the money they get for them. That's where the money I spoke of is coming from. We had some action, and quite a few men on the ship were killed. I can say with some certainty that never in life have I experienced anything quite so frightening and yet exhilarating. The roar of the guns and smoke filling the air — screaming and shouting — splinters flying, and the blood. Fortunately less blood on *Orpheus* than the French ships we encountered, and while I was lucky enough to not get my own self hurt in any way, I think we buried twenty and more men, both French and British. There's still some who's missing arms and legs who won't never sail again. God knows what will happen to them, being put ashore in a hot unhealthy place like New Providence. None of those who have been here before like it, fearing the Jack as they do with good cause. I will try to tell you something of our stay there.

About three weeks back it was, and several days after we escorted the French merchant ships into the harbor at Nassau (that's the city here) I was ashore in a tavern and met a young lady. I know what you're thinking — if she was in a tavern, she weren't no lady. Well, let me tell you. She's just about as nice as you could wish for. And pretty too. Her name's Rebecca, but everybody calls her 'Becca. She says she works for a seamstress making dresses for the rich ladies, but she spent most of the time with me, 'cepting when I was aboard the ship, and some nights when she had to work late. She lives topside in the tavern, but just until she gets some money together and finds a better place. I gave her some money to help her — she didn't ask me for very much, and I didn't have much, neither, and I thought it the least I could do, what with her spending so much time with me. She came here from some place in England — I forget where — I never heard of it anyway — and she has some friends which were already here to help her out. I met them too. Seem nice enough. They actually spent sometime with two of my shipmates from *Orpheus*. A fine sight we made, the six of us parading through Nassau. The people that live here are mostly Negroes, but they talk quite a bit different than the ones at home. Sometimes they're real hard to understand, like they're speaking a different language altogether. Even the white people talk different, unless they're right from England and then they sound like the men on *Orpheus*, which I have learned to understand pretty well. We met a fellow in the same tavern 'Becca lives in that was real friendly to us. He dressed real good and acted like he had a lot of money. Bought us all the drink we wanted and wanted to hear all about the ship and what were our plans. He's the one what told us about the war starting. He came in again, shortly before Coleman and me left on this ship — *Fleur* — just to make sure we were doing good and didn't need anything. We explained we'd be leaving soon for Antigua on this merchant ship with Lieutenant Burns — that's where I am now, by the way, and that *Orpheus* was going somewhere else. A nice man, he was.

I mentioned I'm now on *Fleur*. That's one of the French merchant ships we captured and Lieutenant Burns (he's the first lieutenant from *Orpheus*) is in charge of this ship and the one Mr. Blake, one of the midshipmen from *Orpheus*, is on sailing with us to Antigua. I hope we don't have trouble with weather or the Frenchmen; nobody 'spects we'll be seeing any Americans yet since we only went to war a month and more back, and my shipmates tell me, don't have no warships yet — leastways, none to speak of. We hardly got enough men to sail the ship. Most of them are either French and can't talk English, or landsmen pressed in New Providence who don't know the difference 'tween a jib boom and a spanker. Lieutenant Burns took me as captain of the maintop, and my friend Bob Coleman came as captain of the foretop. He's got the same trouble as me; trying to teach the Frenchies how to work aloft without they don't speak English. The landsmen we got are so scared about being aloft they won't let go of the jackstays to do their jobs. Puts me in mind of poor Tyler when he first come aboard. I doubt they'll ever turn into seamen. We been two days out, now, and Coleman and me pretty much got to do everything ourselves. They ain't learning nothing. It won't be pretty if we get into it with weather or enemy ships before we reach Antigua. This ship has cannons, but they look pretty run down. I doubt they'll fire. One of the gun captains from *Orpheus* been working pretty much full time on them since we left Kingston and he ain't so sure he can shoot them without they'll blow up.

I don't know when you'll ever see this, as it has to be carried by a ship England ain't at war with, and it seems like England's getting into a fight with more people than ever she should. God bless you both and your prayers for me will surely help.

Your faithful and loving son,
Isaac Biggs
July 31, 1812

PART THREE

On Board
GLORY
August - November
1812

CHAPTER TWENTY

Schooners on the Hunt

" 'Vast heaving there, you lubber. Ain't you got eyes in yer head?"
Mr. Halladay had no patience for ineptness, and the display he
had just witnessed proved the point he made as often as anyone
would listen, namely that farmers from Virginia made for poor
sailors — even a farmer who had been at sea for nigh on to six
months. Never mind the fact that the time was just before eight
bells in the middle watch and it was darker than ever, the moon
having set early last night.

The object of his attention was a Virginian who had left the
farm and sought the excitement of life on a privateer. He showed
up in Baltimore with high expectations a week after war was
declared, and with the help of a sailor's rendezvous in a Fells Point
boarding house, wound up in a queue for signing on *Glory* shortly
after she was launched. With a pressing need for men, the skipper, a Chesapeake waterman named Cressy, had signed the
Virginian over his mate's protestations. After shaking down the
vessel for about two weeks, Cressy left to take command of a letter
of marque trader where there was more opportunity for riches. A
former merchant captain was available in Baltimore and was
engaged as skipper for the upcoming cruise. He had gray hair,
though he was only approaching his fiftieth year, and had captained a variety of vessels in the Atlantic trade for over twenty-five
years. Before that, he had sailed with the Continental Navy. His
name was Jedediah Smalley.

Captain Joshua Abrams had put together a small fleet of privateers to harass British shipping, take prizes, and pay back a little of the misery the Royal Navy had dealt the American sea trades.
Not only would his efforts enrich the crews and investors, but
would assist in the war effort by reducing the ships available to the
British for transporting goods as well as taking men of war from

duty potentially damaging to the Americans and forcing them to escort their own merchants. He had found backing for three ships, all sharp-built schooners, and would add to his little fleet should additional backers turn up; when the word of their successes reached Baltimore, he knew the merchants would be clamoring for the opportunity to participate in the effort. For the most part, the Baltimore merchants, farmers, and gentry were eager to participate in the war, and the opportunity for profit. They had little time for the whining and anti-war merchants of Boston who lined their pockets daily with British silver despite the embargo of English goods. Because Willard Halladay felt the same way, he had sailed with Cressy as mate, and had stayed aboard *Glory* in spite of potentially greater opportunity available if he went with his former captain. Halladay was glad of his decision in spite of having a number of landsmen, like the Virginia farmer, aboard, and he liked the new captain. He saw early on that Smalley was a fine sailor who likely would not blanch in the face of cannon fire, and had won the respect of his crew from the start with his bold tactics and skill at handling men.

Now *Glory*, under Captain Smalley, with *Freedom* and *Bill of Rights*, under Captains Abrams and Tom Stebbins respectively, raced through the night to put themselves in position to find fat British merchants unescorted by the Royal Navy. None of the ships showed a light, and unless seen from close aboard, they were quite nearly invisible; only their sails made a dim glow, reflecting the light from the star-filled Caribbean night. The whisper of their bows cutting the through the water was broken by Mr. Halladay's voice, as it carried across the sea.

The lubberly farmer-turned-sailor was properly chastised, the situation rectified and the three ships continued silently on their way south, making good time through a moderate sea with a favorable half-gale broad on their bows. Halladay heard his name spoken quietly from aft, and turned to look toward the small quarterdeck.

"Mr. Halladay." He heard it again, recognizing the speaker as Captain Smalley, virtually invisible in his black coat, and moved at once to join him by the schooner's wheel.

"I probably needn't remind you that we don't want to make our presence here too obvious. Please keep your voice and your men under control. I think it would be helpful to our success if we let the men know what lies in the offing. With the war so new, and this our first cruise, many of them don't have an inkling as to what we're about, save taking prizes. I don't doubt their performance when we fight; I have seen that now twice on the way here.

The two vessels we took off the Carolinas did not offer much of a fight, and, if you recall, their captains were mightily surprised when we told 'em of the war. I don't 'spect any vessels we encounter down here'll be better informed, but there might be a frigate nearby. We are in their waters now, and might could meet up with one quite without warning. We shouldn't be caught all ahoo, and the men need to be alert. After they's had their breakfast we will assemble them amidships and tell them what we're about. Have the petty officers alerted for that, if you please." The captain, having shared the thought with his First, turned his attention back to the helmsman and his ship, leaving Halladay to return forward and see to the watch on deck.

The morning watch would be called soon to start the day's routine; eating their morning scouse and fruit, swabbing down the decks, recoiling halyards and sheets, and ensuring the guns were ready for use. They would also assume the responsibility for the handling of the schooner while their shipmates went below to eat their own breakfast and swab out the berthing deck. The day's routine continued after the hands were fed, with guns drills and instruction in hand to hand fighting with pikes, cutlasses, and muskets. Maintenance, repairs to the ship and rigging, knotting and splicing, and a little horseplay followed. While this was not the American Navy, Joshua Abrams insisted his ships be run in a smart, organized, and seaman-like manner, and engaged captains who felt similarly. Other privateers in the rapidly growing fleets were slovenly by contrast, and Abrams felt that their future successes would likely not measure up to his.

The mate moved around the schooner in the pre-dawn darkness with the easy familiarity born of having been on the vessel even before she had finished building; he knew every rope, pin, hatch and spar as well as his own wife's body, and had trained, in the scant time available, most of the hands to be equally comfortable with the ship so that thought would not be necessary in an emergency. Halladay and Smalley had talked often enough to convince the mate that they shared the same ideas politically as well as the feeling that a war with England had been inevitable. The two men also shared similar backgrounds, having sailed in the Continental Navy, Smalley as a mate then captain, and Halladay as an able seaman.

"Where're we headed, Mr. Halladay?" The question came out of the darkness and at first the Mate didn't recognize the voice.

"What's that?" Halladay sought time to put a name on the disembodied voice.

"Where are we goin' in such an all-fired rush? We don't usually carry this much sail through the night without we're headin' somewhere in a hell of a hurry."

"Oh, Johnson, it's you. I didn't smoke your voice right off." Johnson, a lanky young waterman from the Eastern Shore of Maryland, was captain of the starboard watch and had come on deck early to see what was going on before he relieved his counterpart, captain of the larbowlines. "We're headin' down towards Antigua, where the Brits got most of their ships. See if'n we can catch us a fat merchant what ain't been told about the war yet . . . like them two back off the Carolinas. Captain plans on telling all hands about it this morning. I guess you'll hear more then. You know Captain Smalley; he likes for the crew to know what the plans are so they can act smarter if the balls and splinters start flyin'. Should be a fine opportunity, you ask me. We'll all be richer — a lot richer, less'n I miss my guess — in a few days' time."

"I like the sound o' that. I won't say nothin' to my boys; I'll let Captain Smalley tell 'em the good news. I best be gettin' aft to relieve Little now, or he'll be whinin' all day about my bein' late." The sailor made his way aft with the same ease his mate had shown, and disappeared into the pre-dawn gloom.

The schooner's crew had by now fallen into a traditional at-sea routine with only minimal haranguing from the mates; the watch relieved, decks were scrubbed and sanded, breakfast was piped and the watch below made order out of the chaos in the berthing deck caused by a spot of nasty weather recently encountered which stirred the berthing area the way a cook would stir of pot of soup. Clothes and sea chests, boots and still strung hammocks shared the cramped quarters with the off-watch, a parrot, and a small dog, who had acquired the unlikely name of Rufus. To the men scrubbing the berthing area deck, it was apparent that Rufus was not a sailor, and extra effort accompanied the additional complaints sparked by evidence of the dog's unseaman-like behavior.

"All hands on deck! Assemble by division amidships. Lively now." The inescapable voice of the mate rang throughout the ship urging the men to "move smartly." Buckets and swabs were left where they fell, hammocks in the process of being unshipped were dropped as if they were on fire and the men tumbled pell-mell out of the hatches to find their division-mates and make more-or-less straight lines forward of the quarterdeck in the widest part of the ship. The crew was larger than normal due to the shipping of extra hands for manning prizes, and the men jostled one another for space. Captain Smalley stood silently by the helmsman, watching the proceedings, and waiting for Halladay to indicate that the men were ready for him.

"The hands are mustered, Captain, all save those on lookout and on the wheel. Also two below with the heaves — either drunk up a week's worth o' grog they been savin', or really are laid low genuine." Halladay snatched off his hat, a habit born of and carried unconsciously from his early days as a seaman, as he delivered his report. His dark hair, streaked with gray as was his beard, blew awry in the easy breeze and stuck out at odd angles, unnoticed, when he returned his hat to its place aloft. His penetrating eyes, whose stare had unnerved more than a handful of sailors over the years, were focused on his captain.

"Aye, then. Let's get started." Smalley stepped forward to the edge of the quarterdeck, and stood facing his crew, his legs braced against the easy roll of his ship, and his hands clasped firmly behind his back. The tails of his black coat whipped unheeded around his knees in the stiff breeze.

"Men, you have been assembled so that I can outline broadly for you what we're about here, and what Captains Abrams, Stebbins, and I hope to accomplish before this week is done. You may wonder why we carrried a press of canvas throughout the night. Captain Abrams intends to find us a passel of British merchants headin' to Antigua with stores for the Leeward Island Station and take 'em before they can find out that they're at war with America. It's likely they'll be unescorted by the time they get here and the pickin's ought to be rich. We need to sail fast as ever possible to get us into position, and then lay in wait for 'em to come along. Some of you will be named prize crews to sail what we take into an American port, so you'll be gettin' home faster than the rest of us. But you'll be responsible for gettin' the prize to an American port so's it can be condemned and sold, so your shipmates'll be countin' on you for their shares. It's also possible that we could sail into a neutral here in the West Indies where the American Consul, if they be one, could handle the whole thing for us. That'll be up to Cap'n Abrams, though, not me. It'll be right important for each of you to do your job good as you done off the Carolinas a few weeks back. Now get back to your work, and keep a weather eye open."

The silence broke like a summer thunder squall; everyone was talking at once. The cleverer among the men were figuring aloud the value of the potential prizes and each man's share; others listened to them, the excitement of action and riches further animating their joy at the prospect of wealth. The balance just chattered, sounding for all the world like a pack of monkeys in the jungle. The mate let them vent their excitement for a few moments, then his booming voice thundered out.

"Silence fore and aft! They won't be no prizes if you lubbers don't get your lazy arses back to work and keep the barky a'sailin'. Save your dancin' and cavortin' 'til we're done with this work and you gots your prize tickets in hand. For now, the starbowlines got the watch, larbowlines report to your petty officers for the day's work. Dismissed." Halladay's strength manifested itself even with his easy manner and casual stance, fists balled on his hips and legs spread against the motion of the schooner. His voice carried authority now rather than menace but most knew that in spite of his easy going habits, slackers would see a completely different side of the mate.

The hands moved off, still discussing the potential riches that lay only a few days distant — practically just over the horizon. *Glory* returned to her routine, her sharp clipper bow knifing cleanly through the rolling Caribbean as the few white wind-driven clouds raced her through the blue brilliance of the clear morning sky, mirroring the crisp white capped waves contrasting with the glorious blue of the water.

CHAPTER
TWENTY-ONE

The Night Watch

"You think tonight's gonna be the night, Cap'n?" Willard Halladay leaned on the weather rail, absently scratching his beard, and spoke quietly to the man standing next to him. When not on the quarterdeck, Captain Smalley was approachable by his officers in a casual way; this was one of those times. He thought for a minute or two before answering his mate.

"Who knows, Mr. Halladay? We got to get a little lucky here, but they's bound to be ships comin' into Antigua sooner or later. Let's just hope it's sooner — an' that we see 'em. They could be swingin' to their hooks in English Harbour 'fore we know they've got by, but I think, and I guess so does Cap'n Abrams, we're on their course into Antigua."

"Aye. Seems to me any ship bound into Antigua from the east or the north got to pass within a cannon-shot of here. Now we just got to wait for 'em to show, eh, Cap'n? I collect that's the drift of Cap'n Abrams' plan?"

"You'll get your action again, quick enough Mr. Halladay. I would guess they won't keep us waitin' more 'n a day or two." The captain looked aloft as he finished speaking.

"Should be about time for the signal." Halladay glanced up at the main crosstrees just as three bells sounded, marking an hour and a half into the middle watch.

Joshua Abrams, in command of the three Baltimore privateers, had a standard nighttime procedure which consisted of each ship showing a lantern aloft at every turn of the glass during the dark hours. It allowed the schooners to cover a vast amount of ocean, spreading out as they did, but it kept them in visible contact without showing continuous lights. Should a potential prize show himself during this time, an additional light was shown next to the standard one, its orientation indicating whether the stranger was to weather or leeward, and summoning the other two ships to join with all haste.

As if in response to his comment, a lantern appeared at the tops'l yard on the mainmast, moving forward and aft of the topmast to ensure it's being seen. After a few moments, it was doused, leaving a darkness so profound that one could doubt it had ever existed. A lookout on the crosstrees of the foremast hailed the deck.

"Light forward, half a point to wind'ard. 'Nother to leeward, near on the beam. Singles both."

"Old Tom Stebbins gettin a little for'ard of his position, looks like." Captain Smalley spoke with amusement in his voice; he had nothing but the highest respect for his fellow captain, and knew that being a few degrees for'ard of where he was supposed to be was not going to cause them to miss any ship that might cross their part of the ocean. Captain Smalley chalked it up to enthusiasm on the part of the crew of *Bill of Rights*. He had high confidence in the small fleet's ability to find the British, and having found them, take them successfully.

"Aye, but shouldn't matter much, Captain. When those Brits' tops'ls come over the horizon, like as not they'll be forward of us, headin' for English Harbour quick as they can." The mate had echoed his captain's thoughts. Smalley nodded silently in the dark, and turned to move aft to the quarterdeck.

Over his shoulder he said, as he disappeared into the gloom of the night, "I'm going below, Mr. Halladay. Call me at once should anything be sighted — by anyone — if you please."

Halladay grunted "Aye" and continued to stand at the rail for a few minutes more. Then he too moved off into the night, heading forward to check the men on his watch. His bulky form moved with surprising grace and he tugged with his strong arms and large hands at each piece of running rigging he passed. It was a habit born of years at sea on vessels large and small.

The lower lookouts appeared alert, he was gratified to see; even with the prospect of lucrative prizes likely to appear at any moment, lookouts at this point in the middle watch tended to nod off from time to time. Halladay spoke to the man standing on the lower shrouds, receiving a response quickly. The two men in the bows were chatting quietly, looking forward, one to larboard and one to starboard, as they had been trained. He came around the leeward side of the fo'c'sle and went aft, checking the larboard lookout as he passed.

"How 'bout it, Mr. Halladay. We goin' ta catch us another prize soon?" The voice came from a small knot of men, haulers all, hunkered down in the waist of the ship. They were on call should a sail need to be trimmed or changed. They talked among themselves to help stay awake. Tonight there would be little likelihood of shortening down, as the ship was already down to just its fore and aft sails and a single jib, and the foresail had a single reef tied into it. Since they were not in any hurry now, but rather just holding a station while they waited for a suitable prey to turn up, speed was not an issue. However, should a British ship, or two or three, appear, the reef would be shaken out, tops'ls, stays'ls and jibs set, and the schooners would maximize their speed to cut them off, chase them down, or engage them as their positions dictated. And that would be the call for all hands. Halladay stopped and peered into the dark, trying to identify the speaker.

"I 'spect so. Leastways I hope so. Cap'n thinks it could be right soon. Aye, a ship could come through this water any time now. Those of you going to relieve the lookouts, stay sharp, and don't dope off. Tell your mates in the larbowlines the same thing when they come up to take the watch."

"Aye, aye, Mr. Mate. Nobody's sleepin' here — too much to think about, what with all that prize money just awaitin' for us to pick it up. Be just about as easy as fallin' overboard, I reckon." Halladay recognized the second speaker as his favorite farmer-turned-sailor from Virginia. "We been talkin' about the things all that money gonna buy us. Me, I was thinkin' I might even go back to Virginia and fix up the farm some, buy me some new slaves, and be a *gentleman* farmer. I think I might do that right fine. My missus'd like that too, I'm thinkin'. Course, if the prize share's enough, I just might take me a *new* missus, a lady befittin' my status as a *gentleman* . . ." The Virginian's sentence drifted off, as his mind was filled with images of his 'new' status, his new wife, and his big plantation, formerly a modest and struggling farm.

"Don't you spend all that money yet, sailor. You got a lot o' haulin' and heavin' yet to do and with luck, some boardin' and fightin' 'fore you'll even get you a smell o' a prize share — an ever' man-jack o' you got to do your jobs righty-oh on top o' it. And you ain't gonna get rich in one cruise — if'n you live through it. You can mark my words on that. It surely ain't goin' ta be easy as 'fallin overboard', just a' cause them two off'n the Carolinas struck without which we hardly fired a shot, any o' you what thinks 'at way'll be in for a surprise like you never thought possible." Halladay's rebuke created a silence among the men. He hoped it would give them time to think about what he had said, and possibly encourage them to give an inspired performance when the time came. He continued aft while the impact of his words was still ringing in the men's ears, and before they had time to begin chattering again about their anticipated earnings.

The mate stepped onto the quarterdeck, his seaman's eye seeing immediately that all was well. The quartermaster at the wheel looked alert, keeping an eye on the compass set in the binnacle and the mains'l's eerie glow of reflected starlight. The bosun was nearby, and the log slate showed an entry for the last turn of the glass. As if to solidify his impression, the voice of one of the lookouts forward floated back with an "All's well for'ard," and was echoed by his starboard and then larboard counterparts. The watch continued for another two hours; the larbowlines were called and took over, allowing their mates in the starboard watch to go below for rest for as long as they could, or at least until 8:00 AM when they would be turned out again. The men going below barely heard their mates begin again the noisy process of cleaning the ship's deck and taking their turn on the pump handles for the standard watch-and-watch pumping of *Glory*'s bilges.

As two bells sounded, the single lantern was carried aloft, indicating again that all was quiet and *Glory*'s lookouts had sighted no other lights. The officer of the watch awaited the cry from his lookout forward, maintaining the solitary status of the three American privateers. It came.

"Light to leeward, three p'ints abaft the beam, single light." The third mate, who had the watch, waited for the rest of the report. When it wasn't forthcoming, he bellowed to the tops'l yard. His high pitched nasal voice carried easily to the foretop.

"What about a light to windward? Look sharp, man, and make your report. Do you see *Freedom*'s light?"

"Nothing, sir. No lights to wind'ard 'tall. Dark as the insides of a whale out there." The third scratched his chin while he digested this report. He had been on deck last night before the middle watch and knew where the other ships were supposed to be. What could be have happened that *Freedom* wasn't showing the requisite light from her mainmast? They had heard no gunfire, which, with *Glory* being to leeward of Abrams's schooner, would have been clearly audible. The half-gale had been steady from the northeast with nary a shift for the past twenty-four hours as was common in these waters. The mate could come up with no reason why the light should not be shown. He decided Captain Abrams had indeed shown the light, and the lookout on *Glory* had missed seeing it. He would handle the inattentive sailor personally, bringing him before Captain Smalley only if he insisted that there had been no light. He had ways of disciplining seamen that would not bother the captain, who most certainly had more important things on his mind.

Aye, he nodded to himself, *that's what I got to do. No point in disturbing the captain or the mate for something I can handle me own self.* He turned around, looking for a sailor in the watch.

"You there, get aloft and relieve the lookout at the fore crosstrees," the third ordered the nearest man, "and tell him to git his arse down here to me quick as ever he can."

The junior mate paced up and down on the quarterdeck while he waited for his orders to be carried out. He had managed to work himself into quite a rage by the time the unfortunate seaman showed up and said "Sir?"

Third Mate Phineas Tillet turned and began berating the man standing before him. His small eyes burned with fury at this man who was trying to make him look bad, and in this, his first cruise as a mate. He pointed an overlarge nose at his hapless victim.

"You slab-sided fool. Your momma know she give birth to a blind boy? Any idiot could o' seen that light from *Freedom*. Why, lookouts been seein' them lights all night long. Why'd you miss it now, on my watch? You know which way is for'ard, lad? And wind'ard? All you hadda do was look. I don't think Cap'n Abrams decided not to show a light just acause you was on watch. I'm gonna keep you up there the rest o' the watch, and most o' the day's well. Your eyes gonna be burned out lookin' inta that sun all day, and by suppertime, by the Almighty, you'll . . ."

"Light for'ard, half a point to wind'ard. Single . . . now there's another . . . showin' above the first." The cry from lookout on the foremast silenced all conversation for a heartbeat. A ship, potentially a prize, had been seen by *Freedom*'s lookouts, and from the position of the lights, to the weather of all the ships. Third Mate Tillet changed his course abruptly, regaining his voice and galvanized his watch into action.

"You there, messenger, respects to Cap'n Smalley, and there's the signal sighted from *Freedom* showin' a vessel to her wind'ard." Raising his voice to the men perched high up the mainmast, he shouted, "Show two lights to leeward, to *Bill o' Rights*, second atop the first. In the waist, there. Shake out that reef in the fores'l, and look lively 'bout it. Call the watch below. All hands on deck to make sail."

The action on *Glory* was duplicated by the men on *Bill of Rights* as the two schooners came alive. There was little noise save the cracking of canvas as sails were hoisted, and a brief snapping and popping as an over eager quartermaster began bringing *Glory*'s head closer to the wind before being ordered to do so and before the heavers in the waist were ordered to "Trim 'er, oh . . . heave together, now!" A quick correction by the third eased the ship back off a trifle and the sails filled with a satisfying *whoomp*.

Captain Smalley appeared silently on the quarterdeck, taking in the action going on around his ship in a glance. He saw Tillet had the watch, and while he knew his third mate was a fine sailor, he was a little green in his role of ship's officer, and would bear some watching as *Glory* came to life at the hands of her well-trained sailors.

"Mr. Tillet, I assume you have called the watch below to make sail. Did you signal Captain Stebbins to leeward?" Smalley was pretty sure the answer would be "Aye" to both, but his skill and attentiveness could not let the questions go unasked. He was not disappointed, and noted with some satisfaction that already the recently relieved watch was climbing out of the hatches, and were being directed by Mr. Halladay to their sail handling positions. He soon felt the schooner respond to her greater sail area, and quietly spoke to the man at the wheel.

"Bring her up some, lad, about a point." Turning to the third, he added, "We're coming up, Mr. Tillet, start trimming the main and fores'ls." He stood with his face to the wind for a moment, feeling its force and direction.

"Up another point, if you please, quartermaster. Mr. Tillet, we'll bring her a trifle higher." Raising his voice so that it could be heard forward, against the wind, he shouted, "Mr. Halladay, you may set stays'ls, jibs and flying jibs, now, if you please."

Setting the tops'ls now would hinder the vessel's ability to sail sharply to windward, and while off the wind, they would add a few knots to her speed, he wanted to drive her to weather as fast as ever she would go now to join Captain Abrams sailing some four leagues ahead and to windward. He knew Tom Stebbins on *Rights* would be doing the same thing, and although he could not see the other ship, he also knew that they too would be racing to windward to carry out Abrams's plan of action.

CHAPTER
TWENTY-TWO

Retribution

Dawn found the two schooners still racing to windward, their bows cutting cleanly through the turquoise Caribbean, bones in their teeth and sails straining at their sheets. On board *Glory*, the excitement was high, men leaped to carry out orders — anything to speed the ship on her way to their waiting riches. The water foamed inches below the lee rail, and as the sun hit the spume, it showed a brilliant white in stark contrast to the blue-green of the undisturbed sea. *Glory's* wake streamed straight out behind her, a delicate white feather laid on the sea, the only sign remaining of her passage. Next to *Glory*, *Bill of Rights* paralleled her course half a league to leeward, and a satisfying league astern.

Captain Smalley smiled as he looked astern, knowing the frustration his friend Tom Stebbins must be feeling, seeing *Glory* a league ahead of him. The relative speed of the two ships and the abilities of their crews had been a source of continuing good-natured bickering between the two captains since first they sailed together, and as luck would have it, most of the opportunities they had had to prove the argument either way had shown *Glory* as the more ably managed, or at least the faster. Today was no exception, and Smalley and his mates continued to urge the men to their tasks, albeit unnecessarily. The captain looked aloft, his gaze taking in the sails and their set, and more importantly, the lookouts, ensuring their eyes continuously scanned the horizon. He had expected the cry of "Sails!" for a while now; *Freedom*, in sight since dawn, still flew the hoist indicating "Enemy sighted to windward." The lower part of the flag hoist, indicating the distance and relative bearing, changed periodically, and now showed "two . . . three," signifying that the enemy was two points off the weather bow of the sighting ship, in this case, *Freedom*, and three leagues distant. Smalley fully expected his lookouts to see the ships from the masthead at any moment. He was not disappointed.

"Sails, two ships of sail, three points to wind'ard." The cry, expected though it was, startled both Captain Smalley and Willard Halladay. Halladay grabbed a glass and fairly leaped into the rigging, heading to the top of the ratlines on the mainmast, to confirm the sighting. His agility for a man of his size and years continued to surprise many on board. He called down to the deck, his voice carrying clearly over the wind.

"Aye, Captain. There appears to be two, separated less than a league. Tops'ls and courses I can see. I'd guess French-built by the shape of the stays'ls. Little shiver in 'em, sloppy or short crew'd be my guess. And no flags showin'." The completeness of his mate's report satisfied Smalley, who mentally ran through the plan Abrams had imparted to him and Stebbins. Suddenly he remembered to let Abrams know he had sighted the enemy.

"Quartermaster, a hoist to *Freedom*, if you please. 'Enemy in sight, three then six'. He turned, checking to see if Stebbins had seen the ships as well, and if he had put up the appropriate hoist. As he watched, the flags climbed to *Bill of Rights'* main top, whipping initially, then stiffening in the wind as they gained the height of the mast, reading essentially the same as the ones now flying at *Glory*'s masthead. Smalley glanced back at *Freedom*, saw his and Stebbins' hoists had been acknowledged, and motioned for the quartermaster to retrieve the flags.

"Mr. Halladay, a moment, if you please." The captain, the tails of his black coat whipping in the breeze, waited while his mate stepped to the windward side of the quarterdeck, and continued, "I think we might bear off a trifle so as to cross their bows and get to the weather of 'em. We'd gain some speed, and perhaps more important, the weather gauge on 'em when the shootin' starts. What would you say to that?" On *Anne*, or any of the host of merchants Smalley had captained, he had developed a policy of consulting his officers when he made a decision of this nature — something he had seen one of his Continental Navy captains do quite successfully. Halladay seemed not surprised at the query and, understanding his captain's mindset, looked at the situation as it was developing, then glanced back at *Rights*. He tugged for a moment at his beard, then smiled, the corners of his eyes crinkling.

"I think a couple of points might do the trick, Cap'n. My guess would be that Cap'n Abrams'll hold his course, then come up 'round they's sterns. If us and *Rights* go off some, we'll cross ahead of 'em, and put ourselves to wind'ard. We'll have 'em right between us. If we're gonna fight, we can make 'em fight both sides at once — give 'em something to think about afore they heave to and strike."

Smalley nodded at his mate's corroboration of his idea, then turned again to the quartermasters at the wheel. "Ease her down two points, if you please." He turned forward, and seeing his third mate, raised his voice. "Mr. Tillet, start your sheets; we're coming off a trifle. Stand by to set tops'ls."

The order created a flurry of activity in the waist of the schooner. Men took hold of the main and fores'l sheets, and under the direction of Tillet, began to ease them out, as the vessel's head moved further away from the wind. Additional men were standing by the ratlines, awaiting the order to move aloft and set tops'ls. Having eased the great main and foresails, Tillet looked aft for Smalley to signal him aloft. He got a nod from the captain, and he and his topmen were in the rigging, while Halladay moved forward to supervise the heavers on deck. Captain Smalley looked aft at *Bill of Rights*, tearing through the sea like a ship possessed. He could see her men aloft, already removing the gaskets from the two tops'ls. It would be a toss-up as to which ship had their small square sails flying first. He watched as Stebbins' crew heaved the tops'l yard up the mast, the sail billowing out beneath it. He could hear the orders being given on his own ship, and heard the main tops'l snapping as it began to feel the wind. He turned. The foretops'l yard was two-blocked, and the braces were being hauled to bring the yard around to where the sail would fill properly. The bowline was kept taut as the yard moved, requiring the coordination of two gangs of heavers on deck.

Suddenly, the sail filled with a loud *whoomp*, and the sheet was trimmed to maximize the set of the sail. A second *whoomp* indicated that the main tops'l had likewise been properly set, and the schooner began to respond to the additional drive provided by the new sails; her lee rail, previously just above the foaming water, was now wet, with the foam running down the deck in a great rushing gout. The waves broke over the weather bow, and the wind carried the stinging spray nearly to the mainmast. Smalley smiled in spite of himself; this was what these Baltimore schooners were all about! He had never been on a ship that moved like *Glory* and her sisters.

They would close those ships and be in position to start an action, should one be called for, before dinner was finished, with the afternoon to bring it to a conclusion. A good day's work for anyone, he thought.

The vessels were now visible from deck; when the privateer raised herself on a wave crest, most of the hull of the leader could be glimpsed, at other times, only her sails were seen. Smalley and Halladay could see that the course they set was just about right; they would pass ahead of the two ships about half a league, while Abrams' *Freedom* would pass astern, the schooner having already tacked over to a new course. Apparently, Abrams had seen what his two other ships were doing and agreed, picking up his part in the move to position himself to their leeward.

Jed Smalley smiled inwardly as he recalled the plan of battle, if such a scanty and rather general concept could be called a plan, that Abrams had outlined to his captains before leaving Baltimore. Minimum shooting was the object; the Americans had no desire to damage their prizes to the extent likely in a running battle. The best scenario would be for the British merchants to strike as soon as they realized what was happening. Smalley was pretty sure shots would be necessary — if only to disclose their intentions, but hoped they would be more for show than harm. There was never a doubt that the three privateers would take prizes; the doubt concerned what would be left of them when the Americans boarded.

"Signal from *Freedom*, sir."

Smalley looked at the schooner sailing close to the wind on the opposite tack. Signal flags from her crossjack yard stood stiffly in the wind. The quartermaster who had mentioned it stood with the signal book in hand, waiting for the captain's acknowledgment.

"Aye, lad. What's it say?" The captain had a pretty good idea, but this signal book was different from ones he had used in the merchant service, having to do with battle plans, guns, and strategies. Abrams had developed it from one used by the Navy.

"It's directed at both us and *Rights*, sir. Says we're to fire when in position on the lead ship. *Freedom* will fire from leeward thereafter. Wait a moment, sir, there's another hoist . . . this one's not in the book, Cap'n; it's all letters. Says 'Aim low'. That's it, sir." The quartermaster looked questioningly at Smalley, awaiting a response.

The gaunt face split into a smile showing uneven teeth through thin lips that gave the appearance more of a grimace than a smile. "Show our number and 'Understood', quartermaster." He turned to Halladay, still on the quarterdeck.

"Looks like Captain Abrams must have made up his mind they're Brits, and appears he still has his sense of humor. Be sure our gunners know to fire into the hull if *Freedom's* on t'other side of their target, Mr. Halladay. You should have the hands piped to dinner now, even though it's still early. I want them fed afore we start shootin'. Soon as they've had their vittles, we'll clear for action."

"Aye, Cap'n. I s'pose it wouldn't do to lay a shot or two into Cap'n Abrams, now would it. I'll be sure it don't happen." Halladay's eyes sparkled, indicating a smile; his beard hid his mouth. He turned to instruct the Bosun to alert the cook and pipe the off-watch to their noontime meal. Grog would not be issued prior to the action, but the evening ration would be increased to offset the loss of this important staple in the life of a seaman. Halladay knew the cook would grouse at having to feed the men early, but he discounted it immediately; cook always groused at anything out of the norm, and after all, it was only an hour or so early. By the normal dinner time, the whole crew would have been fed and ready to take their action stations.

Captain Abrams, following a long tradition in most navies as well as the more organized private vessels, had established a very strict quarters bill for all his ships; every man jack had a specific position and job, all designed to fight the ships more efficiently. There were, for example, five gun crews for the deck guns, each with a gun captain, six seamen, and a boy to run the powder charges from the magazine to the gun. The long gun, mounted on a circular track amidships, had a larger crew. Others were assigned to handle sails, both on deck and aloft. The surgeon, assisted by the steward and carpenter, waited in the cockpit for casualties, while prize masters — on *Glory*, there were two, and on Abrams schooner, *Freedom*, there were three — filled in where necessary, replacing dead or wounded officers and petty officers as required. Captain Smalley could not think of any improvement to be made in this plan, and routinely trained his crew in their duties. They would all be tested soon enough in an action likely to be more demanding on the little schooners than any they had seen so far —

certainly than the last prizes they took which struck without a shot fired. He again reviewed in his mind the fighting of the ship, and satisfied that all would work out to his satisfaction, went below to see if his steward could put together some vittles for himself before he cleared for action.

To his pleasure, the table was set in his cabin — his sea chest served as the dining table — and the steward was standing by with a plate of chicken for his meal. Not the usual fare, but it certainly would suffice today. He had barely begun to eat when there was a knock at his door, and Third Mate Tillet stuck his head in. His voice put Smalley in mind of a stuck door being forced.

"Beggin' yer pardon, Cap'n. Mr. Halladay's compliments and it looks as if the Brits are gonna put up a fight. Would you come on deck, sir, quick as ever you please?"

By the time Smalley arrived on the quarterdeck, men were standing by their guns, and the hand weapons for boarding had been laid out by the mainmast. He looked at the two ships, now about a league off his larboard quarter, to windward. Both had raised British ensigns and men could be seen hurrying about on deck, and aloft as they set additional sail. *Rights* was close astern and slightly to leeward. He noticed Stebbins had already cleared for action and his windward guns were run out.

"You may pipe the men to quarters, Mr. Halladay, if you please. We'll take in the tops'ls and flying jibs now also."

The mate waved at the bosun, who instantly brought his pipe to his lips and blew the shrill notes that the men had been waiting for. Smalley realized that at least half his crew had not yet eaten, but it seemed to be of little import to them, given the likelihood of action, and more importantly, the prizes. The men aloft, coordinating with the heavers below, had the tops'ls almost under control; several of the more aggressive of the topmen were riding the tops'l yard down and gathering the sail in as it went slack in the bunts. The guns were run out of the open gun ports to weather, and as soon as the schooner eased her angle of heel, the leeward ports would be opened and those guns run out. The petty officers were moving through the vessel, encouraging the men and lending a hand where needed. Smalley knew that they would be cleared and ready for action in record time this day, and he nodded, almost to himself, in satisfaction. Seeing that *Glory* had crossed the bows of the two ships and now, with the weather gauge, was in control of the situation, he turned to the man at the wheel.

"Quartermaster, bring her down three points. Your course will parallel the British ships for now. Mr. Halladay, do not ease the sheets. My intention is to slow *Glory*, then when the first ship comes within range of the starboard battery, we will wear and fire as we cross her bows. If *Rights* does the same, we should give them something to think about. Cap'n Abrams on *Freedom* will see what we're about and support our move, I am sure."

Glory bore down, now less than half a league from the first British ship, and slightly ahead of her. Smalley could see the activity on the vessel, and wondered if they would fire first; his schooner was certainly in range of their guns. He suddenly realized that Stebbins had the American flag whipping from his mainmast, something he had neglected to think of. He turned to his mate.

"You may show our colors, now, if you please, Mr. Halladay." The mate looked at the captain, then glanced aloft; the captain followed his gaze and saw that his mate had already taken care of it.

"Thankee kindly, Mr. Halladay. I am glad you took the liberty . . ."

His words were cut off by a thunderous *boom* from across the water. He looked quickly at the British vessel. A huge cloud of smoke hung briefly over her bow before it was blown away by the wind. Looking forward, Smalley and Halladay saw a small geyser thrown up in front of their ship.

"We will bear off, now, and you may have the gunner fire as the starboard guns bear. Stand by to wear ship."

Halladay's bellow forward was overshadowed by another *boom*, but this one was not from the British ship. Tom Stebbins had fired the first American shot of the action, and his ball found its mark. Splinters flew from the bulwark of the Englishman, and even against the wind, the men on *Glory* could hear the cries of the wounded on the ship to leeward. *Glory* wore around, her heavy main boom flew across the deck, and the sails refilled with a satisfying *whoomp*. With their course almost directly downwind, the leeward gunports were now also open, and the guns run out.

The after guns, starboard side, found the target first, and each spoke in turn, belching smoke and flame and more importantly, an iron ball. The first shot was short; the gun captain had been overly concerned about firing low so as not to shoot over the ship and into *Freedom*, and the ball splashed half a length from the target. The next ones, however, found their mark and thudded resoundingly against the hull.

Now the forward gun was firing, and then the long tom amidships spoke with its deeper voice. Suddenly, a huge *boom* came from the British ship, greater by far than any of the preceding, and the second gun from the bow exploded, throwing men and iron into the air. Screams, punctuated by shouted orders from aft, added to the cacophony. Smalley saw it happen, but was unsure if a ball from *Glory* or *Rights* had done the damage. Regardless of whose shot it was, he was pleased, none-the-less, and spoke to the mate.

"Mr. Halladay, we will bring her back around to larboard, if you please. Signal Stebbins we intend to board. We should be able to catch them before they have restored order. Have the boarding party armed and standing by, and put some marksmen in the foretop with muskets as soon as the ship comes about."

The helm went down, and *Glory* rounded up smartly, passing stays as only a fore-and-aft rigged vessel can, coming back across the bows of the Britisher some one hundred yards distant. The swift schooner passed down the windward side of the larger ship, wore around again and wound up just off the vessel's quarter, paralleling her course. Neither ship fired a shot, though it was apparent to Smalley that the British master was doing his best to reorganize his crew and bring another gun into action. The fact that the ship was a merchant with only four guns for its own protection, combined with what appeared to be a short crew prevented him from fighting effectively. It surprised the captain that his opposite number didn't strike, faced as he was with overwhelming odds and guns that were old and obviously poorly maintained. It had become apparent that the explosion of the forward gun was not caused by a shot from either *Glory* or *Rights*; it simply blew up when the crew tried to fire it, and this of course, did nothing to inspire his crew to load and fire another.

Smalley saw that his boarders were standing by in the waist. Half a dozen seamen were scrambling up the windward ratlines with muskets strapped across their shoulders. He looked aft; *Rights* was now half a mile behind and firing into the hull of the other British ship. He noted that Stebbins was also receiving fire in return, but his ship looked unscathed. The American fire, either from *Rights* or *Freedom,* had taken down the main topmast of the second British merchant, and Smalley wondered to himself if she were short handed as well, how the master had managed to get men aloft to deal with the snarl of rigging as well as maintain sporadic fire from the main deck. He was still puzzled as to why these two were fighting at all, unless their masters thought a Royal Navy frigate might come along and help out.

Feeling a hand on his elbow, Smalley turned as First Mate Halladay gestured to the British ship, now nearly alongside. They could see a fevered bustle of activity amidships on the vessel, and realized they were trying to get a gun loaded and run out.

"Bear off. Bring us alongside quickly, now." Smalley spoke to the men on the big wheel and the schooner bore down on the ship, rapidly closing the few remaining yards separating them. "Standby with the grapnels — look lively there!" The ships were separated now by only half of the schooner's length, and the size disparity was more pronounced than before. The closer they got, Smalley realized, the more likely it was that the shot, if the British did in fact fire, would fly harmlessly over the schooner's much lower deck. No sooner had this thought crossed his mind when the amidships gun on the British ship fired with a thunderous roar, momentarily deafening Smalley and most of the men on *Glory*'s deck. The ball flew through the air six feet off the deck; it cut one of the starboard main shrouds as cleanly as though a knife had done it, and flew on, decapitating Third Mate Phineas Tillet, albeit less neatly. His headless body landed athwart the starboard nine-pounder, and what was left of his head rolled into the windward scuppers, the sightless eyes open in a gruesome stare. Nobody had time to grieve over the death of the third mate; *Glory* was alongside and the grapnels were sailing through the air. The boarders, led by prize master Tom Corbett, were at the schooner's bulwark, poised to leap the rail and clamber up the side of the larger ship. Already, the men in the foretop were firing, causing the men on the British ship to seek cover. There were only a few left in the Britisher's waist when the cry went out. Smalley and Halladay realized simultaneously that the officer they saw on the British ship wore the uniform of the Royal Navy — the ship was not a simple merchant vessel at all. Halladay spoke first.

"Well, that's why they fought us — they's Navy. Must be bringin' they's own prize in, and didn't want to give 'em up without they fit us. Musta' figgered we'd run off, bein' smaller 'an 'em. Guess they's got a surprise comin'."

By way of an answer, the captain turned toward the waist of his vessel and fairly bellowed, "Boarders away!" The two men stood on the quarterdeck, watching as the tough Maryland watermen swarmed aboard their prize. They met little resistance; the officer they had seen wearing the single epaulet of a Royal Navy Lieutenant was running forward from the quarterdeck waving a sword and screaming for his men to fight; most had laid down their arms, while a few tried to stem the tide of *Glory*'s sailors. He saw one of his men go down, a man named Samuels, he thought, and then the swarm of Glories had rounded up the Britisher's crew remaining on deck and faced the lieutenant with the sword. Realizing he was unlikely to prevail, the man wisely lowered his sword and doffed his hat to Smalley's second mate, Jack Clements, who had been leading the afterguard of the boarders. A cheer went up from the Americans and one of their number went aft to the taffrail to lower the British ensign. In fact, the man cut the halyard with his cutlass, and Smalley watched it flutter out behind the vessel, caught by the wind, before it fell into the sea astern.

CHAPTER TWENTY-THREE

A Reunion

"Have the commander brought aboard *Glory*, if you please, Mr. Halladay. And have the men over there check the below decks for hold-outs and cargo. Pass the word for the bosun, and let us see if we can do something about that starboard shroud." He saw that the surgeon's mates had already removed Tillet's body from the gun carriage and his head from the scuppers and presumed that the sailmaker was preparing a canvas shroud for its burial.

After some time, Halladay reported back to his captain.

"All the crew been found, sir. You was right on the mark. We catched a fair group hidin' out below — Frenchies as well as Brits, and they wasn't in no mood for a fight, I'm thinkin'. We gots 'em bein' watched 'midships. The cargo, what there was of it, was spices, tobacco, and a small amount of sugar. 'Cordin' to one of 'em, most of it already been off loaded when the Limey's first took the vessel. Corbett and his men are aboard, and the carpenter has looked at most of the biggest damage and said she's seaworthy. That damage what been done when the for'ard gun blew up wasn't too bad, 'ceptin' o' course the gun ain't fit for nothin' save heavin' over the side. 'At gun blew itself up; wasn't our shot what did it. Probably why them lads wasn't too keen on firing another 'un."

Most of the damage had been done by several shots from *Glory* striking the ship just above the waterline, the mate concluded, and he had put a crew, supervised by his carpenter's mate, to work repairing those holes. Some of the men had helped Samuels back to the schooner, carefully handing him down to the lower deck, where the surgeon looked at his wound. Not life threatening, but painful, Samuels would be returned to duty in a fortnight or so with a nasty scar on his thigh that would most likely enable him to drink for free in waterfront taverns for some time to come, as his story was told, and enhanced by the passage of time.

Suddenly, Smalley realized that he was not hearing any more firing from astern, and he turned to look. Both *Freedom* and *Bill of Rights* were tied alongside the other British ship. From what he could see, there was some action on deck, but with two boarding parties fighting against a short-handed crew, he figured it soon would be over. Hearing a quiet "Ahem" behind him, he turned, and found himself face to face with a strangely familiar man in the uniform of a Royal Navy Lieutenant. The lieutenant, obviously overwrought, blustered, saliva collecting at the corners of his mouth as he struggled to regain some of his dignity.

"Sir. I am Lieutenant Joseph Burns of His Majesty's Navy, and commander of the British vessel *Fleur*. While I know your country has most recently declared war against England, I most strongly protest this act of piracy on the high seas. You certainly do not appear to be a Naval ship, and as the rag-tag collection of civilians you most closely resemble, you can have no use whatever for this vessel. I demand that you release my men and ship at once so that we may return to our business of delivering this ship and the other vessel astern to Antigua."

"Lieutenant Burns, I am Captain Jedediah Smalley, commander of the schooner, *Glory*. We are sailing in company with Captain Joshua Abrams, under a commission as a private armed vessel from the President of the United States of America, Mr. James Madison. As such, we enjoy much the same status as a naval man of war, as far as you are concerned. I would be interested in knowing why a rather raggedy merchant is being sailed under the command of a Royal Navy officer, and why you have such a variety of additional men at your command. As to "piracy," your words must ring hollow as the practice is certainly not foreign to English ships; your country has been stopping and stripping crew from American vessels for . . ."

With the words "stripping crew . . ." it suddenly dawned on Smalley where he had seen this pompous lieutenant before; he had boarded *Anne* in the Atlantic just two years past and pressed three of Smalley's sailors on the pretext they were Englishmen avoiding service in His Majesty's Navy. He stared at Burns for a long moment, recalling the incident in which not only had three of his men been kidnapped, but one of his men shot dead by a Royal Marine. As he spoke his lips formed a thin line and his deep set eyes glowed like two coals as he recalled the incident, then a sparkle developed in them, and a tiny smile played at the corners of his mouth as he was struck with the irony of his present circumstance.

"It seems the tide has turned, Mr. Burns. Do you recall when last we met?" Seeing a puzzled look on the man's face, he continued. "No? Well, perhaps I can refresh your memory. I was in command of the American merchant vessel *Anne* which was stopped by your frigate *Orpheus* about two years back. I believe your parting words to me, if my memory doesn't fail me, were something to the effect that we colonists were going to be put in our place and it was your hope that you would be involved in the doing. It would appear the shoe is on the other foot; unfortunately you will not be returned to your ship. You will remain aboard *Glory* in confinement until I can get you to an American port where you will hopefully be imprisoned until the hostilities between our countries end. Good day to you. Mr. Halladay, have this man taken below and confined where he will be safe from any harm."

Smalley turned away from the English officer, who was by now purple with rage and speechless at this turn of events. Nobody, least of all some upstart from America, acts this way to an English officer, but here it was, and he was impotent to do anything about it. Halladay took the English officer by his elbow, and gently led him below. Unintelligible utterances, more closely akin to choking noises, dribbled from the lieutenant's mouth as his brain struggled to equate the facts before him with his own long-standing beliefs.

Smalley, only dimly aware of the disposition of Lieutenant Burns, was watching a knot of men on *Fleur*'s deck. They seemed to be having a lively discussion with one of the captured British sailors. Suddenly, *Glory's* second mate accompanied by one of his boarders and another, apparently a British seaman, detached themselves from the group and leaped the ship's rail, landing on *Glory's* main deck. They headed aft toward Smalley and Halladay, led by Jack Clements, whose gangly form and impishly smiling face gave no hint of his mission.

"Cap'n, this cove claims to be an American, and wants to sign on with us. Sounds enough like one to me, but I don't know if'n you want to sign on a sailorman off'n a Britisher. Might be a spy or somethin'." He winked at his captain, and shoved the seaman in question forward.

"My God, it is you, Cap'n Smalley. I am Isaac Biggs. I sailed as captain of the foretop on *Anne,* sir. Pressed by Lieutenant Burns into the frigate *Orpheus* two years and more ago. Do you remember me, sir?"

Now it was Smalley's turn to be thunderstruck. He stared at the man, while a flood of memories of the old *Anne* flooded back. His satisfaction at confronting the man in charge of the British seagoing press gang was prize enough, but liberating one of the pressed men was a bonus he hadn't expected. Many pressed seamen are not soon heard from.

"Welcome aboard, Biggs. Of course I remember you." He turned to the second. "This man is no more a spy than you are, Mr. Clements. Sign him into the ship's articles . . . Wait a moment, Mr. Clements." He paused, thinking. He looked sharply at the American sailor. "As I recall, Biggs, you had been studying some navigation with Mr. Clark back on *Anne.* I would doubt you've had much opportunity to keep up with it in the Royal Navy, but mebbe you kin remember enough to be of some help. And I reckon Mr. Halladay might help refresh them skills." Seeing the confused look on Biggs' face, he continued.

"I have no third mate, Biggs. Tillet was killed in the action with *Fleur.* I am sure Captain Abrams will have no problem with it, if you're interested in filling Tillet's berth."

Now Biggs was speechless. When he found his wits, he smiled broadly and bobbed his head, his curly hair bouncing, his eyes alight with joy. "Yes sir, Cap'n. I would be most grateful for that. I won't let you down, neither, sir. Thank you. And I'll work real hard at gettin' back my navigatin' quick as ever I can, sir."

"Very well, then. Get whatever slops you have and Clements, here, will show you to Tillet's berth." Smalley dismissed the men by turning back toward the prize. The sailor who had accompanied Clements and Biggs from the prize looked at Biggs now in a new light, appraising him as possibly the luckiest man in the West Indies. It was unusual enough for a pressed sailor to be rescued, but by the captain under whom he'd served, and then be made an officer into the bargain!

Halladay stepped to the rail next to Smalley. Waiting until Clements and Biggs were out of earshot, he ran a big hand through his beard, trying to put his concerns into words without appearing to question the decision of his captain. A scowl crossed his face like a shadow, then passed. After hesitating, he determined that the only course was to say it straight out.

"Cap'n, I know it ain't my place to say nothin', but they's men aboard qualified to fill Tillet's berth. This Biggs fellow might be gonna have a problem with some of 'em, bein's how he ain't been aboard but a few minutes." Halladay tried as tactfully as he could to suggest that Smalley's decision was wrong, but the captain would have none of it.

"You mark my words, Mr. Halladay; that man is a natural leader, and unless I'm getting forgetful, he'll do just fine. He sailed with me first as able seaman on *Anne*, and worked his way to captain of the foretop. And he convinced the mate to teach him navigatin' on top of it. He's a fine sailor, and men work willingly for him. If my memory ain't gone, I was lookin' for a third mates' berth for him then. He don't know 'bout bein' an officer, but I think you can help him out with that."

Realizing his captain's mind was set, Halladay nodded and said, "Aye, that I can. Looks like Mr. Corbett's got his crew ready to sail that vessel, now, sir. Should we cut 'em loose?"

"If you please, Mr. Halladay. Have the men stand by to bring *Glory* about. We shall see what is happening with the other ship. 'Pears as though Stebbins and Cap'n Abrams have got everything under control, but we'll have a look."

Captain Smalley watched as his mate gave the orders to retrieve the grapnels and as the ships separated, he shouted over the water to Mr. Corbett, the prize master on *Fleur*.

"Stay hove to for a bit, Corbett. We'll be back with instructions in a trice. We've got to figure where Cap'n Abrams wants to take the prizes." A wave from Corbett acknowledged his understanding, and he quickly sent men aloft to furl tops'ls and tie a reef into the forecourse. As *Glory* slipped away to windward, *Fleur* was brought 'round closer to the wind where she would lie hove to until Smalley returned with orders.

By the time *Glory* arrived at the second British, formerly French, and now apparently American ship, all was quiet. Activity on both *Bill of Rights* and *Freedom* indicated that they were getting ready to cast off from the larger ship. The English colors had been removed from her, and an American flag fluttered in the now gentle breeze from the mizzentop. As Smalley watched from his quarterdeck, a flag hoist climbed to the top of *Freedom*'s mainmast. The quartermaster was at the captain's side with the book before the flags were two-blocked. A look from the captain was all the prompting he needed.

" 'Heave to. Well done. Captains repair aboard'. . . that's it, sir." The quartermaster closed the book, keeping his finger in the place in case more flags appeared.

"Very well. Thank you. Mr. Halladay, you may have the bosun pipe secure from quarters. Have my boat crew assembled and put the cutter overboard as soon as we are hove to, if you please. I have been summoned aboard *Freedom*. Stay hove to with *Rights* and the prize, as I expect I shall be back promptly with Cap'n Abrams' instructions. You can use the time to get our new third mate acquainted with the schooner and the men. I will conduct a burial for Mr. Tillet quick as ever we are underway again."

After the schooner was hove to and order restored, Smalley watched as the boat was rigged to a tackle from the foremast gaff, swung out, and lowered into the water to leeward. He noted with satisfaction that his cutter was ready a full two minutes before Tom Stebbins' crew had his boat ready. He sent below for his hat, and after jamming it onto his head, climbed over the schooner's bulwark and stepped onto the larboard channel for the main shrouds. When the cutter rose on a wave, he stepped in as smoothly as a younger man might have, and told his coxswain to carry him to *Freedom*, lying hove to a scant musket shot away.

CHAPTER
TWENTY-FOUR

Arrival and Shore Leave

By the end of the second week in September of 1812, Abrams' schooners had escorted their prizes to the southwest corner of the recently independent nation of Haiti, on the island of Hispanola, where Captain Abrams believed there to be an Haitian prize court which he hoped would fairly adjudicate their prizes. After discussion with his captains, he had made the decision not to sail the prizes back to a U.S. port as their letter of instructions had indicated; there were simply too many British warships in these waters and sailing a lightly armed prize through them would be perilous at best, as he had so recently proved to the British. Yes, they agreed, better to get the vessels into friendly — or at least neutral — hands as quick as ever possible. Had they been traveling alone in fine weather, *Freedom, Bill of Rights,* and *Glory* could have made the trip from the north coast of Puerto Rico, east of the Mona Passage, in under a week. As it was, they had a week of unusually contrary winds and generally inclement weather which caused the square-rigged merchants to sail a course well off that which would take them through the Mona Passage and then west to Haiti, and with the short-handed crews on both prizes, setting a press of canvas when the wind did turn fair was out of the question.

Smalley, as well as the other captains, and most of their crews were frustrated and generally short-tempered by the time the little flotilla turned the corner of Haiti and set their course for Port-au Prince. Maintaining constant vigilance for not only British men-of-war, but also for additional merchants which might be added to their prize fleet, had contributed heavily to the men being out of sorts. The captain's normally gaunt face seemed even more drawn, his eyes deeper into their sockets.

Only one person on *Glory* would have been happier had the journey taken longer, or a British frigate appeared out of nowhere. Lieutenant Joseph Burns, late of His Majesty's Navy, remained confined below. He was allowed one hour per day topside, and that with an armed guard. After about a week at sea, the sailor with his musket was excused from guard duty and Burns could move freely about the deck. Their arrival in Port-au-Prince meant nothing to him but further confinement and the likelihood that Smalley would not ask him for his parole to be left ashore in Haiti. He had spent the bulk of his time on *Glory* hatching plans to escape, either in Haiti or at sea. So far, there had been no opportunity for the latter, and the plan he had devised for the former depended on a host of chance happenings in his favor. Unlike his shipmates on the schooner, Mr. Burns was not a happy man as *Glory* and her sister privateers escorted their prizes into the harbor at Port-au-Prince.

Setting their anchors in the clear waters of the harbor, the schooners and their prizes created a minor sensation among the townspeople, and most certainly among the officials of the city. Having seen the American flags flying from all ships, the city fathers knew prizes would be auctioned off after their condemnation by one of Alexandre Petion's prize courts, and that meant fees and commissions for them. In addition, it was likely that the buyers of the vessels would be the mulatto gentry planters and merchants who had ascended to the top of the Haitian hierarchy after leading the rebellion which had killed most of the white French some five years previously. Those who survived the massacre escaped the island, leaving most of their possessions behind for the rebels. The tavern and shop keepers knew that their businesses would increase dramatically with the plethora of sailors heading for the pleasures that Port au Prince offered, and soon a festive air filled the city, echoed by the men on the ships; they were looking forward to getting ashore for the first time since leaving Baltimore. Of course, there was also the matter of the prize shares. The men knew they would see no cash until their return to Baltimore, but they would be able to draw advances against their share tickets which according to the scuttlebutt, would be distributed as quickly as the sales were consummated.

"Deck there! Small boat approaching . . . looks like some dandy in the stern sheets." The watchman halfway up the foremast rigging hailed the petty officer stationed in the waist of *Glory*. "Looks like another headin' fer *Fleur*. Looks like they's all black men — crew and passengers alike."

"Boat ahoy! What be your business?" The petty officer hailed the boat closing *Glory* and waited while a hasty conference was held between the "dandy" and what could only have been his assistant. The end result was a friendly wave from the boat, with broad smiles all around. The men on watch had summoned Mr. Halladay, but as yet, he had not appeared. Watch petty officer Johnson picked up a musket, as did one of his men, and leveled them over the bulwark at the approaching boat.

"Stop there. Don't come any closer, or you'll have the devil to pay, and no pitch hot." He waited, and was rewarded with more broad smiles and friendly waves. Still the boat continued. "*Alto,*" he shouted, trying some of the little Spanish he had command of, and thinking to himself, if they don't speak English, they *must* speak Spanish. The oarsmen hesitated. He was getting through! But there it must end, as he was unable to call to mind any more of the language. Fortunately, it was unnecessary.

"What's your problem, Johnson?"

Halladay's arrival startled the petty officer, so intent was he on the boat approaching. He collected himself and explained to the first mate, who was watching the boat with some interest. He finished his concerns with ". . . and they're all black as night, crew an' them in the fancy uniforms as well."

"Johnson, this here's Haiti. Ain't no white folks here at all far's I know for the last four or five years now. They was all killed or run off when the locals rebelled and decided they wasn't goin' to have the Frenchies in charge no more. These coves here look like some kind o' harbor officials, be my guess. Probably comin' to get a fee or see if we're carryin' disease. They's a lot of disease, includin' the Yellow Jack, on some o' these islands. Let the fancy-pants and his mate aboard, but keep them others in the boat." He thought a second, then added. "And keep the boat layin' off a half a length or so. I'll step aft and fetch Cap'n Smalley. Keep 'em here 'til he comes to greet him."

The mate moved off, the boat came alongside, and the coxswain shouted up to the deck in a language Johnson did not understand. The American had no idea what was said, but he knew that "fancy-pants" could not get aboard without they dropped him the man-ropes. Once they were provided, and without further comment or fuss, "fancy-pants" scampered up the side and stood expectantly on the schooner's deck. He looked around, smiling broadly, obviously waiting to be greeted by someone in authority, and hardly noticed Johnson in duck pantaloons and patched jersey. He called down to the boat in the same language used by the coxswain which Johnson and his men still did not understand, and the other man climbed out of the stern sheets and up the ladder. Johnson motioned the boat away from *Glory*'s side while the two men conferred quietly.

"Cap ee tan?" The second arrival spoke to Johnson.

"I ain't the Cap'n, nor do I have any want to be him. He'll be right along, though. You gents just stand fast here." Johnson's words drew more blank looks from the visitors, but over their shoulders, he saw Captain Smalley and Halladay heading toward the group. "Here's the 'Cap ee tan', now." The dandies followed the American's outstretched arm, and seeing the two men approaching, stepped toward them, babbling excitedly in their language.

The blank look on both Smalley's and Halladay's faces dismayed the men; surely men educated enough to be captains would speak a civilized tongue! The frustrated officials spoke more rapid fire patois, raising their voices to assist in the Americans' comprehension.

"I think they're talkin' in French, or somethin' close to it. Mr. Halladay. I got precious little of it myself, but I believe they's some French sailors on *Fleur* we might get some help from. I'll see if I can make 'em understand we're gettin' an interpreter, and you send a boat over and tell Corbett to send over one of his prisoners to help us out here."

"Aye, Cap'n. On my way." The mate welcomed the opportunity to distance himself from the politics and procedures that appeared to be looming on the horizon. He had no trouble facing down an enemy frigate, or even leading a boarding party, but he wanted no part of this diplomatic nonsense, especially in some language he did not understand. He stepped quickly to where one of the schooner's boats was secured, grabbed the crew and went over the rail. Smalley was surprised to see his mate personally handling such a trivial errand, but assumed it was another example of Halladay's conscientious attention to detail.

"Gentlemen," Smalley turned his attention to his visitors. "Won't you please join me in my cabin for a glass?" He accompanied his words with gestures, first to the officials, then to himself, and finally, he pantomimed raising a glass to his mouth. All the while, he smiled warmly, and motioning to the men to follow, headed aft. He glanced back once to ensure they were, and continued below. Having heard that "things" were going on up on deck, the captain's steward had set out on the "dining table" the cut glass decanter and glasses. Smalley was pleased to see that a passable port was in the decanter. He sensed that these two emissaries would likely be offended at something less.

The port was drunk to a pantomime of gestures; neither Smalley nor his guests could understand one another, and eventually, the effort proved too much, and silence ensued. After what seemed like an eternity to the captain, a discrete knock announced the return of his first mate and a French petty officer from *Fleur* who spoke passable English. The French sailor bowed and greeted the Haitian officials and Captain Smalley, each in their own language; he then explained to the Americans that while these two "apes" spoke Creole, a "much lower dialect of the mother tongue," they could manage to make themselves understood in French, given the *extraordinaire* patience of "your 'umble interpreter." Halladay beamed, and Smalley immediately took hold of the situation. He suggested to the French sailor that calling the officials "apes" served no purpose whatever, and "If you think you might make yerself understood, let's get on with it." The French sailor, reddened and nodded, turning to the two Haitians.

After seemingly interminable prologues, the diplomats began to explain the purpose of their visit; not only was there a port charge for the ships, but if the "larger ships were to be sold here, monsieur, there would, of course be a great deal of difficulty with local laws, but we are in a position to be of some help, should there be the right incentive."

Smalley smiled at his mate, and nodded his understanding. Then he answered.

"Of course, gentlemen, I am but one captain of several. You should be dealing with our commodore, Captain Abrams on *Freedom.*" He waited while the French sailor translated, then continued. "He can discuss his plans for providing for our own crews. As to the sale of the ships, our prizes, Cap'n Abrams is of the belief that one of your prize courts will handle that. I believe he plans to handle personally disposition of the foreign crews in due course."

The Haitians stood abruptly, apparently miffed that it took this long to tell them they were in the wrong place, dealing with the wrong captain. They uttered something which caused the French sailor to color noticeably, but not translate. Within minutes, they were over the side, taking the prisoner from *Fleur* with them, directing their crew to pull for the schooner commanded by Joshua Abrams. Neither official had looked nearly as dignified while going over the rail as when they had arrived, and indeed, the junior of the two nearly fell out of the boat as it shoved off, but their stiff attitudes gave no hint of embarrassment, if in fact they felt any. Halladay was laughing so hard he had tears cutting a path through the salt crust on his cheeks before they disappeared into his beard. Smalley continued watching with a neutral expression, but the sparkle in his eyes betrayed his own enjoyment of the situation.

Later in the afternoon watch, the lookout called to the deck. "Signal flags on *Freedom*." The captain was called, after the quartermaster was found and without even looking in the book, told the watch that the flags meant "Captains to *Freedom*." Smalley appeared in his standard rig, including his hat and black frock coat, and was rowed the few hundred yards to Abrams' ship.

His return was cause for most of the hands to appear on deck, more than a few in their shore gear. The sailors pressed as close as they dared to hear what their captain would say to Mr. Halladay; there was barely a sound, save the creaking of leather "shore-side" footwear, and the occasional grunt as someone got elbowed by his mate who tried to get within earshot. The men in the front ranks heard, and let out a lusty cheer; the word traveled quickly to the rest — there would be leave for the starbowlines and idlers at once. Larbowlines would go tomorrow! The schooner's boats were pressed into service and without delay, nearly half the *Glory's* men were on their way to the taverns, shops, and brothels of Port au Prince. Those who could not get into the first boats and had no stomach for waiting, hailed passing small boats and began negotiating for transport ashore.

Isaac Biggs, watching from a perch atop the number two gun, could not help but compare American order and discipline with that of the Royal Navy, his home for the past two years. He could not fathom what might be Captain Winston's reaction to this unruly mob; of course it was unlikely that Captain Winston would ever be in a position to react to such a display — it just would not occur. There were many other dissimilarities as well, most notably the total lack of flogging on the American privateers; indeed, Biggs was not even sure there was a cat o' nine tails aboard *Glory*. It was fine with him. These American sailors didn't need to be flogged to do their duty; they were all fine seaman, most of whom had been to sea since boys, and respected their captain and mates because their leaders earned it, not because they flogged the crew into submission. Biggs thought he would like to stay on the privateer. The word among the crew, and indeed, Mr. Halladay had pretty much confirmed it, was that they'd be back in Baltimore before the end of November, giving them a cruise of less than one hundred twenty days. He hoped that perhaps Smalley would sign him permanently as third mate, recognizing the progress he had made with his navigation and learning the skills of the quarterdeck. He thought of the men he would never see again from *Orpheus:* Toppan, Wallace, Coleman, Bosun Tice, and old gunner Chase. Some of the midshipmen weren't half bad boys, he thought. Too bad they'll not get the chance to sail on a ship where pride, not fear, was the prime motivator. Suddenly he jumped to his feet.

"Wait a minute." He didn't realize he was speaking aloud. His eyes lit up as he smacked a fist into his other hand. "Coleman's right over there locked down in the hold of *Fleur*. I 'spect he'd come sail on *Glory*, given the chance . . . Mr. Halladay. Could I speak to you for a moment?"

"What's on yer mind, Isaac? I was just about to get into my shore rig. Ain't you heading ashore your own self? I'd reckon 'bout half your starbowlines are drunker than billy goats, by now."

"Aye, Mr. Halladay. I am goin'. Just got to thinkin' though. There's a mighty good topman over there in *Fleur*. Man named Coleman. He was on *Orpheus* and captain of the maintop. He might sign on *Glory*. Bet he'd jump at the chance."

"'Spect as how he would. I know I would sign on even as a seaman afore I'd stay locked up in the hold of some ship. How do you know he won't cause no trouble . . . an' what happens if we run into the Royal Navy or some British merchant? You think he'd fight his own people? I don't know, Biggs, he might be a problem lookin' for some place to set a hook, but if'n you think he's so good and won't be no trouble, I'll mention it to Cap'n Smalley, see what he thinks."

"Thank you. I think he'd be right at home on *Glory* — fit in real good and, like I said, he's a fine sailor. Ain't got no love for the Royal Navy, neither."

Willard Halladay nodded and headed below; Biggs sat down on the gun carriage again, smiling at the prospect of seeing his friend and former shipmate again.

"Biggs . . . How does it feel to be back on a Yankee ship again?" Isaac turned at the strong, aristocratic English accent, and looked right into the face of Lieutenant Joseph Burns, Royal Navy. Habits die hard, and Biggs leaped to his feet in the presence of an officer, surprised at his sudden appearance. The Englishman, dressed in a soiled shirt and equally stained breeches, smiled at him. "It would appear we've changed roles, now, eh, Biggs? Here I am being watched by some rag-tag sailor with a gun while you are an officer on the vessel. A fine turn of events, wouldn't you say?"

"Yes, sir, I would." To Biggs, Burns was still an officer, still to be called 'sir' and still to be feared. His disheveled appearance, torn stockings and obviously drawn face diminished not a whit his bearing and demeanor as a lieutenant in the Royal Navy. "I guess it was my good luck and your bad luck that *Fleur* didn't make it to Antigua. Sorry about the guard, but I guess Cap'n Smalley ordered that started up again now we're in a harbor. Are you going to be put ashore here with the others, sir? "

"I am really not certain, Biggs. Your Captain Smalley has not asked for my parole here and seems committed to the notion that I should be taken to America to be held until the hostilities end." All the while Burns was talking to Biggs, his eyes darted everywhere watching the shoreline and taking in the lack of activity on *Glory*'s deck. The sailor assigned to guard him was leaning casually against the foremast, smoking a pipe and studying what he could see of the town of Port au Prince; his musket rested on the fife rail several feet away.

Seizing the opportunity, Burns vaulted over the rail and hit the water with a loud splash, stroking strongly for the shore as soon as he surfaced. Hearing the splash, his guard grabbed the gun and ran to the side the of schooner. He sighted the musket over the rail on the Englishman's back, cocked the weapon, and waited for a clear shot at his charge. As the hammer fell, Biggs grabbed the barrel of the gun, knocking it sideways and spoiling any chance the sailor might have had to shoot the British lieutenant.

"What's the point, sailor? What are you gonna prove by shooting the man in the back? Let him go. If he makes it to shore, there's others there he's got to get around. You may see him yet again."

"Aye, sir. I understand, but Mr. Halladay's gonna have my arse for lettin' him jump. He ain't as easy goin' as you, Mr. Biggs."

"I'll tell the mate. He ain't gonna give you a bad time. If you'd been on a British Navy ship, though, you'd be given a floggin' you probably wouldn't live through . . . and me beside you. Go on 'bout your business now, while I go find Mr. Halladay."

CHAPTER TWENTY-FIVE

A Waterfront Tavern

When the noise and fighting died down and order was restored in the tavern, the four men, who only moments before had been sitting around a table, stood their chairs back up and picked up the two tankards that had overturned in the scuffle, signaling the barmaid to refill them. A drunken topman from *Freedom* had insisted that the commodore's ship was better sailed, with a better crew than any of the other schooners; naturally any crewman not on *Freedom* took immediate and physical exception to the statement. Soon it didn't matter which ship someone was from, if they were within reach, they got hit. A free-for-all ensued, and even two of the men sitting at the table had become involved; it would have been impossible not to with the entire tavern a sea of swinging fists, bottles, chairs and the occasional knife. The three mates dining with Captain Smalley, assisted by the local constabulary, cleared the room out to the dirt street, and once there, the fighting seemed to wither and die. Discussions immediately ensued among the now friendly sailors as to which establishment would next be blessed with their presence.

"When will the ships be condemned and sold, Cap'n? We've been here nigh on to two weeks, and I'd o' thought those ships would be handled by now. I thought the prize court would condemn 'em right quick, bein's how they probably ain't real busy right now." Second Mate Jack Clements, still standing and dusting off his shirt while dabbing at the trickle of blood on his chin, spoke freely to his captain. Halladay and Biggs, the latter still tucking in his shirt, waited for Captain Smalley to answer. They were ready to get back to sea, and each had wondered how many men they would be leaving behind, or bringing back aboard incapacitated from the kind of activity they had just witnessed.

"Cap'n Abrams said it's done, Mr. Clements. Everything is taken care of now, and I 'spect we'll be gettin' under way in the next two or three days. Some Haitian judge has already signed the condemnation order and the buyers likely will sign the sale tomorrow, I'm thinkin'. It was our good luck that that planter fellow showed up when he did, and wanted both vessels; otherwise who knows how long these monkeys might have danced us around. They still gettin' used to their independence — only been 'bout five years now, and they think everyone's out to get 'em. I guess havin' one o' they's own tellin' 'em to get it done helped more 'n' a little." Smalley smiled at the thought; it was the first time he had found anything cheering since their first visit ashore. A ray of sunshine was most welcome, as heretofore he, Abrams, and Stebbins had been frustrated, thwarted, and inconvenienced at every turn by the Haitians, who trusted no one, were in no particular hurry, and saw opportunity at every transaction occurring on their island.

"It'll be good to be back to sea again, I'll warrant," he continued, as anxious as his mates to get this business over and get back to harassing the British. "Willard, do you think you'll have men sufficient to sail *Glory?* Seems like whichever of 'em's not in the local hoosegow's been hurt or got sick with somethin' or other. Maybe we ought to start roundin' 'em up in the morning."

Halladay's eyes grew serious as his mind, fuzzy from drink, struggled to return to the business of the ship. "Aye sir. I had figured to be doin' that anyway. Take Biggs, here, with me. Them what's aboard now ought to stay there, I'm thinkin'."

Smalley nodded at his mate, and looked at Biggs, a scowl crossed his face, giving away the fact that he still didn't completely forgive the man for preventing the sentry from shooting the escaping Lieutenant Burns. Biggs had stood in the cabin after the event for some time while Smalley gave vent in an uncharacteristically loud voice to his wrath, something Biggs had not seen even once in the years he sailed on *Anne* with the captain. All manner of thoughts went through the young man's mind as he listened to the captain's rage, the foremost concerning his newly acquired status as an officer.

The upshot of the event was that Smalley felt cheated out of bringing the British officer to the United States for holding and perhaps confinement. Biggs had managed to calm his captain down, at the same time, saving his job as third mate, by pointing out that it was he, Biggs, who had served close to two years on a British frigate under Burns, and all the animosity had worn away. After all, Biggs added, didn't their Methodist parsons teach them that to forgive is divine? Finally, Smalley regained his composure and dismissed his third mate, allowing the incident to pass, and the business of the ship resumed. He did, however, send a small party of sailors, led by First Mate Halladay, ashore with instructions to find the British officer. A two-day search of Port au Prince turned up no sign of the escaped Lieutenant Burns, and Smalley reluctantly had given up hope of catching the man. Either he was drowned 'in his effort to swim ashore, or had successfully evaded his pursuers.

"Mr. Clements, that'll put you aboard and makin' sure that those what come aboard, stay. Also, you might see Cap'n Abrams' purser and draw some cash, as I 'spect we'll be needin' some stores and provisions. And see that the carpenter has got that pump fixed right this time, or he'll be in the bilge with a bucket for an hour each watch." The tone in Smalley's voice belied his words, and Clements and the others knew their captain's good mood had not played out. Dinner would be pleasant, now that the more boisterous of the tavern's patrons had moved on.

The four men enjoyed their meal, relishing the unique island cooking heavy with the influence of the French who had occupied Haiti until the rebellion. The barmaid kept their tankards filled with ale, and the conversation flowed evenly.

"Mr. Halladay tells me you think there's a topman from the British frigate might want to sail with us, Mr. Biggs." Smalley's casual remark had caught the third mate off guard; he had assumed that, having heard nothing further since he mentioned it to Halladay, the matter had died when the prisoners were transferred from *Fleur* to the beach, and given their parole.

"Uh, aye, sir. I sailed with him in *Orpheus* for all the time I was aboard. A fine sailor he is and good with the men as well. One of the few, if memory serves, what didn't get a taste of the cat, 'least while I was aboard. But I thought all the British and the others was put ashore, long as they agreed not to ship out on a man o' war."

"Aye, they were indeed put ashore, and on their parole on top of it. After all, the ships couldn't very well be sold with them still aboard! Since it is likely we'll be sailin' short-handed in a few days, I would take any of 'em which wants to sign on, and which 'pears to be able. Your man included. They's only a few places where they might be layin' up, given that they ain't got any money, and Mr. Halladay, here, can likely help you find 'em while you're collectin' the rest of the Glories. Any o' the others from that crew 'at you know and who knows a bowsprit from a sheet block, why, bring 'em along. Same wages as the rest and a share of future prizes."

"What about when *Glory* puts back into Baltimore, sir? What of the British crewmen then?"

"What of 'em? I reckon they's damn near as many foreign sailors workin' our vessels as American right about now. Least 'ways, they's a lot of Britishers — come over to American ships to sail without fear of the cat, and for better wages, I'd guess — and the war be damned. Shouldn't be a problem there." Halladay answered the question, but Smalley nodded his agreement, and added his own observation.

"We won't be gettin' back up to the Chesapeake for another few months anyway. No tellin' what'll happen by then. Our business for now is down here and those men can help us out. We'll worry 'bout Baltimore when we raise Cape Henry over the horizon. I don't 'spect the owners'll have a fight over some British sailors aboard — probably enjoy the thought of them raisin' Cain with their own countrymen."

"What of me when we get back to Baltimore, Cap'n? Will I be stayin' on *Glory* as third? From what I've seen in the month and more I been here, I'd like it fine. She's a fine ship 'at sails better 'an anything I ever sailed, save the fishin' schooners I sailed as a boy with my Pa on the Banks." Biggs had been giving this matter some thought and decided — with the help of liberal quantities of rum and ale, and the casual setting — that now might be as good a time as any to collect some insight on his future.

Smalley accommodated him, with a thin smile, and a genuine warmth in his eyes. "Long as I have *Glory,* Biggs, you got a berth. You keep studyin' your navigatin' and the business of the quarter-deck, and they's no reason you got to stay as a third mate; no sir, you could see second, first and even master down the road were you to apply yourself and learn from men like Halladay and Clements. You need have some ability with numbers and the like, but I'd warrant you could manage it."

Isaac Biggs beamed, briefly picturing himself as captain on his own quarterdeck. How proud would Mother and Father be then, assuming they were still alive. At this, a shadow passed over his face, as he thought of how long it had been since he had seen his folks, and he resolved to get himself to Marblehead quick as ever he could when they returned to America. But he couldn't escape the sincerity of the captain's compliment, even though, he reckoned, by morning the words would only be a dim buzz, and hard to remember, but right now, they sounded mighty good. Maybe this was worth the two years he spent as a pressed seaman on a British frigate; *Glory* was a fine sailing vessel with an even tempered captain who was first a sailor, then an officer, and the prospect of prize shares was appealing. Thinking of prize shares, Biggs' face again clouded over briefly as he recollected the prize shares he was owed by the Royal Navy from the capture of the French merchants.

Well, he thought, I *had figured to use that money to get myself off the frigate, and here I am, off. Pounds well spent, I guess; I'm on an American ship jest as I wanted, and I ain't got the money, but I reckon I'll manage fine. Things have took care of themselves, more or less like I figgered. Mebbe I'm even better off than I figgered to be.* He suddenly realized the captain was speaking and refocused his eyes and attention on the man.

". . . have more important things to do than sit here with me." Captain Smalley spoke to all of them. "I'm going to go back out to *Glory* and see to some paperwork. I'd warrant you gents can find something or someone to amuse your own selves for the remainder of the evening. Mr. Clements, I 'spect I'll be seeing you on deck first thing?" The tone Smalley used made the observation rhetorical, and Clements nodded, mumbling "Aye" or something similar through drink thickened tongue and lips. The sparkle in his eyes seemed brighter, perhaps fueled by the rum he'd been drinking and he fingered the gold ring in his ear. He unfolded his tall frame, and as he started to rise, pushed back his chair so that it fell over with a crash; it went unheeded. The others rose as one and wove their way out the door, separating to go their own ways once on the street.

CHAPTER TWENTY-SIX

New Hunting Grounds

"Heave around together . . . put your backs into it . . . listen to the fiddle, you left-footed lubbers, and step like you'd been to sea once before." Winning their anchor and making sail had always been chores that Halladay hated after a prolonged period ashore. It seemed like all his men staggered and stumbled, and the concept of walking the capstan around or heaving on the mains'l halyard together was totally foreign to them. Once they sobered up and worked through their monstrous hangovers, they would once again function like the smooth working, well-trained crew they in fact were. Right now, he'd be just as happy with sober, untrained farmers — at least they could listen and be shown.

Several days after the officers had dined together ashore, most of the crew had been found and *Glory*, *Freedom*, and *Bill of Rights* had severed their tenuous relationship with the shore to sail smoothly out of Port au Prince harbor, looking for all the world like innocent, albeit rakish, coastal schooners carrying goods between the islands. No flags flew at their mastheads as they sailed a generally northwesterly course.

Abrams had decided to try their luck above Cuba, sailing through the Windward Passage and up towards the Bahamas. With Britain's northern West Indian fleet sailing out of Nassau, he figured to have some degree of success. He admonished, perhaps unnecessarily, his captains to "Mind the shoals up there — water's thin as a whore's virtue in places." Their plan was essentially the same as it had been; they would sail in a widely spaced line across the wind so that the lookouts could cover a huge amount of ocean. At night, the standard light signals would be used should any potential prizes be spotted. He had met with his captains on *Freedom* the day before departure. After discussing their next area of operations, he hauled out a small trunk and set it on the deck of the cabin.

"Gentlemen, here it is. Some of the fruits of our labors. You and your crews all will share in this, as you know, and I have had Richards, my purser, go over the accounts in the greatest detail." With a grand flourish, Abrams opened the chest, and as the bright sun, streaming in through the skylight, hit the contents a radiant glow emanated from within. Smalley and Stebbins watched as the lid came all the way up and saw the chest was filled about three-fourths of the way up with gold coin, some loose, and some apparently in small leather bags.

"We're not going to distribute that before we get home are we, Joshua?" Tom Stebbins had done this before, and knew from sad experience that paying out prize shares to a crew in foreign ports would result only in a lot of heartbreak, not to mention broken heads. No, it was more prudent to hold the shares until such time as the ship returned to her home port and the crew paid off. Besides, the owners would handle the distribution along with the courts, and it was only in the most unusual cases where the captain paid out cash.

"Not on your life, Tom. You know me better'n that. No, I will give each of you your ship's share to hold aboard until we get back to Baltimore. That way, if something happens to any one of us, the other crews' shares aren't lost as well. We should have more'n we do here, but those damn Haitian agents had a fee or commission comin' out ever' time I turned around. When that judge told me to negotiate the sale of the two after he condemned 'em, I knew I was in for a devil of a time. If it wasn't the port authorities themselves, it was the merchants. A trial, by all that's holy. I'm telling you, that's the last time I want anything to do with sellin' prizes. The owner's agents and court clerks who do that work earn their fees, they do, and you won't hear me begrudgin' them again. After dealin' with these thieves here . . . I'm tellin' you, what a misery!" Captain Abrams shook his head as if to clear the memory of the frustration.

Jed Smalley, like most privateer captains, had never been involved in the sale of prizes and could only imagine what Abrams was talking about, but he had a good idea from the brief exposure he'd had to the "port officials," that the negotiation with the arrogant and determined ship brokers must have been a frustrating affair indeed. He was pleased to see the results here on the deck before him, and knew the money would be a godsend to most of his men's families, his own included.

Abrams explained again the way the shares were to be divided between the ships and then between the men, all in accordance with the vessel's Articles of Agreement. Naturally, the owners' shares came out first and would be maintained aboard *Freedom.* Under normal circumstances, where the owners had an agent in residence in any but their home port, the captain would be advanced funds for provisioning the ship, paying the crew and the like, while the balance would be retained for payment by the owners upon the ship's return. Since there was no U.S. ship's agent in Port au Prince, Captain Abrams had wisely decided to take the money in gold, and not trust to the wiles of Haitian bankers or brokers. The balance of the funds, after the owners' shares, were for the officers and crews of the three schooners, and it looked to Smalley like quite a tidy sum.

Yes, indeed, he thought. *This money, along with the shares from those two we sent into Charleston, will go a long way.* A captain only gets paid when he is in command of a vessel, and prior to the start of the current hostilities, the shipping business had pretty well ground to a halt. Smalley, like many of his colleagues, had used up much of his resources just keeping body and soul together. In fact, he had been in Baltimore at the start of the war, planning to take command of a merchant bark bound for France. Of course, that was forestalled by the declaration of war, and Abrams, an old friend, sought him out for his privateer fleet.

Having gone over the accounts most carefully with his captains, Joshua Abrams had his steward bring in two canvas sacks. When he left, Abrams began counting the gold and placing small stacks in each bag. When he was finished, each captain knew his ships' share and agreed the distribution was equitable. Further distributions would be made by the individual masters, but on a basis consistent with the practices of the infant privateer fleet. There were always discretionary shares for captains to award for particularly deserving crew members, but fairness generally prevailed.

Smalley, like his friend Tom Stebbins, had brought *Glory's* share back to his cabin and stowed it carefully in a concealed locker behind his gimbaled cot. He had instructed Willard Halladay previously about the locker so that its contents could be salvaged should anything happen to the captain.

Smalley reflected on this as he watched Tom Stebbins work *Bill of Rights* up to windward of his schooner. The wind was freshening, and the spray flew down both ships' decks whenever their bows caught a wave just so.

A little cool water, hard work, and sunshine will help them sink those hangovers faster, he thought as he noticed that still the men seemed sluggish in moving about the vessel. Already, he knew that a dozen and more had left their breakfast in the wake, victims of the unpleasant mixture of too much rum and choppy seas. Clements had the watch, and Smalley turned to him.

"What's the final tally, Mr. Clements? How many did we leave ashore, and how many do we have which are unfit for duty? I don't mean those I know are suffering the ill effects of drink, just the ones too hurt to work."

Clements' eyes were clear and showed their usual gleam that appeared always ready to burst into genuine mirth. "We didn't leave but five ashore, sir, not countin' the three what come down with the Yellow Jack an' expired. As to the live ones, I don't know where they got off to. Biggs and some others must o' looked in ever' whore house and tavern one end o' town to t'other without they didn't find no trace of 'em. We got two men from the prize, Coleman — he's the one what's a friend of Biggs' — and another man. I don't recall his name — somethin' Irish, if memory serves. Seems like a fair hand though. Doctor checked 'em both out, and they's healthier 'an most. More 'n I can say for the three he's got in hospital; a broke arm, a knife wound, and one down with somethin' the surgeon ain't yet figgered out. I'm thinkin' it's the Jack again, but he ain't sayin'. Report is that 'ceptin' for the last, they'll all survive and be back to duty with a few days." The second himself sported the remains of a raspberry on his jaw, a souvenir of a bar brawl.

"Well, I guess that's not too bad a loss, considering we was in that pest hole over three weeks. I've heard of worse, you may be sure. I collect Mr. Halladay has assigned the new men to watches and quarters stations?"

"Aye, that he has, sir. Coleman's in Biggs' starboard watch, and the other's been assigned to the larbowlines, my section. Biggs was right pleased to have that fellow aboard. Seems they was friends right off, when Biggs got hisself on that frigate. Less'n we take more'n a few prizes ourselves, we should be all right for hands."

"Thank you, Mr. Clements. Keep her in line with the others. Your course is northwest, a half north until we turn up to the Passage. I will be below. Send for me as soon as we're clear to harden up and beat into the Windward Passage, or at once should there be a signal from *Freedom* or you sight a strange ship."

"Aye, sir. By my reckoning, we're likely a couple o' hours and more from layin' the center of the Passage, even favorin' the eastern side. I collect we're goin' to stay tight in with the others 'til we're clear?" Clements wanted to be sure he understood the orders for the group. On the quarterdeck there was no time for his usual irreverent attitude, and he listened soberly to his orders.

"I think we'll be fine about three or four cables apart, as we are now, Mr. Clements. With this breeze, we should be layin' Cap-a-foux by supper time or sooner." Smalley turned and folded his lanky frame into the companionway, and Clements noticed him starting to remove his black coat as he disappeared into the gloom of the dark lower deck.

CHAPTER TWENTY-SEVEN

New Men Aboard

" She sure don't sail like anything I ever been on, Tim. You?" Two men were standing at the rail on the leeward side of *Glory* as she raced through the white topped seas, ducking occasionally as one came aboard, and laughing as they did so.

"Not in life, Robert, me friend. Once as a boy I sailed on a wee packet in the Irish Sea — a lively vessel she was by my eyes, but by all the saints, she'd be hard pressed to match this 'un, she would. Why she fairly flies, she does. I wouldn't want old Gunner Chase breathin' down me neck whilst I was tryin' to lay a shot into this ship; I reckon she'd be nigh impossible to hit clean, save with a lucky shot."

Robert Coleman laughed, and turning to his friend, spied a familiar face topped with curly dark hair coming towards the pair from aft.

"So that's what happened to you, Isaac. I was sure they'd grabbed you up and flung you into irons, the way they marched you off'n *Fleur* when she was taken. Then not seein' you in the 'old with the rest of us, nor ashore in 'aiti when they put us on the beach, we was sure you'd come to no good. So 'ere you are, on this fine sailin' vessel with us, an' out to take some prizes. That fellow what brought us aboard — what was his name Tim, 'alladay, wa'n't it? He's first lieutenant aboard 'ere, Isaac. You probably already run into him too, once or twice, eh?"

Biggs smiled at his old friend. Then lines appeared in his narrow forehead as he grew serious. "Coleman, you got a lot to learn. First off, they ain't no first lieutenant on *Glory*; she ain't in the Navy. She's what's called a private armed vessel, I'm told — same as a privateer, I reckon. Owned by a bunch of businessmen in Baltimore, Maryland, and out to catch British shipping. Halladay, why he's first mate, pretty much the same as Mr. Burns was on *Orpheus*, but he ain't Navy. Mr. Clements is second mate, and I'm third." Coleman's eyes widened in silent response to this last revelation. He sputtered, about to say something, but Biggs pressed on. "So you can't call me Isaac when they's anyone around — wouldn't be respectful, even though we been friends and shipmates longer than anyone else aboard. How'd you feel 'bout taken British prizes?"

The two British sailors were silent for a moment. Then the short older sailor with Coleman pushed himself off the bulwark. He wore a handkerchief tied around his neck and a none-too-clean striped jersey. Isaac remembered Coleman had referred to his friend as "Tim" and had noticed his pate was as smooth as a cannon ball, his tarred pigtail being about all the hair he had. It was he who answered the third mate.

"I 'member you from *Orpheus*, Biggs . . . I mean *Mr.* Biggs, and sorry I am about that, sir. An' give you joy of your good fortune, sir. I'm Tim Conoughy, gun captain late of the Royal Navy, and considerin' what the Royal Navy put me through, I ain't got a care, to be sure, 'bout takin' British prizes, an' the more the merrier, I say. That boyo what brought us aboard said we'd get prize shares long as we fought, and that sits just fine with me. O' course I wouldn't mind takin' a Frenchy should one turn up along the way. I'm guessin' they don't signify, though, eh? How 'bout you Robert?" The diminutive Irishman's eyes twinkled with glee as he spoke, his whole body seemed animated with his joy of being on this fleet American schooner.

"I could surely do with some prize shares, my own self. Not a farthing to me name. That's a fact, it is." Coleman turned and stared out over the lee side of the plunging, racing, schooner at the distant land fading into the evening darkness. After a few moments, he looked at the third mate and smiled.

"You don't have to worry 'bout me, Isaac. I 'eard from Mr. 'alladay you was the one what got me aboard 'ere and off'n that stinkin' island where we was dropped from *Fleur*. I ain't gonna be a problem for you, an' I got no desire to get back aboard a Royal Navy ship — probably get flogged 'round the fleet for desertion, I reckon. So I'm 'ere to stay. I think this'll be a fine berth for me — even if she ain't got much of a top 'amper for me to work in."

"Aye, flogged we'd be, and that's fer certain, Robert. An' Tice would love the chance to turn his bully-boys loose on us, seized up to the grate like a couple sacks o' meal. I can hear the cat singin' in me head, I can. Makes the stripes already on me back sting just thinkin' about it, by all that's holy." Tim shook his head, his pigtail whipping left and right as he did, and, pointing a long thin finger at the guns looked hard at Isaac. "I 'spect I can be of some help to you boys here with these guns, Mr. Biggs. They look pretty much the same as most I seen, 'ceptin' that 'midships mounted piece. That's a piece o' work, by the saints."

"Aye, that's the Long Tom. Makes a terrible racket when she fires, but loaded right, I collect she does some heavy damage. I ain't seen it my own self yet, but we got some months afore we head home, so I 'spect there'll be chances to use her. You check with Mr. Clements, the second, and let him know you understand these things. I 'magine he'd welcome a hand."

The Irishman headed off in search of the second mate, his gait showing clearly that he'd spent most of his life at sea, while Biggs and Coleman caught each other up on what had happened to each since the trio of privateers had taken the two British prizes. After Isaac had finished telling of Burns' escape, Coleman clapped him on the back.

"You done right in not lettin' that cove shoot Lieutenant Burns, Isaac. Would'na been right, bein's 'ow 'e was willin' to risk a swim to shore and then 'idin' in the town. An' shootin' 'im wouldn't change nothin' what 'appened with the Cap'n and Burns on that other vessel — what' you call 'er? Righty-o, I remember, *Anne*. I don't 'alf blame the cove for wantin' to risk a swim to get 'isself out of the 'hold. I'm telling you, Isaac, bein' in that 'old with the 'atch battened down tight wasn't no pleasure, and I'd o' thought of swimming for it meself given the chance. Some of those Frenchies and wharf rats we shipped in Nassau got to fightin' and afore we knew it, they was two of 'em dead. Them boys on deck come down and drug 'em out, but still it was some strain for coves used to bein' topside. The landsmen set up a wailin' and carryin' on fit to wake the dead. After what I guess was a couple of weeks, they let us up on deck. Said we could work the ship if we wanted to stay topside; if we didn't want to work, then back into the 'old. They was a few of us woulda' worked for Satan 'isself afore we'd go back down that 'ole again. Conoughy was one stayed topside, and a few others. After we was ashore in Haiti, some cove come and asked if any would like to sign on a schooner; Tim and me, we jumped, 'specially since the cove askin' called for me by name. Not many come, though. One or two went to one of the other vessels, but for the rest, I guess they didn't want to sign on to fight they's own kind and gave they's parole to stay ashore in Port au Prince. There's a place I won't miss! Why, there wasn't a friendly face anywhere I looked, an' those people'd rob a man blind, 'ceptin' none of us 'ad nothin' to rob!"

"Well, I am surely glad you're with us. *Glory* and the others are fine vessels 'at'll sail the bottoms off'n most anything comes along. I 'spect you'll get to see her at her best if ever we raise another ship." He stopped and, seeing Willard Halladay approaching, called out to him.

"Mr. Halladay, this here's Coleman, the fellow I sailed with on *Orpheus* and then *Fleur*. He's a fine able seaman and I'd be pleased to have him in my watch. The other fellow, Conoughy, he knows something about guns, being as how he was a gun captain on *Orpheus;* probably be of use to Clements. I sent him off to find him and tell . . ."

Halladay laughed. "Ease up Mr. Biggs. I've already took care of it. Coleman, here, is in your watch, and I'm right pleased to know 'bout the Irishman. You might recall, Isaac, that I went and found these lads after you convinced Cap'n Smalley to ship 'em." Turning to Coleman, he continued, "You got to get aft and sign the ship's Articles so as to make you a part of the crew. I reckon it was pretty much the same in the British ships, wa'n't it?"

"Aye, sir, it was to be sure. I'd be 'appy to sign 'em. Where's the purser's office? I collect 'e'd be the one to see?"

"No, Coleman. We ain't got a purser aboard; only one in the group is on *Freedom* with Cap'n Abrams. Cap'n Smalley an' me do all the paperwork, so you just get yourself aft and I'll be right along." The two mates watched as Coleman moved aft to the edge of the quarterdeck, still in awe of the way this little schooner sailed. "I think he'll fit right in, Biggs. Seems a fine lad. You were right in pressing the Cap'n to sign him."

"Thank you, Willard. I surely hope he won't disappoint."

CHAPTER
TWENTY-EIGHT

Encounter at Sea

The change of the watch at midnight found the three schooners almost through the Windward Passage; the wind was, as usual here, steady and strong, whipping the sea into a nasty, wet chop, which built on the tops of the rollers being pushed into the Passage from the Atlantic. The shores being close at hand on either side caused back currents and confused the normal direction of the waves, adding to the sloppiness and making the decks of the privateers constantly wet. The sky overhead was clear with an abundance of stars and a bright quarter moon, the air was cool, and with the constant spray lashing anything topside, the men being relieved to go below were looking forward to the warmth of their hammocks. Most had, by now, worked through the ill effects of three weeks ashore, and were functioning as was expected.

Smalley had been on deck since supper; his black coat glistened wetly in the starlight, but he barely noticed the wetness on it or the deck, so intent was he on moving his ship safely through these dangerous waters. He had become one with his schooner. He felt her every lurch as her bow slammed into a wave, or in areas of cross-seas, when a wave smacked the side of the ship. *Glory* was making fine time, behaving like the lady she was, and handling this nasty stretch of water with aplomb, albeit wetly. He saw the others, ghostly in the starlight, were doing as well, and holding their position in the loose formation in which they sailed. Both were, like *Glory* shortened down to a mains'l, reefed fores'l and single jib. They were in no rush, but Smalley knew that had they been in a stern chase, all the ships could, and would, carry more sail, likely up to tops'ls and flying jibs. These schooners were built tough, and thrived in strong breezes and choppy seas.

Through the middle watch the privateers beat their way toward Great Inagua Island, and then to the Atlantic Ocean. The sky lightened with the dawn, slowly at first, then more rapidly, and almost suddenly, the sun rose from the sea into a cloudless sky. At first, the ships glowed in the soft early light, then, as the fiery ball continued to rise, the light became harsh, turning the sea to the east into a dazzling array of diamonds. The lookouts aloft had to squint their eyes to tiny slits and use their hands to block the sun. The vessels bore off to pass between Great Inagua and the eastern end of Cuba, preparing to add sail, and start the routine of another day at sea.

"Sail ho! Broad on the weather bow . . . looks to be 'bout seven or eight leagues distant." The cry of the forward lookout interrupted the morning ritual performed by the on-deck watch, scrubbing down the decks, recoiling all sheets and halyards and putting to rights anything knocked askew by the night's wet weather. All hands stopped what they had been doing to look up, as if by looking at the man aloft they could divine what he saw.

Third Mate Isaac Biggs, who had the watch, called to his messenger and sent him below to inform the captain. He then ran forward and jumped into the foremast rigging, climbing with a speed and skill born of years as a topman. When he got to the yard and stepped from the rigging to the cap, the lookout moved to make room for him.

"There, sir, you can make out her tops'ls clear as day." The man on watch at the foremast cap had been alert, and indeed, only the upper works of the strange ship were visible. Biggs studied what he could see with his glass, but from only her tophamper, he could make no judgment on her nationality. Looking down at the quarterdeck, he saw that Captain Smalley was on hand, his frock coat flapping in the wind as he strove to button it, and his hair askew; he had not taken the time to tie it back as he normally did, nor had he taken the time to clothe himself in more than his britches and coat. Biggs watched as the captain cupped his hands to his mouth, and faintly heard his voice.

"What have we got, Mr. Biggs? Can you make her out?"

Biggs turned and took one more long look with his glass, and then stepped off the mast cap onto the backstay. He slid down to the deck in seconds and strode quickly to the quarterdeck.

"She's too far off yet to make out her colors, Cap'n, if she be showin' any. 'Pears to be square-rigged, and I think I made out the top of a mizzen, makin' her a three master. She showin' tops'ls fore an' main, bare spar aft. She's downwind, on t'other tack, and still six, maybe seven leagues off. Her course'll close with us if'n she don't harden up or wear."

"Very good, Mr. Biggs. . . quartermaster, show the flags for 'Unknown vessel sighted five, seven' if you please." The captain needed to let the man in charge of the little squadron know that the three-master was five points to his weather, seven leagues distant. He reached inside his coat for something, then realized he had no shirt or jacket on under it.

"Messenger, kindly step to my cabin and have the boy fetch me my watch, quick as you can now." He glanced at the sun, giving him a rough idea of the time, and turned back to his third mate.

"Mr. Biggs. It is possible we could be in action by mid-day. We will need to alert the gunner, bosun, and, of course, Mr. Halladay, if you please. You might also let Cook know that he will be feeding dinner early and then have his galley fires doused."

As in the past, and on most every fighting vessel of every nation, news of the sighting and the possibility of a prize spread throughout the schooner in seconds, and before Biggs could get past the main mast, Halladay, accompanied by the gunner, arrived on deck.

"Ah, Mr. Halladay, I had just sent Biggs off to find you. We have a vessel bearing down on us from just for'ard o' the beam. Appears not to be in any great hurry as yet, but they may not have seen us. Best we are prepared." Turning, the captain spoke to the quarter-master. "Have we a response from *Freedom* yet, quartermaster?"

The sailor looked again through his glass at Abrams' schooner. As he watched, flags climbed up the main mast and whipped in the wind until they were secured; once tied down, they stiffened and the quartermaster read them and opened his signal book before answering the captain.

"Just now, sir. Cap'n Abrams says 'Good job. *Glory* to investigate. *Freedom* and *Rights* to aid.' That's all, sir."

"Very good. Mr. Biggs, you may bring her up a point to north-west by north, if you please. And we'll shake out that reef and set the flying jibs."

"Aye, Cap'n." Biggs gave the orders to the helmsman, and stepped forward to shout to the men amidships to trim sails as the schooner responded to the helm. Halladay was already starting the topmen on shaking out the reef and setting the additional jibs ordered by Smalley.

Gradually, the two vessels closed. Beating to quarters became a formality; most of the men were already at their assigned fighting stations when the bosun's pipe trilled. As the square-rigged stranger closed the separation to about a league, Smalley showed his colors. The American flag produced a like response from the larger ship, and a Dutch ensign fluttered to the mizzen gaff.

"Just as you thought, Mr. Halladay." Smalley gave his mate an acknowledgment of his earlier assessment. Since no one was currently at war with Holland, she presented neither a threat nor an opportunity. Watching the ship closely to smoke the ruse of false colors, Captain Smalley instructed his mate to continue to close, but keep the guns manned, ports closed, and watch for a trick.

Now only half a league away with no sign of hostility, the Dutch merchant bore up and backed her tops'ls, clewing up her courses and furling jibs as she did so. Smalley brought his schooner to within a cable length of the Dutch bark.

"You want I should heave to, Cap'n? Appears he wants to talk to us." Halladay never took his eyes off the other ship, and as Smalley agreed, he saw the Dutch captain climb up on bulwark with a speaking trumpet.

"We are the bark *Alkmaar*, Dutch, but out of Naples, Italy most recently, and bound for St. Maarten. We are stopping in Port au Prince first. I am Captain Willem Van Aschwin. I see you fly the American flag. Where are you bound?"

Smalley stood at *Glory*'s bulwark, cupped his hands to his mouth and replied, "We are working our way up towards Nassau. Have you seen any British shipping, Captain?"

"Ya, we passed a British frigate, a thirty-six, two days back. She was headed south of here, my guess to Antigua. We did not speak her, and saw no others."

"Thank you, sir. We wish you God's speed on your journey. Be careful in Port au Prince. Those port officials will try to take the very gold out of your teeth, and smile whilst they're about it. Keeps a man on his toes, I'll warrant."

"Thank you, Captain, for the warning. I have had the pleasure of dealing with those same officials in the past. And a good voyage to you as well, sir."

With that, the men of *Glory* could hear a babble of commands in Dutch emanating from the quarterdeck, and while the orders were totally unintelligible to the Americans, their meaning was immediately made clear when the tops'ls were braced around, courses let go, and jibs set on *Alkmaar*. She bore off, handled in a most seaman-like manner, and with sails filling, lumbered on her way toward the Windward Passage, and Port au Prince.

"Too bad the Dutch can't build a sweet-sailin' vessel, ain't it Cap'n? Those sailormen over there look like they know what they' doin', but that barky just can't manage a fathom above seven or eight knots, even in this breeze. Those boys would like as not give an arm just to sail a day on *Glory*. 'Course then they'd not likely get back aboard that barge." Halladay had a fine eye for ship's lines, and even though most sailors knew about "slab-sided, Dutch-built luggers," the mate's observation caused most within earshot to pause and watch *Alkmaar* slog off toward the narrow cut between Cuba and Haiti that would ultimately take her to St. Maarten, while *Glory*, *Bill of Rights*, and *Freedom*, in sharp contrast, sailed smartly a little north of west.

CHAPTER
TWENTY-NINE

Home

"There it is, Isaac, Cape Henry, Virginia. I'd warrant there was a time not so long ago you'da never figured to see that — leastaways not this close." First Mate Willard Halladay and Third Mate Isaac Biggs stood by the rail at the fo'c'sle watching the land grow larger on the larboard bow. By now, trees and different colors, denoting sand, rocks, and fields could be distinguished. Many of the crew had rushed to the deck when the Cape was sighted just as first light broke across the water. They had been gone for almost four months, and were as excited as children to be close to home again; their excitement was of course augmented by the thought of the payment they would receive when they cashed in their prize tickets which would be awarded by the owners. While this indeed was their native soil, they were another day or possibly two with a fair breeze before they would set foot on it.

The two mates had been watching the land grow larger since Biggs had been relieved from his watch by Mr. Clements and Petty Officer Johnson. When Biggs remained silent, Halladay paused in the lighting of his pipe, and looked at him. The third responded in time.

"Aye. That's a fact. They was several times I figgered we'd none of us be seein' America, let alone Cape Henry. When those two British fifth rates surprised us was one. I guess we should figger on seein' some a' them more and more, now we're at war with 'em. I never thought we'd get away from 'em. I can't help but think 'bout those poor bastards on *Bill of Rights*; loosin' her fore topmast to a parted shroud was a piece of bad luck. What do ya s'pose would a happened if Cap'n Stebbins hadn'a been able to out-sail that frigate? I reckon they'd only be two o' us makin' the landfall, huh?"

"Don't give Cap'n Stebbins all the credit for gettin' away. If Cap'n Smalley hadn'a come 'round when he did and take on the frigate, I 'spect *Rights* would be sunk or burned, one. When yer old shipmate Conoughy took off the Britisher's bowsprit and jib boom with our 'Long Tom', I 'spect that they's cap'n thought again 'bout tryin' to catch some small fish like us — found out we had some sting in our tail, he did. That Irisher earned his keep that day, by my eyes. And the only reason *Rights* could outsail that frigate was the English cap'n couldn't go to weather without his foremast would go by the boards — with no for'ard stays at all. Cap'n Stebbins showed real good smarts in headin' up to wind'ard. Outfoxed them Britishers good, he did. Course, them not bein' able to hit much with those twelve pounders helped a lot too. I guess we won't never know why the other man o' war didn't come after us. God Awmighty, that would have been a trial."

Halladay shook his head at the thought, as if to clear the image from his mind. He continued. "But I wasn't thinkin' so much 'bout that little set-to as when you was on one o' them Britishers yerself. You'da not been seein' America again for a long time, I'd reckon. I heard 'at they send 'em back to England after they's finished a tour in the Leewards. They might not get back to this side o' the pond for a couple o' years."

"Aye, that's a fact. I recall *Orpheus* was s'posed to be goin' home to get refit this summer. But I had figgered a way to get my own self off'n that ship with my prize shares from *Fleur* and the other Frenchies we took. Then you come along. Worked out anyway, it did. I got off, but never got my British shares. Cap'n Smalley told me I'll be getting' shares from those three we took after we left Port au Prince. So I got some money on top of it. I aim to head up to Marblehead and surprise my folks. They must think I'm dead by now, what with the war and all. I writ to 'em, but I don't 'spect they ever got any o' my letters. You figger *Glory*'ll be in Baltimore for a while — long enough for me to get up north and back?"

"No tellin' what'll be going on. That merchant out of New York we spoke only last month said they was more an' more Brit men o' war sailin' along our coast tryin' to close down the ports. One thing 'bout war, Isaac, you never know what's comin' over the horizon. I collect from talkin' to the Cap'n that you folks up in New England got no stomach for fightin' the British . . . 'ceptin' he don't seem to feel that way. Said somethin' 'bout another revolution to prove the first."

"I heard from some of the men on *Orpheus* that there was more

American sailors in the British Navy than there is in the American Navy. And the most of 'em got there same way I did. Either picked off'n a ship at sea like me and poor Tyler and Pope, or else grabbed ashore by the press gangs. That don't sit right with me, Willard; I'm in this war now, and I aim to see it through. If Cap'n Smalley ain't got a berth for me, they's bound to be a berth I can fill on some other ship. My feelin' is that helpin' take British ships evens the score a little, but they's still a lot o' Americans sailin' in the Royal Navy, gettin' flogged for no reason and killed fightin' against some Frenchies they ain't got no fight with. Now with us at war with England, well, . . ." He stopped and looked hard at the first before continuing. A tiny line of spittle had formed at the corner of Isaac's mouth; he ignored it and gave his anger and frustration free rein. "How 'bout that, Willard? Americans on British ships bein' made to fight against they's own. I can't quit now; I aim to make 'em pay, for me and 'specially for poor ol' Tyler."

Cape Henry slipped by to leeward, and the three schooners hardened onto the wind, leaving Cape Charles to weather as they moved gracefully up the Bay. The mates' conversation ended as their attention was needed to handle the schooner as she leaned into the breeze, her bow knifing cleanly through the short chop of the shallow water. Land passed by gradually, and Halladay, when he had time, pointed out landmarks to the third mate; this was all new to Biggs. He had only sailed out of Salem and Boston, passing these waters well offshore. He was surprised by the size of the Chesapeake, but could not believe that it might take them two or even three days to sail to Baltimore if the weather turned on them. A fair breeze and no mishaps would put them into Fells Point by supper-time tomorrow, but the Chesapeake in November can conjure up conditions to try the patience of anyone. Dead calms, howling gales, and thunder storms, even the occasional early snow, can cause a delay for as long as Mother Nature wants.

By the time the hands were piped to dinner, they were beginning to feel the whim of the Lady as the breeze died, and to avoid being carried back on the tide from whence they had come, Smalley ordered his vessel anchored. The others followed suit, and with sails still set, the three privateers floated above their reflections in the mirror-like Bay, anchor hawsers held taut only by the force of the current as it parted before their sharp bows on its way to the Atlantic.

With the turn of the tide later that afternoon, the wind returned, riffling the surface. As they once again began to sail up the Bay, the lookouts called out that two schooners were bearing down on them. American flags showed at the masthead of each of Abrams' vessels, and while there were no colors visible on the two newcomers, their hulls and rigs made them not only American, but sisters to *Glory, Bill of Rights,* and *Freedom.* Abrams sent up a signal calling for his little squadron to heave to, and the two southbound schooners, their hulls gleaming black, rounded up and hove to alongside.

"Is that you, Abrams?" The voice that floated across the water was gravelly and carried easily to all three ships. "Jack Lockhart here. Headed out to see what you left us out there. Did you have good success?"

"Aye, that we did, Jack. Those are mighty fine lookin' vessels. You'll do well. You might keep your eyes open when you get out there; we had a run-in with a pair of fifth rates. One might be a little wary of taking you on — we did some damage to her, but none-the-less, I'd keep a weather eye peeled. What's happenin' at home?" Abrams voiced the question on everybody's minds, and the good-natured chattering going on between the ships stopped while several hundred sailors listened for the answer.

"Things are going quite nicely for us on the water; back in August, you might have heard, one of our heavy forty-fours whupped a British frigate pretty well — *Constitution* it was, and Cap'n Hull did such a good job on the Brits he had to sink their ship, *Guerriere*; wasn't enough left to sail in. I'm afraid things aren't going quite as well with the folks on the frontier, though. The damn Brits massacred everyone in Fort Dearborn, then took Detroit. I guess *Constitution's* victory helps even the score a little, but I fear there's to be more trouble out west. Josh Barney on his privateer *Rossie* have sent in nigh on to eighteen vessels, mostly to Boston and Newport, and Tom Boyle on *Comet* done pretty good too. Fact is, more an' more sharp-built schooners are clearing every month to have a go at 'em. They been having such good success, seems like everyone wants to join the action. I surely do hope they's some left for us!"

"I'm pleased to hear that the Navy is doing well, and that the good citizens of Baltimore are helping out. I 'spect we'll be into Fells Point midday tomorrow, if the breeze holds. Don't know if we'll turn around or not; maybe we'll be a-joinin' you sooner than later. Good luck to you, Jack; keep your eyes open." Abrams waved his hat and called for *Freedom's* sails to be trimmed. She bore off and headed north again, leading her two sisters smartly up the Bay, as Lockhart's schooners headed south for the open Atlantic.

Darkness fell, bringing the November chill with it, and the schooners continued to make their way up the Chesapeake in the still flukey breeze. The wind, what there was of it, seemed to be playing games with the homeward bound sailors; it would blow strongly then die down, or shift to cause the vessels to bear off in order to maintain even their limited speed. As the hands were piped to supper, the rains started, with all the fanfare associated with a November squall — high shifty winds blowing the rain horizontally in sheets accompanied by brilliant lightning and thunder that put one in mind of crashing nine pounders firing at point blank range. Smalley, as well as his fellow captains, shortened sail, knowing as sure as the water was salty, that they'd be shaking out reefs again in no time.

By the time the hands were called for the midnight watch, Mother Nature had again shown her fickle side. While both watches were on deck, Smalley returned to full sail, and when Biggs went below to catch a few hours sleep before being called again at four, he saw the captain smiling as he felt her again driving through the waves and chop left from the sudden squall.

He must be as happy as the rest of us to be gettin' home, thought the third mate as he headed below. *I wonder if I'll be able to get up to Marblehead. . . I wonder how my folks are makin' out . . .* He was still thinking about going home when the easy rolling motion of *Glory* carried him gently and soundly to sleep.

First light saw most of the crew on deck, those with the watch carrying out their normal morning routine, the rest watching the familiar shore slip past. Halladay grabbed Biggs by the elbow, turning him to look at the shoreline to leeward.

"There's Annapolis up there, Isaac. Capital of Maryland. You can make out the sunlight shining off'n the top of the dome on the capitol building . . . there . . . there, do you see it? Looks like the top hamper of a frigate in there, too. Wonder which one it is. We're nigh on to turnin' Bodkin Point into Baltimore. At this rate, and if'n the wind holds like she is, we'll be into Fells by dinner-time."

"A fine thought, Willard. It'll be good to put my feet onto

American land again . . . been a while, you know." Biggs, having never been into Baltimore, did not share his shipmate's excitement about each landmark they passed. He was also tired, and while he was sincere about his desire to be on American soil again, his first thought was a fine meal followed by a full night's sleep. Then he would look into getting himself to Massachusetts and home.

Smalley was again on the quarterdeck, and Biggs, not yet relieved for breakfast, stood silently by the helm while the captain surveyed his ship, the shoreline, and the sky. When finished, he spoke quietly to his third mate.

"Mr. Biggs, you may bear off a point. We'll head for that headland yonder, and bear off more when we're past it. That's home for most of these boys. Even with this breeze we should be at the dock in Fells Point by dinnertime." The captain had obviously caught some of the crew's excitement, and was himself eager to be again on American soil — even though, like his third mate, home was another five hundred miles further north.

Having carried out Smalley's orders, Biggs checked that all sails were pulling properly and the schooner was making her best speed in the wind they had. It would never do to delay his shipmates' homecoming by even one minute; nor would it do any of them any good if they entered the harbor of their homeport looking like some rag merchant sailed by farmers. Obviously the bosun felt the same way. He was moving about the main deck encouraging his men to make *Glory* look as sharp as possible. With glances to windward and leeward, Biggs and Smalley could see similar activities on *Bill of Rights* and *Freedom*. They would make a fine spectacle sailing past Fort McHenry and into Fells Point.

Several hours later, as Fort McHenry appeared on the lee bow, Biggs was joined by his old shipmate from *Orpheus*, Robert Coleman. For several minutes they watched in silence as the star-shaped fort grew larger. Finally, Coleman looked at his former shipmate, and shook his head.

"I'd a never thought I'd be doin' this, Isaac . . . I mean Mr. Biggs." He corrected himself with a smile, knowing that their prior experiences allowed him the familiarity with his third mate, at least in private. "Me sailin' into an American harbor, and on an American vessel on top of it. Wonder what ol' Jack Toppan would say to that?"

"Oh, I 'spect he'd likely laugh some 'bout it. But whatever he had to say, you can be sure you'd hear him! Seriously, what do you plan to do when we get in, Coleman? You gonna stay here on *Glory* or go ashore or what?" Isaac had been puzzling this same question himself, but had not voiced it since the night in Port au Prince.

Coleman toyed with his earring absently as he watched the fort slip by in silence; he had certainly given that very question some very serious consideration, but as yet had not come up with an answer.

"I ain't figgered that one out, yet, Biggs. I likely'll stay at sea. Where, though I ain't any idea. You figger Cap'n Smalley'll let me stay with *Glory*?"

Before Biggs could answer his friend, someone cried out from the foremast rigging, "There she be, boys!. The dock at Fells Point. Lookee there, will ya? Looks like the whole town's turned out to greet us in!"

Naturally, everyone looked, and sure enough, the docks were crowded with people. Some were standing in groups listening to someone speak while others seemed to be parading up and down the dock and the nearby street yelling and carrying on. There was a noticeable police presence as well. Suddenly, a few people on the pier noticed the three schooners sailing toward the Fells Point docks and yelled and pointed. The words were unintelligible to the men on the ships, but gradually, most of the men and women ashore stopped to watch the privateers come in. "Huzzahs" rang out as the vessels approached the pier.

"What do you s'pose that's all about? It surely ain't for us; no one knew when we were comin' in." Smalley ruminated half to himself, but also half to Halladay who was standing by the helmsman as the schooner closed with the dock. Realizing they were fairly close, and that the other two vessels had reduced sail already, the captain spoke aloud to his mate.

"You may hand the fores'l, now Mr. Halladay, if you please. And stand by the main. I will wait till *Freedom* and *Rights* get tied up, then we will come in alongside on the stays'l alone."

"Aye, sir . . . in the waist there . . . let go the fores'l and drop 'er. Lively now. Mr. Biggs, Mr. Clements, encourage those men to step along."

The fores'l swung out and shivered as the sheet was released, and suddenly came down the mast. The men leaped at the foot of the sail and hauled the now docile canvas into neat fakes, securing it in a seaman-like fashion. The speed dropped precipitously as the sail area was reduced, and the schooner came abreast of the dock, and continued past.

Smalley watched as first Abrams, then Stebbins brought their ships in and passed lines ashore to willing hands. Smalley realized he would be tying up outboard of *Bill of Rights,* and was about to mention it to the mate when a mighty roar went up from the crowd on the pier. More "huzzahs" could be heard from parts of the crowd, this time accompanied by applause. It was apparent the good people of Baltimore had just discovered what ships these were and where they had come from.

The men on *Glory* could not take the time to watch what was going on on the dock; soon enough they would be a part of it, but now their full attention was focused on handling the big mainsail and stays'l on their own ship. The main came down smoothly when ordered, was furled onto the boom, and Smalley instructed his helmsman to "Bring her 'round, son, smartly now."

With her speed reduced to scarcely more than headway, *Glory* came around and headed back up toward the dock where her sisters were now secure. Hands on *Rights* waited for lines, and as *Glory*'s bowsprit swung out to pass the long main boom of *Bill of Rights,* Smalley ordered the stays'l dropped, and his schooner ghosted into her place alongside. Lines were handed across and secured. They were home.

The din on the pier had increased in volume, and the men on *Glory* noticed several scuffles breaking out here and there in the crowd. Biggs and Clements, standing amidships saw an elegantly dressed gentleman in a gray suit climb awkwardly over the far bulwark on *Rights* and continue across the deck toward them. When he had come across the breadth of the inboard privateer, he began to mount the bulwark with the obvious intention of boarding *Glory.*

"Just a minute, there, sir. May I ask yer business before you come aboard?" Biggs was taking no chances. He looked at Clements who smiled and spoke to the gentleman.

"Please come aboard, sir, and welcome. Biggs here's new aboard. We rescued him off'n a British prize. Isaac, this here gent's one o' the owners of *Glory*. Go fetch Cap'n Smalley, quick-like, an' tell 'im Mr. Meade's come aboard."

Biggs' departure for the quarterdeck covered his embarrassment at almost forbidding entry to the vessel's owner. Before he stepped onto the quarterdeck, Smalley and Halladay were already heading forward, having seen Meade clamber over *Glory*'s rail.

"Come with me, Mr. Biggs. I'll introduce you to one o' the owners. He should know the third mate anyway." Smalley was smiling as he spoke, and Biggs turned to join the two men.

"Captain, a pleasure to welcome you home, sir. And give you joy on your successes. I heard from Captain Abrams about your splendid voyage, and I believe we have already received notice that the British vessels you took — the ones I believe Captain Abrams said were north of Cuba, have safely reached Charleston and the court has already begun the condemnation process. With those and the others you took you and your men will be quite well off from this trip, I'd warrant, sir."

"Thank you, sir, for that. I look forward to giving the hands their shares. They've earned 'em, that's for sure. Tell me, what brings all these good people out to the dock today? It couldn't be our arrival, since no one knew when we'd be comin' in." As if to make its presence even more keenly felt, the noise from the crowd grew increasingly louder, and even two ships out from the pier, the men had to raise their voices to be heard.

"Why, my goodness, don't you know? No, of course you don't. How could you? You've been at sea." Meade smiled at Captain Abrams. "We received word only last night that our frigate, the USS *United States,* a fifty-six-gun vessel under Stephen Decatur, I believe, not only prevailed in a meeting with HMS *Macedonian* of the Royal Navy, but that Decatur sent her into Newport with a prize crew. Truly a marvelous victory! The people are delighted to have some good news, after the disasters we keep hearing about from the frontier. Things have been rather dismal here-abouts of late, save for the successes of the Navy, and of course the private vessels."

"We passed Jack Lockhart down the bay a bit. He mentioned that things weren't going well out west. I surely am glad the Navy is enjoying success. Small wonder these good people are celebrating. Think of it! A Royal Navy frigate brought into Newport with a prize crew — that had to be a telling blow for the Brits. What are your plans for us now, sir? We do need some refit time, but I know my lads would welcome the chance for another cruise."

"After you have tended to your ship and hands, sir, we — that is the other investors and I — would like you to join Captains

Abrams and Stebbins and ourselves at the Anchor and Owl just across the way there. We have a great deal to discuss, both about your most recent voyage, as well as the future. Until then, I will say 'good-day'."

With a tip of his hat, Meade was over the bulwark and headed back across *Rights'* deck. He met another gentleman, also elegantly dressed as he stepped onto the dock from the now-rigged gangplank, and together they pushed their way through the crowd, heading for the tavern across the street.

Biggs and Clements, now joined by Coleman and Conoughy, looked at each other in silence for a moment; then all of them began talking at once.

"Isaac, what do you think of that! A British frigate being sent in with a prize crew! What a telling blow that must have . . . " Clements stopped short, suddenly realizing that there were two British seamen standing close aboard. His look gave away his confusion at his own words. Conoughy laughed and waved a hand dismissively at the second.

"Don't you be thinkin' of us now, Mr. Clements. You're likely righty-oh. The Navy bringin' in one o' the King's finest must o' been a telling blow to the likes o' Cap'n Winston and Lieutenant Burns."

Clements smiled his thanks and continued excitedly. "I'm headin' down to Annapolis just as soon as ever we get our tickets cashed out. Joinin' a Navy ship, I am. This privateerin's fine work, but they ain't no glory like that in it. No siree. I got me some cash — or I will have, and now I aim to . . ."

He was interrupted by Coleman, whose own excited voice drowned out the second mate's.

"I'm thinkin' young Tim Conoughy and me'll join on with you. Ain't a lot of work 'ereabouts for a topman — nor a gunner — an' that's all Tim and me know. This privateer work's fine, and don't make no mistake, Isaac, I surely do appreciate your getting me off'n that island and out from under Cap'n Winston and his officers. It's just that all's I know is working aloft and all that Tim 'ere knows is guns, and they ain't enough guns for him to do his job on."

Tim Conoughy added his confirmation. "Aye, Mr. Biggs. By the eyes of me sainted Mother, I wouldn't want you to be thinkin' we ain't grateful for what ya done for us. It's like Coleman 'ere says; we need to be on a ship-rigged vessel. This 'ere little schooner sails like the wind itself, she does, but they ain't not nearly guns enough for my taste. I'm thinkin', I am, that sailin' on an American ship could be right satisfyin'. So Mr. Clements, if'n you don't mind, I'm lookin' to tag along too."

"'Ow 'bout it, Isaac? You're a topman just like me. You gonna stay 'ere on *Glory* or come with us to do some real fightin'?" Coleman looked at the second, and winked.

"Not now I ain't a topman, Robert; I'm a mate. But as to stayin' or goin' it's neither one, I'm thinkin'. I still got to get myself to Marblehead and see my kin. They got to be thinkin' I'm dead bein's how I been gone two years and more, and I don't reckon they got any of my letters. After I done that, why then I guess I'll see what's up in Boston for me and find me a berth. Soon's we get our prize tickets cashed in, I'll have me some money and that'll help gettin' me up to Massachusetts. Maybe buy me a horse to ride."

Clements smiled at the third mate. His eyes crinkled and his ever-present smile broadened. "Well, we gonna be together a few days more, boys, while we wait on our tickets. You all got time to change your minds, if'n you got a mind to change. Har har." He laughed at his little joke; the others just shook their heads and went to see to their duties. Isaac smiled inwardly as he thought of seeing his parents again, and headed forward to oversee the furling of *Glory's* jibs.

AUTHOR'S NOTE

Prior to and during the early days of the War of 1812, the sea was a perilous place to find oneself, particularly if one were a merchant seaman of virtually any nationality. The likelihood of being pressed into service in the Royal Navy was a reality and the constant and growing need for seamen to man their warships created in the British naval mind all the justification necessary to stop merchant ships of both England and others and help themselves to a few sailors. Desertion and death (from disease, battle, and poor medical practices) were the primary factors creating this need.

The characters in this novel are imaginary with a few exceptions; Adm. Lafory was indeed the commanding officer of the British Leeward Island Station, headquartered in Antigua. There was a Royal Navy frigate named *Orpheus* on the Leeward Island Station, but she was commanded by Hugh Pigot, a worse flogger than even the fictitious Captain Winston. While the officers and men who people the ships are fictitious, I have tried to maintain the accuracy of job descriptions, ranks, and relationships between ranks. Ship's routine has been portrayed accurately as well.

The operations of the privateers depicted within these pages and which sailed from Baltimore early in the War are essentially a composite of actual Baltimore "sharp-built" schooners. Their owners sought letters of marque and reprisal immediately after the war began and sent these fast able vessels out to harass and capture British shipping. And where better than in the West Indies?

Bringing a prize in for condemnation and sale was a real problem for the captains of the privateers, and short of sending them back to America (a poor choice due to the likelihood of recapture), only countries neutral to the combatants or allies of the privateers were able to be of help. Further adding to the difficulty was the fact that the United States had to have a treaty in place allowing for such action.

In the tale preceding, the privateers bring their prizes into Port au Prince, Haiti, for adjudication by the prize courts operating there under the direction of Alexandre Petion in Port au Prince, and Henri Christophe in the north. It is unlikely that this actually happened during this period, although Toussaint-L'Overture did indeed cause prize courts to be operated on British and American principles and it is known that, during the Quasi-War with France, the United States ships did, in point of fact, avail themselves of their services.

Fells Point on Baltimore's Harbor (now the Inner Harbor) was a popular facility and departure point for the privateers, and while many were built on the Eastern Shore, most wound up operating out of Baltimore. This fact was a major consideration in England's later (1814) choice of Baltimore as the target of siege after Washington DC., as well as for the attacks and raids on the Eastern Shore before and after their failure at Baltimore.

William H. White
Rumson, NJ
1999

Following is a selection from

A Fine Tops'l Breeze

the second book in the War of 1812 Trilogy
by William H. White

© William H. White 2000

The storm was ferocious, and would be remembered by the locals as one of the worst of the decade. The wind drove the tops of the powerful waves into the air, giving the horizontal rain a curiously brackish taste as it stung the faces of anyone unfortunate enough to be outside. The low sky was filled with racing, heavy clouds roiling and tumbling in from seaward, it's tone matching that of the sea and the Bay. Waves crashed on the shoreline, their white spray and foam the only bright relief in the monochromatic gray of the late afternoon in early March.

As the surf pounded Cape Henry and spilled huge rollers into the entrance of the Bay and beyond into Hampton Roads, a small schooner rigged vessel, shortened down to a few scraps of canvas staggered out from behind the lee of Cape Charles and into the maw of the storm.

"I don't reckon them Brits'll be any too anxious to be out here lookin' for the likes o' us'n, Mister Blanchard. You likely can set your mind at ease 'bout that." Warrant Bosun Clements smiled as he shouted through the storm into the face of the young midshipman clinging desperately with both hands to the windward main backstay. The water — a mix of rain and salt — dripped off his eyelashes and nose; wiping them would require him to let go of the backstay. A deluge of the same mixture was pouring down his collar, adding with cold, wet clothes to his misery. Jonas Blanchard had been the senior midshipman on the frigate and was now in command of this pilot schooner, commandeered by Captain Stewart to sail out and warn any American vessels they saw about the tightened blockade. The bosun's words, if indeed the young captain even heard them, did little to ease his abject fear; never in his short career as a sea-going man had he experienced anything like this. It would be only through divine intervention that they survived this holocaust of raging seas and wind. Never mind the British; they were the least of his worries now. Blanchard remained mute, but it did register in his mind that Clements and some of the other men on this little cockleshell seemed unconcerned about the weather; in fact they seemed to welcome it as a guarantee that the British ships effectively closing the Bay would be off station, allowing the American ship to slip through the cordon unnoticed. The storm, combined with the rapidly falling darkness, would cloak the little schooner in invisibility, and it seemed likely to most of the seafaring men aboard that, as long as this worst of Mother Nature didn't sink them, it was reasonable that the British blockaders wouldn't.

They cleared the Cape and the full fury of the storm driven seas met their sharp bows. Clements again put his face close to his captain's. "I'd suggest that mebbe a lookout aloft for'ard might be a worthy pursuit, Mister Blanchard. No tellin' what we might find out yonder, an' surely better to see them afore they see us'n. I can take care of it for you if you wish, sir, seein' as how you're a mite busy right now."

The midshipman's only concern at the moment was ensuring that no one or nothing caused him to release his grip on the windward backstay. He looked at Clements, at first not comprehending his words. Finally the words sank in and he nodded, opening his mouth to speak. Unfortunately, his lunch rather than words came out, and since Bosun Clements was directly to leeward of the young man, he received most of Jonas' offering. Clements' face darkened briefly, then split into a grin as he wiped the front of his tarpaulin coat with his sleeve.

"You jest stay here, sir. You might consider moving to the leeward side if'n you feel that comin' on again." He smiled and added, "Or you might go below," knowing that the smells and close atmosphere of the lower deck would surely inspire the midshipman to even greater levels of seasickness. Blanchard nodded again, but remained stationary, and Clements left the quarterdeck, following the lifeline forward.

No sooner had a lookout taken up a tenuous position in the fore crosstrees than a hail faintly reached the deck. "Deck . . . two p'ints ta wind'ard . . . one . . . this way. . ." The words blew away before they reached the deck, but Robert Coleman, topman, heard most of them and waved at the quarterdeck to get Clements' attention. He pointed to windward, and jumped into the weather shrouds, heading aloft himself.

"Looks like it might be a brig, but ain't no flag I can see. She's makin' 'eavy weather of it, like us. Looks like she's lost a fore topmast and the yard. She's runnin' off afore it, 'bout a league off. Likely she'll pass astern, and busy enough so's they might not even see us." Coleman thought for a moment, then added, "An' if'n they did see us, I don't reckon they's much what they could do 'bout us. 'Pears they got they's hands full without addin' a little schooner to they's worries."

Clements nodded, and ordered the schooner hardened up some, taking the waves more on the bow, but hopefully lessening the likelihood they'd be seen by the brig. He grabbed the wheel to steady himself as a green wave rushed down the deck, knocking two men off their feet and continuing on to the quarterdeck. The water swirled around the feet of the watch before running off the leeward side of the deck taking with it anything loose. Midshipman Blanchard groaned, and tightened his grip on the backstay.

The brig, still showing no colors and shortened to a reefed main tops'l, was now visible from the deck, and true to Coleman's report, her fore topmast and the tops'l yard swayed drunkenly over the leeward side of the vessel. There were men aloft obviously working as best they could at freeing the dangerous spars before they did more damage to the ship. It was apparent she was running for the protection from wind and seas offered by Cape Charles and had no interest in the schooner heading out, if indeed the brig's crew even noticed it, being as busy with their own problems as they were. The unknown vessel passed comfortably astern of the Americans, and they continued on into the deepening night and the raging storm.

By morning, most of the worst had passed, and while a still large sea was running, the wind had abated and the schooner was showing jibs, a reefed fores'l, and a full main. They had made some southing and tacked at sunrise to gain a further margin of open water between themselves and the British blockade. And Midshipman Blanchard was over the worst of his seasickness. He had not left the deck all night, knowing that to be below would be more than his heaving stomach could stand. Jack Clements handed him a pewter cup half filled with strong coffee.

"Drink this down, sir. It'll likely fix you up jest fine. Gonna be a fine day, good breeze and once she backs around to the nor'west, we'll be seein' flatter seas." The acting first smiled at the young man. The color had returned to Blanchard's face, and he no longer found it necessary to maintain his grip on the backstay.

"Thank you, Mister Clements. I'll expect I'll be able to get a sun line presently and work out a latitude for us. We must have made a fair piece to the south during the storm. I collect you have sent lookouts aloft?" A nod from the former bosun indicated he was still ahead of the younger man, but his eyes crinkled at the corners as he smiled at the midshipman's return to command.

Clements turned and headed forward to oversee repairs to the minor storm damage the schooner had sustained in the early morning hours. He passed the gunner, Tim Conoughy, checking the vessel's single four-pounder cannon lashed down amidships.

"Everything righty-o with your toy gun, Tim? Surely glad that little fellow was lashed tight last night; woulda made a hell of a mess if she'da broke loose."

"Aye, Mister Clements. 'Pears she weathered that recent bit o' unpleasantness just fine, by me lights. I was just awonderin' now we're out, where're we gonna get us back in? I mean, if we're out 'ere to tell other vessels 'bout the blockade, what're we tellin' 'em 'bout where to go?"

"Don't you worry none 'bout that, Tim. Mister Blanchard got it all figgered out. Said somethin' 'bout New York or Connecticut, depending on where we could get in."

"Aye, an' it's righty-oh you are. I guess it ain't for me to worry 'bout. It's surely a puzzle to Missus Conoughy's boy though why I can not get meself on a vessel with some guns. Seems they ain't been but a moment or two when I coulda done some good ever since I left the service of the King. Thought I was gonna be righty-oh on that frigate, and now this. What 'appens when we get to New York or the other place you mentioned?"

"Reckon they'll tell us then, Tim. Right now, we got other things to get done. Think that little gun'll fire if'n we need her?"

"Aye, she'll be a firin', for all the good it'll do. One gun . . . and a wee little four-pounder inta the bargain . . . what do they 'spect me to do with this?" This last was under his breath. Tim had volunteered for the berth on the schooner, but was beginning to have doubts. Well, at least he was at sea, and not holed up in Norfolk with all them other coves. And he might get a real warship that might even get to sea when they got into wherever it was Clements said.

The wind backed later that afternoon, and as Clements had predicted, flattened the waves as it filled in from the northwest. The sunset, when it came, was brilliant red, orange, and violet and turned the clouds remaining from the storm into an artist's palette; the colors reflected onto the sea, giving the steady ground swell an eerie, molten appearance.

They sailed to the north, keeping a sharp lookout for any vessels — American to warn, and British to run from; the crew fell into a comfortable routine. And Jonas Blanchard ran a taut ship. He knew he had a fine crew, and looked to this commission as his stepping stone to lieutenant.

About the Author

Photo by Tina/Visual Xpressions

William H. White, a life-long sailor and amateur historian, has been a commercial banker, professional photographer and served as an officer in the U.S. Navy during the 1960s. He is involved in both sail racing and cruising, primarily on the East Coast in one-designs and offshore boats. He resides in New Jersey with his wife of thirty-three years. They have three grown sons. *A Press of Canvas*, his first novel, was born out of his love for history and the sea.

About the Artist

Paul Garnett began drawing before he could write his name. He was a shipwright on the vessel *Bounty* built for MGM's 1962 remake of "Mutiny on the Bounty" and his paintings have been published twice by the foundation which now owns the ship. His art has also been showcased on A&E's television program "Sea Tales" and by *Nautical World* magazine.